egl.
6)14

DATE DUE

AUG 2 1 2014	
DEC 3 0 2014	

BRODART, CO.   Cat. No. 23-221

LITTLE
BIG
MAN

LITTLE
BIG
MAN

A NOVEL BY
THOMAS BERGER

A DIAL PRESS TRADE PAPERBACK

LITTLE BIG MAN
A Dial Press Trade Paperback Book

PUBLISHING HISTORY
Delta Trade Paperback edition / October 1989
Dial Press Trade Paperback edition / July 2005

Published by
Bantam Dell
A Division of Random House, Inc.
New York, New York

Chapter 1 and part of chapter 2 originally appeared in the March 1964 issue of *Esquire* magazine in slightly different form.

Copyright © 1964 by Thomas Berger
Introduction copyright © 1989 by Brooks Landon

The Dial Press and Dial Press Trade Paperbacks are registered trademarks of Random House, Inc., and the colophon is a trademark of Random House, Inc.

ISBN: 0-385-29829-3

Reprinted by arrangement with Delacorte Press/Seymour Lawrence

Printed in the United States of America

Published simultaneously in Canada

July 2005

30 29 28 27 26 25
BG

To Mary Redpath

CONTENTS / *Little Big Man*

	Introduction by Brooks Landon	xi
	Foreword by a Man of Letters	xix

Chapter

1	A Terrible Mistake	1
2	Boiled Dog	21
3	I Make an Enemy	35
4	Pronghorn Slaughter	45
5	My Education as a Human Being	51
6	A New Name	65
7	We Take on the Cavalry	79
8	Adopted Again	97
9	Sin	109
10	Through the Shutter	123
11	Hopeless	137
12	Going for Gold	143
13	Cheyenne Homecoming	157
14	We Get Jumped	173
15	Union Pacific	187
16	My Indian Wife	205
17	In the Valley of the Washita	223
18	The Big Medicine of Long Hair	243
19	To the Pacific and Back	265
20	Wild Bill Hickok	279
21	My Niece Amelia	295
22	Bunco and Buffalo	311
23	Amelia Makes Good	329
24	Caroline	341
25	Custer Again	353
26	Trailing the Hostiles	367
27	Greasy Grass	381
28	The Last Stand	401
29	Victory	415
30	The End	431
	Editor's Epilogue	439

Introduction: The Measure of Little Big Man

HAD THOMAS BERGER never written anything other than *Little Big Man*, he would have earned a respected place in American literary history. Just as surely as there can be no single "Great American Novel," *Little Big Man* has by now been almost universally recognized as *a* great American novel, and while its genius was not immediately apparent to large numbers of readers or to all initial reviewers, that genius has now been recognized by some two dozen scholarly studies and uninterrupted popular sales in the more than forty years since it was first published. As L. L. Lee so accurately observed in one of the first articles to give careful consideration to *Little Big Man*: "This is a most American novel. Not just in its subject, its setting, its story (these are common matters), but in its thematic structures, in its dialectic: savagery and civilization, indeed, but also the virgin land and the city, nature and the machine, individualism and community, democracy and hierarchy, innocence and knowledge, all the divisive and unifying themes of the American experience, or, more precisely, of the American 'myth.'" Surely Frederick Turner was correct when he concluded in a 1977 reassessment of *Little Big Man* for *The Nation* that "few creative works of post–Civil War America have had as much of the fiber and blood of the national experience in them." It now seems safe to predict that *Little Big Man* the novel will match its survival skills against those of Jack Crabb, its 111-year old protagonist. And in some ways, *Little Big Man* must be acknowledged as Berger's greatest novel, the one in which he took on the sweeping matter of his American literary and mythological heritage and made a lasting contribution to both.

Little Big Man is a story purporting to tell the "truth" about the old American West. It is ostensibly transcribed from the tape-recorded reminiscences of "the late Jack Crabb—frontiersman, Indian scout, gunfighter, buffalo hunter, adopted Cheyenne—in his final days upon this earth." That Jack's final days come some 111 years after his first, and that he claims to have been the sole white survivor of the Battle of the Little Bighorn, puts this "truth" in some doubt. Equally strong and contradictory evidence exists that the last of the old-timers is hopelessly senile and that he is a fiction maker as concerned with developing his own story *as a narrative to be read* as he is with relating the incidents of his life. Furthermore, Jack's narrative comes to us through the patently unreliable editorship of one "Ralph Fielding Snell," a fatuously gullible and weak-minded self-professed "man of letters," who not so incidentally reveals a number of parallels between his life and that of his narrator. Snell, who does admit to some doubts about Jack's story, also admits that he passes on its claims only after his own emotional collapse of some ten years, and his foreword and epilogue contain numerous hints that this emotional condition persists.

Yet against all of this postmodern self-reflexivity stands the disarming realism of Jack's tale, the authority and credibility of his voice. The action in *Little Big Man* is episodic, its story a macaronic of historical events and personages, its atmosphere the swirling myths that transformed people and events into America's defining epoch: the West. What unites the disparate threads of the novel's action and its swings between the antithetical world views of white and Indian cultures is Jack's voice and vision as he takes his place in the great American literary tradition started by James Fenimore Cooper with his character, Natty Bumppo—the legendary Leatherstocking.

Significantly unlike Leatherstocking, however, Jack can be counted on to describe frontier life with both humor and accuracy. Whatever else may be said of Jack Crabb, let there be no doubt that *he gets things right* whenever he speaks of customs or events in the Old West. Indeed, Jack's description of Cheyenne life draws heavily from anthropological studies such as E. Adamson Hoebel's *The Cheyennes: Indians of the Great Plains* and George Bird Grinnell's *The Fighting Cheyennes*. Likewise, when Jack speaks of Custer or the cavalry, the fine points and drawbacks of specific handguns, the growth of frontier cities, or other matters of white culture, he is equally accurate and often insightful. There is simply no way of knowing how many of Jack's experiences Berger directly or indirectly drew from other sources. Acknowledging many of those sources, Berger says of his research: "After reading some seventy books about the Old West I went into a creative trance in which it seemed as though I were listening to Jack Crabb's narrative." The brilliance of *Little Big Man*, however, has much more to do with Berger's principles of selection, combination, and comment than with the diversity and accuracy of his sources.

And it should not be overlooked that Jack also consistently offers a folksy-sounding but astute critical commentary on the *literature of the West*. Indeed, one of the wonderful ironies inherent in Berger's structure is that Jack, the ostensible man of action, reveals much more literary sophistication than does Snell, the ostensible "man of letters." Just as surely as Jack's account of his life explores the nature and importance of western myths—both white and Indian— it also explores the linguistic and literary mechanics of myth-making, whether in history, anthropology, journalism, or the novel itself.

Berger has so crafted Jack's voice as to make it at once a part of and comment on the process through which the Old West has been created for the public by language. First and foremost, Jack is a *storyteller*, with his primary allegiance to language rather than to history. Actually, as Berger would no doubt specify, history *is* language, and perhaps nowhere is this more true than in the case of the "history" of the American frontier. One of the most appropriate ways in which Berger designed *Little Big Man* as the "Western to end all Westerns" was to make Jack's voice and character such an obvious pastiche of fact and fantasy, of literary myths and received truths. From Cooper onward the literature of the frontier has been filled with seemingly crude and unlettered characters who ultimately drop their rough personae to reveal either noble birth or genteel background and education. Berger plays against this specific western convention by keeping Jack's persona scrupulously democratic and unprivileged while allowing just enough narrative sophistication to show through to call Jack's true nature into question.

One of Berger's most significant stylistic accomplishments is the creation in Jack of an "unsophisticated" colloquial voice that captures the essence of the American frontier vernacular but escapes its limitations. The vernacular ring to Jack's voice rises primarily from a smattering of well-codified colloquialisms: "commenced to," "a deal of," "they was," "knowed," and so on. Combined with Jack's use of natural, historically appropriate metaphors and the accuracy and specificity of his details, this technique more than masks the sophistication of Jack's narrative technique. Using relatively few of these colloquial code words, Berger efficiently imparts backwoods credibility to Jack's narration without limiting the precision of either his syntax or his diction.

In fact, what is most remarkable is that Jack's voice rings so true while also containing so many unexpected signs of sophistication. Included in his vocabulary are such unlikely terms as: "recumbent," "quandary," "signification," "obdurate," and "circumferentially." And more significant than this erudite vocabulary are the delightful precision and rhetorical craft of many of Jack's sentences, such as this one:

> As I say, none of us understood the situation, but me and Caroline was considerably better off than the chief, because we only looked to him for our upkeep in the foreseeable future, whereas he at last decided we was demons and only waiting for dark to steal the wits from his head; and while riding along he muttered prayers and incantations to bring us bad medicine, but so ran his luck that he never saw any of the animal brothers that assisted his magic—such as Rattlesnake or Prairie Dog—but rather only Jackrabbit, who had a grudge against him of long standing because he once had kept a prairie fire off his camp by exhorting it to burn the hares' home instead (p. 23).

Even Ralph Fielding Snell calls attention to this phenomenon, inviting his readers to consider a number of specific seeming inconsistencies in Jack's narration, including the fact that while Jack's own voice is often ungrammatical, his representation of Custer's speech or of Indian discourse is always impeccable (pp. xxx–xxxi).

Berger's game here is a complicated one: By having Snell point out the seemingly surprising flashes of sophistication in Jack's narration, he alerts us to the possibility that the entire narrative is a hoax; however, by calling attention to this verbal phenomenon, Snell diverts our attention from the even more unlikely aspects of Jack's voice. The interplay between editor Snell and narrator Crabb can only remind us of that between editor John Ray, Jr., and narrator Humbert Humbert in Nabokov's *Lolita*. But just as surely as Jack's voice belongs to the chorus of recent voices announcing that literature is a delightful hoax, it belongs to the chorus of "historical" voices determined to tell the way the Old West actually "was," quite different enterprises united only by the medium of language.

What is perhaps most interesting in Jack's voice is its ability to transcend cultural issues in pursuit of larger truths. This ability to synthesize the vagaries of his experience into larger propositions about reality does not make Jack wise, as the pattern of his personal disasters starkly attests, but he persistently pursues the grail of understanding, even when at considerable personal cost. He mulls the ironies of frontier conflict and routinely plays devil's advocate to some of the most dearly held received truths of western lore, matching the wondering charm, escaping the sentimentality, and surpassing the wisdom of Huck Finn, another of Jack's literary forerunners.

Finally, Jack is able to cast even the most famous battle in the history of the Old West into unexpectedly philosophical terms, seeing it for its unity rather than its conflict:

> Looking at the great universal circle, my dizziness grew still. I wasn't wobbling no more. I was there, in movement, yet at the center of the world, where all is self-explanatory merely because it *is*. Being at the Greasy Grass or not, and on whichever side, and having survived or perished, never made no difference.
>
> We had all been men. Up there, on the mountain, there was no separations (p. 435).

It is through observations such as this that Jack transcends some of the limitations of both white and Indian worldviews, coming to understand, as Frederick Turner puts it, "both myth and history as radically human constructs."

Although in many ways the story of Jack's narrative is more fascinating than the story of his life, one aspect of that life is particularly significant: Jack's quest is always for freedom. All the self-reflexive or meta-literary elements in this novel finally exist to direct our attention to the relationship between language and freedom. And it is in this light that *Little Big Man*, a literal model of the traditional "captivity narrative" most directly dramatizes Berger's fascination with the ways in which language serves to make captives of us all.

In this one fundamental respect, Berger's contribution to the literature of the frontier strikes a radically new note. Whether by virtue of a noble primitivism, as in the case of Cooper's Leatherstocking, or by virtue of an opportunistic amorality, as in the case of most of the frontier characters of the southwestern humorists or the "wild and woolly" heroes of the Beadle dime novels, or Huck Finn striking out for new territory, the western hero has been at bottom the very exemplar of individual freedom—often of anarchic freedom. Deadwood Dick, for example, is beyond the reach of almost all obligations because he has survived hanging as a thief, a feat Jack approaches by surviving at the Little Bighorn.

What finally distinguishes Jack from Deadwood Dick and his other American literary predecessors is that *he is not free*: he may escape the trappings of captivity, whether at the hands of the Indians, the Pendrakes, or of commerical creditors, but Jack remains the slave of his own standards—his haunting sense of obligation to definitions. Jack repeatedly states his admiration for others who understand real freedom, but Jack cannot himself escape the bonds of his own definitions. As he diagnoses his own problem when he runs away from the Pendrakes, intending to return to the Cheyenne: "God knows I thought enough about it and kept telling myself I was basically an Indian, just as when among Indians I kept seeing how I was really white to the core" (p. 143). No matter how desperate or low his situation, Jack maintains his faith in codes of conduct but he cannot reconcile the competing claims of the Cheyenne standards—which he understands and respects—with white standards—which he simply cannot keep from measuring himself against, no matter how unjustified or contradictory he knows them to be. When Jack opens his narrative with the claim "I am a white man and never forgot it," he refers to his personal curse more than to a matter of racial pride.

The problem is that Jack's sense of himself always looks beyond the concrete satisfaction of his very real accomplishments to the impossibly abstract ideal of civilization; Jack judges himself not as a man but as a *white* man. Hard-nosed pragmatist or cynic in so many things, Jack is a sucker for the ideal of civilization and progress even though he finds the reality inexorably disappointing. For him, Mrs. Pendrake emblemizes civilization, even when her actual conduct profoundly disillusions him:

> She always knowed the *right thing* so far as civilization went, like an Indian knows it for savagery. . . .
> I figured to have got the idea of white life, right then. It hadn't ought to do with the steam engine or arithmetic or even Mr. Pope's verse. Its aim was to turn out a Mrs. Pendrake (p. 115).

The point of all of this is that while Jack's sensibility is beyond sentimentality in most matters, at heart it is hopelessly romantic in its acceptance of the myth of progress and civilization, the myth of white culture that steamrolled the West. Intellectually, Jack is all for the Indian concern with what *is* as opposed to the white preoccupation with how things *should be*, but his commitment never grows firm enough to afford him any satisfaction.

The one seeming exception in Jack's life demonstrates the true extent of his misery. On the night of his Indian son's birth, the night before Custer's attack on the Cheyennes camped along the Washita, Jack achieves his greatest moment of personal freedom, overcoming his white sense of morality to fulfill his Cheyenne obligation to his wife's sisters. Before making love to the three sisters, Jack faces his usual dilemma ("my trouble lay in deciding whether I was finally white or Indian") but for once manages to suppress his "white" standards: "There could be no doubt that I had once and for all turned 100 percent Cheyenne insofar as that was possible by the actions of the body. . . . No, all seemed right to me at that moment. It was one of the few times I felt: this is the way things are and should be. I had medicine then, that's the only word for it. *I knew where the center of the world was*" (p. 240).

Once, but not for all. The key phrase in Jack's reverie is "insofar as that was possible by the actions of the body," and what he fails to achieve is liberation through the actions of the mind. Custer's attack shatters his peace, destroys the world whose center he had just found, and throws him back into the clutches of white standards and expectations. Appropriately enough, the only real and lasting triumph in Jack's life must be created and measured in accordance with those white standards. That triumph is his "uncorrupting" of the young whore Amelia, the one hoax in his life that really succeeds, based as it is almost entirely in the abstract ideals of white society, and carried off almost entirely through the medium of language.

In fabricating the new Amelia, Jack most closely approaches the ideal of white society symbolized for him by Mrs. Pendrake. In this one area Jack manages to free himself from culturally imposed definitions and to act not as some standard of conduct dictated, but as he chose. His explanation reveals a momentary insight into his own ever-losing struggle with absolute definitions. Acknowledging the suspect nature of Amelia's claim to be his niece, Jack defiantly states that since all of his "real" families had been torn from him by disaster, he had earned the right "to say who was or wasn't my kin" (p. 334). For once Jack manages to define a situation. But when Jack records his satisfaction at Amelia's success, he measures his pride in cultural rather than personal terms, judging his success at arranging her respectability "about as high as a white man can aspire."

Jack's *achievements* are Cheyenne, his *aspirations* are white, and therein lies a kind of captivity against which his shiftiness has no power. What may be the most significant of the many levels of meaning in *Little Big Man* is not that Jack survives but that he suffers—ever victimized by his own hypostatization of "white ideals. Jack displays many of the afflictions of Nietzsche's man of *ressentiment*, fighting and scheming for physical freedom but always hobbled by his own sense of impossible obligations. The moment of his greatest victory also reminds us of his ultimate submission to the tyranny of self-imposed definitions, just as the Indian victory at the Little Bighorn marked the end of the Plains Indian way of life.

BROOKS LANDON
University of Iowa

Foreword by a Man of Letters

IT WAS MY PRIVILEGE to know the late Jack Crabb—frontiersman, Indian scout, gunfighter, buffalo hunter, adopted Cheyenne—in his final days upon this earth. An account of my association with this remarkable individual may not be out of order here, for there is good reason to believe that without my so to speak catalytic function these extraordinary memoirs would never have seen the light of day. This apparently immodest statement will, I trust, be justified by the ensuing paragraphs.

In the autumn of 1952, following an operation to correct a deviated right septum of the nose, I convalesced in my home under the care of a middle-aged practical nurse named Mrs. Winifred Burr. Mrs. Burr was a widow, and since she has by now herself passed away (as a result of an unfortunate accident involving her Plymouth and a beer truck), she will not be hurt by my description of her as stout, over-curious, and spiteful. She was also incredibly strong and, though I am a man of some bulk, when washing me tumbled me about as if I were an infant.

I might add here, in acknowledgment of the current fashion in literary confession, that from this treatment I derived no sexual excitement whatever. I dreaded those ablutions and used every feasible device to gain my freedom from them. Alas! To no avail. I believe she was trying to provoke me to discharge her—a self-damaging enterprise, since nursing was her livelihood. But Mrs. Burr was one of those people who indulge their moral code as a drunkard does his thirst. Her late husband had been an engineer of freight trains for thirty years, and hence her idea of an adult male American was a person who wore sooty coveralls and a long-billed cap made of striped pillow ticking.

She did not think my physical disrepair serious enough to require a nurse (although my nose was swollen and both eyes black). She disapproved of my means of life—a modest allowance from my father, who was well-to-do, afforded me an opportunity to pursue my literary and historical interests with relative indifference to, and immunity from, the workaday world, for which, notwithstanding, I have the greatest respect. And, as one might expect from a widow, she took a dim view of my bachelorhood at the age of fifty-two, and went so far as to let drop certain nasty implications (which were altogether unjustified: I was once married; I have numerous lady friends, several of whom came to call during my period of incapacity; and I do not own a silk dressing gown).

Mrs. Burr gave me many an unpleasant hour, and it might seem strange that I let her figure so largely in the limited space of this preface, the purpose of which is to introduce a major document of the American frontier and then retire to my habitual obscurity. Well, as so often happens in the affairs of men, fate uses as its instrument such an otherwise unrewarding person as my quondam nurse to further its inscrutable aims.

Between her attacks on me with the washrag and her preparations of the weak tea, toast, and chicken broth that constituted my sustenance during this period, Mrs. Burr was driven by her insatiable curiosity to poke around the apartment like a common burglar. In the bedroom, she operated under the guise of her merciful profession. "Got to get some clean puhjommas on yuh," she would say, and deaf to my instructions, would proceed to ransack every drawer in the bureau. Once beyond sight, however, she pretended to no vestige of decency, and from my bed I could hear her assault, one by one, the various enclosures throughout the other rooms, desks, cabinets, and chests—many of them quite valuable examples of Spanish-colonial craftsmanship which I procured during my years in northern New Mexico, where I had gone to strengthen my weak lungs on high-altitude air.

It was when I heard her slide back one of the glass doors of the case containing my beloved collection of Indian relics that I was forced to protest, even if the vibration of a shout did make my poor nose throb in pain.

"Mrs. Burr! I must insist that you let my Indian things alone!" cried I.

She shortly appeared in the door of the bedroom, wearing a mag-

nificent Sioux headdress, reputedly the war bonnet of the great
Crazy Horse himself, for which I paid a dealer six hundred and fifty
dollars some years ago. I was too agitated at the moment to appreciate the sheer visual ludicrousness of this fat woman under that
splendid crest. I was too shocked by her heresy. Among the Indians,
eagle feathers belonged exclusively to the braves, and a squaw
would no more wear a war bonnet, even in jest, than a modern
woman would climb into her husband's athletic supporter. Readers
will pardon the uncouth comparison; yet it is not unjustified, for
there are few lengths to which our women will not go (the pun is
intended), and what Mrs. Burr was actually doing, albeit unwittingly, was to dramatize the malaise of our white culture.

She whooped and performed a crude war dance in the doorway.
That person's energy was astonishing. I dared not protest further,
for fear she might take offense and damage the rare headdress,
which was almost a century old; already some of the eagle down
had been shaken loose and floated about like the seed-carrying para-
chutes of that woodland plant which bursts to perpetuate its race.

By remaining silent and averting my eyes, I discovered the way to
survive Mrs. Burr's bad taste. Failing to elicit another sound from
me, she at last replaced Crazy Horse's bonnet in the cabinet and
came back to the bedroom in what with her passed as a reflective
mood.

She seated herself heavily on the radiator cover. "Did I ever tell
you when I worked on the staff of the old-folks' home in Marville?"

A more sensitive person would have taken my murmur as adequate discouragement, but Mrs. Burr was immune to subtlety.

"Seeing them Indin things recalls that to my mind." She cleared
her throat with a disagreeable sound. "There was a dirty old man
there, claimed to be a hundred and four years old. I will say he
looked every bit of it, I'll say that for him, nasty old customer,
scrawny as a bird and with skin like wornout oilcloth, he couldna
been less than ninety even if the other was a dirty lie."

In trying to reproduce Mrs. Burr's speech I know I am quixotic:
the best I can do is describe it as the vocalization of maximum ill
will.

"Anyways, the other thing he claimed to be was a cowboy and
Indin-fighter from the olden time. They watch a lot of tellvision up
there, old Westerns and such, and he was always saying that's junk
because he went through the real thing. Rotten old bum, used to

just ruin it for them other old folk, if they paid him any mind, which they didn't usually. He had wandering hands, I always used to say, the old devil, and you couldn't come and tuck the blanket around his ancient legs in the wheelchair without he'd try to get one of them little birdie claws down into your boozum. Say, he had a pinch, too, if you bent over nearby to get a pillow off the floor. Imagine, with a woman of my age, although of course I was younger then, that being seven years ago, and the late Mr. Burr was known to say, when he'd had a few, that I never cut the worst figure. But to get back to the old repperbate at the home, he claimed to be at Custer's Last Stand, which I happen to know was a durn lie because of having seen a movie of it in which all was killed in some fashion. I always say, the Indin is the only real American when you get right down to it."

So much for my nurse. *Requiescat in pace*. A week later she left my employ, and it was midway in the following month, I believe, that I read the notice of her fatal accident. I flatter myself that I am not the sadistic bore who so often writes our prefaces and uses them for self-indulgence. I see no reason to take the reader with me on every twist and turn of my search for the individual who proved to be the great frontiersman.

For one thing, as soon as Mrs. Burr saw my interest in the "dirty old man who claimed to be an Indin-fighter," etc., she led me on a long, squalid, and fruitless chase through the obstacle course of her memory. For another, none of the staff at the institution for the aged at Marville (where I went as soon as my nose had recovered its normal shape) had ever heard of the person in question, whose name Mrs. Burr had rendered as "Papp" or "Stab" or "Tarr."

Nor did the "cowboy" references ring a bell. And as to the alleged great age of my subject, the physicians laughed in my face; they had never known an inmate to survive past 103. I received the definite impression that they were determined to preserve that record and might give the quietus to any arrogant old codger who tried to better it—like all such institutions they were terribly overcrowded, and the wheelchair traffic was a real terror to pedestrians on the gravel walks.

I was apprised by the state welfare bureau of the existence of similar facilities for the superannuated at the towns of Carvel, Harkinsville, and Bardill. I journeyed to each of them and held many interviews among both staff and aged—some of these would make good stories in themselves: I talked to one old-timer, who had a bass voice and wore a bathrobe, for half an hour under the impression that she was a man; I even found several gaffers with Western reminiscences, to which they gamely continued to cling after a shrewd question or two exposed the imposture. But no Papp or Stab or Tarr, no 111-year-old survivor of the Battle of the Little Bighorn.

I might be asked at this point how I could justify my apparent belief in the veracity of Mrs. Burr's statement that there was such a man as Papp, or, accepting that, in the authenticity of his story to her? It is true that I am given to acting on impulse, and having the means to do so, I do not apologize for this foible. It is also true that, as might be surmised from the reference to my Indian collection, which is worth thousands of dollars, I have a passion for the Old West. Finally, in my possession is an Extra edition of the *Bismarck Tribune*, Dakota Territory, July 6, 1876, containing the first casualty list for the Custer massacre, and *on that roster are the names of Papp, Stab, and Tarr.* They are entered as having been killed, of course, but owing to the mutilation of the bodies, few could be identified with certainty.

Stab, I at first feared, must be eliminated for the reason that he was an Arikara Indian scout. Had Mrs. Burr's old man been an Indian surely she would have said so; on the other hand, she did make reference to the old-timer's skin: "like wornout oilcloth"; although she neglected to specify the color. Of course, not all Indians are brown—not to mention that none are actually red.

But I have broken my promise not to digress. . . . It was not beyond the realm of possibility that Papp, say, or Tarr—or even Stab—had survived that terrible carnage and for his own peculiar reasons evaded the notice of the authorities, the journalists, historians, etc., for the next three-quarters of a century—perhaps had amnesia for most of those years—and suddenly chose to reveal himself at a place and time in which he would be disbelieved by his ancient fellows and attendants of the sort of Mrs. Burr. It was not impossible, but, I decided after months of fruitless search, highly unlikely. Besides which, Mrs. Burr herself had last seen the individual in question in 1945. As unreasonable as it might be for a man to live to 104, how much more absurd to survive to 111!

Downright ridiculous, in fact. I made the mistake when calling on my father to collect my monthly stipend—he demanded that regular personal appearance—I made the error of responding honestly to his query: "What are you up to this month, Ralph?"

He viciously bit into his cigar holder. "*Looking for a one-hundred-and-eleven-year-old survivor of the Battle of the Little Bighorn!*"

Luckily, at that point one of his flunkies entered the office with dispatches from Hong Kong concerning the hotel my father proceeded to build in that colony, and I was spared further aspersions on my alleged weak-mindedness. My father was nearly eighty years old. He and I had never been close.

Just at the point at which I was about to throw up the game and begin, instead, serious work on my long-deferred monograph on the origins of the Southwestern *luminaria* (the Christmas lantern comprising a lighted candle in a paper bag filled with sand), projected several years before during my residence in Taos, N.M.—I was just perusing my notes on the subject when I received a curious letter, which looked very much like a hoax.

Deer sir I hurd you was trying to fine me—I reckon its me you was trying to fine on account I never hurd of ennybody else among these here old burned out wrecks at this home who was ever a hero like myself and partipated in the glorus history of the Olden Time Fronteer and new them all Genl Custer, Setting Bull, Wild Bill, that mean man Earp, etc or went through the socalled Little Bighorn fight or Custers Last Stand.

I am being held prisoner here. I am One Hundred and 11 year old and if I had my single action Colt's I wd shoot my way out but I aint got it. Being your a riter and all I will sell my story for 50 Thousand dollar which I figure to be cheap considering I am probly the last of the oldtimers

> Yr Friend
> Jack Crabb

The handwriting was vile (though not in the least feeble) and took me all day to decipher; the redaction published here can be described as only probable. The letter was written on a sheet bearing the rubric of the Marville Center for Senior Citizens, which as we have seen had been my first port of call and yielded negative results. The request for fifty thousand dollars suggested the work of a potential confidence man.

Yet the next day found me, at the end of a hundred-mile drive through scattered cloudbursts, maneuvering my Pontiac into one of the spaces marked "Visitors" in the asphalt parking lot at Marville. It was early afternoon. The administrative director looked slightly vexed to see me again, and downright contemptuous when I showed him the letter. He put me in the hands of the chief of the psychiatric section, forthwith: a whey-faced person named Teague, who impassively studied the gnarled calligraphy on my document, sighed, and said: "Yes, I'm afraid that's one of ours. They occasionally get a letter past us. I am sorry that you were inconvenienced, but be assured this patient is altogether harmless. His suggestion of violence in the last paragraph is fantasy. Besides, he is physically debilitated to the degree that he cannot leave his chair without an attendant's help, and his apperceptive faculties have degenerated. So have no fear that he can make his way to the city and do you hurt."

I pointed out to the doctor that Mr. Crabb's threat, if so it could be called, was directed at the staff of the Marville Center and hardly towards me, but of course he merely smiled compassionately. I am not without experience of these gentry, having done my stint at fifty dollars an hour, twice a week, for several years when I was a decade younger, without the least diminution of my nightmares and migraine headaches.

"Nevertheless," I added, "I *must* insist on seeing Mr. Crabb. I have just driven a hundred miles and given up a morning that had more profitably been spent with my tax accountant."

He instantly acquiesced. Members of his profession are very easy to impose one's will upon, so long as one does so in economic rather than emotional terms.

We went up one flight and walked a good half mile, corridor upon corridor; the psychiatric section was the newest part of Marville, all tile and glass and philodendrons: indeed, it resembled a greenhouse, with here and there a clump of old bald heads like mushrooms among the foliage. We reached a glassed-in balcony full of geraniums. Early December had established itself outside, but by means of the thermostat Marville maintained an internal summer all year round. I was suddenly shocked by a dreadful illusion: in a wheelchair, with its back to us, stood an abominable black bird—the largest turkey buzzard I had ever seen. Through the window it directed a raptorial surveillance on the grounds below, as if in search of lunch, its naked, wrinkled little head trembling ever so slightly.

"Mr. Crabb," said Dr. Teague to the bird, "you have a visitor.

Whatever your feeling towards me, I'm sure that you will be very polite to him."

The buzzard turned slowly and looked over its sloping shoulder. My horror decreased at the sight of a human face rather than a beak—withered, to be sure, and covered in Mrs. Burr's wornout oilcloth with many seams, but a face, indeed a furious little face, with eyes as hot and blue as the sky above a mesa.

"Boy," said the old man to Dr. Teague, "I took a slug in the ham once near Rocky Ford and cut it out myself with a bowie and a mirror, and the sight of my hairy behind was a real pleasure along-side of looking at what you carry on top of your neck."

He spun the chair around. If as a bird he had been large, as a man he was distinctly undersized. His feet were positively minuscule and shod in saddle oxfords, I suppose for the horsy connotation. What I had taken for swarthy plumage was in reality an old swallow-tailed coat, gone black-green with age. The temperature in the solarium was high enough to force a geranium's bud, yet under his coat the old man wore a stout woolen sweater over a pajama coat of flannel. His trousers were pajama bottoms, and where they rode up his skinny shanks one could see gray long johns making a junction with black stockings.

His voice I have saved till last. Imagine, if you can, the plucking of a guitar the belly of which is filled with cinders: a twangy note that quickly loses its resonance amid harsh siftings.

Dr. Teague smiled with all the compassion of his repressed malice, and introduced us.

Crabb suddenly slipped between his brown gums a set of false teeth that he had been concealing in his hand and bared them at the doctor, snarling: "Git on out of here, you lanky son of a bitch."

Teague let his eyelids descend in amused tolerance, retracted them, and said: "If it is satisfactory to Mr. Crabb, I see no reason why you cannot talk quietly here with him for half an hour. You might drop by the office on your way out, Mr. Snell."

Jack Crabb squinted at me briefly, spat out his teeth, and put them away in an inner pocket of the swallowtail. I felt uneasy, knowing that everything depended on my ability to create a rapport between us. As soon as I had distinguished man from buzzard, I believed absolutely that he was everything he claimed to be in the letter. Yet I determined to move with caution.

He again put those remarkably blue eyes on me. I waited, and waited, and let him stare me down.

"You're a sissy, ain't you, son?" he said at last, not however unkindly. "Yes sir, a big fat sissy. I bet if I squeezed your arm the impression would stay there for a long time like it was made of tallow. I knowed a fellow looked like you come out West and went among the Kiowa and they tied him up and let the squaws beat him sore with willow sticks. You got my money?"

I realized that the old scout was testing me, and therefore I failed to show I had been offended, as indeed I had not been.

"Why did they do that, Mr. Crabb?"

He grimaced, which involved the total disappearance of his eyes and mouth and most of his nose, only the very end of which protruded like one fingertip of a clenched fist wearing a shabby leather glove.

"An Indian," he said, "is crazy to figure out how a thing works. Of course, not everything interests him. What don't, he don't even see. But they was interested in that sissy, all right, and wanted to see whether he'd cry like a woman if he was beat. He never, though the marks showed on his back like they was flogging a cheese. So they give him presents and left him go. He was a brave man, son, and that's the point: being a sissy don't make no difference at all. You got my money?"

"Mr. Crabb," said I, somewhat relieved by the story though it still seemed obscure to me, "we'll have to get straight on another point: my means are very modest."

He replied: "If you ain't got money, then what have you got, son? Them clothes don't look like much to me." He took his cane from the back of the wheelchair, where it had been hanging, and poked me in the midsection; fortunately the tip was covered with a rubber crutch-end and did not hurt, though it left smudges on my beige weskit.

"We'll discuss that later," I had the shrewdness to say, finding a wicker chair behind a rubber-plant grove, drawing it into the open, and placing myself in it. "First, I hope you won't be offended if I check your story for authenticity."

The statement elicited from him a prolonged dry laugh that sounded like the grating of a carrot. His little yellow head, naked as a foetus and translucent as parchment, fell onto his chest, and my heart gave a great jolt of apprehension: I had discovered him too late; he had fallen dead.

I rushed to the wheelchair and put my hand upon his wrenlike chest, then my ear. . . . Would that my own heart beat so firm and true! He was merely asleep.

"I wouldn't like to see you misled by your own enthusiasm," said Dr. Teague a few minutes later, seated behind his metal desk, on which was mounted a fluorescent lamp supported by a great derricklike structure. "I remember your Mrs. Burr, who was a member of the janitorial staff rather than a nurse. She was discharged, I believe, for supplying certain patients with intoxicants, foremost among them being Jack Crabb. While an occasional draught of something mildly alcoholic might have a favorable physical effect on the aged, assisting in circulation, a strong drink can be very deleterious to an old heart. Not to mention the psychic effects. And I think that Mr. Crabb's paranoid tendencies are quite apparent even to a layman."

"But he *could* be a hundred eleven years old. Can you grant me that much, Dr. Teague?" asked I.

Teague smiled. "Curious way you put it, sir. Mr. Crabb is so many years old in reality, and it has nothing to do with what I will grant or you will accept. There are certain techniques by which medical science can determine the approximate age of a man, but those means lose precision as the subject grows older. Thus with a baby—"

I got out my handkerchief just in time to catch a sneeze. I had thought as much: an aftereffect of those wretched geraniums. And my prescribed nose drops were a hundred miles away. My straightened right septum ached; the incision had hardly healed. Yet there was a moral lesson in this eventuality. I remembered Mr. Crabb's story about the unoffending chap who was beaten by the Indians, and belatedly understood it: each of us, no matter how humble, from day to day finds himself in situations in which he has the choice of acting either heroically or craven. A small elite are picked by fate to crouch on that knoll above the Little Bighorn, and they provide examples for the many commonplace individuals whose challenge is only a flat tire on a deserted road, the insult of a bully at the beach, or a sneezing spell in the absence of one's nostril spray.

I filled my hand with water at Dr. Teague's stainless-steel washstand and sniffed some up my nasal passages. It was a stopgap remedy and not very efficacious. I sneezed regularly for the next forty-five minutes, and my nose swelled to the size of a yam, my eyes narrowed to Oriental apertures. Yet my will never wavered.

Dr. Teague's interest proved to lie exclusively in the subject of money, or more properly, Marville's general and the psychiatric section's particular shortage of that supreme good of our culture. Medical science could determine a baby's age for almost nothing; for an old man it took money. Wheelchairs required money. Attendants like the late Mrs. Burr, not to mention genuine nurses, had to be paid. Even those detestable geraniums apparently strained the budget.

I had never before realized that my father was on intimate terms with a number of state legislators. Whatever Dr. Teague's proficiency at his own trade or science or swindle, he gave evidence of being a gifted student of politics. The upshot of our little session in his office, in which every item but ourselves seemed to be fabricated of metal, was that I agreed to discuss with Father the advisability of increased appropriations for senior-citizens' centers. On Dr. Teague's part, he would, pending receipt of sufficient money to schedule certain chemical and X-ray tests to determine the calcium content of Jack Crabb's ancient bones, tentatively estimate the old scout's age to be "ninety plus."

I doubt whether Crabb in his prime, with his Colt's Peacemaker, could have done better against Teague. I decided that I could discharge my obligation by writing my father a letter. Whether he acted on its suggestions, I do not know. He never mentioned it on my regular appearances. The zeal of Dr. Teague, of course, and that of the director, his instigator, never flagged during the five months of my almost daily interviews with Jack Crabb. I cannot recall making a trip through the corridors in which I did not encounter one or both. The exchange became habitual: "How does it look, sir?"

"Encouraging, Doctor."

I have not been back to Marville since the early summer of 1953, at which date they were still asking.

Now a few words on the composition of these memoirs. In their original form they consisted of fifty-seven rolls of tape recorded in Mr. Crabb's voice. From February to June, 1953, I sat with him every weekday afternoon, operating the machine, encouraging him when his enthusiasm flagged, now and again putting pertinent questions that aided him in clarifying his account, and generally making myself unobtrusively useful.

It was, after all, his book, and I felt peculiarly honored to have rendered it my small services. The locale of these sessions was his tiny bedroom, a cheerless enclosure furnished in gray metal and looking onto an airshaft up which noxious vapors climbed from the kitchen two floors below. The glass-enclosed balcony on which I had first met him would no doubt have been more comfortable but for my allergy to its flora, not to mention the possibilities it afforded for interruption by the other old people and members of the staff.

Then too, Mr. Crabb was visibly failing during these months. By March he had taken permanently to his bed. By June, on the final tapes, his voice was hardly audible, though his mind continued vigorous. And on the twenty-third day of that month he greeted me with glazed eyes that did not alter their focus as I crossed the room. The old scout had reached the end of his trail.

After checking out of the motel in which I had resided for five months, I attended the subsequent funeral, at which I expected to be sole mourner, since he had no friends; but in actuality most of the other ambulatory inmates were present, wearing, after the fashion of old people at such functions, expressions of smug satisfaction.

The obsequies were held on June 25, 1953, which happened to be the seventy-seventh anniversary of the Battle of the Little Bighorn. In death as in life, Jack Crabb seemed to specialize in the art or craft of coincidence.

As to the text: it is faithful to Mr. Crabb's narration as transcribed literally from the tapes. I have subtracted nothing, and added only the necessary marks of punctuation: when the latter sometimes seem sparse, my motive has been to indicate the breathless rush in which these passages emerged from the speaker. I have made no attempt to reproduce the old scout's peculiar voice or pronunciation, lest the entire book resemble the letter which he wrote me from Marville.

He was a gifted raconteur and had a keen ear: in no other fashion can I account for certain inconsistencies. You will notice that while the direct narration, *in propria persona*, is ungrammatical, a cultivated character such as General Custer speaks in the formal style. And Indian discourse in translation appears impeccable as to grammar and syntax. Indeed, in his own speech Mr. Crabb is not always uniform, using "brought" and "brung," say, or "they was" and "they were," interchangeably. But listen occasionally to individuals of the lower orders among your acquaintance, your garageman or bootblack—he knows the rules of civilized rhetoric; has not, after all, been living on the moon; can, if he wishes, speak well, and sometimes may if only to elicit a gratuity. It is clear his habitual idiom is a product of the self-indulgent will.

You may question Mr. Crabb's having in his untutored vocabulary such a word as "apprehension." But it must be remembered that the frontiersman of yore received his rude culture from many sources: for example, Shakespearean troupes traveled to the farthest outposts; as did ministers of the gospel, with the King James Bible in their saddlebags. Then as we shall read, under Mrs. Pendrake's tutelage young Jack was exposed to Alexander Pope and no doubt other notable poets as well.

I think you will agree that Mr. Crabb is astonishingly circumspect as to language. Occasional uncouthness, yes. Consider the man, his circumstances and time. But his attitude towards women has an old-fashioned gallantry to it: romantic, sentimental—to be honest, I think it even cloying at times. He may have overdrawn his portrait of Mrs. Pendrake, for example. I suspect she may have been no more than the trollop each of us has encountered now and again in his own passage through life. My own ex-wife, say—but this is Mr. Crabb's book and not mine.

However, when not giving direct dictation, Jack Crabb, man to man, was probably the foulest-mouthed individual of whom I have ever had experience. He was incapable of speaking one entire sentence that could be uttered word for word from a public platform or quoted in a newspaper. It was "Hand me the _____ microphone, son. . . . I wonder when that _____ nurse is bringing the _____ lunch." So I must ask the reader to make his own substitutions when in the course of the narrative Mr. Crabb represents himself as saying to Wyatt Earp, in that famous confrontation down on the buffalo range: "Draw, you goddam Belch, you." Be assured the idiom was far stronger.

One more note: the word "arse." Like so many amateur writers —and he thought of his spoken narrative as eventually appearing in letterpress—Mr. Crabb was frequently threatened with loftiness, but this is not a sample of it. No, he believed this term to be the polite locution for the derrière, that which could be pronounced anywhere without offending. You will notice he often puts the other form into the speech of those he regards as particularly boorish.

So much for that. A decade has passed since Jack Crabb spoke into my machine. In the interim my father at last died of natural causes, and thus began a protracted legal battle over the inheritance between myself and an alleged half-brother, illegitimate, who appeared from nowhere. Which should not concern us here, were it not that I subsequently suffered an emotional collapse that rendered me *hors de combat* for the better part of ten years. Hence the long delay between this book's conception and its dissemination.

I have said enough, and now shall relinquish the stage to Jack Crabb. I shall pop back in the briefest Epilogue. But first you must read this remarkable story!

RALPH FIELDING SNELL

LITTLE
BIG
MAN

CHAPTER 1 *A Terrible Mistake*

I AM A WHITE MAN and never forgot it, but I was brought up by the Cheyenne Indians from the age of ten.

My Pa had been a minister of the gospel in Evansville, Indiana. He didn't have a regular church, but managed to talk some saloonkeeper into letting him use his place of a Sunday morning for services. This saloon was down by the riverfront and the kind of people would come in there was Ohio River boatmen, Hoosier fourflushers on their way to New Orleans, pickpockets, bullyboys, whores, and suchlike, my Pa's favorite type of congregation owing to the possibilities it afforded for the improvement of a number of mean skunks.

The first time he come into the saloon and started to preach, that bunch was fixing to lynch him, but he climbed on top of the bar and started to yell and in a minute or two they all shut up and listened. My Pa could handle with his voice any white man that ever lived, though he was only of the middle height and skinny as a pick handle. What he'd do, you see, was to make a person feel guilty of something they never thought of. Distraction was his game. He'd stare with his blazing eyes at some big, rough devil off the boats and shout: "How long's it been you ain't seen your old Ma?" Like as not that fellow would scrape his feet and honk his nose in his sleeve, and when my brothers and sisters carried around cleaned-out spittoons for the collection, remember us kindly for our pains.

Pa split the collection with the saloonkeeper, which was part of the reason he was let to use the place. The other part was that the bar stayed open throughout the service. My Pa wasn't no Puritan. He'd take a shot or three himself right while he was preaching, and was never known to say a word against the drink, or women, or cards, or any of the pleasures. "Every kind of sport has been invented by the Lord and therefore can't be bad in itself," he would say. "It's only bad when the pursuit of it makes a man into a mean skunk who will cuss and spit and chew and never wash his face." These were the only specific sins I ever heard my Pa mention. He never minded a cigar, but was dead set against chewing tobacco, foul language, and dirt on a person. So long as a man was clean, my Pa didn't care whether he drank himself to death, gambled away every cent so that his kids starved, or got sick from frequenting low women.

I never suspected it at that time, being just a young boy, but I realize now that my Pa was a lunatic. Whenever he wasn't raving he would fall into the dumps and barely answer when he was spoke to, and at his meals he was single-minded as an animal in filling his belly. Before he got religion he was a barber, and even afterward he cut the hair of us kids, and I tell you if the spirit come over him at such a time it was indeed a scaring experience: he would holler and jump and like as not take a piece of your neck flesh with his scissor just as soon as he would hair.

My Pa was making out right well in that saloon—although it is true there was a movement afoot among the regular preachers to run him out of town because he was stealing their congregations aside from them middle-aged women who prefer the ordinary kind of Christianity that forbids everything—when he suddenly decided he ought to go to Utah and become a Mormon. Among other things he liked the Mormon idea that a man is entitled to a number of wives. The point is that other than cussing, chewing, etc., my Pa was all for freedom of every type. He wasn't interested himself in having an additional wife, but liked the principle. That's why my Ma didn't mind. She was a tiny little woman with a round, innocent face faintly freckled, and when Pa got too excited on a day when he wasn't going to preach and work off his steam, she would make him undress and sit in a barrel-half and would scrub his back with a brush, which calmed him down after about fifteen minutes.

Pa took us all to Independence, Missouri, where he bought a wagon and team of ox, and we set out on the California Trail. That was near as I can figure the spring of 1852, but we still run into a number of poor devils going out on the arse-end of the gold rush that started in '48. Before long we had accumulated a train of seven wagon and two horse, and the others had elected Pa as leader, though he didn't know no more about crossing the plains than I do about the lingo of the heathen Chinese who in later years was to work sixteen hours a day building the Central Pacific Railroad. But given to shouting the way he was, I think they figured since they couldn't shut him up, might as well make him boss. Then too, every night stop he would preach around the fire, and they all required that, because like everybody who gives up everything for the sake of one big idea, they periodically lost all of their hopes. I ought to give a sample of my Pa's preaching, since if we don't hear from him soon we'll never get another chance, but it wouldn't mean much a hundred year away and in a Morris chair or wherever the reader is sitting, when it was originally delivered by evening on the open prairie next a sweetish-smelling fire of dried buffalo dung. It might seem just crazy, without showing any of the real inspiration in it, which was a matter of sound rather than sense, I think, though that may be only because I was a kid at the time. The ironical thing is that my Pa was somewhat like an Indian.

Indians. Now and again, crossing the Nebraska Territory, following the muddy Platte, we would encounter small bands of Pawnee. Indians was Indians to me and of course as a kid I approved of them generally because they didn't seem to have a purpose. The ones we saw would always appear coming over the next divide when the train was a quarter mile away, and would mope along on their ponies as if they were going right on past and then suddenly turn when they got alongside and come over to beg food. What they wanted was coffee and would try to get you to stop and brew them a pot, rather than hand out a piece of bacon rind or lump of sugar while rolling. I believe what they preferred even better than the coffee, though, was to bring our progress to a halt. Nothing drives an Indian crazy like regular, monotonous movement. That's why they not only never invented the wheel, but never even took it up after the white man brought it, as long as they stayed wild, though they were quick enough to grab the horse and the gun and steel knife.

But they really did favor coffee, too, and would sit on their blankets, nodding and saying "How, how" after every sip, and then they chewed the biscuit my Ma would also hand out, and said "How, how" after every swallow of that as well.

Pa, as you might expect, was much taken with Indians because they did what they pleased, and he always tried to involve them in a philosophical discussion, which was hopeless on account of they didn't know any English and he didn't even know sign language. And it is a pity, for as I found out in time to come, there is no one who loves to spout hot air like a redskin.

When the Pawnee were finished they would get up, pick their teeth with their fingers, say "How, how" a couple of times more, climb on their ponies and ride off, with never a word of thanks; but some of them might shake hands, a practice they were just learning from the white man, and as anything an Indian takes up becomes a mania with him, those that did would shake with every individual in the train, man, woman, and child and baby in the cradle; I was only surprised they didn't grab an ox by the right forefoot.

They never said thanks because it wasn't in their etiquette at that time, and they had already shown their courtesy with them incessant "how-how's," which is to say, "good, good." You can look the world over without finding anyone more mannerly than an Indian. The point of these visits had somewhat to do with manners, because these fellows were not beggars in the white sense, the kind of degenerates I seen in big cities who had no other means of support. In the Indian code, if you see a stranger you either eat with him or fight him, but more often you eat with him, fighting being too important an enterprise to waste on somebody you hardly know. We all could have run into one of their camps, and they would have had to feed *us*.

This entertaining kept getting bigger every day, because I figure one Pawnee would tell another, "You ought to go over to that wagon train and get some biscuit and coffee," and as we traveled with them ox only about two miles an hour when moving, and stopping to brew coffee slowed it down even more, we was in range of the tribe for several weeks. Larger and larger bands would show up, including women and even infants in seats fixed up on lodgepoles trailing behind the horses, the so-called travois. So by the time we reached Cheyenne country, in the southeastern corner of what is now the state of Wyoming, and it started all over again with a new tribe, everybody in the wagons had used up their coffee, making that the principal supply we intended to lay in on the stop at Fort Laramie at the junction of the Laramie and North Platte rivers.

At Laramie, though, they had run out of the beans and did not expect another shipment for a week, that being some years before the railroad. Oddly enough my Pa would have been willing to wait, but the others were hot to get on out to California, being they was already three years behind time.

Jonas Troy was an ex-railway clerk who had come out from Ohio. I remember him as wearing a little fringe of beard and having a skinny wife and one kid, a boy about a year older than me, a very nasty child who tended to kick and bite when we fell out at play and then when you got him back would cry.

"Indins," said Mr. Troy, "like whiskey even more than coffee, so I heard. Besides, it's easier to serve. You don't have to stop rolling, just tip the jug."

Troy and my Pa at this minute were standing in front of the stores at Laramie that were built into the inside of the stockade wall. Must have been a dozen people passed them during the time they arrived at that decision who could have told them otherwise and saved their lives—trappers, scouts, soldiers, even Indians themselves —but of course they never thought of asking: Troy because he believed in anything thought up by himself and confirmed by my Pa, and Pa because on the basis of his encounters with the Pawnee he figured he knew an Indian to the core.

"Sure," said Pa. "I can tell you, Brother Troy, that the nature of the fluid don't concern the redman. It is the act of libation itself. Remember it is written in the Book of Mormon that the Indin comprises the lost tribes of Israel. That accounts for my difficulty in speech with them noble specimens along the Platte, knowing not a word of Hebrew though I intend to give it study when we reach Salt Lake. But the Lord has enabled me in His inscrutable wisdom to communicate directly, heart to heart, with our red brothers and what I hear is love and justice commingled."

So they bought a number of full jugs from the traders and shortly thereafter we pulled away from Laramie without any coffee. I can still recall seeing the fields on the west side of the fort covered with junk throwed away by others who had gone before: oak tables and chairs, bookcases with glass doors, a sofa covered in red plush. . . . It's a wonder what some people will want to take across thousands of mile of buffalo grass, desert, river, and mountain. There was even a lot of books laying there, all swoll up from the weather and bust open, and my Pa took time to run through some of them in hopes of finding the Book of Mormon he talked about but actually had not ever seen a copy of, having got all his information on the Latter-day Saints from some traveling tinker who come in the saloon in Evansville and was drunk at that. As a matter of fact, now that I look back on it, I don't think my Pa knew how to read, and such parts of the Gospel as he could quote he had heard from other preachers when he was still a barber.

A day or so from the fort, on the south side of the North Platte, still in rolling grass country though up ahead the bluffs began and beyond them the Laramie Mountains showed peaks of snow, and the date I reckon to have been in early June, we had our chance to give Troy's theory a workout. For here, from the direction of the river, their ponies' feet still dripping water, come a band of about two dozen Cheyenne braves. The Cheyenne is a handsome folk, often tall and straight-limbed, and like all great warriors the men tend to be vain. As courtesy would have it when upon a visit, these fellows were all decked out in bead necklaces and breastplates of joined bones, and their hair was braided with that ribbon the traders carry. Most of them wore a single eagle feather, and one a plug hat of which the crown was cut out so his head could breathe.

As usual, they had appeared of a sudden over a bluff when the train was at the distance of about a quarter mile. You will seldom encounter a party of Indians moving along a flat space; they go along level ground, of course, but the usual white man won't catch them at it. Even after I lived among redskins for some years I couldn't explain how they know when other people are in the neighborhood. Oh, they drive a knife blade into the earth and listen at the haft, but you can't generally hear your prey unless it's galloping. Or they might pile up a little cairn of stones at the top of a divide, and with that as cover for their head, spy around it down the valley. But the plains is one swell after another, like ocean waves frozen in position, and since all you can see from one rise is the intervening stretch to the top of the next, you will miss whatever is beyond it. And the Indians don't pick every divide; just certain ones; yet when they do look, they generally see something.

Troy's idea about serving the whiskey from the rolling wagons was a bust before it was tried. A moving wagon of that era was about as steady as a sleigh being drug across a field of dry boulders, and the bumping was enough to shake a piece of bread to pieces before it reached your mouth, let alone a drink of any description. Besides, the Cheyenne were in a formal mood and dismounted soon as they reached us, coming over to shake hands first, so we surely had to stop.

The fellow in the plug hat was their leader. He wore one of those silver medals that the Government give out to principal men at treaty signings; I think his showed the image of President Fillmore. He was older than the others and he carried an ancient musket with a barrel four foot long.

Now I haven't referred to her before, but my eldest sister was six foot tall and, being very strong of feature, she was still unmarried at more than twenty years of age: a great big rawboned girl with a head of flaming orange hair. She used to spell Pa in driving the ox team and could throw a whip better than any of the men except Edward Walsh, who was an Irishman out of Boston weighing two hundred pounds and as a Catholic never cared for Pa's preaching but was tolerant about it since other than his family there wasn't any more of his own kind along; the others tolerated *him* because he was so big.

This sister's name was Caroline, and on account of her size and doing a man's work, she wore men's clothing on the trail—boots, pants, shirt, and flop hat—although there were those who thought the worse of her for it.

A very athletic person and a stranger to fear, she hopped from the box to the ground on the Indians' approach, and Plug Hat marched up to her, sticking out his brown right hand while the left held the old musket across his front and also kept his red blanket from falling off.

"Right pleased to make your acquaintance," says Caroline, who is a deal bigger than the old chief, and gives him a grip so hard you can see the pain travel up through his hat and down the other arm. He almost lost his blanket. His chest was naked underneath, and that's how I saw his medal and also a scar across his belly that looked like a weld on a piece of iron. That provided the name he was known by among the whites, Scar Belly, though among the Cheyenne he was called Old Lodge Skins, Mohk-se-a-nis, and also Painted Thunder, Wohk-pe-nu-numa, and I never did know his real name, which among Indians is a secret; and if you find it out and call him by it he will at the least be terrible insulted and at the worst have ten years of bad luck.

Old Lodge Skins (at present he didn't identify himself, which always seems irrelevant to an Indian, but I was to see a lot of him in afterdays), when he recovered from Caroline's shake, give a speech in Cheyenne, which was one phase of his courtesy and the other was that in between sentences he said the English words he knew, "god-dam" and "Jesus Christ," which he had been taught for a joke by earlier immigrants and the soldiers at Laramie, and didn't of course understand was cursing and wouldn't have known if it was explained, on account of Indians don't have swearing in their languages though they have lots of things that are taboo: for example, after you are married you can't mention the name of your mother-in-law.

My Pa was standing alongside Caroline, and I don't recall what it was upset him most, the swearing or the attention my sister was getting, but he pushed out in front of her, saying, "If you was looking for the wagonmaster and spiritual leader of this flock, that be me, Your Honor."

Him and Old Lodge Skins then shake hands, and the latter fetches from a beaded pouch he carries in the vicinity of his belly a filthy, tattered hunk of paper on which some other white wag had scrawled the following:

This heer is Skar-gut he is a good indun and takes a bath unse a yar wether he needs it or not he won't cut your thoat under enny condishun so long as you keep a gun on him his heart is as black as his hind end yer fren

BILLY B. DARN

The chief evidently figured this to be a recommendation, because he looked right proud while my brother Bill was reading it aloud on request of my Pa (that's the reason I said earlier I don't think Pa could read himself; but it's more than a hundred year ago and I don't remember everything).

Pa was a considerate person to strangers, especially if they was savages, so he pretended the note said something good and invited the whole bunch to come have a drink, which I don't believe the Cheyenne understood right off. "Whiskey" they would have known, but Pa put it some long way, "potation" or whatever—and they still didn't get it when Troy and our men broke out the jugs. You see, an Indian figures no white man in his right mind would give them liquor unless he had a running start. The traders always left the whiskey negotiation till last, brought out the barrels, and rode off fast as they could go.

Indians are first to admit they can't hold their liquor, and even in those early days some of the chiefs tried to keep it from their young men, though a redskin leader has only advisory power which is frequently ignored. Old Lodge Skins could not believe ten white men, counting the larger boys, half of them unarmed and with only two horses and having seven wagons full of twelve women and girls and eight smaller children, would feed whiskey to two score Cheyenne braves on the open prairie. If he had, he would have warned my Pa before he took a drink, because Indians are fair that way. They don't feel any guilt about what they do under the influence of liquor, regarding it as a mysterious sort of power like a tornado—and you don't see reason to blame yourself for knocking a fellow down if a high wind picks you up and throws you into him; although if you see it coming you would tell him to move clear. So with an Indian when he hits the booze, if he hasn't anything against you.

Old Lodge Skins took the tin cup my Pa handed him and drained it in one swallow, as if it was water or cold coffee, tilting his head back so far the plug hat fell off. The drink was already down his gullet before he altogether comprehended the nature of it, and you might say simultaneous with that recognition he became instantly drunk, his eyes swimming with liquid like two raw eggs. He fell over backwards on the earth and kicked his feet so hard one moccasin flew off and hit the cover of our wagon. His musket dropped, muzzle down, and packed some dirt in the end of the barrel, of which we'll hear more later.

Meanwhile our men politely ignored him and passed on to the other Indians. Not having brought out more cups, they handed around the jugs, grinning and shaking hands, and Troy thought his idea was proceeding so well that he started a practice of slapping the braves on the shoulder as if they was saloon cronies. Now I could see, at the age of ten, that the Cheyenne didn't get the import of that: giving him a present with one hand and striking him with the other, and both by an individual of a different race, would call an Indian's whole code of manners into question, as it would with a horse you fed and flogged at the same time.

The others weren't so quick to fall drunk like Old Lodge Skins, with whom it was more the surprise than the beverage. Having seen him, they were somewhat prepared—well as a redskin can ever be—and went under the influence by stages: sort of pathetic gratitude when they was handed the jug, puzzlement when Troy hit their shoulder, then a slow beginning of elation when the stuff hit the stomach—all this fairly quiet, except of course for the "how-how's" and mutterings of satisfaction.

We might still have got away after everybody had one round apiece, but Old Lodge Skins come back to life, got up, and indicated he would swap his pinto pony, his plug hat, his Government medal, his musket, in fact, everything down to the breechclout, for a second swallow.

"Never mind that," says Pa. "It ain't going to cost a desert patriarch nothing to partake of our hospitality. I just wish I could talk Hebrew." With that, he hands the chief a whole jug all for himself.

Troy gives seconds to a flat-nosed brave and claps his back. This fellow, whose name was Hump, swallows slow, licks his lips, hands back the jug, grimaces like he smells something stinking, then begins to howl like a coyote under a full moon. Everybody else is still quiet at this point, so it sounded funny, and Old Lodge Skins takes a breath between pulls at his own jug and looks glassy-eyed at Hump, which seems to annoy the latter, for he draws his iron tomahawk and starts at the chief, who lifts up the ancient musket and fires it at the other, but the earth, remember, is packed into the muzzle and the barrel peels back, like a banana skin, almost to the lock.

Nevertheless, Hump is scared by the explosion and also unable to reply in kind because he doesn't possess a firearm himself, but only a bow slung over his shoulder along with a quiverful of arrows. He turns slowly, licking his lips, and sees Troy, who is handing refreshment to a young brave called Shadow That Comes in Sight (these names I learned later). Hump studies Troy's back for a spell, then pats him with the left hand like Troy had done him, at which the white man turns, hearty as a fellow at a lodge meeting (he and Pa and our others have ignored the gunshot), and Hump plants the hatchet blade into his forehead. It was one of those trade tomahawks of which the reverse of the head is a pipe that can be smoked by boring a hole through the handle.

Troy looks cross-eyed for a minute at the wooden grip that extends over and parallel to his nose, then Hump withdraws the weapon, letting his victim go over backwards spewing blood. Shadow That Comes in Sight, wearing a numb look, catches up the jug from Troy as the latter goes down. Hump claws at Shadow, who smashes him in the face with the stone vessel, so hard it breaks and they are both dripping with spirits. Hump's right nostril is severed from his nose except for a little skin string, and there seems to be a general net of gore containing his entire face, but he joins Shadow, now that their point of difference is soaking into the ground, in a fresh assault on the nearest jug.

From this juncture on, the altercation becomes general and the noise very barbaric: yells, howls, squeals, and screams, the snicker of steel on bone, the mushy murmur of flesh being laid open, the blast of gunfire, and the wind of arrows as they left and the whonk of their arrival.

The women and us kids stayed back by the wagons, and though I could not make out my Pa in the middle of the pack, I could hear his yawp above all that din: "Brethren, where have I failed?" Then he gargled on a throatful of fluid and blew out his spark. Next time I saw him, on the morning after, the arrows staked him to the ground like a hide stretched out to dry. Yet he still wore his scalp, for this was whiskey and not war, and not being in their right minds, the Indians didn't take trophies. They fought among their own likewise as with the whites, and Pile of Bones blew out the back of White Contrary's head with a cap-and-ball pistol and his brains run out like water from a punctured canteen; he swayed for a long time before he dropped, retaining the jug that had cost him life itself, and Pile of Bones had to hack it from the hands of a corpse.

Walsh, who being Irish had hit the spirits in the wagon before he went to serve the Cheyenne, pulled a knife from his boot, but it got turned in the rush upon him and pierced his own belly; he was dying with terrible sounds. Otherwise, our fellows went down without resistance. Farthest out, I could recognize Jacob Worthing by his boot-bottoms, with the new soles put on at Laramie. John Clairmont, an Illinoisan, lay with his head pointed towards the wagons; I knew him by his baldness. And from the center of the tumult already over, sprouted a little thicket of arrows from among the matted grass. These turned out later to be fixed in my Pa, although at the time I didn't know that but saw the feathered ends as a type of prairie bush.

For a while after the whites were disposed of, the Cheyenne that were left kept sucking at the jugs and paid no mind to the women and children. Which explains how Worthing's wife and kid were able to get away: she picked up her boy and started running, with the wagons as cover between them and the Indians, towards the Laramie Mountains, snow-capped so far away though near-seeming the way eminences are on the prairie. You could see the Mrs. and child for onto a mile, intermittently between their sinking into swells and then coming into sight again on the upward slope; finally they disappeared over a bluff and I have never heard of them from that day to this. The rest of us just stood there dumbstruck, not even crying.

But little Troy at this point up and made a desperate move. He run out to his daddy's body, took a butcher knife off a scabbard in its belt, and stuck the side of a tall Cheyenne who was singing a drunken dirge in between pulls of a jug. An Indian admires that kind of ginger in a kid, and if this particular specimen had not been liquored up he might have give him a present and a strong name, but he was in the demon's grip, and raised the lance on which he had been leaning and drove the boy off the ground on its point, which come out the back of his blue shirt directly, accompanied by a great blossom of scarlet. The Cheyenne kicked him free, and he struck the prairie with the sound of a wet rag being slapped onto a bar-top.

The boy would run from a lad his own age but took on a six-foot savage. As to yours truly, I believe at that time the other children looked on me as a bully though I was underweight and no bigger than a sparrow, for I was the youngest in my family and knocked about a good deal by my brothers and sisters, for which treatment I would pay back them to whom I was not kin. But seeing white men get punishment of this fashion from Indians, I have to admit I let the water drain into my pants.

About a dozen Cheyenne were still conscious when the whiskey was all gone, though some lay flat as the dead and wounded and put a glazed stare upon the sky. Others sat upon their skinny haunches, looking glassily into the crotch, and some whined like injured hounds. Old Lodge Skins was squatting there with his seamed face turned towards Caroline. After all that turmoil, in which, having his own jug, he had not participated except perhaps to set it off, he was yet trying to figure out what her game was, and on my sister's part she was studying him, I think right through the worst of the carnage. Since a year or so back, she had been a peculiar type of person, somewhat forward with the male sex but on the order of another man rather than a harlot.

Hump busted the last jug with his hatchet and run each fragment over his tongue. His nose was dripping fresh blood from where that nostril had since come altogether off and got lost, and his chin ran red, subsequently dyeing his bone breastplate, but he was basically a friendly-looking Indian even now. He had the widest mouth I ever saw on a human being, and his nose, broad to begin with, was smashed more so. For a Cheyenne his eyes were large. He put them in our direction, going over us one by one.

It is true that save Mrs. Worthing and her boy, nobody tried to get away; and except for young Troy, none did any fighting back. You didn't see no rifle-shooting pioneer women with our train. Even Caroline did not know another weapon than her bullwhip. Which she had been holding all this while in her left hand by the stock, the long tail trailing on the prairie behind her. She had no lack of targets to crack it at, but just stood peering at the old chief.

One of our couples was originally out of Germany, called by everybody Dutch Rudy and Dutch Katy, simply the two of them without offspring. Round, pink-faced individuals, two hundred pounds apiece and losing not a gram in those weeks upon the trail, on account of they had brought their wagon filled with potatoes. I could now see Dutch Rudy's belly rising like a hillock from the plain, some yards out. Dutch Katy was leaning against their wagon, two along from ours, wearing her blue sunbonnet, and where her hair showed it was pale and fine as cornsilk. Like all women of them days she was more or less shapeless in her dress, except there was a lot more of her. She was a great hunk of flesh, and on her is where Hump's eyes came to stay after their travel.

Across he staggered, and Katy knowed it was for her and started to appeal in Dutch, but as after a bit it was clear he didn't mean to kill her, or not anyway until he had his pleasure, she went down on the ground slowly as if melted by the sun, and Hump ripped at the gingham and stuffs beneath until he laid her thick flanks bare, pressing his swarthiness between them, him all dirt, blood, and sweat and coughing like a mule. Dutch Katy, like all her countrymen, had always been a maniac for keeping clean. She used to wash at every stop, going in the river while wearing a loose dress for modesty, and had had some close escapes from the quicksand of which the Platte was full. I remember once they had to throw a line over her and draw her out by ox.

This event touched off a general movement by the Cheyenne towards our women, and since there was more of the former than the latter, again the strife began which had so lately ended over the whiskey, and again Indian felled Indian, but enough was left to mount the widows of Troy and Clairmont, and the Jackson sisters—

and if you think there was outcry on the part of the victims, you are wrong; while those who were not raped stood watching those who were as if waiting their own turn, their children clustered around them.

Now Caroline at last woke up when Spotted Wolf come towards my mother. She shouted at Old Lodge Skins, who simply grinned in answer. My fifteen-year-old brother Bill, and Tom who was twelve, they broke and run under the wagon, among the buckets hanging there.

That left me, with my wet pants, and my sisters Sue Ann, thirteen, and Margaret, eleven, and we was hugging Ma.

Caroline tried once again to get the chief's intervention, but it's likely that he never knew what she wanted and it's sure he could have done nothing if he had, and the shadow of Spotted Wolf, an enormous Indian, was already across us and we could smell his stink. My Ma was praying in a low moan. I looked up and saw the Cheyenne's face, which was not wearing what you generally think of as a cruel or indecent expression but rather one kind of dreamy and genial, like he had every O.K. for his lust.

At that moment the black lash of Caroline's whip snaked around his throat, drawing up the bear-claw necklace there, and he went over backwards, cracking his head on a rock and didn't get up.

"You go with the kids to climb in the wagon, Ma," said Caroline, coolly withdrawing her whip into a big loop. "None of these individuals will trouble you further." Caroline was completely self-possessed as she said this; she was as arrogant as my Pa.

Old Lodge Skins was pointing at the unconscious body of Spotted Wolf and laughing his guts out. That irked Caroline, but also pleased her, and she flicked her whip sort of flirty at the chief. He flopped onto his back with his arms crucified and laughed his old mouth, dark as a cave full of bats, into the sun. His foot was still bare and his busted gun lay near him like the skeleton of an open umbrella.

Ma did what Caroline said, gathered us kids together, including the two cowards down among the ox dung, and we went into the wagon, where we found room for all of us though there really wasn't any, what with the furniture, boxes, and bags that represented our worldly goods. Tom's shoe was in my face, rather nasty considering what he had walked in, and I was wrapped around a barrel now full of crockery but which had once held salt-fish and never lost the aroma, but we was lucky to be alive, so you didn't hear no complaints.

All afternoon we stayed there; it was like being closed up in a bag lying in the sun, because the junk in the wagon bed cut off the air without insulating any. Outside the noise died away within an hour, and when after midafternoon Bill took nerve to raise the side canvas and peep from under, he reported no one standing within the range of his eye.

We then all shivered at the squeak of somebody climbing into the box out front, but Caroline soon poked her head in through the puckered opening and said: "All quiet, folks. You stay where you are and don't worry none. I'll be sitting right here all night."

Ma whispered: "Can you do anything for your poor Pa, Caroline? What become of him?"

"He is stone-dead," said Caroline, plenty disgusted, "and all the rest along with him, and I got enough to do right here without keeping the buzzards off them."

"You know," said Ma, addressing us all, "if he had had time to learn the Hebrew lingo he would have been all right."

"Yes, Ma'm," answered Caroline and withdrew.

I managed after a while to drop off and wrapped around that barrel I stayed asleep till dawn, at which time Sue Ann poked me awake with a spade handle maneuvered through the baggage. They were all the rest of them up and out, and I crawled forth sore of body but empty of mind until I touched the earth and heard the sound of shovels. The surviving women—and that I believe was all of them, for they had been smart enough not to resist, and when finished the drunken Indians had been too weak for further mayhem and collapsed—were digging graves with the help of the older children.

Already before dark on the afternoon before, what with the hot sun, the coyotes and carrion birds had got quick wind of the matter and paid the field a visit. The results was fairly evil. Now with people moving, the birds wheeled high and the coyotes sat out on the prairie just beyond gun range.

The Cheyenne were all gone, and their dead with them. When I asked Caroline, who claimed to have been awake all night and would know, she said: "Don't you worry none about that, but go and help the folks with Pa."

It was then I saw my Pa for the last time, as hitherto described.

Ma and the rest of the family unpinned his body from the ground, and we lowered him into the shallow grave dug by Caroline and filled it in, which took quite a few shovelfuls, as I recall, to cover the end of his nose. Nearby, Dutch Katy was performing the same service for Dutch Rudy. She was wearing a fresh dress and her fair hair was dark with wet: it was plain she had already been down to the river for her bath. I won't say I never saw a dirty German, but the clean ones go to an excess.

Now we was just finished putting our menfolk under the sod, when someone looked up and shrieked like a crow, and there was the Cheyenne coming down the rise. There was now but three of them, Old Lodge Skins and two braves, the latter each leading four riderless ponies. They showed no preparation for violence, but this second appearance was too much for most, and for the first time our people began to yell and cry. Back under the wagon went Tom and Bill. Caroline was the exception. I remember while grabbing onto her bony hips in my own fright, looking up at her face I observed a rather keen look about the nostrils like a horse's when he smells water.

The other two, with their herd, stayed back some thirty yards while Old Lodge Skins rode forward on his brown-and-white pinto, which had painted rings around the eyes. He put up his hand and orated for about fifteen minutes in a queer falsetto. His plug hat was a little more crushed than yesterday but otherwise he appeared in perfect shape.

It was strange how in no time at all everybody went from fear to being excruciatingly bored, and the very women who yesterday had been helpless victims and just minutes earlier were howling in fright, now began to advance on him threatening with their fists and saying: "Git on out of here, you old skunk!" Which shows something about the way a female is put together; she will suffer any outrage so long as it is interesting, but bore her and she don't know fear.

But Caroline spoke up. "Settle down, now," said she, swaggering out in front of the crowd. "Don't you understand they come back for me? That's what the horses is for, to pay for hauling me off. You noticed yesterday, didn't you, that I wasn't touched while all that nasty business was being done to *you?* They was saving me, was what they was doing." My sister's cheeks were a deal more ruddy than the sun could be held accountable for, and she was tossing around her copper hair like the flies was at her face.

"Now, you'd better let them take me," she went on, "unless you want to get kilt like the men."

"But Caroline," Ma asked plaintively, "what in the world do they want you for?"

"Probly torture me in various devilish ways," Caroline answered very proudly. I thought it a strange thing to boast about, myself, but held my peace, because what I could see was that my sister reminded me of nobody so much as my Pa. That poor thing was determined to be extravagant.

The Widow Walsh then said: "Ah, go on, then. I ain't stopping them," and turned away, the rest of the women with her. They had lost their men and been raped and were stranded in the wilderness, and there was no way back but that by which they had been months in coming, so they could hardly be much moved by what happened to one girl.

Old Lodge Skins was impassively sitting his horse, watching us through droopy eyelids. On the wooden saddle hung his shield, round, made of hide, and adorned with ten black scalps. In place of the blown-up musket he now carried a lance from the shaft of which dangled a couple more hanks of hair. He wasn't a bad-looking dog, or hadn't been in his youth, anyway, whenever that was; his braids now were shot with gray and the muscles of his limbs were stringy. It is hard to tell an Indian's age, but he must have been within smelling distance of seventy. He grew a big nose with a long, hooking sweep to it, and the ends of his mouth had slight upward twists, whereas his eyes was sad. He generally wore a sort of good-natured melancholy as to expression. You couldn't say he looked dangerous in any wise; indeed, it was rather Caroline who seemed savage at this juncture.

She had been a tomboy but was getting on in years, and the men never took to her back in Evansville except as a pal. She had got a crush on the local blacksmith, a widower of forty, and hung around the forge, but as far as he went was to let her hold a horse's hoof while he shoed it. Then there was some farmer's son: I think for a time they spread manure together, forked hay, and the like. Not even them drummers who came and went, of whom it was said they would screw a snake if somebody'd hold its head, paid her attention as a woman. White men had never done much good for her, you see, and now Pa and the others with the wagons had got themselves killed.

I mention this to explain Caroline's peculiar manner at that time. I think she was also humiliated at not having been raped.

"Well, Caroline," said Ma, standing there in her long, washed-out dress and sunbonnet; she looked like one of them little dolls you can make out of a hollyhock blossom with a bud for its head. My Ma was small, not far over five feet, and I reckon my lifelong shortness is due to hers. "Well, Caroline, I expect we will have to go back to Laramie. I'll tell the soldiers and they'll come to fetch you."

"I wouldn't count on that," replied Caroline. "Indins know all about how to hide their tracks."

"Well, then," Ma said, "you must drop a button now and again, or a piece of your shirt, to lay a trail."

Caroline impatiently scraped the sweat from her forehead and wiped the hand on the butt of her jeans. She believed, I think, that Ma was trying to diminish her danger and self-concocted glory, and the direct result of that was the cooking of my goose.

"Maybe they won't hurt me permanently," said Caroline. "Maybe they'll hold me for ransom. I don't expect to be murdered, or why would they want Jack to come along, too?"

That awful whimper, I discovered after a bit, was issuing from my own throat. Hearing my name had set it off.

To her credit my Ma went up to Old Lodge Skins's horse and begged him not to take me, on account of I was her youngest and only ten years old and skinny. He nodded with sympathy, but when she was done he beckoned to his followers, who rode in and tied all eight horses to our wagon as if the deal had been closed. Even then the subsequent events might have failed to transpire had not the Cheyenne hung around for a bit in the hopes they would get a cup of coffee! Indians simply never understood whites and vice versa.

"Bill will take one of the ponies and ride back for the soldiers fast as he can go," Ma said, giving me a great hug. "Don't think bad of your Pa, Jack. He done the best he could, given his vision. Maybe by taking you and Caroline, the Indians are trying after their own fashion to make up for what they done yesterday. I don't think they're bad people, Jack, or they wouldn't have brung the horses."

There you had it. Nobody thought to ask Caroline how she knew what the Cheyenne were up to without speaking their language.

There was a time when I suspected my Ma actually wanted to get rid of us, because the soldiers never came; which was before I found out, some years on, that Bill rode back to Laramie, sold the horse, got a job with the traders, and not only never reported about us to the Army but also never rejoined the wagons. No, my Ma was well-meaning but ignorant. My Pa was crazy and my brother was a traitor. Then there was Caroline. They weren't much of a family, I guess, but then I was not with them long.

Ma give us each a kiss, and Caroline mounted one of the ponies brought by the Indians, pulling me up behind. The other kids waved in silence, Bill with a dirty, scared grin. Old Lodge Skins, dawdling about nearby on his horse, grunted quizzically and covered his lips. I didn't know then that this is how Indians show astonishment—their mouth falls open and they cover it so their soul can't jump out and run away.

He thereupon gave evidence of wanting to make another speech, but Caroline motioned him to come on, dug her heels into the mount, which was skittish owing to its unfamiliarity with white hindquarters, and we went off like a cannon shot, heading north.

At top of the rise, she pulled in on the rawhide bridle and waited for the three Cheyenne, who weren't in no hurry, I'll say that for them. Then we rode on down to the river, which was yellow and swollen from the spring rains, and swam the ponies across, I holding onto the tail of ours and spinning behind like a lure on a fish-line.

CHAPTER 2 *Boiled Dog*

ON THE OTHER SIDE of the river, Caroline fetched me up on the pony's rump again, and said in a new sappy, romantic way that would have been pathetic were I not numb from fear and now swamped with the muddy water of the Platte: "Maybe, Jack, I'm going to be an Indin princess in feathers and beads."

I never had rode horse much before, and already it was beginning to get me in the crotch and hams from jolting up and slamming down at every stride; and if I dug my heels into the beast's yellow haunches, he would blow out his belly and try to shiver his arse out from under mine. I had not made a friend in that animal, which was a pity being as he was my sole means of support in a vast and alien land populated by savages.

One of the latter came up alongside us at that moment, namely Old Lodge Skins himself, whom the river crossing had changed as to personality. I later found he had a special feeling about the Platte, regarding it as the southern boundary of his territory and when on the other side felt foolish and irresponsible, whereas when north of it came back to normal, whatever that was. Anyway, once he rode in out of the water, he gave us a stern look from under his hat, pointed back over a bony shoulder protruding from his blanket, as if to say "Get behind," and trotted his animal up the bank.

We followed, our horse making the bluff in a couple of tries owing to his double load—not that I was that much extra weight, but rather because he never lost an opportunity to let me know I was an imposition.

Now when Indians travel, they go every which way according to their personal taste. Them two braves who had come with the chief didn't cross at the same place as us. One rode down a hundred yards and swum his pony over, and the other went upstream for about a mile, then the river took a bend and he went around it out of sight. I guess he knew a better place. We didn't see him again for an hour, until we come over a rise, and there he sat on the earth, his mount grazing nearby. Old Lodge Skins passed him without so much as a look, and the brave returned the compliment. The latter started singing, though, in an awful moaning fashion that we could hear for a long time thereafter, when so far off he looked like a tiny bush.

After I had lived some time with the Cheyenne and learned their peculiarities, I remembered that incident and realized that the fellow had been in a "mood." Something had offended him—maybe the river crossing he used had turned out to be full of quicksand or a frog on the shore called him an insulting name—and he moped along full of depression, and deciding to die, he sat down and began to sing his death song. In the old days before the coming of the whites, other than in battle Indians never kicked off except from shame. But the white men brought a number of diseases—like smallpox, which wiped out the entire Mandan nation—and that took the point away from dying for moral reasons, so it was cut out for the most part, although some willful individuals like our friend might try upon occasion.

Apparently it didn't work this time because I saw the same fellow next day in camp, where he was peering into a little trade mirror and plucking out facial hair with a bone tweezer. His vanity had got the upper hand, so he must have recovered by then.

The riding got somewhat easier because the chief proceeded in a slow walk and every half mile or so stopped altogether, turned to us, and made certain hand signals accompanied by noises in his heathen tongue—communications which Caroline interpreted as statements of admiration for herself and suchlike rot. Then he would stare sadly at us for a minute and head on.

Now I better explain part of the secret at this point, as long as you understand what neither Old Lodge Skins nor me got the hang of it until quite a spell afterward. As to Caroline, well, it's useless to speculate about what she thought she knew or what she imagined, because they was always all mixed together.

The main thing was that the chief *had not made a deal to buy me and Caroline back at the wagons.* What he done instead was make a long statement on the massacre, excusing the Cheyenne from any responsibility for it; but to be decent, because he liked white men still at this time and he also figured to get blamed when the story reached the troops at Laramie, he brought them horses to pay for the men that were killed.

So there we were, what with Caroline's taste for romance and the gift for jumping to conclusions she inherited from our Pa, trailing Old Lodge Skins across the prairie under a terrible misapprehension. The chief thought we was following him to get more reparation and the speeches he made at them stops was to protest against the injustice of our hounding him like coyotes, who will sometimes follow you for miles.

Caroline stared at him in love, and that poor Indian interpreted it as the look of ruthless extortion. In later years I grew greatly fond of Old Lodge Skins. He had more bad luck than any human being I have ever known, red or white, and you can't beat that for making a man likable.

As I say, none of us understood the situation, but me and Caroline was considerably better off than the chief, because we only looked to him for our upkeep in the foreseeable future, whereas he at last decided we was demons and only waiting for dark to steal the wits from his head; and while riding along he muttered prayers and incantations to bring us bad medicine, but so ran his luck that he never saw any of the animal brothers that assisted his magic—such as Rattlesnake or Prairie Dog—but rather only Jackrabbit, who had a grudge against him of long standing because he once had kept a prairie fire off his camp by exhorting it to burn the hares' homes instead. Which it did, turning away from his lodges after coming so close the tepee-skins was scorched. Ever since that incident the rabbits all knew him, and when encountering him alone would stand up on them enormous hind legs and say: "We think bad thoughts for you." They would also call him by his real name, which is as malicious as you can get, and go bounding off, showing white or black tail as the case may be, for both families had it in for that particular Indian.

And I'll say this: I never in my life saw more examples of that animal than when in the company of Old Lodge Skins. Let the toe of his moccasin protrude from the tepee, and up they'd leap for miles about, numerous as sparks when you throw a horseshoe in the forge.

But the one defense a redskin has against the kind of harassment me and Caroline was, unbeknownst to us, dealing to our host is loss of interest. If an Indian can't accomplish his purpose with reasonable haste, it bores hell out of him and he will forget it immediately. He is interested only in a going proposition. So with Old Lodge Skins, who after a bit tightened the scarlet blanket around him, which under a hot sun kept him cooler than had he exposed his naked back, and rode on as if he was the only living individual north of the River Platte.

The third brave (counting as second the fellow sitting back a ways under the illusion he was dying) specialized in being always a half a mile off, to the left, right, or ahead. I guess he was looking both for enemies and something to eat. At any given time the Cheyenne was over-furnished with the first and had too little of the second.

In such fashion we proceeded towards the Cheyenne camp, which I reckon to have been not more than ten mile, as the arrow flies, from the Platte in a direction north by northeast; but it took our little party three or four hours to get there, owing to the chief's warped manner of navigating so as to discourage me and Caroline.

The sun still held itself a hand's width above the horizon, but the prairie underhoof was slowly turning purplish. A person who knows that land can fix his look on a square foot of turf, never turning to the sky, and tell you the hour of day at any moment from the general cast of light upon it. I mean a white man. An Indian don't keep that sort of time because he ain't, in the white sense, ever going anywhere. You can imagine Columbus saying, "I better get started: it's 1492 and I got to get across the ocean blue before midnight on December 31st or else America won't be discovered till '93," but a redskin computes in another fashion. The sign-language term for "day" is the same as for "sleep." Now, looking at a patch of earth, an Indian would see which animals had stepped there during the past two weeks, what birds had flown overhead, and how far it was to the nearest water—this in addition to a lot of supernatural stuff, because he does not separate the various types of vitality one from the next.

So if I say Old Lodge Skins went along in a coma, I mean as far as we were concerned. He knew where he was, all right, and at one point caught the attention of the scouting brave—whose name I might as well give: Burns Red in the Sun—pointed ahead to rising ground, and showed a hooked finger. Burns Red traveled in from the left flank and slipped off his pony, undoing the single rein of the rawhide war bridle from his belt and tying it to a lance which he drove into the earth. He dropped his blanket and stripped off his leggings. In his breechclout and carrying bow and arrows, he snuck up the long swell of which we others waited at the foot, flopping to his belly just before the point of divide. The grass hereabout had been trampled flat by a great herd of buffalo and not long before, it not having sprung back yet, and you could see him snaking all the way until his moccasin soles tipped up and disappeared.

Shortly there came on the wind, blowing from him to us, the *thunnng, thunnng* of two arrows leaving the bowstring, a rush of little hoofs, and then Old Lodge Skins trotted up and over, me and Caroline naturally hard behind. There, squatting at a buffalo wallow half filled with water, was Burns Red in the Sun. Alongside him lay a pronghorn antelope whose panting throat he was in the act of cutting, the animal having been felled but not killed by a shaft to the left haunch. The other shot had missed altogether; still, Burns Red had done a nice piece of work, creeping to within fifty feet of the little pack, the remaining four of which were now at the distance of a quarter mile and still going. That creature can run.

The next thing Burns Red did was to cut off that black and white rosette of tail from the antelope's behind, which he would keep for decoration, it being a cunning little item. Then he slit open its chest at the division between the ribs, and plunging in his fist, he ripped out the gory heart, hot and still palpitating. This he shoved at me.

At the sight of that dripping offal, I shivered off, but Burns Red seized my nape with one hand and pushed the heart in my mouth with the other. That was actually a mark of preference, for he was mighty fond of fresh antelope heart himself, to which he owed his prowess as swiftest runner in Old Lodge Skins's band, but of course I didn't know that then. However, I was scared of Burns Red in the Sun, who had the peculiarity mentioned in his name, as many Indians do though some others are almost black, and to protect his cheeks he daubed them with a coat of clay that dried a wolfish gray-white, from which his eyes peered little and glittering like a serpent's.

So I gnawed off a hunk of bloody heart, which was not the easiest work owing to the stringy vessels that run through it, and he relieved me of the rest and gulped it right down. My nausea disappeared once I fully swallowed the raw morsel, the taste of which I can only describe as live and fleet. Immediately the calf-muscles of my legs started to hum like plucked bowstrings and I felt I could have caught the wind had not we all mounted again, Burns Red with the antelope carcass leaking gore on the rump of his pony, where he toted it.

Old Lodge Skins had detected the beasts on the other side of the hill, though there was no way he could have seen them. He had a gift for that sort of thing, which was unusually acute even for an Indian. The way he knew was having dreamed it. He was dreaming as he rode along that day, right in the middle of the prairie. He didn't need nighttime or even to fall asleep.

Not long after shooting the antelope we arrived at the Cheyenne camp, which had located on a little creek about as wide as a gun-stock and was shaded by no more than three cottonwood, two of which were only saplings. We pulled up on the knoll above, so as to give them time to identify us as ourselves rather than Crow come to run off the Cheyenne ponies. Old Lodge Skins was full of such courtesies—which is what this could be called, because nobody around that camp was ever alert for intruders; at least once a week they were successfully raided by horse thieves from enemy tribes, sometimes in broad daylight.

What could be seen from the knoll was as follows: a couple of dozen hide tepees, pitched on the right bank of the stream. In the meadow beyond, a pony herd of some thirty head. In the water itself, a number of giggling, bare-arsed brown children slapping water at one another. A bunch of able-bodied young men sitting around smoking and fanning themselves with eagle feathers, a few others strutting up and down wearing finery before a group of womenfolk pounding something on the ground. A couple of young girls towing in from the prairie a buffalo robe full of the stacked dry dung of the same animal, the so-called chips used for fuel on the plains being there was little wood available. A heavy-set female chewing soft a hunk of hide. Others going for water and hauling bundles and mending lodge skins and making moccasins, sewing leggings, fringing shirts, marrowing bones, grinding berries, stitching beads, and the rest of the duties to which an Indian woman gives herself from dawn until she lies on her robe at night and her man mounts her.

As we come down to the creek nobody in camp paid the slightest notice, but when Burns Red in the Sun, who rode last, splashed across with the antelope slung behind, it created quite a stir among the women. I found out later that band hadn't had a bite of meat for about ten days and was feeding on prairie turnips and old rawhide and considering the chewing of grasshoppers like the Paiutes, which to an Indian is about as low as you can get. This was in late spring, when in those days the plains were ordinarily hairy with buffalo, and if you recall, the grass on the hill near the water hole had been beaten down by a great herd. Yet Old Lodge Skins's bunch hadn't ate flesh for more than a week. That's what I mean about their bad luck.

Now a special mention to their dogs. Little as the band was, they had thirty or more mongrels, the prevailing color of which was pus-yellow though every other hue was also represented, including a good many of the spotted variety. This crowd kept up a constant din at all times, snarling, barking, howling, quarreling among themselves, so that they were generally worthless as watchmen, even in the nights, which they would spend answering the coyotes who wailed from the bluffs while the Pawnee snuck in and cut out a dozen ponies without drawing a growl.

These dogs met us at the creek, swarming among the horses' legs and jumping at the antelope's head as it swung lifeless above them. But they was also wary of the rawhide quirt strapped to Burns Red's left wrist, which he flicked negligently at them like a horse scattering flies with his tail, so though they clamored and snapped their fangs, they didn't actually bite nothing. The secret to enduring an Indian dog is to ignore his noise; he hasn't got much worse. I didn't learn that right off, and had some bad times, as right now: there was one dirty white dog, with red eyes and a slavering mouth, who decided to give me his preference over the antelope carcass. He crouched below our pony's left haunch, and while studying my face, slowly rolled back his upper lip at the same time as his lower jaw fell away, making all in all a very savage exhibition of yellow ivory. Caroline had to elbow me in the ribs so as to draw breath, I was hugging her that tight.

"Now don't shame me before our friends, Jack," said she, straining to smile at the Cheyenne women crowding round, none of whom however give us yet a glance. I believe at that point Caroline had already begun to lose her nerve. I don't know what exactly she had thought she was getting into, but at the first sight of an Indian camp the stoutest heart is likely to quail. Without experience of them, you tend to think: well, I see their dump, but where's the town? And the smell alone is very queer: it isn't precisely a stench as white people know one, but a number of stinks melding together into a sort of invisible fog that replaces the air, so that with every breath you draw in all the facts of life concerning mankind and the four-footed animals. Right now it had a principal odor, owing to our pony staling under us at the very moment. Except in the case of such a particular event nearby, no smells predominated. You was just completely in another type of existence from the first minute your lungs filled with that atmosphere.

But, like anything else, living in it made it your reality, and when next I entered a white settlement, I missed the odor of what seemed to me life itself and felt I would suffocate.

Burns Red in the Sun dismounted and stalked proudly around camp, leaving the throng of women to dispose of the antelope, which they fell on and skinned in the time it takes to fill and light a pipe, and began to butcher with like speed. As to Old Lodge Skins, he walked his pony to a big but shabby tepee the cover of which, in between where it was patched, bore faded blue-and-yellow drawings—stick-men, scratchy animals, triangle-mountains, button-suns, and the like—got down, handed the single rein to a boy who was standing there in a leather breechclout and nothing else but moccasins, and ducking almost to his knees so his plug hat would clear and holding it besides, went in through the entrance hole.

"This here," says my sister Caroline, "I believe, is home." What I could see of her face when she turned in the saddle, looked definitely peaked. "But," she went on, "would it be seemly for us to foller him indoors? That's the question."

"Caroline," I answered, "I am raw and sore from this riding, and my Pa is dead and my Ma is far away, and that white dog is still alongside watering at the mouth. I am scared to get down."

At that some of my sister's spirit returned. "I sure won't let a dirty little dog stop me," she said with heat, and having flipped her leg over the saddle, raking me with a bootheel in the process, she dropped to the ground. The dog ignored her utterly. Taking her cue from the chief, she also give her rein to the Indian kid, who was staring at me out of his bright black eyes. For racial reasons I didn't take to him, but I jerked my thumb at the dog, who was waiting for nothing in the world but my coming down where it could conveniently get at me.

Being a shrewd lad, he got the idea and fetched the cur a foot in the rump that sent it whining off. So added to my natural bias against him was that favor, and I hopped to the ground with my nose lifted and on the strength of spite trailed Caroline as she took a big gulp of air and entered the lodge.

It was marvelously dark in there, coming from the outdoor brightness of afternoon, and whatever you could see owed to the presence of a little buffalo-chip fire in the center of the floor and such light as fell through the smokehole at the top of the cone. Now if the outside smell was remarkably ripe, you could never recall it after one whiff of indoors a tepee, where it was like trying to breathe underwater in a swamp.

After a while I could make out a stout woman stirring a pot over the fire, but she didn't lift her head at us. All round the circumference of the lodge were dark forms, their heads against the skin wall and feet pointing towards the middle, which closer inspection showed to be not persons recumbent but hairy buffalo robes. It was so dark we had to traipse from one to another, never knowing but that the next might be occupied by some savage who might take the intrusion very ill. We had half-circled the fire before locating Old Lodge Skins, whose bed was directly opposite the door. He was sitting silent there, and Caroline almost fell over him, catching herself at the last minute on a tepee pole from which was dangling a number of skin bags and bundles containing such few private possessions as an Indian owns.

The chief held a stone pipe which had a wooden shank a foot and a half in length and was decorated with a series of brass tacks that winked in the firelight. We just stood watching him, on account of having no place else to go. He filled his pipe bowl from a little leather pouch and then the stout woman put a stick in the fire until it caught and blew it into a burning coal, fetching it to him, who thereupon lighted up, sucking so hard his cheeks caved in like a skull's. Owing to the length of the stem, it was powerful hard to keep one of them pipes going, but he got it to where he was satisfied, then all at once shoved it towards Caroline.

My sister, mannish as she tended to be, however had not smoked nor chewed her life long. She admired the pipe kindly and passed it back to Skins. The chief correctly supposed she didn't savvy what was wanted, and indicated with his fingers she should sit down upon the buffalo robe at his right. Then Old Lodge Skins leaned across and placed the end of the stem in her mouth, while mimicking with his own lips the action of smoking.

Caroline accepted the mouthpiece and went to puffing according to Old Lodge Skins's model. Of course, to her this, I believe, was a type of sexual ritual or the like. The chief, however, was muttering incantations against what he thought was her bad medicine directed at him, and the fact that she had taken the pipe encouraged him to believe that his charms would work, because an Indian holds by smoking above all things.

Old Lodge Skins finally took the device away when it got to where she was expelling only a thin vapor, and Caroline gasped and chewed awhile on her neckerchief. She was panting for a goodly time after, but never passed out and didn't puke. Caroline was a pretty tough old girl.

The chief now loosened the ashes in the pipe bowl and poured them out on the toes of Caroline's boots, so as to give her bad luck, only we didn't know that at the time. Then he stoked up again from his beaded pouch with what was actually in small part tobacco, the rest being made up of red-willow bark, sumac leaves, the marrow from buffalo bones, and several other ingredients. Indians of course invented the habit of smoking, and almost nothing else.

By the time he had smoked his own bowl out, Old Lodge Skins changed his whole style. He grinned, he spoke a good deal of Cheyenne in an affable tone, and he said something to the woman at the fire that was apparently orders, for she left directly and come back with a fresh hunk of antelope from the carcass earlier referred to.

This moon-faced woman hacked up the flesh and threw it in the pot with the mess already simmering there. I figure it was on account of the smell that while the meal was cooking a bunch of Indians began to show up at the tepee. First come that boy who took the horses, and then another stoutish woman who from the back was a dead ringer for the cook, and a tiny girl wearing not a stitch and a slightly bigger lad likewise; next appeared a fine tall fellow about twenty-five years of age; and finally Burns Red in the Sun, the breadwinner himself, still in his mask of clay, and just behind him a procession beginning with a slender woman with a great fall of loosely braided black hair and eyes soft as a doe. Three or four kids followed her, the oldest about six.

These people squatted around the circle of the lodge wall and had eyes for nothing but that pot. Most of them brought their own wooden bowls and some had spoons of the same or else horn. They never uttered a sound, and not once did they so much as glance at me and Caroline.

After a bit the cook ladled out a bowl each for my sister and me, and then the others gathered around and got theirs. Old Lodge Skins didn't eat a thing, just sat there on his buffalo hides and looked grand.

Now it happened that I remembered how the redskins that had come to our wagons always said "How, how" when they ate biscuit and drank coffee. I still felt mighty uneasy about the whole situation, and though I was terrible hungry, that meal did very little for my peace of mind: it was pretty strong, I'll tell you. The antelope chunks weren't too well done. Indians don't have a prejudice against grease, on the one hand; and on the other, they weren't given in those days to using salt. Along with the meat was some chokecherries all cooked to a mush, and a root or two that didn't have a taste until you swallowed it and it fell all the way to your belly and gave off the aftereffect of choking on sand.

But, as I say, I recalled that courteous remark and put it. I wanted them people to like me. They weren't paying no attention to us yet, but I had seen how Indians could change. "How, how, how," said I, right to Old Lodge Skins. It took a bit of nerve. Caroline give me a poke, but the chief was considerably pleased.

In fact, he shot it right back at me, "How, how," and then spoke something that turned out, after I learned to parley in Cheyenne, to be my first Indian name: Little Antelope, which was *Voka* in that lingo and sounded like a cough. As a name it had no undue importance since I got several more in time, but was a start. At least I hadn't been scalped for uttering the sentiment, which I had considered not unlikely, for you probably ain't got no conception of what it resembles to be a boy of ten newly joined a pack of barbarians.

And Caroline got a favor, because while the chief was grinning at me, I saw her fish a big hunk of meat from her bowl and slip it outside under the tepee skin, where a dog could be heard to gnaw it up straightway, because you never find a nook or cranny in an Indian camp that don't have a dog right at hand.

I figure it was the colorful aspect of the Indians, along with their cruelty, that she had been attracted by back at the wagons; but the longer we stayed with Old Lodge Skins, the more commonplace the life of a savage seemed. For it is true that an Indian can slaughter a person one minute and the next sit down to his grub as quiet as a clerk in the settlements. He don't make the separation between the various endeavors that a white man does. Indians are altogether different from anybody you ever knew.

Next thing, the chief said a word to the cook—because as he admitted later, his feelings towards us was really mixed: we would appear to him by turns benign and malevolent. Right then he was kindly disposed to us on account of our breaking bread, or rather antelope, in his tepee, which does an Indian so much honor that the host never takes a bite till his guests are finished; that's the reason Old Lodge Skins himself wasn't eating. As I say, the chief gave word to the cook and she beckoned to me to come along with her, which I did in some apprehension and passed while making the half-circle of the lodge all them Cheyenne chewing like goats. When we got outside through the door hole, the sky was about half along towards dark with great purple smears in the west, separated each from the next by streaks of vermilion.

I'll tell you I was not awfully interested in scenery at that age, and the reason I was looking to the sky could be laid to the reappearance, no sooner than my head cleared the tepee flap, of my enemy that white dog. I was trying to ignore him, but he seized my trouser cuff and proceeded to chaw on it, and he might have ate me up had not the woman looked back at that point.

She was Buffalo Wallow Woman, Old Lodge Skins's wife, and the other inside who favored her was her younger sister, White Cow Woman, who according to the Cheyenne practice had come along with her kin when the latter married and was obliged in the same degree as the proper wife to make herself available to the chief for all the purposes to which an Indian puts a female.

Anyway, Buffalo Wallow Woman laughed, and pointing at the dog, put a question to me. Taking my tearful look as sufficient answer, she picked up the animal, who thereupon howled with anguish which availed him nothing. For directly Buffalo Wallow Woman carried him inside the tepee, where she busted his skull with a stone hammer, rolled him through the fire to singe his hair, chopped the carcass to a number of bleeding hunks, then into a kettle they went to boil. This was the work of as many moments as it takes to tell it, for she was a plump and powerful soul, and smiling all the while.

Old Lodge Skins was looking proud enough to bust. There isn't any better eating to an Indian than dog, and white dog is the very best of that. To show you how high they regard this victual, they had had no fresh meat for more than a week yet forbore from touching their dog pack.

I'm afraid that me and Caroline failed to understand the honor we was being done at that juncture. My sister stood fast at the massacre of people, including her own Pa, but when it come to seeing that ugly dog butchered before our eyes, she began to sway on her crossed legs and try to swallow her fist.

That was when Old Lodge Skins all at once looked at Caroline and sneezed so hard his plug hat slipped down over one eye. He sneezed again, and off it fell entirely. Twice more he spasmed in his big nose—it sounded like the barking of a fox—and his braids flew and his medal leaped up, falling back with a *thunk* against his breast-bone.

Now the whole pack left off stuffing grub down their gullets and gawked at us like they should have when we first appeared but I guess failed to because, having minds of one track, they was fascinated with the prospect of eating that antelope. The pretty woman with the doe eyes went so far as to come and set right on Caroline's very buffalo skin and peer incessantly at my sister, who had all she could put up with just in trying not to vomit on account of the white dog, who you could already smell in the steam from the pot, sort of the odor of a wet overcoat hanging near a fire to dry.

Shooting Star was that woman's name and she was the wife of Burns Red in the Sun and had give birth to the several children she had brought to the chief's tepee, including one tiny baby in a cradleboard hanging from a lodgepole, who had beady little black eyes like a bird. His contraption was arranged so he could water without being took out of the sling.

The curiosity of Shooting Star served to take Caroline's mind off the perturbations of her stomach, and she summoned her strength to say: "Right proud to meet you, Mrs.," offering one of her big paws to shake on it. But what the Indian woman did instead was reach into the fork of my sister's jeans and feel there, then the same with the chest of her shirt. Concluding which, she spoke one word to Old Lodge Skins: "*Vehoa!*" and clapped a hand over her own mouth. The chief followed suit and was joined by everybody present in the same gesture.

Sooner or later an Indian will sneeze when he is near a white woman. Some say that is due to perfume or talcum powder, but I never saw my sister use anything on herself but yellow soap.

However you want to explain it, that was the first time any of the Cheyenne knew Caroline for a girl.

CHAPTER 3 *I Make an Enemy*

THE DIFFERENCE BETWEEN men and women is very important to the Cheyenne—more so than the distinction of the dead from the living, as a matter of fact—and they was satisfied to have established it insofar as my sister went. Besides, the antelope was all ate up at that moment and the dog wasn't quite ready. So the rest of the Indians come crowding round us to exercise their curiosity.

This was mannerly by their lights. They restricted themselves to peering, for the most part; and some handled our clothing, but never touched flesh. I believe could we have understood Shooting Star's remarks, we would have heard her in so many words apologize to Caroline for the laying on of hands—which was justified by the facts derived from it. I mention this because, being white, it always seemed marvelous to me that savages was not inconsiderate except through ignorance.

Particular attention was of course paid me by the kids. Little Horse, that boy who had cared for the ponies—I sure made a big hit with him from the first. As I have said, I did not take to him; but even at that age I was shifty, had to be, else I wouldn't have survived a decade let alone more than a century, and so when I saw him admiring my boots, I stripped them off quick and offered to hand them over. But the thought of confining his feet in such fashion is one of the many things that scares an Indian, so he pretended not to get the purpose.

The dog was served up directly. Fortunately it was a small animal and had to go around to many eaters, although as guests me and Caroline got the largest chunks. The Cheyenne proceeded to stay up to midnight, it must have been. When I say that, I mean various of them came and went, new individuals entered the lodge and inspected my sister and me, certain Indians rolled up in their buffalo robes and went to sleep right alongside groups of others chattering and laughing (for contrary to white opinion nobody is more sociable than a redskin when among his own). Some sort of activity continued for hours during which the fire continued to blaze: the women, for instance, went about their chores and Old Lodge Skins smoked four or five pipefuls with divers of his cronies. One of the latter was Hump, of all people, who other than a big scab on his nose looked very fit and grunted at me and Caroline in a friendly manner. I don't know whether or not he recognized us from the day before, but he was very decent about not blaming us for his having committed rapine and murder—which is how an Indian would look at it.

As to Caroline, she sat on her robe in pretty much of a daze from the time of Shooting Star's investigation and even ate her dog in the same spirit. Old Lodge Skins paid her no more attention at all. He wasn't insulting, just not interested.

At length the fire dwindled because Buffalo Wallow Woman wasn't throwing any more chips on it, having gone to a well-deserved bed if I ever saw one. As I found out the next day, me and Caroline had hers, next to that of Old Lodge Skins; so she displaced one of her kids further on, and so it went around the circle like musical chairs until my admirer Little Horse was short man and had to go next door to the tepee of his brother, who was none other than Burns Red in the Sun.

Eventually my sister and me was sitting there alone looking at the dying fire, from which the smoke clumb in a skinny thread to the hole at the junction of the lodgepoles and there met the night, a sky colored dark blue, rather than black, by virtue of a dust of yellow stars.

Next to us, Old Lodge Skins was taking his murmurless rest, his hat dangling overhead from a rawhide line, the silhouette of his big beak pointing up in the perpendicular. You could hear a number of strong breathings but no snores, on account of Indians are trained from birth not to make noise when there ain't a purpose to it. Also a faint sifting now and again as a last piece of buffalo dung dissolved into ash.

It was queer to be there, but speaking for myself no longer scary. You may think the worse of me, away from my home such as it had been and my father killed and all, but I had begun to feel as though it wasn't so desperate. It was warm in that lodge and the people had turned out to be tolerant. If they hadn't offered us violence that night, I couldn't figure them doing it next day: you don't feed a fellow by dark and then murder him next morning. On the other hand, though, you couldn't get away from the fact they wasn't white.

"A penny for your thoughts, Caroline," says I to the slumped figure of my kin, whose jaw was in her splayed hands and whose hat was way down to her fanned ears. She appeared very glum in the shadow, and her voice sounded in the same vein.

"Savages ain't much of a lot, Jack," she answers, inconsiderately loud, I thought, with her hosts trying to catch their sleep. "See how they done in that little dog? Following which they was feeling me as if maybe I was next for the pot, though I never heard Indins was cannibals. I don't think you can count on them, Jack." With a grunt she struggled to get her soles to the ground, which ain't the easiest thing when you have had your rump on it for some hours with your legs crossed.

She repeated almost the same remark, with a significant difference that did not strike me at the time: "You better not count on them, Jack"; and stumbled stiff-legged towards the door flap—I figured, to go relieve herself before bedding down for the night. For myself, I determined to hold it till morning because of being scared of the roaming dogs outside.

Well, that was the last I saw of Caroline for a time. She went over to the meadow, cut a pony out of the herd, rode away, and it was years before I ran into her again, which event we will come to in order. Meanwhile, you have to understand I considered her for a spell as missing and then forgot about her altogether. Nobody could say I owed her more.

I probably could have heard the hoofbeats as she fled had I not fell asleep directly, there being little else in the way of wrapping so cozy as a buffalo robe when you get the hang of it. Though at first it tends to be stiff on the skinned side, whereas the hair on the other is rough as a brush, it soon cleaves to the body from your natural warmth and becomes as if you have growed it on yourself.

Next thing I knowed, that young boy Little Horse woke me up in the dawn. "Come on," he indicated; and shivering off the remains of my sleep, which wasn't hard to do because of the cold of that time of morning, I followed him out to the field where the ponies was pastured. There was markedly fewer than when I had seen the herd the day before: Caroline's theft of one was nothing to what some Ute had come and stole a little later on, or maybe it was the Pawnee this time. Anyway, unless Old Lodge Skins's crowd went out soon and stole some horses back, they would all be walking.

Little Horse already knowed, as an Indian would, that Caroline had run off and figured correctly that I was going to stay and be part of the tribe, having no alternative, and he had woke me to go with him because that was the duty of the boys of my age: tending the ponies first thing every morning. Which is to say, he knew more about me than I did myself at that moment, but his grin was in no wise mocking or mean as we left the tepeeful of sleeping Cheyenne grownups. Indians don't rise especially early when nothing's doing, except for the boys.

Outside the dawn was blue, and chill to go with it. I hadn't had one particle of my clothes off for a couple days, and not washed for the same space of time, enjoying my deficiency. I mention that because I recall thinking about it and feeling luxurious. Even as a small boy, a white man gets that sort of idea when he goes among Indians: What the hell does anything matter? I'm with savages, don't have to wash, can go to the toilet right where I stand, and so on. My point here is that, on the contrary, a Cheyenne takes a bath every day in the nearest water, and even if they hadn't observed that custom, there would have been another requirement to take its place. If you're a human being, you can't get away from obligations.

On the route to the meadow, me and Little Horse encountered various other lads going to the same chore, aged eight to twelve; and on account of the thefts, there was so few ponies left that the herdsmen almost outnumbered the stock. Our job turned out to be leading the animals to the creek for watering. After which we took them to a new pasturage, for they had ate quite a bit of grass from the old one, and after all, the plains belonged to us far as the eye could see.

Little Horse and the other boys did a lot of gassing and laughing among themselves, and for all I know it might have been at my expense. I was alone insofar as wearing pants, shirt, boots, and hat; but after we rehobbled the lead mare to keep the herd from straying and went back to the creek and stripped down to take that bath I mentioned, I was distinguished only by my skin, and when we come back out of the water—which was fairly cold to start with but warmed once you were in, especially because of the horseplay that Indian boys give a lot of time to—why, I left off all my duds except the wool pants. Gave everything away, in fact, which made me a lot of immediate friends.

When we got back to the lodges, the recipients went inside and brought out Cheyenne stuff in return. That was when I finally took off the pants and got into the buckskin breechclout that one of the boys give me, and secured it with the belt I had from another. Also put on moccasins; and received a dirty yellow blanket from a tall kid named Younger Bear, who accepted my trousers and straight-way amputated them for use as unjoined leggings, throwing aside the waist and seat. Nobody had use for the boots, which just laid there on the ground and were left behind in the same position when the camp moved away. If an Indian isn't interested in an item he does not so much as see it, will stumble over it repeatedly without ever considering he might kick it aside.

We never did get breakfast that first morning, for the simple reason that there wasn't any food to be had. The antelope had been ate up totally the night before, and they couldn't afford to do in no more dogs for a spell, seeing as how the ponies was fast disappearing and a certain number of pack animals was required when camp moved. Also Caroline had not returned—for I still thought she might be back at that point; though never once did I entertain the idea she might be killed—and I had nobody to jaw with in my own language.

But before the sun had got far through the sky, I had learned quite a vocabulary of the sign lingo and conversed with Little Horse on such things as could be expressed with the hands. For example, you want to say "man," so you put up the index finger, with the palm facing inside. Of course I was considerable assisted in learning the lingo by Little Horse's habit of making the sign, then pointing to the thing itself. The motion for "white man," a finger wiped across the forehead to suggest the brim of a hat, was somewhat difficult to savvy owing to Little Horse himself wearing the felt hat I had discarded. He kept running his finger along the brim and pointing at me, and I first thought he meant "your hat," or "you," before I got it straight. The sign for plain "man" naturally meant "Indian man."

For "Cheyenne" you run the right index finger across the left as though striping it, for the distinctive arrow-guides used by all Cheyenne was made of striped feathers from the wild turkey. By the way, in their spoken language Cheyenne don't ever call themselves "Cheyenne" but rather *Tsistsistas*, which means "the People," or "the Human Beings." What anybody else is doesn't concern them.

After our bath, them boys fetched bows and we played war in and out of a buffalo wallow near camp, shooting one another with arrows that didn't have no points. And then we did some wrestling, at which I was none too good and somewhat shy to try too hard, but after getting badly squeezed, I turned to boxing and bloodied at least one brown nose. The latter was the property of Younger Bear, and the event caused him to receive a good deal of jeering, because I'd say Indians are given to that trait even more than whites. I felt sorry for Younger Bear when I saw the ridicule I had let him in for.

Which was a big mistake: I should either never have hit him in the first place or after doing so should have strutted around boasting about it and maybe given him some more punishment to consolidate the advantage: that's the Indian way. You should never feel sorry about beating anybody, unless having conquered his body you want his spirit as well. I didn't yet understand that, so throughout the rest of the day I kept trying to shine up to Younger Bear, and the result was I made the first real enemy of my life and he caused me untold trouble for years, for an Indian will make a profession of revenge.

The next thing I remember us boys doing was to go and play camp with a number of little girls. This game is a mimicry of what the grownups do. The girls set up miniature tepees and the boys act like their husbands, going out on war parties and having mock buffalo hunts in which one boy, playing the animal, carries a prickly pear at the end of a stick. The hunters shoot their arrows at this fruit, and are considered to have brung the buffalo down if they strike the target. Whoever misses, the buffalo lad gets to swat on the hind end with the prickly pear. You can see that whatever the Cheyenne do has a threat of pain in it, if not the realization thereof.

In the earlier doings I had fell in on equal terms, but it wasn't so when it came to play camp, and that I believe was due to Younger Bear, who was by common consent war chief of that establishment on account of he could shoot an arrow exceptionally well and he was very convincing when braining a make-believe foe with a nasty-looking war club he had fashioned himself. That's the way a man gets to be a war chief among the Cheyenne: he can fight better than anyone else. He is a chief only in battle. For peace they have another kind of leader. You take Old Lodge Skins, he was a peace chief. The principal war chief of our bunch was Hump. These fellows got along fine, except you'll recall at the whiskey fight as soon as they had a few in their belly, they went for each other. However, when Skins's gun blew up, they forgot about it and went their separate ways.

Anyhow, Younger Bear was at about eleven years of age already very well advanced towards his true profession, and he was a big tall fellow who walked with his chest arched out. I'll say this about the fight I had with him: he could have killed me except that he knew nothing about boxing. But his ignorance wasn't my responsibility; I ain't never been big, but I'm shrewd.

In those first days I was dependent on what the other boys would lend me: bow, arrows, and the certain type of stick they ran with between their legs as if it was a pony. But when it came to war games under Younger Bear's direction, off they'd ride, even Little Horse, leaving me behind with the girls and the littler kids who were supposed to be the babies of the play camp. Now after them boys did that until it got to be a habit, they started to call me "Antelope Girl," because there I was, helping to dismantle the toy tepees, which is women's work.

The sun dance was another adult pursuit the children mimicked in play camp. The boys would drive thorns in their flesh, tie strings to them, and drag around prairie-dog or coyote skulls. I might have got desperate enough to try it myself, had I not already at that early age worked out the following proposition: a white man is better than a redskin, who is a savage. Why is he better? Because he uses his wits. Centuries earlier the Indians had learned you could move heavy objects by rolling logs under them, yet still by the time I lived among them they had never cut a cross section through one of them logs to make a wheel. You can see that as either invincible ignorance or stubbornness; whichever, it's just barbarous.

I did go behind one of the play-tepees and experiment with a thorn, but no sooner than the point touched my flesh I turned yellow. I never could get interested in hurting myself. So I got an arrow, stole a real one with an iron trade point, and wore it in two with a jagged rock. Now the Cheyenne make a chewing gum from the evaporated juice of the milkweed. Buffalo Wallow Woman give me some, but I put it into my belly button rather than my mouth, and stuck in it the end of the arrow shaft that ends with the feathers. The other part, that with the iron head, I fixed so it appeared to issue from the cleft of my arse, the breechclout being drawn aside in accommodation. It looked as if I was fairly skewered through the middle, at an angle of forty-five degrees. When I was all prepared, I come out from back of the lodge, walking funny with my rump cheeks tight, and secretly supporting the feathered end with a hand to my gut as if to catch the pain—that was an infraction of the rules, for the idea is to show a manly indifference to the hurt, but I figured the act would be spectacular enough to cover up an incidental.

I was right. The girls saw me first and slapped their mouths so hard it's a marvel their front teeth stayed tight. And then the boys, with their miserable little thorns and them tiny animal skulls. In chagrin Coyote ripped his out of his back and throwed it away, and the blood streamed in scarlet ribbons down to his rump. Little Horse began to dance about and boast how he was my friend. Poor old Younger Bear, he just turned and trudged away, the little skulls trailing along the ground behind him, hopping when they struck a rough, and when one of them caught under a sagebush the rawhide line broke rather than his skin.

From here on I was on equal terms in the war games, and before long Burns Red in the Sun made me a little bow. Burns was Old Lodge Skins's son by one of his earlier wives now dead. My own position turned out to be orphan attached to the chief's lodge, which gave me the right to benevolent consideration from the whole family just as if I was related to them by blood. Almost every tepee had a similar lad, though the rest was pure Indians. The women were obliged to give me clothes and food, and the men to see I grew up into a man. I don't recall my race being held against me while I was small. Caroline, for example, was never referred to—for one reason, because it was a great shame to Old Lodge Skins that he had smoked a pipe with what turned out a female. In the very old times the Cheyenne would not smoke when a woman was even in the tepee; they tied up the door to keep them out.

Another reason why it was easy for me to melt into that tribe was that none of the Indians wanted to think about the incident of the wagons. As we have seen, my brother Bill never reported the massacre to Fort Laramie, and the soldiers didn't come, so the Cheyenne had no worry about that. What bothered them was that while drunk they had nearly killed some of themselves; that's the worst thing a Cheyenne could do: kill another Cheyenne. Being drunk is no excuse. It is always regarded as murder, and the murderer rots inside his guts, giving off a stink to other members of the tribe, soiling the Sacred Arrows, and driving the buffalo away. Such a fellow cannot smoke the pipe, nor will anyone eat from a dish he has touched; he is generally run out of camp.

Now I know at this point you figure you have one on me. The way I described the whiskey fight, it looked as if some of the Indians *were* killed: for example, I surely said Pile of Bones blew off the back of White Contrary's head and the latter's brains run out. I swear that insofar as anybody could have told on the spot, that is what happened. But imagine my surprise when on that first morning in the Cheyenne camp, directly after the bath we boys took in the creek, who should show up waiting for us to take him to his horse but White Contrary, big as life and twice as ugly, and showing in no particular that he had ever been hurt. I trailed along behind him, taking a special interest in the back of his head, but if there was a hole in it, you couldn't prove it by me. I saw a louse or two crawling along the part of his braids, but not even a crust of dried blood. And it was White Contrary, all right, for he had an unmistakable wart on the left flange of his nose.

Maybe you are beginning to understand, when I pulled the arrow-out-of-arse trick, why it didn't occur to none of the children that I was hoaxing them. That is because Indians did not go around expecting to be swindled, whereas they was always ready for a miracle.

CHAPTER 4 *Pronghorn Slaughter*

IT AIN'T BAD to be a boy among the Cheyenne. You never get whipped for doing wrong, but rather told: "That is not the way of the Human Beings." One time Coyote started to laugh while he was lighting his father's pipe, because a horsefly was crawling on his belly. This was a serious failure of manners on his part, comparable to a white boy's farting loud in church. His Pa laid away the pipe and said: "On account of your lack of self-control I can't smoke all day without disgusting certain Persons in the other world. I wonder if you aren't a Pawnee instead of a Human Being." Coyote went out upon the prairie and stayed there alone all night to hide his shame.

You have got to *do things right* when you're a Cheyenne. A baby can't cry just for the hell of it—the tribe might be lying in concealment at the moment and the sound would give away their position to the enemy. Therefore the women hang them cradleboards on bushes some distance from camp until the youngsters inside develop the idea that crying don't do no good, and get the habit of quiet. Girls need to be trained to control their giggle. I seen Shadow That Comes in Sight line his little daughters up before him and tell them funny stories at which they was supposed to restrain laughter. At first they all flunked, shrieking like birds; then they got so as to only smirk and simper; and finally, after many sessions, they could hold a stony look towards the most hilarious joke. They was free to enjoy it but not to make a demonstration. At the proper time they could laugh their guts out, for an Indian loves his humor and Shadow That Comes in Sight was a great wit.

Other than for that special instruction, the Cheyenne didn't run a school. They never read nor wrote their language, so what would be the purpose? If you wanted a point of history, you went and asked an old man who kept it in his mind. Numbers got boring when you run out of fingers, so to report the size of an enemy war party you had spotted would go something like this: "The Ute is near the Fasting Place Butte. They are as many as the arrows that Sticks Everything Under His Belt shot at the ghost antelope in the time when the cherries was ripe." This being a famous story, everybody in Old Lodge Skins's crowd would know within one or two the number of Ute referred to—and in a moment of emergency, when a person tends to fear the unknown, they could connect it up with something familiar.

A Cheyenne believed his animal was also Cheyenne and knew it. "Tell your pony," Burns Red would say, "that the people will talk about his bravery all over camp. Tell him stories about famous ponies and their exploits, so that he will try to do as well. Tell him everything about yourself. A man should keep no secrets from his pony. There are things he does not discuss with his brother, his friend, or his wife, but he and his pony must know everything about each other because they will probably die together and ride the Hanging Road between earth and heaven."

The trouble with me was that I felt like a damn fool, speaking to a dumb beast. That's the difficulty in being white: you can't get away with much. Nobody expects more of an Indian; with him fool things are, so to speak, normal. You'd be disappointed in an Indian if he *didn't* talk to horses, the way I look at it, for he is born crazy. But being white, I knowed too much even at the age of ten.

You understand that I can't give no day-to-day account of my upbringing. It must have took a couple of months to learn to ride without being tied on, and longer to get real proficient with the bow and arrow. But now I got to go back to that very first morning and wake up Old Lodge Skins, who we left dead to the world. That Indian got up intending to fast for twenty-four hours. He had had another dream about antelope. Coming on top of the one of the day previous, it meant he had to get to work.

In the afternoon the chief went up the creek maybe three hundred yards and just beyond the brush erected a little tepee about the size of the play-lodges we kids had, just big enough for him to sit in. He went inside at sunset and did a number of secret things till dawn the next day.

While he was in there, throughout the night certain other Cheyenne would go and beat upon the outside of the tepee cover. What went on here concerned the preparation for a gigantic antelope surround. If when them other men pounded on the lodge skin any quantity of antelope hair fell off the cover, the hunt would be successful.

While this was taking place, a party of Ute run off the whole horse herd, and next morning the only Cheyenne ponies left was the few that their owners had tethered right outside their tepees. However, quite a mess of antelope hair was laying on the ground about the medicine tent, so the lookout was good.

Old Lodge Skins emerged from the little tepee next morning. He looked somewhat different from usual in that his eyes seemed to be focused miles away in whatever direction he turned. He was carrying two short black poles, each with a hoop on its end and decorated with raven feathers, and when he walked into open country, the whole camp trooped along behind—men, women, children, and dogs. I have told about antelope as we encountered that little herd the day before at the buffalo wallow: they can run a mile in one minute and will stampede on a change of wind.

This quick beast has one flaw against living to old age: he is nosy. Show an antelope something that flutters and he can't resist it. That is the practical side of those poles-and-wheels that Old Lodge Skins was carrying: the Cheyenne called them antelope arrows, and they were deadlier than if equipped with iron points, for they made the skittish beast so curious he would run himself and his kin into suicide for a closer look. Admitting that, there was still a lot to a surround that made no sense except as magic.

I suppose we must have walked three miles out in the prairie—everybody except one decrepit old woman and a warrior who stayed behind because he had the sulks. At a certain point on a space of flatland we stopped, and Old Lodge Skins set down on the prairie. He had left behind his plug hat, and wore two eagle feathers braided into his hair. Now the unmarried women come up before him, and he chose the stoutest two by waving the antelope arrows at them, sort of charming them into sitting alongside him. One girl was average fat, but the second was so chubby it took a keen watch to find the features of her face; her eyes was like little seeds.

Set a fat girl to catch fat antelope, was the idea.

Them braves that still kept their horses now mounted, and the rest of us fell in on either side of the chief and the fatties so as to make a half-circle with them in the middle. Two other girls, skinnier people, suddenly grabbed the antelope arrows from Old Lodge Skins and dashed away on diverging tracks like the legs of a V with him at the point. Off go the horsemen in pursuit, the two leaders overtaking the girls and swiping the medicine sticks, then riding on still along the V legs, holding up the little wheels with the raven feathers fluttering. Now a single antelope come into sight on a roll of ground about a quarter mile ahead of the riders, in the exact center between their two files, on a dead line with Old Lodge Skins's position. Like men, grazing antelope put out sentries. These here signal the herd by putting up their white tails like signal flags. What would you think a pronghorn scout might do when he saw twenty Cheyenne galloping on either flank and a bunch more standing in the midst of the prairie around an old Indian and two tubby maidens?

Well, this one stared so hard you would have thought his ears might shoot off his head. Meanwhile the riders was reaching his lateral. He looked left and he looked right, but them equal forces emanating from the flanks sort of compressed his attention back to the middle, and even at the distance you could see him quiver from the haunches though his yellow cheeks and black muzzle was froze in wonder.

Old Lodge Skins set within the red blanket, the white plumes on the ends of his two feathers blowing in the soft wind. The two fat girls was still as mounds of earth, nor among the pack of dogs did one cur so much as show a tongue; they was also Cheyenne.

That scout moved forward, placing each dainty hoof as if it was a separate decision, his white neck-bands puffed out like a collar of shirring. Along the crest behind him appeared a margin of little horns, followed at length by little tan heads, staring our way. The forward horsemen gained the rise and went over, the funnel they made ever widening, with its neck pointing to Old Lodge Skins sitting way back here in the crescent of his tribe. There was only enough riders to indicate the lines of flank, with full space between each Indian to let through a nation of antelope, but these beasts, being charmed, had no mind to escape.

Down the slope trotted that sentry; behind him the horizon was full of animals, with more crowding over. He came a hundred yards on, and still there was no end to the massing herd, forming the shape of a huge arrowhead back of his lead, aimed at Old Lodge Skins. Cheyenne and animals were harmonizing in a grand rhythm, for which the old chief beat time. I guess the gods was supposed to have writ the music. If you don't like that aspect of the affair, then you'll have a job explaining why maybe a thousand antelope run towards ruin; and also how Old Lodge Skins could know this herd would be in this place, for no animal had showed a hair before he sat down on the prairie.

The lead riders, with the staffs and wheels, having reached the end of the herd out there and crossed behind it, changing sides one to the other, galloped back to Old Lodge Skins and gave him the medicine devices. There was now a magic line tied round the antelope, and with a wand in each hand, the chief began to draw it in.

He flang up his arms, and the whole vasty herd began to run, its head some seventy yards out, its tail just coming over the rise. A good three hundred yards of prairie was jammed with animals, haunch to haunch; with the width of the mass at the rear covering about the same measure east to west: an enormous heaving wedge of pure antelope. We people now stirred, extending the crescent horns, rounding out the base of the V into a U, and the beasts came towards a living corral of which the walls was Cheyenne—men, women, children—made solid by their outspread blankets and the dogs between their legs.

Half along the left arm of it, I tried to cock an eye on that first sentry, but he was gone in the rush as faster animals overtook him, and soon all particularity was lost in the churning of numberless legs and clouding dust. The chief waved his wheels as the leaders reached the entrapment, and they diverted left, but there met the Cheyenne fence; then to the right with similar dismay. He crossed the wands twice, and the eyes of the foremost beast followed suit, nose snorting, and it locked hoofs and went to its knees, forming a hurdle for those hard behind, which they failed to negotiate.

This pile-up happened right before me, and from there on it was sheer panic as beast clumb upon beast and butted each other's brains out, goring one another's bellies, and some just plain trampled into the earth. We closed in then, and the horsemen completed the great circle, everybody with a club or hatchet or maybe merely a big stone, but no kind of projectile for this tight work. I'd say it took a good hour to beat every last antelope to death though we was swinging incessantly, and a number of animals died of their own efforts.

At no time did Old Lodge Skins put down his wands, but rather kept on gesticulating till no beast lived to see them; that was his duty and obligation, and he took no part in the killing. So far as I went, I had not the strength at that age to do much damage even to such a fragile animal, but joined my efforts to the general mob, pounding a rock at tan hide wherever an opening showed. I might have struck Younger Bear once or twice in the confusion, for he was very near me. That boy tried to break an antelope's neck with his bare hands, like some of the stronger men could, by twisting its horns. He couldn't manage it, and finally had to sink his hatchet between the ears, and its starting eyes welled with blood from the inside and its tongue retched forth and it died.

CHAPTER 5 *My Education as a Human Being*

YOU MIGHT HAVE NOTICED that Old Lodge Skins started out as a buffoon in this narrative. Let me say that was true only around white men. Among the Cheyenne he was a sort of genius. It was him who taught me everything I learned as a boy that wasn't physical like riding or shooting. The way he done this was by means of stories. I reckon he told me and the other children many a hundred such tales, and sometimes the grownups would listen too, for he was held to be a wise old Indian and wouldn't have lived to his ripe age had he not been.

I'm going to tell you two of his tales. One of them saved my life when I went on my first horse-stealing raid. The other, which he spoke at a council-meeting with some Sioux, will give you a better idea of the difference between red men and whites than anything else short of having lived as both, like me.

Several snows had fell and melted since I joined the Cheyenne, and I must have been going on thirteen years of age. We boys was playing war one day and Younger Bear, growing taller by the month, shot a blunt-head arrow with such force that when it struck a lad called Red Dog in the forehead he was knocked cold. I believe it had been aimed at me, but I was ever a shifting target. Old Lodge Skins happened along at the moment in the company of an Indian by the name of Two Babies, who was naked and painted black from head to toe and going out to take an enemy scalp in accord with some vow.

Two Babies just walked by in a kind of trance; but when Old Lodge Skins saw Red Dog laying unconscious, he leaned over him and said: "Come on and eat!" The lad woke up instantly, and the chief sent him over to Buffalo Wallow Woman for a meal, which will cure an Indian of almost anything.

Then Skins said to Younger Bear: "It is a brave warrior who tries to kill his friends." And the Bear was full of shame.

Old Lodge Skins spread his blanket on the ground, and we all sat around him. His braids was wrapped in weasel fur, and he wore a sort of little scarf ornamented with the old-time beads that dated from before the whites come with their glass jewelry: these was fashioned from the purple section of the ocean shell, and since the Cheyenne lived in the middle of the country, they must have reached the chief by a long history of trading, starting maybe a century or so back when some coastal savage in Oregon or Massachusetts cracked open a clam, sucked down the rubbery meat, and fell with his stone drill to fashion something cunning from the shell.

The chief said: "I'm going to tell you about a warrior who loved his friends. This happened many snows ago, when I was a young man. In those days you seldom saw a gun among us, because we did very little trading with the white men and of course other Indians would keep what firearms they could get hold of. We didn't even have many iron arrowheads, and in battle we would ride up close to the enemy, hoping to get shot by his arrows so as to get some of those iron points."

He laughed heartily, and pulled up his legging to show his right calf and its mass of ancient punctures.

"There wasn't any other way to get them at the time. For horses, we would generally go south to the land of the Snake People, for they are great riders and have the best ponies. It is said the reason for this is that they mate with horses, but I have never seen this with my own eyes." The Comanche is who he was talking about, the world's finest riders, excelling other Indians; and whether or not they coupled with mares, I know for a fact they mounted their own women stallion-style, from behind, neighing and snorting; they was all horse-crazy.

"Sometimes we would not really need the horses but would go just for fighting, because the Snakes are a brave people and it lifts your heart to see them come charging, particularly on an early morning when the sun is still a young man in the sky; later on, when he is middle-aged, it gets too hot in their country and you can see why years earlier the Human Beings ran them down there and kept this place for ourselves, which is perfect."

Talk of war always cheered Old Lodge Skins. He'd lose several decades right in front of you, his eyes would heat up and his cheeks filled out, and he'd positively chortle at a specially gory turn.

"One time a party of six Human Beings was after horses in the Snake Country: Hawk's Visit, Little Robe, Horse Chief, Iron Shirt, Crazy Mule, and Little Man. With them also was a man called Hairy, of the Arapaho who you know have always been our friends and usually camp with the Human Beings. Now this party had started out with the intention of capturing wild horses rather than stealing those of the Snakes. Otherwise Hairy would not have gone along, because the Arapaho were at peace with the Snakes that year.

"Near the headwaters of the Washita, our men came upon the trail of a big Snake village and determined to raid it after nightfall, although they had no guns and only a few remaining arrows and could not fight long if the Snakes caught up with them afterwards.

"Having located the camp, they hid until dark. Then they crept in and stole a herd of beautiful ponies. Hairy did not take part in this raid, owing to the treaty his people had with the Snakes. He waited outside camp, holding their own ponies for the Human Beings, and when they came driving the herd he went with them. They rode all night and half the next day without stopping until the sun stood where he could have looked right down the smokehole of a tepee. By then they had reached the Stinking Creek, where a horse can drink but not a man. So they watered that herd.

"But they had not been able to ride fast, having to drive the stolen horses, and before they left the Stinking Creek, the Snakes arrived, in a number that was more than ten for every Human Being also including Hairy. Our men mounted their ponies and went up onto a little knoll, then killed the animals to make a fortification, stripped off their leggings and shirts, and singing their songs, prepared to die.

"Before the Snakes charged, a chief of theirs named Moon rode up near enough the knoll to be clearly seen and said, in the signs: 'You Plenty of Tattooed Marks,' which is how the Snakes call our friends the Arapaho, 'why are you stealing our horses with the Striped Arrow People? Your tribe and mine are at peace. Are you a bad person?'

"Hairy stood up and answered: 'I did not enter your camp nor did I steal your horses. These are my friends. I have lived with them, eaten with them, and fought alongside them. So, although it is true that I do not have a quarrel with you, I think it is a good day to die with them.'

" 'I hear you,' Moon signaled back and joined his people, and they charged the knoll, killing Iron Shirt, Hawk's Visit, and Little Robe, but the remaining four fought so bravely that the Snakes retired, having lost several of their own, with some others wounded. Then the Snakes charged again, but with only about ten of their warriors instead of the whole party, and Hairy was killed with a lance through the chest, but he put his last arrow into the neck of the man who did it as he was being ridden down. The Snake toppled off his horse, grasping the mane, and in its rearing and plunging the pony kicked Crazy Mule in the stomach and another Snake leaned over while galloping and brained him with a war club. Also Horse Chief was given a bad wound, from which he soon died.

"Now only Little Man remained alive, and he had no more arrows. He had to wait until a Snake shot an arrow at him so he could pull it out of his body and shoot it back. In this fashion, he had killed one of the riders and wounded another as the charge went over the knoll. But now the Snakes were coming back from the other side, six or seven of them, riding down on him with their short lances.

"The first Snake had just gained the crest when Little Man seized a blanket from the pile of clothes our people had discarded, and shouting 'Hu, hu, hu!' he flapped it at the pony's head, scaring the animal just enough so that it faltered from the proper line of charge, and the lance missed Little Man, making a long rent in the blanket, instead. Grasping the rider's belt, Little Man pulled him from the back of the pony. The Snake no sooner struck the ground than Little Man made three quick knife cuts across his throat, but could not take the scalp, for the other Snakes were on him. He leaped upon the pony, and with the captured lance drew so much blood from them that the Snakes retreated across the plain to where their main force was waiting.

"Little Man rode back and forth upon the knoll, singing his death song, while the Snakes held a council. Then Moon came forward and said in the signs: 'You are a brave man. We have taken back the horses you stole and do not want to fight any more. You may go home.'

"But Little Man said: 'I do not hear you.' And Moon went back and the Snakes charged again, this time with twenty men, and Little Man killed several with his lance and went himself untouched. Now the Snakes were really frightened; they had never before tried to fight against such powerful medicine.

"Moon rode forward again and signaled: 'You are the bravest

Striped Arrow Person we have ever seen. Keep that pony you are riding and keep the lance, and we will also give you another horse. Go back to your people. We don't want to fight any more.'

" 'No thank you,' said Little Man. 'All my friends are dead, including one who was loyal to the Human Beings although he was himself an Arapaho. Without my friends I would just sit around all day and weep. You had better kill me, too. It is a good day to die.'

"Thereupon Little Man raised the lance above his head, and sounding the war cry and the name of his people, he charged the entire Snake force. Moon was a brave chief, but when he saw Little Man galloping towards him, shouting those terrible cries, he screamed and tried to run away, but Little Man overtook him and ran the lance halfway through his body, where it stuck. So Little Man drew his knife and continued the charge into the Snake army, who fell away before him. He rode among them like the whirlwind, stabbing and cutting on all sides so furiously as if he had a knife for every finger, and the Snakes were howling in fright though they are a valiant people.

"At last a Snake with a musket shot Little Man in the back, and he pitched to the ground and the Snakes cut off his head. But when they had done that, Little Man's body got up and began to fight again with the knife it still grasped in its hand. And his head, which they mounted on a spear, started again to shout the war cry. The Snakes could take no more. They galloped off fast as they could go, and those that looked back saw Little Man's headless body running after them, waving his knife. Then when they were out of reach, it walked to the top of the knoll and lay down among its friends. Nobody knows what happened to the head, which was dropped by the man carrying the spear when it began to shout.

"Moon recovered afterwards but was humpbacked like a buffalo for the rest of his life. He bore no shame for his running because Little Man had a medicine that day that no Snake could have been expected to stand against. Moon told me this story himself in a later time when we made peace between our tribes, and the Snakes also found Little Man's brother and gave him that horse they had promised, so that they could go again to the place where Little Man died, without being attacked by his body."

I had not seen a white person since Caroline snuck out of camp that night. One time since, when we was camped on the Surprise River and us boys was out hunting prairie chickens, we saw some moving objects a couple miles off that I took for buffalo, but Little Horse, with his Indian eyes, said no, they was white men, that one had yellow hair, was armed with a shotgun, and rode a bay that was slightly lame in the left forefoot; and the other wore a beard and was mounted on a roan with a saddle sore. Also, they was lost, but he could see that the bay had got the scent of water and shortly they would strike the river and know where they was. So we went in the other direction.

There was a reason why we didn't hanker none to meet these whites: it had begun to mean bad luck for the Cheyenne. You remember what happened at the wagon train of my white family: some Cheyenne had almost killed one another. Then some bad things was occurring from time to time down at Fort Laramie, where a number of Indians camped roundabout to trade. A young man might get drunk and take a shot at a soldier or run off with some horses. And once a Sioux come across an old sick cow strayed from some emigrant train, and killed it for its hide. Burned up at this, the Army attacked the Indian camp and several individuals on both sides was rubbed out.

We was sixty-seventy miles away from Laramie on War Bonnet Creek at the time of this incident but knew about it quick enough. Some Minneconjou, which was a type of Sioux or Lakota, come riding in and held counsel with Old Lodge Skins, Hump, and our other principal men. Anybody can attend such a meeting, and can say anything that isn't ridiculous, but generally the chiefs do the talking because they are wiser, which is why they are chiefs.

Luckily there was a man with the Minneconjou who knew Cheyenne, for though the Human Beings and the Sioux been allies for generations, they speak altogether different languages and usually have to converse in the signs as if they had no closer connection than a Portuguee and a Russian. So this man interpreted.

Great Elk, a Minneconjou, stood up and told what happened down at Laramie, concluding: "I have met many Wasichu"—which is how the Sioux call whites—"and drunk their coffee and eaten their molasses, which is good." Here many of the Cheyenne sitting round the tepee said: "How, how."

"But I have never known why they came to our country," Great Elk went on. "First there were just a few of those poor homeless ones, and the Lakota took pity on them and gave them food. Then many came with the ugly cattle that one cannot eat because they have lost their testicles and have tough flesh, being good only to pull the Wasichu wagons which are filled with useless things except for the coffee and sugar and the iron hoops of barrels, from which you can make arrowheads. The Wasichu women are sick-looking and make me sneeze. Then the soldiers came with their big, weak horses; and they have no wife each man for himself but share among them a few women whom one must give a present every time he lies with her.

"If a Wasichu does something that the other Wasichu do not like, they tie a rope around his neck and drop him from a high place, so as to pull his spirit from his body. They talk of the great villages they have in the place where the sun rises, but if that is so, why do they come to our country and scare away the buffalo?

"I shall tell you why: the Wasichu are sick, and if they ever had the great villages they brag about, everybody there has died from lying with those sick women or eating that bacon which stinks, and now the rest come here and if we don't kill them all, they will infect the Lakota and our friends the Shyela."

The latter was the Sioux name for "Cheyenne."

Great Elk sat down then and scratched his lice, and another Sioux spoke to the same effect, and then our Hump stood up to talk. He wasn't much of an orator, but he sure had a grasp of the practicalities.

"If we are going to fight the white man, we had better get some guns and powder. The only place we can get enough guns and powder and shot to fight the white man is from the white man. I do not think that he will want to give them to us for this purpose; we have very little to buy them with even if he would sell them for this purpose; and we certainly can't take them away from him, for if we could do that, we wouldn't need guns and powder and shot for this purpose."

Hump thought for a moment, opening and closing his mouth for air since his nose was permanently obstructed by that damage he sustained at the wagons. "I don't know, either, what the white men are doing here. I think they may be crazy. I think it's better to keep away from them, since we don't have guns and powder and shot."

Great Elk got up again and said: "At the fort was a young soldier chief who said with ten men he could rub out the entire nation of Shyelas, and with thirty men, all the people of the plains. But we Minneconjou, along with some Oglala, rubbed him out instead. This is his ring that I am wearing on a string around my neck. I used to have his finger, too, but I lost it."

Old Lodge Skins finally took his turn, and put on that falsetto that proper oratory called for. The following remarks was developed deep in the chest, but come out high and quavering after having fought a passage through his tightened throat. The first time you heard it, you might have thought the poor devil was dying of strangulation; but it could get the wind up in you once you caught the style.

For a while he flattered the Minneconjou and the rest of the Lakota. Then he reminded them of the Cheyenne theory that they was established in the Black Hills and rich in horses at the time when the Sioux showed up there poor as could be and with only dogs for transport, and the Human Beings took pity on them and give them a horse now and again, which enabled the Sioux to prosper into the great tribe they was at present.

"As to the white men," he said after an hour or so, "among my people it was my grandfather's grandfather who saw them for the first time. His name was Walking on the Ground. In those days our people lived near the Lake You Cannot See Across, in houses of earth, and they raised corn. One morning Walking on the Ground and several other Human Beings were tracking a bear along a creek when they came across the trail of another kind of animal they had never seen before. These new tracks were almost the size of a bear's, but they showed no toe marks and were round and smooth. Our people believed these tracks to have been made by a water-animal, whose toes were joined one to another so he could swim well.

"They followed the trail until they came to a clearing in the forest, and there they saw six of these new animals, and the grizzly bear too, who had also been tracking them. The new animals looked strange to our people. They seemed to be naked, but each one had a different type of fur or skin and another shape of head. Our men then thought they were cousins or even children of the grizzly bear because like him they stood on their hind feet and had bulky bodies and used their front paws like hands.

"But the next moment, the grizzly bear charged the new animals, and several of the latter took from between their legs their penises, which were longer than their arms, put them against the shoulder, and making a great noise, shot flame and smoke at the grizzly and he fell dead.

"Our people were terribly frightened at this and ran back through the forest to their village to tell the others, and the others were excited and had to see these new animals for themselves. So all the warriors in the village went back to the clearing where the animals were and hid in the bushes and watched them. One of the animals stripped the skin off its body and head and our men clapped their mouths in astonishment. But when the animal's fur was off, it looked just like a human being except that its flesh was white and it had hair all over its face. It washed itself in the creek and put its skin back on, and our men then realized that what they thought was its hide was actually clothing.

"Several of the animals had hairy faces, and our people supposed these to be the males, whereas the smooth-faced ones were the females. And they saw that the lightning-shooting sticks were not the penises of those animals, but they sometimes stood holding them between their legs, so it had looked that way.

"Our men drew back into the forest and held a counsel. Hungry Bear said: 'I don't think we should bother these animals or make them angry, because they are very strange and you can't tell what they will do.'

"Black Wolf, who had not been with the first party that saw the shooting, said: 'We could easily kill them, but that white flesh doesn't look as if it would be good to eat, though the skin might make a pretty shirt.'

"But Walking on the Ground, who was very wise, said: 'These animals are not Human Beings, but they are men. You know the old prophecy made by our great hero Sweet Medicine, that a new people would one day come among us, their skins white and their ways odd. And you know that he said they will bring us bad luck. But now they are here, and it is better for us to find them than for them to come upon us by surprise.

" 'Here is what we should do: I will walk into their camp and look at them. The rest of you watch from the bushes. If the white persons attack me, then we must fight them and someone should go back to the village and send the women and children to hide. If I am not attacked, then some of you can also come into camp.'

"Walking on the Ground stripped himself to the breechclout and went alone into the clearing. The first white person to see him started to raise the lightning stick, but another—without hair on its face, so that it seemed a woman—stepped in front of the first and thrust its hand at Walking on the Ground. My grandfather's grandfather stopped and looked her in the eyes, for our people had never heard of shaking hands at that time. Then other white men came all around Walking, and our men in the bushes started to stretch their bows, but soon they saw the whites were not trying to harm the Human Being but rather smiling at him and making talk, and so some of them came out of the bushes and went into that camp.

"The smooth-faced persons turned out to be men as well as the hairy-cheeked, and one of them wore a golden cross around his neck and when he took off his hat his head was mostly bare skin except for a fringe around his ears. He got two sticks and making a cross of them, stuck it in the earth, and then all the white men fell upon their knees while the bald one closed his eyes, folded his hands, and talked. Then the whites showed the Human Beings their lightning-and-thunder sticks and let them pull the triggers, but our people were still scared when the shots came.

"Those first white men stayed in that place for about one moon and started to build a square house of logs. Our people would visit them every day, and the man with the cross would give them presents and make signs that they should kneel upon the ground while he talked to the crossed sticks which were his medicine, and so they would do so to be polite.

"But then one night, while half of the white party was sleeping, the other half killed them and took all their things and burned up the house and went over to the Big Water, got into a boat they had there, and went away.

"That is the truth as it has come down to me," said Old Lodge Skins. "And the same thing happened many times thereafter, whenever the white people appeared. They do not like each other, and sooner or later one will kill the next, and usually not in battle, the way our people do to prove themselves brave and to enjoy the courageous deaths of our enemies and to die on a good day, but rather by shooting in the back or stretching the neck or by infecting one another with the coughing-sickness and sores or making people lose their heads with whiskey.

"But I say they are white, and not like us, and there may be some reason why they act this way that one cannot understand unless he is himself white. If they ever attack me, I will defend myself. But until such time, I will avoid them."

That was when we went up into the Powder River country,

though we wasn't in no hurry and first went south for a day or so along the Surprise River and took buffalo there. Them was the days before the railroad and the professional white hunters, and you could find single herds numbering in the hundreds of thousands, maybe a square mile or more of beasts crowded so thick you couldn't see no grass between them, and the Cheyenne would get them milling and drop one after another with arrow or spear and it would make no appreciable difference in the size of the herd. Then the women would come out for the butchering and when it was done haul the usable parts back to camp on the hide, which was afterward fleshed and stretched on a frame for a robe or lodge cover. We'd eat boiled tongue and roast hump then, the finest grub in the world, alongside which your best beefsteak will taste like a singed bootsole. But it is all gone now.

Now it's true there wasn't no white men up on the Powder, but there was Crow Indians roundabout. The Cheyenne and the Crow was generally enemies, but made a peace some years before when the Government got most of the warring tribes together on Horse Creek east of Laramie and had them sign a treaty not to fight one another. This worked fine between tribes that never came in contact with the next, but didn't last long with them that did, it being normal for a Cheyenne to fight a Pawnee. And if you didn't fight, you'd turn into a woman.

So with the Crow, who was by the way friends of the whites, claiming never to have killed a white man and for that reason they was always let to keep their country. The Crow was brave men when they fought the Cheyenne and Sioux alone, but when they served as scouts for the U.S. Cavalry, they often turned coward. I don't know why.

Anyway, we no sooner had got up to the Powder than some of our men who was out spying come in with the news that a big camp of Crow had been located on the Crazy Woman's Creek.

"If it is a big camp, they must have a lot of ponies," said Hump.

Shadow That Comes in Sight, one of the spies, said: "Those Crow are very rich in ponies. They are the most beautiful ponies I have ever seen. I hid all day in the scrubwood just to look at those ponies."

"I have heard you," said Hump and sighed. The group then went over to talk with Old Lodge Skins, a bunch of us boys following along.

"Do you need ponies?" the chief said after he had been apprised.

Shadow nodded his head very sad, saying: "Never have I been so poor."

Old Lodge Skins asked the same question of the others and got the same answer. Then he spoke, groping within his blanket: "I received this medal for making my mark on the peace paper between us and the Crow. On it is the face of the Father who lives in the main village of the whites. I said that I would not fight with the Crow while the sun still shines forever, and I do not speak in two directions. But none of you made your mark on that paper and none of you wear this medal. I don't think the Father knows who you are. My own favorite type of horse is pinto."

So a party of raiders formed at twilight: Shadow That Comes in Sight, Cold Face, Yellow Eagle, Bird Bear, and Long Jaw. It was autumn of the year, with the nights getting brisk, but of course they stripped to the buff so no clothes would get in the way of their quick work. We boys was hanging around doing little services for these men we admired: honing a knife, filling arrow quivers, and so on, when Younger Bear steps up to Shadow and says: "I am ready to go."

Shadow, cinching up his moccasin, answers, "All right," without looking at him.

Younger Bear says: "I have practiced many times, stealing meat from the women." He was referring to the game we played which like the others trained us for more serious business: the women cut buffalo flesh into thin slices and hung them on rawhide lines to dry in the sun, and we would snake along on our bellies and swipe it, each slice standing for a pony. If the woman saw you, she hit you lightly with a stick and you was counted out. Actually Younger Bear was one of the worst at this game; force, rather than stealth, being his specialty. But he was around fourteen now and he was going to bust if he had to stay a boy much longer.

"I killed a buffalo two days ago," he went on. This everybody knew because his father had gone around camp singing about it after the hunt and then gave a feast.

"I have heard that," said Shadow. "You can come."

"I am the strongest boy in camp," Younger Bear said.

"You also talk a lot," said Cold Face, who was tying a little medicine bundle behind his ear for luck. "We'll stay here and you can go and make a speech to the Crow, who love a big mouth."

"You can come," said Shadow, "if you don't say any more. The Human Beings are the greatest people on the face of the earth, the bravest warriors, have the most beautiful and virtuous women, and live in a place that is perfect. That is known to everybody, even our enemies. A Human Being just *is* and does not have to talk about it."

Now that stuff got my goat even more than Younger Bear's volunteering to join the raid. I liked the Cheyenne and by this time really felt I was maybe a second cousin to them, but whenever I ran into their arrogance it served only to remind me I was basically white. The greatest folk on earth! Christ, they wouldn't have had them iron knives if Columbus hadn't hit these shores. And who brought them the pony in the first place?

I was standing at the side of Little Horse and whispered to him, "I'm going." He said, "I'm not," and left Shadow's tepee. That was the first sign that I can remember he showed of what was to be his life direction.

I stepped up to the men and asked: "Can I go?"

I was in the wrong state of mind for such a dangerous venture, when solidarity is wanted, whereas I was joining out of my difference from my comrades. Them Cheyenne looked at me and then they looked at one another. I was about thirteen, quite the shrimp in build, and I had red hair, blue eyes, and skin that may have been dirty and sunburned and scratched but withal was pale as a fishbelly.

I believe it might have occurred to them right then that the Crow was friends of the Americans, and that it probably was foolhardy to take along on what was only too likely to be a fatal expedition for some, a fellow whose trust wasn't secured by blood. Not to mention an untried kid.

But Shadow says: "All right." You give an Indian a choice and he is sure to take the reckless alternative: he is inclined to let anybody do what they want. Especially the Cheyenne, who don't have initiation ceremonies for a boy. You want to be a man so you try what men do, and there ain't nothing to stop you but the enemy.

CHAPTER 6 *A New Name*

I STRIPPED OFF my leggings and shirt and smeared myself full of black paint so that white hide of mine wouldn't put me at a disadvantage in the moonlight, and Little Horse showed up again, carrying the whole skin of a black wolf that was so big I could get inside with almost nothing hanging out. Which was the idea: the head went right over my own skull, and I looked out the eyeholes.

We started off soon as it was definitely night, seven of us, and rode twenty mile at the trot over a plain of grass; then walked, leading the animals, for say another three. Much of the latter was rough terrain, in and out of ravines filled with scrubwood, and the only light a half-moon that seemed to carry the same cloud across the heavens with it as a shade. I could just have made out my hand at arm's length had it not been blackened. But Shadow moved along right smartly as if it was high noon; and three men behind, I let my horse follow his lead.

We fetched up in a deep draw that went down to the Crazy Woman's Creek, and there across the water were the lodges of the Crow camp, each glowing like a lantern from the fire within, for the older a tepee skin the more it takes on the character of oiled paper and sometimes you can stand outside at night and identify the inhabitants through it. We was still too far away for that, but what I saw was mighty pretty in a toy way, and the wind was moving from them to us, bringing the smell of roast meat. We hadn't ate all day, for you don't stuff yourself when you go to steal horses. Yellow Eagle sniffed alongside me and said: "Maybe we ought to visit first." We could have walked peaceful into camp and them Crow would of had to feed us, for that's the Indian way.

"We'll leave the ponies here," whispered Shadow That Comes in Sight, "and you and you will hold them," touching me and Younger Bear; it was O.K. by me. But Younger Bear began to protest so strongly you might have thought he was sobbing.

Which infuriated Yellow Eagle. I didn't know that man well, who had joined our camp only a few months back, but he possessed a deal of scalps and he owned a percussion-cap carbine, which was a rare implement among the Cheyenne in them days. For a long time that was the only gun in our bunch, and it wasn't no good owing to a lack of the caps, for we avoided the whites, even traders, like Old Lodge Skins said. Elsewhere, though, the Sioux and other bands of Cheyenne were having little run-ins with the Americans along the Oregon Trail, taking their coffee now from the emigrants without waiting for it to be offered and sometimes all else as well. I noticed among Yellow Eagle's collection of hair some which looked too light for Pawnee or Snake ever to have sprouted. The carbine probably came from the same quarter.

The Eagle was burned up at the improper manner in which Younger Bear was carrying on.

"You have lived for enough snows," he scolded him, "to understand that among the Human Beings a veteran warrior knows more than a boy about stealing horses. It has nothing to do with who is brave and who isn't: no Human Being has ever been a coward. You are asked to stay here because someone has to hold the ponies, which is as important a job as going into the Crow camp; and you know that we shall share equally what we capture. I don't hear Little Antelope complain. He is a better Human Being than you, and he is white."

Nobody else said a word and Yellow Eagle had been whispering. Nevertheless an awful silence descended, as if after a riot of noise. Younger Bear had been wrong, but the Eagle turned out more so. Not a word had been said about my race since I joined the tribe, not even by the Bear himself, who hated me. That wasn't done, it could do no good, as the Indians say, and Yellow Eagle no sooner got it out than he knew his error.

"That should not have been said," he told me. "A devil had control of my tongue."

I was getting into the wolfskin at the moment, which I slung behind me while I rode; just aligning the eyeholes so I could see through them. The light was poor and everything looked hairy.

"I don't think bad of you," was my answer, "for you haven't been long with our camp."

"I don't think it is a good night to steal ponies," said Shadow, and started to remount while the others murmured agreement and followed suit.

"No," said Yellow Eagle. "I will take away the bad luck I have brought." He leaped on his horse and rode off in the direction whence we had come.

"I'll stay and mind the ponies," Younger Bear stated contritely, his head down. "With the other one," meaning me.

So he accepted the halters of three, and I took as many, and so nobody could see us against the moon we kept hard against the left side of the draw that was hereabout maybe seven-eight foot deep, adequate to conceal men and animals from anybody on the plain above. The four big Cheyenne walked towards the Crow camp glowing across the water. In a minute you couldn't see them any more nor hear them in two. After a while the moon finally got rid of that cloud and brightened some though not enough to throw a shadow.

I sat down in that wolf suit, which I was glad to have for its warmth alone, and sure didn't grieve none that I was not en route into the camp. On the other hand, if I'd had to go, I couldn't have picked better comrades than them four. I had started to get a glimmering of what the Cheyenne meant when they always talked about dying: I began to understand the loyalty to friends, but what I didn't have was the feeling that I myself was disposable.

Now that the rest had gone, Younger Bear took up his grumbling again.

"They should not have done this to me," he muttered. "I should have gone along. You could hold six ponies alone."

"For that matter," says I, "*you* could hold them all, and I might go."

"You would be scared," he comes back at me. "Your medicine may be big in play camp, but it wouldn't fool a Crow. This is the time to be a man." He was standing there with his chest puffed out as usual, though he wasn't so husky as formerly, having gone into the skinny lankiness of the teen years.

I don't know what I'd have been forced to do at this point so as not to let that Indian outface me—probably would have dropped them halters had he refused to take them, therewith losing the horses, and run towards the enemy camp to join the raiding party, thereby losing my life and throwing those of the others in grave jeopardy.

I was saved in a curious fashion. Suddenly an enormous Crow sprang over the bank onto the floor of the draw and knocked Younger Bear senseless with a war club. This in utter silence excepting the impact of his moccasins on the sand, which was scarcely noisy, and the sound of the club against Bear's head, just a sort of neat *chock!* like when you throw a stone against a keg.

In a flash his knife was out and his left hand drawing Bear's braids tight so the scalp would begin to pull off as it was being cut.

Then I was at the Crow, who hadn't taken notice of me because he maybe thought I was a real wolf that Bear was talking to—an Indian wouldn't have seen that as funny—I was at him and on him as if I was climbing a tree, for he was monstrous large with all his sinews in tension, skin rough as bark. But now I was there, I didn't know what to do with the son of a bitch. I was now too close to shoot a bow, which anyway I had dropped, and I was clawing for my knife but that wolfskin was all bunched up and I couldn't find it.

Of course the Crow was not exactly waiting in amused toleration. The big devil flexed his hide and flung me against the other side of the draw, and I was knocked cold by the meeting of my chin with my own right knee.

I come to within the next second, when the point of his knife had already broken skin above my right ear and begun sawing round towards the back of the head. I started some and the knife scraped bone. That makes the goddamnedest sound, reverberating to your testicles.

Now my hair was longer than when I had been with my white kin, but not nearly so long as an Indian wears his. The reason for this is that it grew naturally like snagged wire: let it go a month and I'd look neither Indian, white, male nor female, but rather like the belly of a goat that had been tracking through fresh dung, for along with the tangle the ginger color would darken, the more the hair, and go to brown, and any kind of animal fat laid on it would streak in green.

That was why I'd hack it off now and again when it got more than halfway down my neck. So this Crow, he was already in the act of scalping me when he hesitated for the briefest space on account of the funny feel of that short hair, which sure belonged to no Cheyenne by birth.

This break in rhythm brought me out of the spell I was under, quietly suffering the top of my head to be sliced off, the warm blood running into my right ear. I couldn't wrestle him, I didn't have no weapon, Younger Bear so far as I knowed was stone dead, and the other Cheyenne was in the village by now, too far away to help, and if I made a noise the rest of the Crow would be roused and murder my friends. This was the kind of thing for which Old Lodge Skins had told us boys that story about Little Man fighting the Snakes. Sooner or later he knowed it'd come in handy. I couldn't let a *Crow* do this to a *Human Being!*

I jerked back and bared my teeth.

"*Nazestae!*" I hissed. "I am Cheyenne!" It would have sounded more impressive could I have afforded to shout it as battle cry; I have explained why I couldn't.

But do you know, with that the Crow pulled away his knife, fell back on his haunches, and covered up his mouth with his left hand. His thumb had slipped on my movement and run across my forehead, opening up a white streak through that paint made of soot and buffalo grease. He didn't understand what I said, for Crow and Cheyenne have different tongues, but he spoke as if in answer to it and in English:

"Little white man! Fool poor Crow! Ha, ha, big fooling. You want to eat?"

He was scared I'd take offense, see, because the Crow always sucked up to Americans, and in his dumb way wanted to bring me over to his lodge. It wasn't his fault, of course, none of it, and that fellow has always been on my conscience. It appeared he was out in the night by himself for some reason when he run across me and the Bear, and worked quiet for he didn't know how many others of us was in the vicinity. But I couldn't have known that at the moment; I couldn't in the time at my disposal explain the situation for him; and least of all could I go as his guest to camp, or even let him talk about it any longer in that loud voice.

So I had to kill him. Murder him, a friendly fellow like that. Shoot him in the back, what's more. In retrieving my wolfskin that had fell off in the struggle, I had found my bow and quiver on the ground. The Crow at that moment was crawling up the wall of the draw to get the pony he had left on the plain.

Three Cheyenne arrows, *thunk, thunk, thunk,* in a straight line along his backbone. His hands lost their purchase and his big body slid down again till his moccasins hit bottom, and it stopped rigid on the incline.

That was the first I ever took a human life, and however it sounds to you, it was one of the best times. I was saving my friends, and you shouldn't never have to apologize for that. And after all, he *had* scalped me almost halfway, which though he later veered friendly left its mark I can tell you. The right side of my face and neck was sticky as molasses with lifeblood—mine, very dear to me—and I was afeared to feel up there in case my whole skull-cover flapped loose. I dropped out of the picture then.

Next time I opened my eyes, I was laying inside a little tepee of brush and alongside me squatted some fellow wearing the top of a buffalo's head, horns and matted hair, and he was singing and shaking a buffalo tail in my face. I had a terrible headache; my skull felt as though it had shriveled like a dried pea. I seemed to be wearing a cap of mud. I tried it gingerly with my fingers, but the medicine man gave a loud buffalo-snort at that moment and spat a mouthful of chawed-up flower petals into my face.

I had been long enough then among the Cheyenne to hold my peace. Besides, the headache gave one great surge and then began to ebb away. I sat up, and Left-Handed Wolf, for that was the medicine man's name, started to dance around the robe where I lay, singing that monotone curing song interspersed with snorts and bellows. And he kept chewing more dried flowers from a little pouch on his belt and blowing them at me from the quarter points of the compass.

Then he leaned over and tapped a little stick on my cranium, and off fell the clay cap in two halves in which a few wiry hairs was embedded. Now my head felt especial cool as if indeed the whole scalp was missing, but he spat some flowers on it and it didn't hurt no more at all.

Now he danced slowly before me and dangled that buffalo tail just beyond my reach. I tried weakly to seize it, but he'd back off a little each time. I felt the strength coming up from the soles of my feet, and when it reached my knees I got up and followed him, still trying to grab the tail that he shook before me while bellowing and tossing his horns. His face was painted black, with the eyes and nostrils rimmed in vermilion.

Wolf backed through the tepee door and I come along, reaching for that tail more and more vigorously, and when I got outside, I saw the whole camp, warriors, women, kids, babies, and dogs, lined up in parallel rows from the lodge entrance to the river. They was all by their presence working for my cure. No Cheyenne suffers alone. I was mighty touched by this display and got the power of it, straightening up my back and walking with almost normal force.

When we reached the riverbank, Wolf said: "Stretch yourself."

I did so, and some black blood started from the place above my temple where the Crow had first inserted his knife, and falling into the water was carried away and lost in the Powder's swift current. Then came the good red blood, which Wolf stanched with dried flowers.

"I am well now," said I. That's the God's truth, and was the end of the incident. Afterwards I looked in a trade mirror and found a thin blue tracing at the roots of my hair, but even that was gone in a day or so.

The moral effects was farther-reaching. For one thing, a crier right away went about camp singing about what a hero I was and inviting people to a feast Old Lodge Skins was holding in my honor. The chief for celebration give most of his horses away to certain poor Cheyenne who didn't have any, and after the eats he made presents to everybody who come: blankets, jewelry, and so on—he ended up almost naked. He also made a speech which from modesty I'll pass up except for the important points.

After recounting my exploit at great length in a poetic fashion that would just sound silly in English, he said: "This boy has proved himself a Human Being. Tonight there is weeping in the Crow lodges. The earth shakes when he walks. The Crow cry like women when he comes! He is a Human Being! Like the great Little Man, who came to him in a dream and gave him strength to kill the Crow, he walks!"

This was exaggerating some, but as I told you I did think of Little Man and jerked away from the knife, which caused the Crow's hand to slip proving I was white. I had told Old Lodge Skins only about the inspiration of Little Man, figuring it would please him. He took it from there.

After some minutes of the foregoing stuff, which didn't embarrass me none, for everybody was beaming at me, including some of the young girls who was allowed to peek under the tepeeskin—I was getting some interest in girls at this point of my life—after that, the chief said:

"This boy's medicine comes from the vision of Little Man. He is himself little in body and he is now a man. But his heart is big. Therefore his name from now on shall be: Little Big Man."

That was it, and that's how I was called ever after by the Cheyenne. True to Indian ways, no one used my real name; no one even knew it. It was Jack Crabb.

The horse-stealing expedition was also in its other respects a job well done. Them four warriors had slipped into the Crow village without rousing a soul and took thirty horses, more or less, driving them back to our camp through what remained of the night into early morning. When they reached where me and Younger Bear was, Bear had come to with a knot on his head but otherwise O.K. Lucky for us that Crow had been wandering without his bow, else we'd both been plugged from the top of the draw and never knowed the difference. So they tied me to my pony and brung me in.

I got four horses from the common loot, thereby becoming a man of certain substance, but had a greater thrill when a little lad, eight or nine, named Dirt on the Nose, asked me: "Now you're a warrior, can I tend your ponies?" Meaning I could stay in bed of a morning now when the kids got up for chores. Maybe I could, but it was not the Cheyenne way to press your advantages. Shadow That Comes in Sight, for example, the veteran warrior who had led the raid, took a share of three horses, kept the least for himself, giving the best to Old Lodge Skins and the next to Hump—not because they was chiefs, for that cut no ice as such; no Cheyenne kissed the arse of authority—but because they had advised him well. Then Bird Bear and Cold Face each give one of their ponies to Yellow Eagle, who though he made a mistake had done the right thing to correct it. Then I gave him one of mine, for the same reason, and since I had been involved. Then I offered another to Left-Handed Wolf, who refused because you aren't supposed to be paid for treatment. But it was O.K. to present it to his brother, which I did.

Therefore I answered Dirt on the Nose in this wise: "Killing one Crow does not yet make me the equal of the great warriors among the Human Beings. I shall still tend my own horses, but you are a good boy and I am going to give you that black I have been riding."

Everybody said: "How, how."

So none of us who took our life in our hands ended up a hell of a lot richer except in pride and honor, but a Cheyenne would die for them things any old day.

Younger Bear never showed up at the feast, I think the reason is obvious. It went on far into the night, and I ate a good deal too much of boiled dog, which was the fare: I had got a taste for that victual by now but had never developed an Indian's capacity for gorging on the one hand, and then fasting on the other. After the shebang was finally done, I went out into the prairie and relieved myself and then set for a spell on a nearby rise. The moon was a hair skinnier than last night, but riding clear. Nevertheless, it would rain towards morning: you could feel that in your nose and through the soles of your moccasins against the old autumn grass and even through your haunches on the ground. Nobody ever told me that sort of thing. You learned it naturally living in our manner, like a man in town knows from the look of a storefront that they sell tobacco inside.

About a mile away, a coyote barked for a while, then yelped, then howled, then whined in several different notes. It sounded like a whole pack, but was just one animal, for they are natural ventriloquists. He was answered from the north by the long, sorry wail of a timber wolf—or Crow raiders imitating the same, for that is one of their specialties; but it continued off and on for an hour in the same location, so must have been the real beast.

After I had sat there long enough to warm the earth with my rump, a rattlesnake come crawling towards me, as they are ever cold and will move right into your bed if you suffer them to do it, for a bit of warmth. But I heard under the wind noise the slither of his dragging length, so counterfeited the flap of an eagle's wing and he reversed himself.

So I, Jack Crabb, was a Cheyenne warrior. Had made my kill with bow and arrow. Been scalped and healed with hocus-pocus. Had an ancient savage who couldn't talk English for my Pa, and a fat brown woman for my Ma, and for a brother a fellow whose face I hardly ever saw for clay or paint. Lived in a skin tent and ate puppy dog. God, it was strange.

That's how my thoughts was running at that moment, and they

was white to the core. Them kids I used to play with in Evansville would never believe it, neither would those with our wagons. They knowed I was always mean, but not that rotten. On the night of my great triumph, there I sat, thoroughly humiliated. Other than for my real Pa, the one killed at the wagons, who was crazy, you could seldom find a man back in town who didn't think an Indian even lower than a black slave.

Right then I heard a sound that made me think the rattler had took a second thought and decided in his slow, stubborn way: what's an eagle doing here in the night? and come back to try his luck again at getting near that warmth.

But it was Younger Bear, sitting down alongside. That shows how dangerous it can be to think white in the middle of the prairie. I hadn't heard him coming. I could have lost the scalp that just was healed back on had it been an enemy.

He sat there some ten foot away, staring into the night and, I expect, thinking red. I didn't say nothing. At last he looked in my direction and said: "Hey, come here!"

"I was here first," says I.

"I got something for you," he says. "Come on over here and get it."

I wasn't taking any of his crap now that I had saved his life, so I just turned away and directly he come crawling to me.

"Here," he said. "Here's a present for Little Big Man."

I couldn't see what he was holding behind his back, and leaned to look, and he pushed the big bushy scalp of that Crow into my face, laughing like hell.

"That's a stupid thing to do," I told him. "You are the biggest fool I have ever known."

He dropped the hair and fell back on his arms.

"I thought it was a pretty good joke," he says. "That is a beautiful scalp and perfumed with musk. Smell it if you don't believe me. It's yours. I took it, but it should belong to you. You killed him and saved my life. If you want me to do anything for you, I will. You can have my pony and best blanket, and I'll tend your horses."

I was still sore at that silly thing he did; although it was a typical Indian joke, it showed bad taste and worse will at this point. I wasn't taken in for a minute by his apparent friendliness.

"You know," said I, "that one Human Being don't pay another for saving his life."

"Yes," answered Younger Bear in a deadly voice, "but you are a white man."

There ain't no curse words in Cheyenne and most of the insults take the form of calling the other guy a woman or cowardly, etc., and even in my anger I never thought of applying those to Younger Bear. Besides, he had a great argument. I had just been in the act of thinking the same thing. Yet you know how it is: there are women who will take pay for letting you on them, but don't call them "whore."

Now on the needle of this Indian, the worse fate I could imagine was not to be a Cheyenne. He had really hurt my feelings. What I should have done was to accept it the Indian way, go sulk and fast until he apologized, which he'd of had to if only on account of my high prestige in the tribe right then. Actually, Bear didn't but half believe in his own accusation. He was jealous and so had thrown me the dirtiest insult he could think up. If I'd played it right it would have got him in the backflash: *he* would have had to prove he was the Cheyenne, for I had done so.

Instead, I said hotly: "That's right, you fool. Since I gave yours back to you, you owe me one life. And you can't pay me off with that scalp nor a blanket nor all your ponies. Only a life will do, and I'll let you know when I want one."

He stuck the Crow scalp under his belt and got up.

"I heard you," he said and went back into camp.

I had said that because I was mad and wanted to play it big. I didn't know rightly what I meant. It was probably a kid's bluff. Myself, I forgot it directly, though remembering Younger Bear's dislike of me well enough for a while: then I forgot that too, for I didn't see no more instances of it. He stopped shooting play arrows at me, put no more burrs under my saddle, in fact seemed to do his best to pretend I was as solid a Human Being as he had proved me not to be.

But the point is that he never forgot what I said on that rise up by the Powder River, and about twenty years later, and some fifty mile away from where we had been sitting that night, he paid me in full.

I have said I was getting interested in girls. Just about the time this began to happen, the situation changed so that I couldn't get near any of the Cheyenne girls of my own age. They had started to get their monthlies and from that time on was kept away from the boys, being always in the company of their mothers or aunts and wearing a rope belt between their legs until they got married. (They wore it after marriage, too, whenever their husband was away.) About all you could do was to show off when the girl you liked was watching. That probably comes as a surprise: you may think an Indian goes at it like a jackrabbit, but not the Cheyenne with their own women unless they are married to them, and since the married men always swear off it before going to war, and we were most of the time fighting, the Cheyenne were pretty hard up for tail at any given time. That's why they was such fierce warriors, or so they believed anyway. I never knew a man who didn't have a special interest in his own member, but to a Cheyenne it was a magic wand.

After Younger Bear went away and I cooled down, I started thinking about a girl named Howaheh—which means, I ask you to believe, "Nothing." When we were littler and played camp, I had frequently been forced to choose Nothing as my make-believe wife, on account of them other boys knew how better to go about getting the good-looking ones for themselves and I was left with this girl, who was fairly ugly. But here lately she had, as young girls will, of a sudden turned pretty as a buckskin colt, with big, shy eyes like an antelope and the graceful limbs of a doe. She always used to like me when I didn't pay no attention to her, but as you might expect nowadays ignored me utterly.

Well, nothing I could do about Nothing right then, so I finally got up and went down into camp. There was a dog awake there, about to howl in answer to the coyote though he knew it was wrong because it might alert prowling Crow to our location, so I said to him: "That's not the Cheyenne way," and he closed his chops and slunk off.

Everybody else was sleeping, the fires all cold. I found my robe, not far from the doorhole, and started to get into it when I realized it must be Little Horse's, for he was wrapped in it, so I moved on to the empty one alongside, though I usually slept to his left.

But he was awake, and whispered: "This is yours."

"It don't matter none," I says. "Stay there."

"You want me to?" he asks, sounding disappointed.

And then I went to sleep, not thinking any more about it. If a Cheyenne don't believe he can stand a man's life, he ain't forced to. He can become a *heemaneh*, which is to say half-man, half-woman.

There are uses for these fellows and everybody likes them. They are sometimes chemists, specializing in the making of love-potions, and generally good entertainers. They wear women's clothes and can get married to another man, if such be his taste.

Little Horse began to train to be a *heemaneh* not long after this incident. Maybe he got the beds mixed up by mistake that night and didn't have anything in mind. Whatever, I personally didn't find him my type.

CHAPTER 7 *We Take on the Cavalry*

THE CROW COME AFTER US on the following day and we had a good war, which was a stand-off as to who won. So we fought some more. And we fought the Ute and we fought the Shoshone, and after trading some horses with the Blackfeet, we fought them too. This fighting was pleasurable to the Cheyenne when they killed the enemy and very sad when vice versa. In the latter event you heard the wailing of mourners from morning till night. For while Indians love war, I don't want you to get the idea they like to lose their relatives to it. They really like one another in the same tribe. And as to the enemy, they hate him for what he is but don't want to change him into anything else.

When the Cheyenne gave the beating there was celebration. If it happened near our camp, the women and children went out and clubbed and stabbed the enemy wounded who was lying about and mutilated the dead, taking as souvenirs such items as noses, ears, and private parts. This was a real treat for them. If you seen as much as I did, you would have like me developed a strong stomach. Buffalo Wallow Woman was sort of my Ma, just a fine soul. I can't count the times when I was small she hugged me against her fat belly, smiling down that moon-face with a sheen of grease on it; or give me a specially juicy piece of dog meat, tucked me in the robe at night, slipped me some Indian chewing gum, did beading on my clothes, and on and on. She was 100 per cent woman, like Old Lodge Skins was all man, and I don't know that you could get near her quality had you boiled down a score of white females for their essence. But now what'd you think when you saw that sweet person ripping open some helpless Crow with her knife and unwinding his guts?

I'll tell you what: after a while, I didn't. The Crow and Ute and Shoshone never protested, on account of they did the same, so what the hell business was it of mine? You recall Old Lodge Skins's attitude towards the whites: their ways were nonsensical to him but he figured they had reasons. I wasn't going to let no Indian outdo me in tolerance. If Buffalo Wallow Woman or some tiny brown-faced kid came in from the field holding a piece of human offal, proud as can be, why I'd say the equivalent of "Swell!"

I had a bigger problem than that. I was still young but had killed my man, so if there was a war of any size I didn't find it easy to beg off. I didn't have no inclination to become a *heemaneh* like Little Horse, though that's no criticism of him. There wasn't any other alternative. What I did try, not being actually a Cheyenne, was to kill as few of whoever we was fighting as practicable; that is, I would go all out if it was a defensive action, but slack off if we was carrying the day.

I tried, that is, to retain some smattering of civilization while doing nothing to jeopardize my barbarian friends. A very thin line to walk. Neither was it always possible to avoid certain savage practices, if you know what I mean. Hell, I guess you don't. All right, then: I didn't go out of my way to do it, but I had to take hair now and again. So long as I've confessed that, you also ought to be told that in such cases the victim ain't always dead or even unconscious, and your knife ain't always sharp and sometimes there is an ugly sound as the scalp parts company with the skull. I kept it to a minimum, but sometimes Younger Bear was close by me on the field of battle, offering no choice. By the age of fifteen he carried so many scalps about his person and gear that at a certain distance he seemed covered all over with hair, like a grizzly.

I don't want to overemphasize this practice. There was another, fortunately for me, that took precedence over it: I mean the making of coups, riding into the midst of the enemy and striking one with the handle of a weapon or with a little stick carried just for that purpose. It is a greater accomplishment than killing him because more dangerous for the practitioner, and if you had to reduce the quality of Cheyenne life to a handy phrase you might describe it as the constant taking of risks.

I could always try to count coups when I wanted to avoid blood-letting, and I often did, though not being among the foremost in that pursuit. To be outstanding at it, you had to be crazy. I held my own and never tried to compete with Coyote, who among the bunch of my age was champion and became a bigger hero for it than Younger Bear with all his hair. The Bear made valiant efforts but at the last minute he couldn't help setting aside his coup stick for his hatchet and instead of touching he would hack. But Coyote rode unarmed into the press of the enemy and, slashing lightly with his little quirt, took coups more quickly than they could be enumerated, and though his adversaries made every effort to take his life, he would generally come back without a scratch, having great medicine.

Now I might go on for hours relating the incidents of war, but whereas they are every one different in the actual occurrence and never dull when your own life is at stake, they have a sameness in the telling. So I won't wear them to the point where you think fighting is as routine as riding on a streetcar. Nor will I go into my numerous wounds, most of which I still bear slight traces of, like faded tattooing.

That same summer that we was up on the Powder, a colonel named Harney attacked the Brulé Sioux in their camp on the Blue River, above the North Platte, and killed eighty. It almost goes without saying that these Indians was friendlies, otherwise the Army wouldn't have found them; and put up no resistance, else they wouldn't have been punished to that degree. Some of that figure was made up of women and children, on account of the warriors retreated from the cavalry charge. That sounds yellow but actually was ignorance. I'm talking about both Indians and whites. A coward kills women, but a soldier of that time at full gallop often couldn't tell them from the braves, and the kids got it from the indiscriminate hail of lead.

As to the fleeing warriors, you got to know Indian ways to appreciate that. When they fight each other, one side charges and the other retreats; then they turn and reverse the situation. This makes for a nice contest in which everybody gets his chance. The Army didn't fight by the rules and no doubt would not have if they knew them, for a white man gets no pleasure out of war itself; he won't fight at all if without it he can *get his way*. He is after your spirit, not the body. That goes for both the military and the pacifists, neither breed of which is found among the Cheyenne, who fought because of the good it did them. They had no interest in power as we know it.

Well, up on the Powder River we heard about this incident even as it was happening, in the Indian way which I have already told you I can't explain, so just accept it as I did. Red Dog mentioned it to me, and for all I know he got it from an eagle, for he was an eagle-catcher, which is a special profession among the Cheyenne. Within a minute or two it was all over camp. The chiefs didn't hold any council this time, because for one thing no Sioux appeared with any project, and for another, it had just gone to prove Old Lodge Skins's wisdom in staying away from white men and thus giving them no opportunity to break any rules.

We stayed the rest of the year up in that territory, which was prettier country than along the Platte, nearer to lodgepoles, fire-wood, elk, and bear, for the Big Horn Mountains rose fifty-sixty mile to the west with their purple base climbing to a silver crown, and they was rich in timber and game and kept the watercourses fresh through the summer from their melting snows. When winter come, we left off fighting on the larger scale, though now and again you might encounter little enemy parties trapping buffalo in the drifts while you was out doing the like, and the whiteness might end up splashed here and there with red.

But sometimes it was just too cold, with the snow up to a bull's shoulders, and I recall once when four of us coming back from an unsuccessful hunt ran across six Crow in a blizzard, we reached wearily for our slung bows, but they signaled: "We'll fight when the weather gets better," and went on. That was a relief: you could hardly see them.

When it got real fierce, when your very speech would freeze as it emanated from your lips and blow back in stinging rime against the cheeks, we hung close to the tepees and ate the dried meat taken the summer before and stored in rawhide parfleches, and pemmican, the greasier the better on account of a bellyful of melting fat will warm you sooner and stick longer than most anything I know. The value of stout women also went up in the snowtime, and I believe it was that winter that that enormous fat girl from the antelope surround ran the price for her hand up to six horses and other gifts too numerous to count (all of which went to her family) and was led to the bridegroom's lodge.

One time when Nothing was outside her tepee gathering snow in a kettle to melt down for water, I slogged over to her vicinity and warbled like a bird, but she didn't take any more notice than if I hadn't been present, and soon her Ma come out and throwed a little bone at me and said go away, bad boy. That was the extent of my love life that winter.

By the thaw we was all, men and animals, pretty well trimmed down to basic muscle and sinew, with our tongues sharp for fresh provender. Spring was really something to look for in those days when you were lean and hungry and young. Old Lodge Skins wasn't the latter by upwards of fifty years, but the sap rose in him before it did in the trees and he got his younger wife, White Cow Woman, with child again. I have previously mentioned only Burns Red and Little Horse as his offspring, because I was closest to them, but there was others around in various sizes, of which I didn't take much notice of the little girls and was banned by custom from doing so with the females of my own age, they being so to speak my sisters; and more was dead.

Shooting Star, Burns Red's wife, was also pregnant, and a lot of the other women after that season of lay-off from war. These new children would make up for our losses in battle, those that were males, that is, and if they grew up. At present there was five or six women to every adult brave. I've slipped by the subject of death as if we won all the time. We lost almost as often; mostly it was an even score in the long run. What made the Cheyenne special was that they were fewer than most of their enemies; always outnumbered but never outfought, as the saying goes.

As to the punishment we sustained, I don't count wounds, and sometimes apparently mortal ones would be cured by the medicine men in the style I've described, but it might give an idea when I say that before the winter closed in, three of those five grownups I went on the raid with were dead: Cold Face, Long Jaw, and Yellow Eagle. Spotted Wolf, who if you recall was going to assault my white Ma when Caroline cold-cocked him, he was killed against the Pawnee in the spring before. These is just to mention some of the names you might recognize. We never at full strength could mount more than forty warriors.

For a long time I believed Old Lodge Skins's bunch was the whole Cheyenne nation, then at least one of the main bands that constitute the tribe, but in fact what it turned out to be was one big family:

most of these folk were related to one another by blood or marriage or adoption, and there was a few stragglers from hither and yon, now and then, but not enough to alter the complexion of things.

A Cheyenne won't pass on shameful gossip about himself or his own. So it was a while before I found out why Old Lodge Skins's camp kept to themselves.

Quite some years back, when Old Skins was a boy, his Pa had killed a fellow Cheyenne in a quarrel over a woman and been exiled from the Burnt Artery band. Him and his relatives took off and lived alone, and at length he died, but the kin had lived so long by themselves that they was leery about going back. They also bore that shame, and when they did run across other Human Beings would rest their chins on the chest and look out of the sides of their eyes if at all. They come to be known as the *tatoimana*, which is to say the Shy Folks.

Now Old Lodge Skins became their leader, having proved himself wise and brave and generous, and the time come when they was invited back to the Burnt Arteries on the occasion of the sun dance where all the tribe joins together. By God if that Indian didn't get into the same kind of trouble as his Dad—a vein of horniness run right through the family—he swiped the wife of a man from the Hair Rope band and though he left two horses as payment the other fellow didn't like the deal and come after him and in the set-to got an arrow through the windpipe and choked to death.

Skins didn't bother to come back to that dance after that, but was joined by the rest of his family out on the prairie and they wandered by themselves again for years. Somewhere along the line they was reinstated. By the time I joined up, they could go to the all-Cheyenne get-togethers but was not encouraged to camp in the Burnt Artery circle. They stayed pretty shy for a long time.

But now that fat girl had got just about the last eligible husband in our camp, for the Cheyenne won't stand for incest and we hadn't picked up any new people since the coming of Yellow Eagle, who was now dead leaving two widows and a tepeeful of orphans which Shadow That Comes in Sight had to adopt.

I don't think Old Lodge Skins can be condemned for deciding to move south again when spring got well under way, though it defied his intention to keep clear of the whites. We had to get some fresh blood before we could let some more, and most of the other Cheyenne was down below the Platte. There were Sioux up around the

Powder, and they was our fighting allies, but Skins was quite the snob when it come to family connections. He never forgot that version of Cheyenne history which he mentioned to the Minneconjou: the Human Beings had horses when the Lakota was still using dogs. He didn't spell it out, but I know he figured the Sioux as lower-class.

That was how the women come to strike camp and make travois of the lodgepoles, on which they packed the folded tepee skins and the rest of the gear, and did the same with the lighter articles onto the bigger dogs, including among the baggage certain small kids lashed atop it, and those of us with horses mounted them and some walked, and in a great messy caravan stretched for a mile, the warriors riding flank, we wended southward, leaving a wide trail of horse dung, wornout apparel, cleaned bones, and the ashes of many old campfires.

I was on the way to becoming a white man again, although I never suspected it at the time.

We traveled all the way to the Solomon's Fork of the Kansas River, in the north of the present-day state of the latter name, and there in a great camp covering a mile or more of bottomland we found the entire Cheyenne nation, who except for us had wintered together the preceding season. That was a mighty assemblage, the biggest I had seen up to that point, and it made me proud: probably a thousand lodges in the configuration of a circle, with the tepees of each band making a little circle within the greater. And all the bands was there: the Hair Rope, the Scabby People, etc., which were hitherto known to me only in narrative, not to mention the military societies such as the Dog Soldiers, who acted as a police force, and the Contraries who do everything backwards.

Old Lodge Skins was sort of uneasy when we was riding in: I could see that, for an Indian's face is as expressive as anybody's when he is among his own, but nobody tried to stop us and nobody came up and asked: "Where are you going? What do you want?" which they would have done to someone who did not belong, and after a while I could see, beneath his chiefly dignity, that the old man was considerable relieved.

Shortly out come some headmen from the Burnt Artery band and greeted him like a brother, inviting our bunch to camp in their circle. The old crime had been washed out. So everything was perfect and they had taken buffalo on a big ritualistic hunt up on the headwaters of the Republican River, so we all had to eat six or seven consecutive meals that day because every Indian who saw you would pull you into his lodge and press a feast on you.

Then there was some speechifying by the orators and songs by the singers, and some dancing by the *heemaneh*—with whom Little Horse now definitely threw in his lot—which was very graceful and well received. And gossip was exchanged on every hand, Shadow That Comes in Sight told his jokes, and gifts were presented back and forth and it got to be a problem to remember what you had left to give the next guy without passing on something you had just received.

I was in the middle of all this. There were those among the new people who sized me up, and I expect some talk went on out of my hearing until they all got it straight, but I never had to undergo one embarrassing moment, except maybe owing to the excess of approval that was manifested after Old Lodge Skins, Burns Red, and Little Horse done their bragging about me.

Everything seemed to be swell, but after purely Indian matters had been pretty well gone over, up came the subject of the whites and that was like a storm sky obscuring the sun. The spring before, there had been a difficulty over four horses which the Cheyenne said were strays found roaming the prairie but the soldiers claimed as their own, so they killed one Human Being and put another into the post guardhouse, where he died. Then in the summer a party of young men came across a mail wagon and asked the driver for some tobacco, but he shot at them, so they put an arrow in his arm and the next day the troops attacked their camp, killing six Indians and stealing their horses. As the Cheyenne was fleeing from this assault, they ran across a wagon train, so they took revenge upon the whites and killed two men and a child.

There had been other troubles, with a chief called Big Head wounded while on a friendly visit to Fort Kearny. The Cheyenne felt especial put upon, for by their lights they had always been amiable to white men. Even after all these bad things, they sent a delegation to see the Government Indian agent and apologized. They also returned a woman they had captured. But you see the complication was this: Indians wasn't ever organized. Them that come in to apologize wasn't the same as what killed the whites. And them that the soldiers usually punished was never the ones who had committed the outrages. The white people on whom the Indians took revenge had no connection with the soldiers.

It was pretty early on that I come to realize that most serious situations in life, or my life anyway, were like that time I rubbed out the Crow: he spared me because I was white, and I killed him because I was Cheyenne. There wasn't nothing else either of us could have done, and it would have been ridiculous except it was mortal.

Anyhow, the Cheyenne now had got to believing they might soon have to destroy all the white men on the plains, an idea that didn't seem altogether preposterous when you saw the size of that camp. Even I got to entertaining the possibility: we could ourselves mount maybe fifteen hundred warriors, and we was now friends with the Kiowa and Comanche who lived just south, and our old pals the Arapaho would help and the Sioux from the north. I was making out all right as an Indian and didn't figure on losing any sleep over what happened to my native race when I thought of how little they had ever done for me. Besides, there wasn't any talk of invading St. Louis or Chicago—or Evansville—which is where white people belonged.

That was before I heard the oratory of the medicine men: two of them, named Ice and Dark. They had great powers. All they had to do was make certain motions towards the soldiers, and when the latter fired their guns the bullets would roll slowly down the barrels and fall harmless to the earth.

I used to stand along the path that Nothing took when she went to the river for water, and as she passed I'd grab the fringe on her skirt and give a little tug, then let go. About the only compensation I got for it was that she didn't show no more attention to Coyote, who was also now stuck on her, than to me. He and I would take turns in paying her notice: such as that if I was waiting for her on the river path, he would let that go and try to approach her when she was gathering buffalo chips. Since neither of us was yet getting anywhere, we wasn't jealous of each other and maintained the neutral relations me and Coyote had always had. You know how it is: you have your friends and enemies, and then there is that host of others you can take or leave: same way among Indians.

I also had developed an Indian sense of time. I must have been about fifteen when we was on the Solomon's Fork, and I had this crush on Nothing but I wasn't any more impatient in regard to it than she was: the Cheyenne take five years or so to court their women and even so I was young to be starting now. I'll bet you never knowed redskins was so slow in this area. But being warriors, the Cheyenne like to keep themselves bottled up. You try fighting sometime after going at it hard and you'll see the point: you'll just want to sleep.

Well sir, it was interesting to be in that big camp with all the activities and pretty soon they held a sun dance which went on for eight days of highly elaborate doings that wouldn't mean anything to an individual not of that persuasion, but it reaffirmed the Human Beings in their sense of superiority, if it was possible to do that when they already never believed they had even close competition. In the self-tortures Younger Bear distinguished himself of course. He ripped the pegs out of his chest within fifteen minutes after their being attached, and had them hooked into new places and hung against the rawhide lines all night long. Next day his whole upper body was like an open sore, and he didn't treat it with salve or mud or anything but strutted around with the blood drying.

Now you might call it typical of the Cheyenne that after all the talk of how they was going to wipe out the whites, and all the ceremony that fitted them to do so, they began to break up the camp and move off with a purpose to keep out of trouble. After all that, it would have seemed like an anticlimax to go and really fight, and Indians, who war among themselves all the time, didn't get no pleasure out of tangling with white men, which was a nasty business even if you won.

The bands traveled individually but for some distance formed two general movements: northward or south, for the tribe as a whole was divided most of the year into a larger segment that roamed as separate parts about the Platte, and another that hung around the fort of William Bent the trader, on the Purgatory and Arkansas rivers down in southern Colorado.

We who followed Old Lodge Skins was of course Northern Cheyenne and now moved with the Burnt Artery band in that direction. I should say before we get too far along that we had done a good bit of business at that gathering and married off most of our available females, whose husbands was now with us. That and his acceptance back into his proper band had put Old Lodge Skins in such a good mood that I figure he would have got into trouble again under the wrong buffalo robe had not camp been struck when it was. I had seen him flickering his ruttish old eyes at several fat figures. I myself as yet didn't have a horny thought towards Nothing, just would have liked to hear her shy, soft voice or draw a peek from them glowing black eyes.

We hadn't got far when our scouts come back with the report of a column of troops about half a day's ride ahead, moving our way. Now at the big camp they had had a few flintlocks, so about three of our warriors was now armed in this fashion, and Hump, who had been waiting for years for this eventuality, wanted to ride on and fight the soldiers. But Old Lodge Skins and the head chiefs of the Burnt Arteries was concerned for the women and children, so we turned and went back south in search of our other folks. Traveling east, we caught up with some of the southern people and reassembled with them again near the Solomon's Fork. It wasn't the whole crowd from before, but we had maybe three hundred fighting men and say ten or fifteen flintlocks which seemed to the Cheyenne pretty formidable armament.

The excitement was so great I didn't have no time to work out my new point of view: I had already decided theoretically, as I said, that the utter annihilation of the paleface on the western prairie wasn't no skin off my arse: I didn't know a white man west of St. Joe except for the remnants of my own family who by now must long have reached Salt Lake. But when I studied that out, I never actually saw myself participating in such a massacre. Now here was a battle coming up with the U.S. Cavalry and I was passing for a Cheyenne warrior of some repute. I had the choice of being a coward or either kind of traitor. I remember wishing we was still fighting the Crow.

It sure was a serious problem, but all the time I considered it I was stripping down, daubing myself with red and yellow war paint, and honing the heads of my arrows on a little whetstone. There are some who in moments of indecision cease all bodily movement so as to give free play to the mind, but I'm the other type: I give employment to my hands, figuring my brain will follow suit. When this don't work, there ain't no reason to believe I'd have got any farther by sitting with my chin on my knuckles.

We sent the women and children off south below the Arkansas, although owing to the confidence the Cheyenne had at this moment they set up the lodges again and left them standing. Then Ice the medicine man led us to a little lake nearby, in which we made ourselves invulnerable by dipping our hands in the water. When the soldiers fired we'd just put up our palms and the balls would barely clear the muzzles and dribble to the ground.

That was when the whole business cleared up for me: I was going to die.

You can go so far with Indians and then that sort of thing comes up. I know the medicine of Left-Handed Wolf had cured me of my head wound, but I believe that happened because I was unconscious during most of the healing, and when you are out of your right mind there don't seem to be any rules as to what is possible. Dead drunk, a man can take a fall that when sober would mash him like a tomato. I don't want to be no bigot: I'm not saying that under no conditions can a rifle ball be stopped by magic. What I'm saying is that it ain't going to be stopped by someone who don't believe it can be done as applied to himself. Which was me. So far as Hump went, or Burns Red in the Sun, or Younger Bear, that was their lookout.

If you been listening close you might have caught me up back a ways in the part about fighting the Crow. That first one I killed had found I was white even in the dark: what about those we rode against in the daytime? I painted my face and body, but how about my red hair? I'll tell you. After all the enthusiasm over my first exploit, I certainly didn't want to mention the peculiar conditions of it to any of the Human Beings, for that Crow's discovery of my race, his friendly ways, etc., would only have confused them to hear about. But when we rode out in war, I had represented my problem to Old Lodge Skins in this style:

"Grandfather," I said, which is how you address a man of his age, "I want to do something and don't know the proper way. I don't want the Crow to see the color of my head, and yet I don't want them to think I have been such a coward as to cut off my hair so I can't be scalped. I am still too young and have taken too few coups to wear a full war bonnet."

The chief thought this over, and then he took his plug hat and put it on my head. It was a bit big and came down to my ears, but all the better for coverage.

"Whenever you fight, you may wear this," he said, "but give it back between times because it goes with that medal the Father sent to me from the main village of the whites."

And that's what I did, stuffing a little padding inside the band so it'd be snugger and tying it to my chin with a rawhide cord. As to the hair on my nape, I'd run the paint up to cover that. I still didn't have no braids, of course, and the Crow probably didn't take me for a 100 per cent Cheyenne, for Indians have sharp eyes even in the press of war, but I could have been a breed.

Now we were about to go against the troops, so I went to where Old Lodge Skins with the other leaders was planning our order of battle, they doing this in a formal way like with a trained army, and I caught his attention and asked for the hat, which he was then wearing.

He drew me aside; in fact, we both mounted and rode up on the bluffs above the river, him on one of his marvelous pintos that did his bidding without a word or touch of the bridle. At the highest point we stopped, and he looked into the distances and remarked there was 250 horse soldiers about five miles off, followed two or three miles behind by a body of infantry. I couldn't see a goddam thing but the swelling prairie.

Then he put his bright old eyes on me and said:

"My son, those are white people that we are going to destroy. This will be the first time I have ever faced the whites as an enemy. I have always believed they had a reason for what they did, and I still do. They are strange and do not seem to know where the center of the world is. And because of that, I have never liked them but never hated them either. However, recently they have been behaving badly towards the Human Beings. Therefore we must rub them out."

He looked sort of embarrassed and scratched his nose.

"I don't know whether you can remember back that far, before you became a Human Being and as dear a son to me as those I made with Buffalo Wallow Woman and the others, filling my heart with pride and bringing honor to my tepee. . . . I shall not speak of that earlier time, which has probably been washed from your memory. I just wish to say that if you do recall it and believe riding against these white-skinned ones would be bad medicine, you can stay out of the fight and no one will think the worse. You have proved many times you are a man, and a man must do what is in his heart and no one can question it."

He wouldn't say I was white, see, but was giving me an out if I wanted one. With his usual arrogance he assumed anybody who had the chance would rather be Cheyenne; but with his consideration, which was no less habitual, he was acknowledging the fact of my birth.

"Grandfather," I said, "I think it is a good day to die."

You tell that to an Indian, and he don't immediately begin soothing you or telling you you're wrong, that everything's going to be swell, etc., for it ain't the hollow speech it would be among whites. Nor is it suicidal, like somebody who takes the attitude that life has gone stale for him, so he's going to throw it over. What it means is you will fight until you're all used up. Far from being sour, life is so sweet you will live it to the hilt and be consumed by it. One time before I joined the tribe a band of Cheyenne caught the cholera from some emigrants and those that wasn't yet dying got into battle dress, mounted their war ponies, and challenged the invisible disease to come out and fight like a man.

I don't honestly know whether I was saying it in the Indian sense, but Old Lodge Skins took it so and give me the plug hat. A jackrabbit appeared at that moment and sat there within easy range, wrinkling its nose at him. He got a bothered look, wheeled, and galloped down to the bottomland. It was several years before I talked to him again.

The troops reached the river about two miles to the west and then began to move downstream towards us. They knowed we was in the vicinity but it held a certain surprise for them to come round a bend of the Solomon and find three hundred Cheyenne horsemen waiting in line of battle, our left flank against the river and our right under the bluffs.

The Human Beings was in full regalia, warriors and ponies painted, feathers galore, a good many in the full bonnet, the sun picking up the gaudy colors and glinting off lance heads and musket barrels. Some of the braves was talking to their horses, those animals prancing and breathing through expanded nostrils as if they was already charging. They smelled the big cavalry mounts and began fiercely to whinny, having the same attitude to them that the human Cheyenne had to the whites.

I was riding a buckskin, one of those taken in that Crow raid, and he was a mighty good animal though having to make his way through life without much commentary aside from the normal greetings. Right now was the closest I ever come to discussing philosophical matters with him. I was real nervous owing to my suspicion that not all my comrades took Old Lodge Skins's position on my presence in the middle of the first rank. Especially Younger Bear, who had been down on the right wing but seeing me rode up and wedged a place for his pony alongside. He was painted dead black from waist up, with vermilion in the part of his hair, his eyes outlined in white and horizontal white bars across his cheeks.

I couldn't tell whether he was grinning at me or just baring his teeth; it was the first notice he had paid me in a long time. I didn't return it; I wasn't feeling at all well, and was sure grateful for the war paint I had on myself. That's the wonderful thing about paint: no matter how you feel inside, you will still look horrible.

Hump and the other fighting leaders was riding up and down the line and the medicine man Ice was also there, uttering his mumbo-jumbo and shaking rattles, buffalo tails, and other junk towards the cavalry, which had stopped a half mile away on the bottom and seemed to be just studying us. I was hoping they would maybe start laughing themselves to death: the soldiers, I mean. Because that's what I was inclined to do. You get this funny excitement before a charge; and the longer it takes to get under way, the more intense it becomes, so that when you finally go, you are doing what you need more than anything in the world at that point.

But add to the situation that I was naked and wearing the plug hat, that we was facing some three or four hundred white men carrying firearms, and that I was in my fifth year of pretending to be an Indian—I found myself laughing my guts out no doubt preparatory to their being filled with hot lead.

However, I did my best to muffle this, so that it sounded like a mumble or a deep guttural chant as a matter of fact, like a natural Cheyenne thing. It seemed to impress Younger Bear, for he took it up, and then the next braves on either side, and pretty soon it was sounding from every chest and had turned into the Cheyenne war song, and we began to move forward on its music at the walk, some of the ponies dancing out but the front rank generally dressed. We was still holding back our power, bottling it up while working the charm, paralyzing them whites by our magic as we walked in the sacred way.

I forgot about myself, being just a part of the mystical circle in which the Cheyenne believed they were continuously joined, which is the round of the earth and the sun, and life and death too, for the disjunction between them is a matter of appearance and not the true substance, so that every Cheyenne who has ever lived and those now living make one people: the invulnerable, invincible Human Beings, of all nature the supreme product.

We had proceeded maybe two-three hundred yards in this fashion, the troops still watching us, obviously charmed like the antelope in that surround and about to be similarly butchered—a number of our warriors had indeed slung their bows and were grasping war clubs and hatchets, expecting to knock the helpless soldiers from the saddle—when there was a multiple glitter from the blue ranks and above our song come the brass staccato of the bugle call.

They had drawn sabers and next they charged.

We stopped. There was six hundred yards of river bottom between them and us. Soon it was down to four, then three, and our singing petered out. The bugle was done by now, and no sound was heard but the thumping of a thousand iron-shod hoofs intermixed with scabbard jangle. And speaking for myself I never saw guidons nor uniforms nor even horses but rather a sort of device, one big mowing machine with many hundred bright blades that chopped into dust all life before it and spewed it out behind for a quarter mile of rising yellow cloud.

Now we was the paralyzed, and froze to our ground until the oncoming ranks was within one hundred yards, then seventy-five, and then we burst into fragments and fled in uttermost rout. The magic, you see, had been good against bullets, not the long knives.

I say "we" for effect. Actually, at a certain razor's, or saber's, edge of choice, I cut clean my Cheyenne ties, pitched Old Lodge Skins's hat to the earth where it was shortly churned into trash by galloping hoofs, and with the free-swinging sash of my breechclout began to scrub the paint off my face, all the while yelling in English, which I hadn't spoke for five years, so some of my urgency went into rhetorical matters.

What do you say at such a time that won't make you sound like more of an Indian? My vocabulary was real limited, what with disuse, and I tell you the imagination ain't at its best when a six-foot trooper, mounted on a huge bay, is thundering down on you with his pigsticker and all around is similar gentry pursuing your late family and friends who is running like stampeded buffalo.

Here's what I said. I shouted: "God bless George Washington!" In between I was scrubbing my forehead on that breechclout flap, for which I had to bend forward in the saddle. Which saved my life, for that big trooper sickled his blade across precisely where my adam's apple would have been under normal conditions. Well, that business about Washington hadn't worked, so as he wheeled for a second swing, backhand, I yelled: "God bless my Mother!"

To evade his savage chop I had to go down on the offside of my pony, Indian-style, clinging by my shins, and rode in a circle while he dogged me all along, slashing the air but it made a fearsome snicker. Meanwhile the rest of the cavalry was pounding by, and I expected to be hacked from behind before this son of a bitch either hit me or understood what I was getting at. For he was big, and I don't care what you say, for every inch a man grows over five foot five, his brain diminishes proportionately. All my life I have had a prejudice against overgrown louts.

This dodging went on long enough and with enough variations so I saw he could never touch me, on the one hand, and would never stop trying, on the other. He wasn't much of a horseman: at the end of every slash the momentum of his saber-wielding arm would pull up the far knee and loosen his seat while the animal veered. He done this once too often, and I poked my moccasin over into his ribs and with a sudden jolt unhorsed him in a clatter of scabbard and spurs and the rest of that overload the soldier boys toted.

I dropped off my pony, trailing the war bridle from my belt, put a knee into each shoulder of that dazed trooper and laid the edge of my scalping knife across his bristly throat—the blunt side, in case temptation offered.

All of a sudden I recalled a number of choice phrases I had heard from grownups around Evansville.

"Now, you ———— ," I says with great energy. "Do I have to cut your ———— throat to get it through your ———— thick head that I'm a ———— white man?"

His dumb look never altered, but he said: "Then why in hell are you dressed like that?"

"It's a long story," says I, and let him up.

CHAPTER 8 *Adopted Again*

YOU CAN PROBABLY READ about the fight in books because it was the first real engagement between the Army and the Cheyenne, causing quite a stir at the time. The soldiers claimed thirty Indians was killed in the saber charge, the colonel reported nine, and the truth was four dead, several wounded. It took place in the month of July, 1857.

That's the kind of thing you find out when you go back to civilization: what date it is and time of day, how many mile from Fort Leavenworth and how much the sutlers is getting for tobacco there, how many beers Flanagan drunk and how many times Hoffmann did it with a harlot. Numbers, numbers, I had forgot how important they was. Kansas had also become a Territory, for all the difference it made to me.

That trooper, whose name was Muldoon, took me to the colonel when the excitement was over, and the way I told it was the Cheyenne had forced me on pain of death to join their war party, after having five years earlier killed my whole family and held me henceforward in brutal imprisonment. Muldoon vouched that I sure could have killed him but refrained from it. With the paint scrubbed completely off, and in a gray wool shirt and blue pants Muldoon lent me from his extras, about eight sizes too big, I appeared pretty harmless.

I didn't have no need to worry. Regarding Indians you could tell anything in them days and have it swallowed, and sooner by the military than the civil, for the reason that a white soldier keeps up his nerve by believing his enemy is contemptible to the point of buffoonery. Some of them troopers thought Indians ate human flesh, for example, and had relations with their own daughters.

So the colonel expressed his sympathies, then tried to get some information out of me as to the location of the Cheyenne lodges and horse herd, as he proposed to burn the first and capture the second, but I acted as if rendered half idiotic by the tortures I had underwent for years and so eluded that. It turned out he found the camp anyway by merely following the trail, and burned the abandoned tepees. I was happy to see that Old Lodge Skins's was not among them; Buffalo Wallow Woman and White Cow Woman must have took time to fold it up before fleeing. From there on, that general trail burst into many little ones, as is the Indian practice for evasion. The warriors, who had gone off to the east, would circle around later. Everybody would get together at some later time when the danger was over.

The Army mucked about that area most of the summer, at one point going as far west as Bent's Fort and seizing the supplies there that was supposed to go as annuity payments to the Indians under the existing treaty, then coming back to the Solomon again. But they never found no more Cheyenne and at length returned to Fort Laramie.

I had of course been with them this while, being looked after by Muldoon, who found it convenient to forget I could have killed him with my hands tied behind me and pretend I was a helpless kid. Well, I let him, for he was a kindly slob. He used to make me wash a lot with strong Army soap, claiming I still stunk like a goat for weeks after I had left the Cheyenne. I believed *he* did, and the rest of them soldiers; but it was just a case of relative smells, I expect, and I could recall what had seemed to me the stench of the Cheyenne camp when me and Caroline had entered it years before.

The other soldiers treated me the same, and other than having to listen to a lot of their stupid talk, I never actually suffered. On a campaign like that was an easier way to break back into white life than any other. At least we was outdoors and slept on the ground, and though that Army grub, chiefly sowbelly and hardtack, was garbage, I shot some game now and again, for I had retained my bow and arrow and my Cheyenne pony, and the soldiers liked red meat too, so that made me quite popular with them though I never talked much, which they laid to my weak-mindedness owing to years of captivity.

You might have thought the colonel would be interested in my experiences of five years' barbarism, but he wasn't. I wasn't long in discovering that it is a rare person in the white world who wants to hear what the other fellow says, all the more so when the other fellow really knows what he is talking about.

I'll say this, my medicine failed when we got to Laramie. I had not had anything in mind when I went white at the Solomon battle, except to save my life while not retreating. I sure didn't figure out what such a decision would entail in the long run. I was away from civilization so many years that I forgot how everything is organized there: you don't just move into someone's tepee and let it go at that.

For example, we hadn't been long at Laramie, where I was still bunking with the soldiers, when the colonel sent for me.

"The records in this department are far from adequate," says he. "The unfortunate incident in which the red fiends assaulted your father's wagons has never been entered, so far as we can determine from our files. I'm afraid punishment of the particular malefactors will be rather difficult owing to the insufficient information you have so far provided as to their identity—this of course added to the problem of laying our hands on the Indians concerned were they even to be clearly identified.

"For as you know they are a wily lot. Eventually, I suppose, we will be forced to kill them all off—I can see no other possibility in the face of their savage obduracy against setting aside the life of the brute.

"So much for those unhappy memories. The important thing is the life that opens before you," and so on, the upshot of which was he sent me east to Fort Leavenworth, the departmental headquarters, with a column that was going there the next day. Leavenworth was on the Missouri River, right near Westport, what was later named Kansas City, and Independence, where my Pa bought his wagon and team of ox. This was civilization, or what passed for it in them days, in the extreme.

I got a choking sensation when I heard the news. There was already so many white men around Laramie you could hardly breathe, and I didn't sleep well in them rectangular barracks, on account of having been trained by the Cheyenne to favor the circular dwelling. I think I have mentioned their feeling about circles, the circle of the earth and so on. They was set against the ninety-degree angle, which brought continuity to a dead stop. Old Lodge Skins used to say: "There's no power in a square."

Now I was going back to a whole world of sharp corners, while somewhere out on the prairie the Human Beings had collected again, and having keened for their dead, was eating roast hump and dreaming and telling stories by the buffalo-chip fire and stealing ponies from the Pawnee and getting theirs stole in return, and Nothing was there in her fringed dress of white antelope.

They knew about where I was, although they might not have been told, the way they knew about everything that concerned their people and nothing else. They wouldn't have heard of or understood the slavery troubles, John Brown and all that was going on in white Kansas at the time.

But I never regretted leaving Laramie as such, which had grown into as ugly a place as you could find—that's what I thought then before I seen many other white places. A lot of Indians pitched their tents thereabout, among them I'm sorry to say certain Human Beings, but they didn't resemble the ones I had known, and the individual tribes was not so important as that they all belonged to a degraded type known as the Hang About the Forts. The free-roving bands didn't think much of them. A good many of these gentry literally just sat around their stockade in their blankets, looking stupidly at what went on, for they was permitted to come and go at will, and if a soldier wanted the space they occupied he would roust them out of it, like shooing a dog. Some did a little trading in second-rate skins, and some prostituted their women, and all of them subsisted on Government handouts give to them for being "friendlies." These last of course was usually less than half of what they was authorized by law, for the Indian agents withheld the rest and sold it to white emigrants or the Army seized it for their own use on account of the quartermaster's stores was generally insufficient owing to crooked purveyors back East or thieving supply officers.

It was also against the law to sell liquor to the Indians, but the Hang Around the Forts was oftener drunk than not, for the troopers would sneak them whiskey in exchange for a roll with their wives and daughters, a sorry lot but presumably better than nothing —few white women was to be had thereabouts. Also the traders did quite a good business in firewater, fairly open, and I never heard they was arrested for it, probably because when drunk the fort Indians was even more harmless than when in possession of their faculties.

I mention this subject because while I was at Laramie I run into someone I knowed from the old days. I had wandered among the

Indian camp out of nostalgia for my old life, but I was about to be driven back to the fort by dirty old squaws trying to sell me mangy buffalo robes and their whoremaster husbands, grinning and sniveling, when I saw a canvas tent pitched there out of which from time to time an Indian buck would stagger and then maybe fall flat before he reached his destination or puke all over the ground.

A number of braves was inside when I poked in, each singing a different song or orating hoarsely to nobody in particular. The smell was indescribable. At the back of the tent was an open barrel with a rusty dipper hanging on it, and alongside stood a white man dressed in filthy buckskins. He looked as if he had never washed his face from the day he was born; you could have peeled the dirt off it like a rind. He also never owned a razor.

"How're ya, partner," says he, showing his mossy teeth. One of the Indians lurched over then, and taking off his moccasins, handed them to this sowish fellow, who after examination of the articles shakes his head. So the Indian pulls off his shirt, which was a gray wool trade item, black with grease, and hands that over.

The white fellow puts up his first finger, with the top two joints folded down, and says: "Half, you brown-arsed son of a bitch. Half, you shit-eater." And half-fills the rusty dipper, and the Indian takes it and pours it down his throat.

"Have one on me," the white man invites yours truly.

I just look at him, and he says: "I don't mean of this horse piss. I got a bottle of the real stuff here." He fetches the same from a sack on the ground, while stuffing into it the shirt and moccasins he has just obtained.

"For that in the barrel I use a pint of whiskey per gallon, add gunpowder, tobacco, sulfur, tabasco, and black pepper, then water it up to level. These skunks don't know the difference. But I swear that this here is the good. Drink up." He pushes the bottle at me.

"No, thanks," I says.

"Well, stay anyway. I don't get much chance for conversation during the day, dealing with these _____." He upends the bottle and lets it gurgle, and one of the Indians sees it and staggers towards him, but he kicks him in the groin and the Indian, who from his braids is a Cheyenne, falls to the ground and passes out. The others don't pay no attention to this incident.

"Of course," the fellow says, lowering the bottle, "I generally goes over to the fort of an evening and take dinner with the commanding officer, a personal friend of mine, but during the day I get pretty lonely. It ain't easy for me to deal with this trash, considering they murdered my whole family in front of my eyes and _____ all the women in it. I reckon when Kansas becomes a state one of these years, I'll go up to Congress for Senator." He took another swallow. "Sure you don't want to take a pull of this? It's still got the hair on it."

But I turned my back on him and, stepping across that recumbent Human Being, left the tent. I didn't drink whiskey as yet, and I never could stand to hear the lies of my brother Bill. I was just grateful he didn't recognize me.

At Leavenworth, quite a big fort, I was quartered with an Army chaplain who had a little house for himself and family. This was a skinny horse-toothed fellow with a wife who resembled him strongly and several fair-haired children who didn't look like either of them. I stayed there for several weeks, during which time whenever the wife and kids was out of the house and I was there with the chaplain, he'd ask me into his office and start talking oily about my spiritual well-being, in the course of which to make his point he'd lay a spidery hand on my knee. I think he was a *heemaneh* though he never went farther. I wasn't sorry to leave when the time come, for in addition to that, his wife claimed I still stunk and made me bathe a lot.

At last I was called in to see the head officer there, a general with whiskers, and he said: "Well now, Jack, we've got a fine home for you. You'll be schooled and get proper clothes and have a splendid father to look after you. You have a lot to catch up with, but you're a bright boy. And if in later years you wish to pursue a military career, to follow the guidon with our brave boys, I'll be glad to let you use my name."

With that he stuck his head into a pile of papers, and his orderly led me outside to where that Army chaplain I had stayed with was talking to an enormous fat man sitting in a buggy.

I just want to say here that was the first and last time I saw the general. Nobody at Leavenworth ever asked me a word about the Indians I have lived among for five years. But neither had it occurred to the Cheyenne to ask me about the ways of the white man, not even when they was being destroyed by them. You got to knock a man down and put your knife at his throat before he'll hear you, like I did to that trooper. The truth seems hateful to most everybody.

So I was brought outside to that buggy, and the chaplain says: "Here's our little savage now."

The other man had a square-cut beard of black, and he wore a black frock coat, but his belly was too great to fasten it across. His fat was hard and not soft, if you know what I mean. The old-time strong men used to be like that, with enormous potbellies that was fat but felt like muscle if you hit them there. I had seen pictures of such, and I thought maybe that's what this fellow was.

So I immediately got the idea we'd be traveling around to the opera houses, giving shows, lifting sixteen midgets with one hand, breaking iron chains and all, for the chaplain says: "Jack, this is the good man who has graciously consented to adopt you. You must honor him as you would your own Papa, for that's what he has become by law."

The fat man glanced at me over his beard, shifted his powerful shoulders, and said in a voice as deep as if it echoed from a canyon bottom: "Can you drive a wagon, boy?"

I admired him and wanted to please, so said: "Yes, indeed, right good."

"You're a liar, boy," he growled. "For where'd you learn to drive a wagon if you have been reared by the Indians? We shall have to beat the lying out of you." He leaned down, grabbed my shirtfront, and lifted me into the buggy with only his left arm. It was like being levered up with the trunk of a tree.

The chaplain squealed: "Oh, Jack, you must be respectful to the Reverend and show him that you learned at least some manners in your short time among us."

That was it: my new Pa was not a theatrical performer but another goddam preacher, as if I hadn't had my quota of them, and his name was the Reverend Silas Pendrake. In addition to that black beard, he had thick black eyebrows, and his skin was white as dried pipe clay. He sure looked mean. I had retained my scalping knife in the waistband of them Army pants I still wore, underneath the shirt, and I considered putting it into his spine as we drove towards the Missouri River. But I was discouraged by the look of his enormous spread, which run about four foot from shoulder to shoulder and almost as thick through. I believed my blade would snap off against it, as if you'd stab a stone wall.

That knife and Muldoon's six-foot clothes comprised my total property. They took my pony when we got to Leavenworth and I never saw it again. I think the chaplain sold it to compensate for my keep, and his tow-haired kids got to playing with my Cheyenne bow and broke it.

At the river Pendrake drove his buggy right onto the deck of a stern-wheel boat that was sitting there. His horse by the way was a big, patient gray animal; and you might figure how strong he was to pull his gigantic owner. That horse was a might leery of me, as I could tell from the curve of his nostrils: I reckon he could smell the Indian on me though I had washed at least four or five times all over in the months since leaving the tribes.

After a while they got that boat going, and it was interesting but I didn't like it much because I remembered Old Lodge Skins would mention that if a Human Being, anyway, went over much water he would die. Of course I had been raised on the Ohio at Evansville, but that was long ago, and the Missouri to look at won't build your confidence. It is always undermining its banks before your eyes, and I reckon that if enough years go by it will have worked its way out to Nevada and be irrigating them deserts.

I ain't going to tell you where we was heading, except it was a fairly prominent town in western Missouri. The reason for my delicacy will be clearly apparent in the sequel, as they say. So we'll just go on here from where we docked after a trip of some hours, and drove off the boat, and through the town to the better section of it, where Pendrake had himself a proper church and next door to it a two-story house of some substance, with a barn in back into which he run the buggy, and said to me the first words I can recall he uttered since leaving Leavenworth: "Do you know how to un-hitch a wagon, boy?"

I had learned my lesson. "No, I don't, sir," says I. "Not a-tall."

"Then you must figure out how to do so," he rumbles, though not nearly as mean as he talked at Leavenworth, and I immediately got the idea that maybe his manner there was intended to offset the mincing ways of that chaplain, so I wouldn't think all preachers was alike. I'll tell you right now about Pendrake: he never seemed to know how to act natural except when eating; otherwise he appeared to be trying to live up to an obligation to someone or something else. I think if he'd of cut himself, he might bleed to death before working it out laboriously that the thing to do was put on a bandage.

Well, it wasn't hard to study out how to unhitch that horse, and aside from tossing his head some, but doing that slow and heavy, the animal didn't give me no trouble, and I got him in the stall. After that was done, though, I was in a quandary, on account of I still didn't have no faith that Pendrake wouldn't take a marvelous price for a bad guess. If I stayed in the stable and he expected me up at the house, there might be hell to pay. On the other hand, if I went to the house, maybe he'd rather I stayed in the barn. I decided for movement, as usual, and headed for the house, but instead of going into the back door which he had used, walked around to the front, thinking I'd avoid him for a time that way and also get the lay of the building in case I'd have to run for it.

I went up on the porch and through the front door, and into a hall where a hatrack stood fashioned of deer antlers, then stepped into a parlor which I expect wouldn't look like much today but it was then a wondrous sight to me with the brass coal-oil lamps and tidies on the furniture to keep off hair-grease, for though Pendrake wasn't exactly wealthy, he sure wasn't seedy like my folks had been and wasn't Army like that chaplain.

Then that great voice said behind me: "You're in the parlor?" He wasn't exactly outraged by it, just dumfounded.

"I didn't break nothing," says I.

I hadn't turned till then. When I did, expecting to see his hulk directly behind me, he was actually farther away than I thought. With that voice of his, he could be a hundred yards distant and still sound on your neck.

But now, between him and me, was a woman with dark-blonde hair drawn across either side of her face and into a bun at the back. She had blue eyes and pale skin, though not the dead white of his, and wore a blue dress. I reckoned she was about twenty years of age while Pendrake was fifty, so believed her his daughter.

She was smiling at me and had teeth smaller than average over a full underlip. She kept looking at me but talked to Pendrake.

"I don't think he's ever seen a parlor before," she said velvety soft. "Would you like to sit down, Jack? Right here," pointing out a kind of bench covered in green plush. "That's called a loveseat."

Pendrake sort of growled deep in his windpipe, not in rage but rather a sort of stupor.

I said: "No thank you, ma'am."

And then she asked if I wanted a glass of milk and a piece of cake. There wasn't nothing I wanted less than milk, for which if I'd ever had a taste I had long lost it, but thought I'd better play along with this girl if I was going to have a friend in that house, so followed on to the kitchen and by so doing got out of Pendrake's way for a while at least, for he went to a room off the parlor where he wrote his sermons and sometimes spoke them aloud; you could hear him rumbling through the woodwork and the glassware would tinkle all through the place.

In the kitchen I met another individual who was friendly right off. She didn't have no other choice, being colored. Though freed, she wasn't acting cocky about it, I can tell you, for it was within the law in Missouri of that day to keep slaves. I guess once you've been one, you always figure you can be made into one again. She got on my nerves slightly, however, with her everlasting good humor, which I suspect was partly fake, and I'd have had more in common with her great-grandpa who carried a spear in Africa. This cook's name was Lucy and she was married to a fellow who worked around the place outside, cutting grass and all, another freedman by the name of Lavender. They lived in a little cottage out beyond the stable, and I could sometimes hear them arguing out there in the middle of the night.

That white woman which I took for Pendrake's daughter was actually his wife. She was older by five or six years than I had first thought, just as he was some younger. Still, there was quite a range between them and I already wondered that first afternoon what she saw in him. And I might as well say now I never found out, either. I reckon it was one of them marriages arranged by the parents, for her Pa had been a judge and such a fellow wouldn't want a saloon-keeper for a son-in-law.

Mrs. P. now sat across the table while I drunk the milk, and impressed me by the interest she took in my early life, or seemed to. Here was the first soul who ever asked about my adventures, which surprised me in a refined white woman in the Missouri settlements, whereas that colored Lucy, though laughing incessantly and saying "Lordy," couldn't have cared less and I knew figured me for a mighty liar.

I saw I had a good thing in my stories, so didn't exhaust them all at once. I also tried to mind the eating manners showed me by that chaplain's wife, where the first time I set down to table I picked the meat off the plate with my hands. I knowed better now and cut that cake Mrs. Pendrake give me bit by bit and daintily inserted it into my mouth on the point of a knife.

When I was done, she said: "You don't know how glad we are to have you with us, Jack. There aren't any other young people in this house. Your coming has let the sun in." I thought it was a pretty thing to say.

Next thing she did was take me shopping for some new clothes. She got her bonnet and parasol, and her and me walked into the commercial part of town, for it was not far and the day was fine weather in early October as I recall. We come across a number of people that Mrs. Pendrake knowed and they gawked at me and sometimes talked with her as to my identity. The women generally made a clucking noise and sort of simpered, though I drew a belligerent look from certain of them who were old maids, schoolteachers, librarians, and such, for I hadn't got a proper haircut in five years and probably had a nasty expression in spite of my efforts to look decent.

As to the men we encountered, I don't believe a one of them could have told you later whether I was tall or short, for they kept their eyes fixed on Mrs. P. She had quite an effect on them. I don't believe I done her justice in the description, which I have tried to tell from my point of view that first day. As I had spent my formative years among the Indians, my basic taste in women was for black hair and dark eyes. She was also supposed to be my adopted Ma, so I was restrained somewhat from looking at her purely as a woman. But it's only fair to say that with white men I reckon Mrs. Pendrake was thought to be indeed a beauty, and most of them we met that afternoon acted like they'd have got down on their knees and hung out their tongues if she'd of asked them to.

CHAPTER 9 *Sin*

OF COURSE I HAD to go to school there in that town, and it may surprise you to hear I didn't mind it much. Sitting on a hard seat for long hours was the worst part, and I wasn't thrilled none by the sour old spinster who taught us, and it was also embarrassing to be put with the tiny children, for I never had much learning up to that point. I could read a little before I went with the Indians, and I could count, and I understood that George Washington had been President though I couldn't have said when.

Let me just say I labored diligently at my studies, and Mrs. Pendrake tutored me at home, and by spring I had advanced in reading to where I could do the work of twelve- or thirteen-year-olds and in composition right well though spelling was never my strong point, but in arithmetic I stayed virtually a baby. But that was ever so many year ago and I didn't go to school long, so if the man who is listening to this story of mine copies it down the way I am saying it, you will read the memoirs of a uncultivated person, that's for sure.

The Pendrakes must have talked some to each other in my presence, but I swear I can't remember any such occasion. As I see them back over the years, we're sitting to supper in the dining room, the Reverend at the head of the table, Mrs. at the foot, me along the side, Lucy putting down bowl after bowl of steaming food. After grace, Pendrake's voice not loud but so penetrating that I reckon it could soften tough meat, he'd dig into his chuck. He was a prodigious eater, outdoing even a Cheyenne in that respect, for while an Indian will stuff himself most wonderful there is much of the time that he has to go hungry; it evens out over the course of a month, say, to somewhat less than the average intake of a white man who never misses his three square.

But Pendrake laid into it day in and day out, and I'm going to tell you what he'd eat on any one of them, for you won't have an idea of that man without knowledge of his appetite.

For breakfast Lucy would fry him six eggs, a great mass of potatoes, and a steak about the size of his two giant hands put together. By the time that was chawed up and had been washed down to his belly with a couple quarts of coffee, she'd deliver the griddle cakes, ten or twelve surmounted by a hunk of butter big as an apple and dripping with molasses. For lunch he'd eat two entire chickens with stuffing, potatoes, couple vegetables, five pieces of bread, and half a pie swimming in cream. In the afternoon he'd make calls on sick parishioners, and they wouldn't never be so under the weather that they couldn't see to it he got an enormous hunk of cake or a dozen cookies along with coffee or tea.

Then came supper. He'd drink a bowl of soup into which he broke so much bread it was more solid than liquid. Next would be a platter of fish, then a huge roast of beef which he would single-handed reduce to the bone after me and Mrs. Pendrake had maybe a slice each; a mountain of potatoes, a swamp of greens, and boiled turnips and black-eye peas and steamed carrots, four cups of coffee and about five pounds of pudding, and if there was any pie left over from lunch, he'd drive that home as well.

Yet for all that gluttony he was the neatest eater I ever seen. He wouldn't put a finger on any type of food but bread; for the rest he used knife and fork as nicely as a woman does her needlework. And when he was through the plate shone as though fresh washed, and such bones as was left rose in a little polished stack in an extra bowl he had Lucy lay by for that purpose. It was a real show to watch him take a meal, and I got some pleasure from filling in the time that way, left over after I satisfied my own appetite.

Mrs. Pendrake only picked at her own victual, which was no wonder because she didn't do no work for which she'd have to eat much. Now I was used to Indian women who stayed busy from dawn until they rolled into their buffalo hides, and before that, my own Ma who even with the help of my sisters complained the day wasn't long enough in which she could finish her duties. But Mrs. P. had Lucy to cook and there was another colored girl who come in frequent to clean though didn't live in, and that Lavender, he did all the gardening and run errands and whatnot outdoors. So here was this perfectly healthy white woman, in the prime of life, with nothing to do except for the hour or so she spent in helping me with my lessons when I come home from school.

Now having been reared by savages, I had manners that may not have been polished but they was considerate. I certainly didn't step up to Mrs. Pendrake and say: "It strikes me you are useless around here." But that's what I thought, and it wasn't no criticism for I liked her and helped her when I could. She had this idea of being my Ma, so to oblige I'd pretend now and again to need mothering.

In the first months of school I took a bit of jeering from the other boys my age for studying with the ten-year-olds. I let it go awhile, and you know how that works: they give it to me stronger when they believed I had no defense, and throwed in some stuff about "dirty Indian."

Finally the whole bunch was waiting one afternoon at the corner of an alley on the route home from school. As I come along, they begun to taunt me for being an Indian, which had a unjust side you might not get until you realize they thought I had been captured and kept prisoner for five year. You might say I deserved their needling more than they knew, but I don't think they should be forgive on the basis of accident.

I kept on walking without comment until one of them stepped out before me. He was about five foot ten at sixteen years of age, and had a few pimples.

"There ain't a day," he says, "when I can't lick a dirty Indin."

I was willing to believe that when it come to fisticuffs, which the Cheyenne didn't practice. Indian boys wrestle some, but as I have indicated to a sufficiency, they don't have much reason to fight among their friends when the enemy is generally just beyond the next buffalo wallow. And when they tangle with the enemy, it is not to show him up or make him eat dust, but rather to kill him altogether and rip off the top of his head.

Thus I just looked at this boy in contempt and pushed by him, and he hit me with his loutish fist underneath my right ear. I must have staggered off to the bias for eight or ten feet, being his hand was large and on the end of a weighty arm, and dropped my books along the way. Them other lads hooted, cawed, and whistled. I hadn't had any action now since the saber charge and wasn't used to it in town like that, a person tending to go by the custom of where-ever he's stuck, so I clumb onto my knees slow, thinking, and that fellow run over and swung his boot in the direction of my hind-quarters.

That puts a man off balance: he should have knowed it if he was going around kicking people, but he learned it then. I just rolled under the lifted foot and pulled the other leg loose. He fell like a bag of sugar. I stuck my hoof into his neck and got the scalping knife from under my shirt. . . .

No, I didn't even scratch him with it. For that matter, I could have let him suffocate had I not lifted my foot off his neck eventually, for it choked his wind and he was turning purple. But I wasn't no Indian, and figured I had proved it by putting my knife away, gathering up my books, and going on.

When I got home the angle of my jaw there below the ear was swoll as if I was squirreling a cheekful of nuts. Mrs. Pendrake saw it right off, and says: "Ah, Jack, I must get you to the dentist."

I says no, it wasn't no wisdom tooth. We was in the parlor then, where we always did the tutoring although it was far from the best place in the house for that purpose because you could hear the Reverend muttering in his study nearby, but I guess she supposed I liked it.

Then what could it ever be, she asks. She was wearing a rich blue that day, which become her a great deal, especially when her eyes in sadness took on the exact shade of the dress. Late in the year the buffalo grass turns tawny and when you are climbing an elevation with the sun slanting on it, that's about the shade of her hair. We was sitting as usual side by side on that plush loveseat, with me as far away as I could get, on account of next to that fine lady I always worried that I still stunk though while I was with the Pendrakes I took a bath every Saturday whether I needed it or not.

"A fight," says I. "A boy hit me there."

She formed an O with her mouth, which stayed half open so you could see just an ivory trace beyond her pink lip, and she put her cool hand on the back of mine. She was trying to be a mother, see, but didn't really know how. For fighting, a Ma will swat at you if you ain't hurt, or doctor you if you are. But Mrs. P. figured the thing was to be sad, for she had an ideal conception of everything.

Here's what I mean when I said I helped her: I let my eyes fall to the swell of her bosom, and I lifted her hand to my jaw.

"How it thumps," she says. "Poor Jack." And you know how

them things go, I couldn't tell if it was mostly her or me, but soon I had my face against her breasts and my thumps was alternating with those from her heart.

I expect you are thinking what a nasty little fellow I was. Well, believe what you like, but remember Mrs. Pendrake was only about ten years older than me. It was hard to think of her as a Ma, but at the same time I never before that moment figured her as a girl if you know what I mean. When it came to idealism, I had quite a bit of my own. I have told you the Cheyenne was prigs, and that fighting takes the same kind of energy as sex. It's peace that is the horny time. Most of them fat merchants in that town was real sex fiends compared to an Indian brave. And them other white boys my age was already slipping into brothels or laying the maids.

With the inactivity I was undergoing and all, and especially that studying—I don't know much about scholars but I should judge them a carnal lot, because in my experience with the life of the mind, though I was interested in it, after a bit a tension would build up owing to the invisible nature of that which was studied. You can't see it nor put your hands on it, yet it claims your absolute attention. It'd make me nervous in time. Then I would think of girls as a relief.

There you have the background to this incident, before which I never had an indecent thought towards Mrs. Pendrake. And you can get off the hook now, for nothing else happened here. She was a fine lady: if I hadn't knowed that otherwise, I could feel it in the hardness of her bosom, which if anything hurt my sore jaw. She was all laced up in whalebone. If Buffalo Wallow Woman pulled you against herself, it had been like sinking into a pillow.

For another, at that moment a little delegation showed up at the house: that boy I had fought, his Pa, and a town constable, ready to hang me, I expect, for assault with a deadly weapon.

Though Mrs. P. as a mother left something to be desired, in this type of situation she couldn't be bettered. In polite relations, as you might call them, she was the Queen of England.

First place, she kept them people in the hall while me and her continued to sit upon the loveseat. I don't mean she said Stay out there; she just had that force of will. So the constable, a beefy individual, filled the whole doorway and if the boy's Pa wanted to say something, had to step aside. They was always bumping into one another. We never saw the boy at all.

"Missus," the constable says, "if it be discommoding to you, why they ain't no reason why we cain't come back another time." He waited for a bit, but Mrs. Pendrake never answered such commentary. "Well then, I got a lad here, Lucas English, son of Horace English what owns the feed store—"

"Is that Mr. English behind you, Mr. Travis?" asks Mrs. P., and then the constable and English, a fellow in vest and sleeve-garters, do that little dance of interchange and Travis drops his helmet, and English says: "Yes'm, and there ain't nothing personally involved in this matter, Mrs. Reverend, for I been obliged to the Reverend for many years for supplying his wants in the way of feed—"

Mrs. Pendrake says there with her cold smile: "I believe you refer to the wants of the Reverend Pendrake's animal, do you not, Mr. English, and are not suggesting that Mr. Pendrake eats oats."

English gasps with false laughter, which gets his hoof further down his throat, and the constable pushes him away and steps into the doorframe.

"It's like this, Mrs.," says he. "There seems to be a fight between two lads. One lad's got him a knife, and according to the statement of the first, says he will get him the other's scalp with it like the redskin practice." He grins. "Which of course ain't within the law."

Mrs. Pendrake says: "The poet tells us to err is human, Mr. Travis. I'm sure the English boy did not intend to use his knife on my dear Jack, but simply to make a childish threat. If Jack can forgive him, I shall not prefer charges." She looks at me and asks: "Dear?"

"Sure," I says, feeling real queer to hear her call me that for the first time.

"Ah then, Mr. Travis," Mrs. P. says. "So far as I am concerned, there's an end to it." And thanked him, and called for Lucy to let them out.

Now I figured after that handsome performance I owed Mrs. Pendrake something. Oh, I suppose even at the time I knew she had never done it for me, though it was obvious to a clever woman like her that I had the knife. She just wasn't going to let no man take her to task even indirectly. The fact I belonged to her gave me absolute immunity, the way she saw it. I had never before known a woman, white or red, who had that type of opinion of herself, which was power though you might say used negatively. Had it been used in the positive fashion, she'd have been manly, but nobody could ever take Mrs. Pendrake for anything but 110 per cent female though you might not confuse her with your Ma.

But right now, I thought I could please her by pretending, anyway, to make that very confusion. It might have been play-acting on her part to call me "dear," but I'll tell you I liked it in front of those slobs.

So I says: "Mother"—"Mother" is what I says—"Mother, which is the poet what wrote that particular motto?"

Well sir, the word did a lot for her, though I might not have pronounced it with much confidence this first time. Of course she didn't let on, but went to a bookcase and brought back a volume.

"Mr. Alexander Pope," she says, "who also wrote: 'Fools rush in where angels fear to tread.' "

She read me some of that man's verse, which sounded like the trotting of a horse if you never paid attention to the words or didn't understand most of them like me. What I did savvy seemed right opinionated, like that fellow had the last word on everything.

My only complaint was that for a poet he wasn't any too romantic. Now you take a boy who lived my kind of life, you'd figure him to be about as realistic as any, if not altogether cynical. That may be so, but it never applied to women, or at least not to beautiful white women who was useless for practical purposes.

I fell into an infatuation for Mrs. Pendrake right then. I guess even at my present time of life, I am still weak on the subject of elegant and gracious ladies. Authority is also involved, as in her handling that constable and feed merchant, and having a knowledge of fine aspects, like the way she held the works of Mr. Pope, with her head inclined against the afternoon sun from the west window so that the margins of her nose and forehead was crystalline and her hair old gold. She always knowed the *right thing* so far as civilization went, like an Indian knows it for savagery. And I saw then that uselessness was a necessary part of it. If you put such a woman to work, you'd lose that which was her special value, like if you made a hitching post of a statue.

I figured to have got the idea of white life, right then. It hadn't ought to do with the steam engine or arithmetic or even Mr. Pope's verse. Its aim was to turn out a Mrs. Pendrake.

I said infatuation, but you can call it love, and directly I was awed by it and moved over to my end of the bench again.

Just about then, while I was sliding my butt across the plush, in comes the Reverend from the door behind us which connected with his study. He had stopped rumbling there when the men had showed up. Now he moves ponderously around in front of us, and for some moments his wife kept reading whatever poem she was on then, so he waited till she was done. Then he spoke to me.

"Boy," he said, real kindly. "Boy, it is my opinion that you have labored earnestly at your studies in these three months since coming to this house." The next thing he done was to falter and stroke his beard. The wonders of this day was never-ceasing. After that first afternoon, he had no more spoke to me than to Mrs. Pendrake in my hearing.

"I do not want you to have the misapprehension," he finally said, "that we here see life as all duty. Therefore tomorrow, which is Saturday, and if Mrs. Pendrake does not require you and if you are favorably disposed to the project, I should be willing to take you fishing."

Now, it being November of the year and while not winter as yet the weather was cold and damp and not the time any sane person would have fished for sport, I lost no time in accepting the invite. Add to the other reasons against so doing that I really couldn't stand the Reverend except when he was eating, and you won't understand why I did until I say that if he seemed to be in his wife's debt, I had just now got to feeling in his.

So there we was, out to the creek next day in fairly miserable weather where the air was like a big sponge full of water and no sooner had we reached the stream when someone squeezed it and rain begun to pour down. We had come out in a buckboard, with Lavender driving and only he had sense enough to bring protection against the inclemency, for he had a big toe that was infallible as a weather gauge.

I could see right off that the Reverend didn't know anything about fishing from the way he put a doughball on the hook—that was what we used, for Lavender claimed he couldn't find worms in late November. And the day was sufficiently unpleasant to drive off a fellow who was crazy for the sport. But Pendrake had said he was going fishing, and that's what he fixed to do, the water swirling around his hatbrim and running off his black coat. He was dressed in his usual, by the way, with no provision for leisure.

Lavender offered us his umbrella in insincere fashion, for which I didn't blame him, but Pendrake said no, he didn't require it, so Lavender kept it over himself and put a blanket underneath a tree and set there and looked at an illustrated paper someone had give him though he couldn't read, but seemed to get more out of it than those who could, for he was laughing at it.

Me and the Reverend went down to the bank a ways along by some willows which was now brown and he says: "What's your opinion of this location, boy?"

"It's as good as any," says I. My hair was all matted from the rain and water coursed down my cheeks; it seemed ridiculous in view of what we was supposed to be doing to have a good time, but I never minded the soaking as such, having been wetted down plenty as an Indian inside as well as outside the lodge, for tepee skins generally leak after they been in use for a while, especially at the seams.

But here he looked at me out of that black beard and said with genuine feeling, for which his voice was less ponderous: "Ah, boy, you're getting wet." With that he drew a big handkerchief and wiped my face right gently.

I guess I can't explain it, but that was one of the truly kindest things anybody's done for me, ever. It didn't matter none that I wasn't distressed or that his sudden discovery of the rain after it poured some minutes might have been foolish. He put his big hand on my damp shoulder and looked sorry out of all proportion. I hadn't seen him straight ever before. His eyes was hazel and didn't have too much of a lid. Without the beard he would have looked to lose much of his force, though he surely had enormous strength of muscle.

"We don't have to stay if you don't want to," he said. "We can go on back. It was an unfortunate idea." He shook his head like a buffalo bull and droplets flung off the beard and he turned away and stared at the muddy creek, and says: "He sendeth rain on the just and on the unjust."

"Who?" asks I, for I didn't know.

"Why, our Heavenly Father, boy," says Pendrake and, closing up grim again, throws his line in the water, which was so disturbed by the pelting rain that the bobber was dancing all the time and you would never tell from it if you caught a whale.

The Indians has always fished with a spear, which is to me a more interesting endeavor than hook and line. Also the rain was now getting to me: I had softened up in only a month or so. However, I didn't want to hurt the Reverend's feelings, so I presented him a bright suggestion.

Acting on it, he had Lavender run the wagon down on the bank, which was wide enough and flat for such accommodation, unhitch the horse and take him back under the tree, and we crawled beneath the buckboard, letting our fishpoles stick out, and thus had a roof against the elements.

Any fool could have figured this out, but the Reverend was greatly impressed by what he called my "acumen." He seemed relieved that I was no longer getting soaked. As to himself, it was more complicated: you see, his trouble was he couldn't allow himself any pleasure aside from eating. He would have preferred to be dripping and uncomfortable—that's the only reason I could dream up as to why we come in the open wagon at all rather than the closed buggy which he also owned. I never could study out why Lavender was there, except that maybe the Reverend was uneasy with me by himself.

It was a tight squeeze for a man of his bulk underneath the buckboard. We set there a time smelling of wet wool, during which the current intermingled our lines and swept them useless into the bank and no doubt soon melted off the doughballs.

At length Pendrake said: "Boy, from what you asked before about the rain, I understand my delinquency." He was cramped in there with his beard against his rising belly and looking on to the stream through the sheet of water coming from above.

"I have left you to live in the ignorance of an animal, though I have been specifically charged with leading men to a knowledge of God. Yesterday," he goes on, "it came to my attention that you are swiftly approaching the province of adulthood, that soon the boy will be the man."

For a minute I was scared he seen me on his wife's bosom and misinterpreted that event.

"Mrs. Pendrake," he began, and I gathered my legs under me in case I had to run for it, "Mrs. Pendrake, being a woman, is altogether innocent of these matters. She was not a party to a lie. Looking at you through the eyes of a mother, she saw no blemish in the boy she knows, and that is a credit to her.

"But I am a man, and as such, no stranger to impurity. I myself passed through the years in which you find yourself. I know the

Devil, boy, I have shaken him by the hand, I have embraced him and smelled his stinking breath and thought it the finest perfume."

He got himself exercised with these remarks and pressed his head against the buckboard floor, squashing his black hat, while the wagon lifted several inches out of the mud.

Then he eased and spoke gentle. "I heard that colloquy through my study door. I am aware that you had the knife, boy, and I can imagine only too well your motive for using it against another. . . . The girl's identity is of no interest to me. I am willing to believe that although you were doing the Devil's work you did not recognize him in his female attire. Does she have velvet cheeks, boy, and satin hair and long-lashed eyes undershot with damask? No matter, behind that mask is a skull of white bone with hollow sockets, and that soft pink mouth is the cave of death."

I just flicked my line as if I had a bite, for whatever could I say to that? As to the girls I had been thrown with so far, they was ten years old in that school class.

"I don't condemn you, boy," Pendrake said. "I tell you I know the fire that rises in the loins and sweeps upward consuming all before it. I know the primitive peoples among whom you spent your boyhood make a sacred thing of this conflagration. But that is our difference, is it not? that we harness our bestial energies. That we do not defile but preserve. Woman is a vessel, and it is within man's power to make that vessel a golden chalice or a slop bucket."

Along about here, Lavender come down to the bank under his umbrella and toting an enormous basket covered with oilcloth. He scrooched down and peeked at us under the wagon.

When talking to the Reverend he assumed a lazy, whiny, idiotic style that I happened to know he reserved for just that purpose, for he was otherwise very sharp though illiterate as I said.

"Your Honor," says he, "would . . . you all . . . be wantin' . . . thisheer lunch?"

"Put it down, that's a good fellow," answers Pendrake in a clipped way that he probably figured would stimulate Lavender to move faster but seemed to have the reverse effect.

When Lavender finally trudged away, Pendrake said: "There is a case in point. Can you understand that Lavender and Lucy would have lived in common, defying the ordinances of God and man, had I not insisted on marrying them?"

I might say at this point and then we won't mention it again, that

I do not know whether Pendrake was Abolitionist or Proslavery. He had freed Lavender, if that meant anything. And if he was Abolitionist, why his reason would have been that freedom would make the colored people less lusty. Now I know you can read in history books that the slavery issue was hot in Missouri of this date, and there was private wars over it and shootings in the dead of night, a reign of terror and so on. Well that ain't no lie, but you could be living right in the middle of it like me and never know it was going on. Remember that next time you read something. I knowed many a man who went all the way across the prairies during the Indian wars and never saw one hostile savage. That's the way reality operates. I wasn't ever interested in politics, so I never saw any. In them days there was always somebody getting shot or knifed, and you wouldn't think nothing of it. And then I have an idea that Pendrake was so respectable that he might not have had to take a loudmouthed stand either way.

The Reverend broke off at that point and pulled the oilcloth from the basket. Lucy had packed us more food than all of Old Lodge Skins's band ate during one whole winter. There was two or three cold fried chickens, a great hunk of ham, about a dozen hardboiled eggs, two loaves of bread, and a chocolate cake, just to mention the larger items.

We hadn't done nothing so far but sit under the wagon, and I wasn't too hungry. I was also feeling a little queasy from being damp in wool; among the Cheyenne you wear leather, which takes the rain almost like your own skin. Or maybe I might have been embarrassed at Pendrake's jawing about matters that should be private. I guess I already knowed it at ten, before I went with the Indians, but I had forgot how the conjunction of men and women is looked upon as dirty by the whites, so they got to involve it with law. Lucy and Lavender shared the same room, but it was against the laws of God and man until Pendrake said a few words over them, after which it was O.K.

Well, it was an entertainment to see the Reverend consume that lunch. I ate a wing, an egg, and a piece each of bread and cake and felt myself uncomfortable full at that. All the rest went soon enough into Pendrake's great belly. What was left of the contents of the basket was a pile of cleaned bones and eggshells within fifteen minutes.

Then he brushed his beard with his fingers, though I never in my acquaintance with him saw him drop a crumb into that underbrush —he was neat about food, I believed, because he wasn't going to let a morsel escape his mouth—and picked his teeth and cleared his passages with a huge draught from a jug of water that Lucy had included.

"It has been a great satisfaction to me to have this talk with you, boy," he says then. "And I hope and trust you will derive some value from it. We have not before had the opportunity to know each other, for while I am your father upon earth, I am much occupied with serving my own Father in heaven. But He is also yours, and in serving him I am serving you, if I do it properly. That effort leaves me little time for the delightful sport we are enjoying today, though to enjoy oneself moderately is surely no sin."

I haven't mentioned how I had to sit Sundays in church and listen to Pendrake's gab. The only consolation was that Mrs. P. had to go as well, wearing her fine clothes, and it was a proud thing to sit alongside the most beautiful woman in town, with the men, including the ancient elders, stealing looks at her and their women all peevish. But them sermons! Pendrake's trouble was he didn't have no fire. Unlike my old man, he didn't get no release from his religion, but rather was further bottled up by it. That might have kept him from getting killed by savages, but maybe it is worse never to open your spirit up to the wind.

Anyway, he always said a good deal about "sin," and what I got to wondering now we was sitting there, was what in his opinion constituted such. You may remember with my Pa it was cussing, chewing, spitting, and not washing your face. It seemed likely Pendrake had another view. Anyway, we obviously wasn't going to catch any fish, and lunch was over, and despite the Reverend's remarks on the satisfaction afforded by our little talk, he was still uneasy-looking. I reckon a man who puts out words all the time gets to wondering whether they are ever being received.

So to oblige him, with the same motive I had called Mrs. P. "Mother," I asked about sin. He wasn't a bad fellow, and he had wiped off my face. I am like an Indian in that if I am treated nice I'll try to make a return.

He had a wider-sweeping definition of sin than my Pa's, and a longer list of specifics than my old man had give, probably because

Pa was an amateur at preaching and couldn't read. For Pendrake's roster wasn't properly his own but rather, as he admitted, that of the Biblical Paul.

"The works of the flesh," answers the Reverend. "And 'the works of the flesh are manifest, which are these: adultery, fornication, uncleanness, lasciviousness, idolatry, witchcraft, hatred, variance, emulations, wrath, strife, seditions, heresies, envyings, murders, drunkenness, revelings, and such like.' "

It was a funny thing, the most important years of my rearing so far had been handled by my second father, who was Old Lodge Skins. Now you take away "envyings" from that list—for he didn't covet much, owing to his belief he had everything of importance already—and you had a perfect description of that Indian's character. Yet he was as big a success among the Cheyenne as a man could be.

As to myself, I had performed only a few of them crimes; on the other hand, I was still young.

For the rest of the day, though, I stayed fairly pure and even extended the period for several weeks on. That's what white life did to me. First time I got soaked in civilization, I come down with pneumonia.

CHAPTER 10 *Through the Shutter*

I WAS REAL SICK, such as I had not been since earliest childhood. I don't mind being wounded, but I hate to be sick. I mean, I don't like to get a wound, but if you have to pay a penalty I'd rather it were that than any type of illness which will put you to bed. I don't care to lay around unless some part of my flesh is missing and I can watch it knitting up.

You see there what I said about penalty. Despite my cynical ways as I approached the age of sixteen, the Reverend had got to me with his bluenose talk, and I had had dreams the night after the fishing expedition, in which I was doing my damnedest, though I knowed it was wrong, to make the golden chalice of woman into a slop bucket like he said.

You might say he give me the idea, just as he give me pneumonia by that outing in the rain, for that's what I had in the morning though at first it seemed like just a cold and I got up as usual. But I felt so poorly at breakfast and got dizzy when Pendrake lit into his great mess of eggs though he was neat as always, so Mrs. P. puts her cool hand against my forehead, which was flushed at the same time that I was chilled to the bone.

Shortly I was back in bed, and an old doc with white whiskers come eventually but he didn't have the medicine of Left-Handed Wolf, I can tell you. I was sick for about three weeks, and understood later that it was believed I should die during the first few days and the Reverend come and prayed over me.

Lavender told me that. He dropped in frequent when I started to improve. I remember the first time I saw him standing alongside the bed as I woke up from the napping with which I put in most of that time, I had the delusion I was back among the Cheyenne. He was

very black of countenance, but the Indians sometimes painted themselves that color: anyhow, he wasn't white.

So I made a remark in Cheyenne.

"Pardon?" says he, widening his eyes, and then I seen who he was
and felt embarrassed.

"Now then," he says, "you just rest easy. Don't you worry none
about old Lavender. He just come to see how you was."

He generally referred to himself in that style, as if he was talking
about a third person. I guess he had some theory that you wouldn't
suffer him to say "I" or "me."

I says: "I thought you was an Indian."

Sometimes one remark will make you a friend, and it generally
ain't planned to do so, for I have found that you can seldom inten-
tionally make up a successful compliment. I don't mean I was enemies with Lavender before saying that; it was rather that we took
each other for granted as kid and servant. I reckon he had come to
visit me out of curiosity.

He says: "I snuck up here while everbody but Lucy's not to
home, and Lucy don't know I did or she'd be riled."

I had a room all my own on the second floor, with a big soft bed
that took me a while to get onto sleeping in without taking down
seasick.

"Ain't you never been here before?"

"I carried up furniture," Lavender says, "and washed the windows, but never come for socializing. I suppose if it be known I was
here now, you might say you ast me."

"Sure," I told him, and then you know how a person will feel self-
pity when he's sick: "I reckon you're the only one who cares
whether I live or die. You're the only one who come."

"You just don't recall," he says. "The Lady was here all the time,
and the Reverend made his prayers and I reckon had he not you'd
be stone-cold and they'd have dug a hole in the ground and drapped
you in and shoveled the earth back on and stomped it down."

"Well," I says, "so long as it didn't happen I wish you wouldn't
go on about it in such detail. Do you figure it was God who saved
me when asked by the Reverend?"

Lavender gets a sly look. "That doctor ain't likely to have done it
when he run Lucy off from giving you any of her tonic what is
made from roots and suchlike and will cure any ailment. I tell you,

there was a time when everything I et turned to poison and my stomach felt like a fishnet. Lucy give me her tonic and inside a week I could chew up and swally a bone like a dog and never tell the difference from a bowl of mush."

I said: "Why don't you set upon the chair there?"

"I wouldn't mind it a-tall," says he and does as much, a little stiff at first and then gradually taking his ease. "Say now, that was a funny thing, you taking me for an Indian. I never knowed they was black."

I just realized I had a mustard plaster on my chest, because it started to itch, and so I was scratching while we talked.

I says: "I saw a Cheyenne dark as you down on the Solomon's Fork. They called him Mohkstavihi, which is the same name they give to any colored person like yourself."

"Black Man?"

"No, Black White Man."

He laughed out loud at that, then stopped short and nodded serious. "I got to burn leaves now," he says and goes out. I wonder if I had hurt his feelings, but it was the truth, which is supposed to make you free.

However, back he come the following day, when Mrs. Pendrake had gone out shopping again and the Reverend was in his study, and this time Lavender never feared Lucy on account of he got bold enough to ask Pendrake's permission to see me, which was granted.

He also took the chair without being asked, which was O.K. by me, for owing to my upbringing I never had no views on how fresh you should let a darky get, though that was a worrisome thing to plenty of whites in Missouri.

It turned out that Lavender was fascinated by Indians. I have said Mrs. P. listened that first day to my experiences, but that was the end of it, so I suppose she did then just to be mannerly. And anybody else I run into would have rather died than asked me about that subject, I reckon.

But Lavender couldn't get enough of it. I would have thought he was going to write a book had he not been illiterate.

After a time he says: "That dark Indian you told me about seeing on the Solomon River, I been thinking on him, and I figure he might be kin." Lavender was a smart fellow; he couldn't read nor write and never had a day of schooling, but he knowed a great deal of things. He started talking now about Captain Lewis and Captain Clark, who we hadn't yet got around to in the school, for their names was new to me.

"Why," he says, "them white men went up the river until it got so skinny they could stand with one foot on the right bank and one on the left, and then found the tiny hole it trickled out of, and could have stuck a finger in it and stopped it off, and you wouldn't have had no more Missouri River but just a big ditch of mud two thousand miles long, dryin' and crackin' in the sun."

I didn't believe him, but later I heard it was true—I mean about Lewis and Clark being real people; whether they could have stopped off the Missouri with one finger was another thing.

"Captain Lewis and Captain Clark took along a colored man named York, and the Indians had never seen a colored man before and thought York was painted black, so would spit on their hands and try to rub York's color off, and when they couldn't, they'd tell all the other redskins for miles around and they would all come and try to rub the paint off him too.

"York was the most interesting thing the Indians found about Captain Lewis and Captain Clark. And you know what he done, for he was right humorous, he told them Indians he had started life as a wild animal and Captain Clark caught him in a snare and tamed him into a man. Then he roared and showed his teeth and the Indians would run away. But they took a great liking to York, give him presents and had him lay with their women so as to get some black babies."

Lavender raised his eyebrows. He said: "Now it is likely if you was to go out there today you would run into some of his offspring, which it looks to me like you done. York was a first cousin to my granddaddy. I believe he was the most famous person in my family."

"It could be," says I.

"The more I think about it, the surer I am," Lavender says, and then he leans over close to me, keeping his voice down: "I don't mind telling you I'm fixing to go out there myself. . . . Now you go and mention that to Lucy and I'll be in trouble."

"You ain't taking her along?"

"That's my reason for leaving," he whispers, while looking fearfully towards the doorway. "You let a woman catch you and you'll have reason to be sorry for it every minute of the day. Now the

Reverend bought me from my old master and he freed me according to law. I have heerd him say: 'No man must own another.' Then he makes me marry Lucy, for I expect he believe it's all right for a woman to own a man. The way I look at it, I had one benefit from law and one defect, so I am even now and before I get to losing I want to go out where they don't have any laws a-tall and are purely savage."

"Maybe we should go together," I said. Until that minute I never had thought of running away from the Pendrakes, for they had treated me well, but I had been in civilization for a couple of months now and still couldn't see no sense to it whenever Mrs. P. wasn't around. Now I was sick in this shameful way: you hadn't ought to be made ill by the rain, which is a natural thing. What it meant was that I wasn't living right. About the only time I felt proper in town is when I throwed that kid Luke English to the ground and went for my knife. And I believed my blood was getting watery from the lack of raw buffalo liver. The only thing I learned so far that seemed to take real root was lustful yearnings, and the Reverend told me they was wrong.

"If you can wait till I am better—" I began.

But Lavender frowned and said: "I ain't going to listen to that talk. The difference between me and you is I am colored and you is a boy. Now nobody has no call to stop a colored man who ain't a slave from running off, but if he takes a boy with him, he got trouble with the law again."

"Listen," says I, "once we get beyond Fort Leavenworth, *I'll* be taking *you*."

That hurt his pride and he mumbled some with his eyes down, and he allows: "Well, I'm going tonight, anyway. I would wait if I could, but I cain't."

"What difference would another few days make?" For I thought to be up within that time.

"Ever hour is a living agony," says Lavender. "It is a monstrosity of nature for man to be ruled by woman."

I figured he got them words from something Pendrake said, so I asked if Lucy give him so much trouble, why didn't he get advice on it from the Reverend?

"Look here," Lavender tells me, "I ain't going to say nothing against your Daddy."

"He is my Pa," says I, "only in that law you was talking about, and it is a wondrous thing how a man can get himself new relatives by signing a piece of paper." It made a real mark on Lavender that I never held a high opinion of law, either, and like himself was a victim of it, though not in his discomfort.

He sort of shrugs with his mouth and says in a low voice: "He ain't going to get none in the usual way."

My back started to ache from a twitch of muscle, and I shifted my position in bed.

"What's that supposed to mean?" But I knowed well enough, and my back felt worse at the new angle.

Lavender winced and drew back. "I don't want to get me in trouble."

"I thought you was going to run off tonight."

He opened his eyes. "That's right," he says and grins in relief. "That's right, I sure am."

"You reach me over that paper and pencil on the desk, I'll draw you a map of where to find the Cheyenne." I told him quite a number of useful items on how to get along with the Indians, concluding with: "Now you can be friendly but don't ever crawl on your belly before a Cheyenne no matter what he does, on account of he'll do it worse then. I mention that because they have lately had a lot of trouble with whites and might carry a prejudice."

"Against white men?"

"Of which you are a black-colored one," I says. "I'm talking of what they believe, which is the truth when you live among them, like law is around here."

I drawed that map, resting the paper against a book. Lavender couldn't read, but he ought to be able to follow the lines of rivers.

"If you was going to wait a while, I'd teach you some of the sign talk and maybe Cheyenne as well," I said.

"No," he told me, "I cain't tarry. But I thank you kindly."

"Hold on," I says as he starts to rise from the chair. "You never finished what you begun before about the Reverend."

Lavender went out and looked up and down the hall, then he come back alongside my bed.

"He don't lay with his Lady," says he. "I expect on account of he is a preacher, but them other preachers in town has children, so it must not be against the law."

"You mean never?" I asks. "For I've knowed Indians who

wouldn't do it for a time because of a dream they had or before a war."

"Never," says Lavender. "Lucy see that in the yolk of an egg. She got the gift of a witch. That's the reason I'm leaving. Every time I go with another woman, Lucy see it in an egg."

Lavender didn't run off that night. He come in to see me again the next day and never even apologized for not carrying out his plan. Instead he talked as if he meant the *next* night, and the same happened the next, and so on. People who *talk* instead of *do* give me a pain in the arse. I reckon Lavender just wanted somebody to complain to, and that's all right, but I wish he would of admitted it. On the other hand, I guess you ought to have a different standard for judging a man who had been kept as slave until the age of twenty-two. It takes him a while to know what's possible, and maybe he should be given credit for just having the idea of real freedom.

Anyways, I oughtn't to protest his staying, for he was the only person in that town I could talk to with ease. That boy I whipped, Luke English, come around to visit while I was sick. He still hated my guts and figured he had been tricked rather than beaten outright —whites always believed that when licked by Indians—but his Pa wanted to suck up to the Pendrakes, so sent him over with a cake his Ma had made. Luke stopped somewhere on the way and tongued off all the icing; which didn't matter none to me, though, because I was still off my feed and couldn't have ate a cannonball like that when well.

As soon as Mrs. Pendrake, who had let him in, went downstairs, Luke started talking indecent. Him and the Reverend could have gone around with a tent show, holding debates on the topic, for they represented the long and short of it.

"Say," Luke remarked, studying round my room with his mean eyes, "you got quite a wigwam here. Did you ever sneak a girl in?"

"Did you?" I asked him in scorn.

"I don't have it so private. I got to bunk in with three brothers. My old man and old lady went at it so hard they have filled the house. I also got four sisters. The oldest is just eighteen. Some feller climbs in her bed every night and has his way with her. Pa don't know what to do about it."

I was taken in and dumb enough to ask: "Why don't he shoot him?"

"Oh," says Luke, cackling, "it's her husband."

He sits down on the foot of my bed. "What's it like with an Indin squaw? I hear they got quite a strong smell. I hear you want one, you throw a bean across the fire and the one it lands near has to go with you even if she's married to the chief. I never had an Indin woman. The ones I seen have been mighty ugly. I'd druther find me a fat sheep if I couldn't get nothing else.

"Course I do all right as it is. The other day I come into the room while the darky girl was cleaning. Nobody else was upstairs at the time, though my Ma and sisters was down in the kitchen. So I was feeling like a piece, and I just throwed that black girl down and put it to her. . . . "

I never did like dirty tales, true or false; if they're any good, they just make you wistful; if not, there's nothing more boresome in the world, I reckon. As to Luke, the more he talked, the more I was convinced that his experience consisted solely of playing with himself to the point of idiocy.

Nonetheless when Mrs. Pendrake come up and asked us both if we'd like a glass of buttermilk and I says no and showed I was tired, and he says yes and she took him off to the kitchen, with him staring at her up and down soon as her head was turned, I was pretty jealous. For you take even a rotten-looking kid like that, he was of the male sex, and Mrs. P. knowed it. She couldn't help reminding you she was a woman. I don't mean she did one thing you could see with the naked eye, and as I have said she was downright cool to most men and acted as if they was standing in horse manure about ten feet below her location.

After enough time for him to have drunk a gallon, Luke come back upstairs, where he had forgot his cap. He was licking his thick lips, which I guess was reasonable enough on account of there was a margin of buttermilk around them. But I had my knife under the pillow, and I remember vowing that if he made one reference to Mrs. Pendrake, I would cut out his black heart.

But he just said: "Well, I'll tell my Pa you ain't going to die from that beating I give you. I ain't got no hard feelings if you ain't. When you get back on your feet I'll innerduce you to a good whore down at Mrs. Lizzie's."

I had been a man before my time, and now I was being a baby

after it, just laid there day after day and when I wasn't being talked to, looked at the ceiling and saw a naked woman imprinted on it. Not Mrs. P., I hasten to say—nor the Indian females I had seen now and again without clothes though the Cheyenne is modest, and you take Nothing, had I come upon her bare it wouldn't have been a striking experience—but rather a *picture* of a nude woman that used to hang back of the bar in the saloon in Evansville years before when my Pa preached there.

Now that is a funny thing that come back to me from a time when it didn't mean nothing. They put a blanket over it during services, and I can recall Bill sniggering and my sisters blushing, but to me it had been right dull: she was fat as to breast and hip, and had one meaty haunch crossed over the other so as to hide her loins. Her nipples was purple, that was all I could have said at the age I had been then, because they reminded me of plums.

But here she was on the ceiling of my bedroom. It went along with everything else in that house, I suppose, the image and not the reality: Mrs. Pendrake's motherhood, the Reverend's spiritual authority, Lavender's freedom, and my woman who had never existed.

At last I got strong enough to take outside walks so long as I dressed warmly, for it was winter now with a fall or two of snow while I had been laid up. And then one afternoon when we had finished our dinner, the Reverend having so far as I was concerned outdone even his own record in laying waste a turkey singlehanded —for Mrs. P. took very little and I was still on soup—Mrs. Pendrake says: "Dear, it might be diverting for you to walk downtown with me. We might take a glass of soda water and buy some new clothes."

I won't go into the shopping, which Mrs. P. accomplished in amazingly short time for a woman though she bought a big load of stuff for both herself and me. I reckon she was about clothes like the Reverend was concerning food: gluttonous but tidy. Nevertheless, I wasn't any too robust yet and even when well I get dizzy in shops. So she noticed that and says: "Now we'll have our soda water."

I had never been in the place we went, which had just been opened up while I was sick, pretty fancy with little marble tables and wire chairs and some brasswork, and there was a big marble bar and on it a vessel like a funeral urn which was silver-plated, with a cupid sitting on top and two elephants' heads projecting from the bowl. In the base of this structure was six or seven knobs under which they'd put your glass, squirt some flavor into it, then stick it beneath an elephant's trunk, turn his ear, and out would come the soda water.

I took an immediate dislike to the fellow who run the place, for he thought quite a lot of himself, wore a brocade waistcoat and a artificial flower in his lapel, and was mighty tall. I guess you'd say he was handsome by the light of some, clean-shaven and with black curly hair. He sure thought so, anyhow. What I didn't like was the snooty manner in which he run a place where women and children went for refreshment.

Now this fellow would draw the soda himself, then put the glasses on a silvered tray which a small colored boy who was dressed like a little Arab, turban and balloon pants, would tote to your table. I tipped the kid a penny the Reverend give me, and he wasn't in the least grateful for it, just bit it to see if it was genuine, and put it in his curly-toed shoe. I done that because I wanted to play the grown man at this point and escort Mrs. P. rather than vice versa, for I was almost sixteen. I was shorter than her while walking, but seated here we was about the same size.

She got the idea, for Mrs. Pendrake knew every minute the exact situation when it come to male and female, and without calling attention to it she slipped me a dollar so I could pay the bill when time came.

It was perfect for about two minutes, me and her together like that, and she called me "dear" a good deal and the cherry-flavored soda that she drunk left a flush on her underlip. I had never seen anything more lovely than her fair face between the fur hat and collar. She and I, we just cared for each other and hated everybody else in the soda shop and maybe the rest of the world thrown in.

Then over comes that bastardly proprietor sneering with his front teeth, though he means it as a smile I reckon, and says to Mrs. P.: "Maybe Buster would like to eat a cake." He didn't talk cultivated like her or ignorant like me, just cheap. He was also the first man I had ever saw who didn't give way before Mrs. Pendrake, but looked at her insolent with his eyelids falling.

In return she faltered towards him, then said to me: "This is Mr. Kane, Jack."

I knowed by then what was manners and stood up so as not to shame her, but he didn't put out his hand nor acknowledge the introduction in any other wise, but went back to the marble counter and fixed a tray of cookies and sweetmeats and had them delivered before me by means of the little colored boy.

"Isn't that kind," said Mrs. Pendrake. She picked her muff from the spare chair. "I wonder, dear, whether while you are occupied with these, you might permit me to finish my shopping. I must make several more purchases and should not forgive myself for tiring you on your first day out."

It was always such a pleasure for me to hear her speak, I sometimes failed to gather the sense of it. So it was now. I didn't realize she was leaving me there until she touched my shoulder and went to the door, having to open it for herself, for that manager kept his back turned then, though a minute later when two ugly, scrawny females who I recognized as the wife of an elder of our church and her old-maid sister prepared to go, he sprang out and in his oily fashion bowed them on to the walk.

Well, I thought, if he thinks he's going to get the better part of my dollar with them cakes, he is wrong. I wasn't hungry, anyway, and grew a little resentful that Mrs. Pendrake hadn't recalled the doctor saying I should go easy on sweets. Feeling sulky, I gazed up to the ceiling of that place and saw my old tormentor, the woman of the saloon picture, printed on it. It must have been the thought of Luke English, for I remembered what he said about the whore at Mrs. Lizzie's. He no doubt had lied, but I knowed where Mrs. Lizzie's was, over a saloon at the other end of town, and there was sure whores there, which you could see hanging in the windows, and sometimes if you was a boy my age they would call down: "I'll grow you up for a dollar."

It'd fix Mrs. Pendrake right if I went over there with her dollar. She hadn't ought to have left me alone, I was thinking. I got up and went to the counter to pay my bill, realizing then that I wouldn't have a dollar left, for that soda water was a nickel apiece and maybe that skunk would charge for them cakes though I hadn't ate a one, and yet I was sort of relieved at not having to go to Mrs. Lizzie's. I was a real mess at that time of my life, never having an idea but it was canceled by the next.

The skunk, however, wasn't there; I don't know where he went, leaving behind an old fellow with a handlebar mustache who allowed my reckoning was already taken care of. So I still had my dollar, which seemed unfortunate when I reached the street, for a great weakness hit me in the hamstrings. I looked up and down for

Mrs. Pendrake, wishing I could see her so I wouldn't have to go no further. There was nothing in the world I wanted so little as a whore at that moment, but I felt it was a challenge once I had got up instead of waiting in the soda-water place.

Then I saw the tracks of her boots in the slush. I couldn't tell you what made them distinguishable from the other footprints; I just knowed them, for I was familiar with her every particular. I could smell a room and tell you if she had been in it during the last two days. That's the one respect in which my senses hadn't got blunted while living in town. Them tracks went along the walk, down to the corner, took a left, north another block, again a left—I followed them though pretending to be dawdling along like a sappy kid—and when they had took that second left onto a residential street running parallel to and behind the block of shops, I understood she had lied.

Halfway along the block was an alley that run back to the commercial street. A cart had been through it but lately, pulled by a mule led by a colored man about seventy years of age: an Indian would have knowed the age of the mule as well.

Anyway, right along this alley had gone Mrs. Pendrake's little boots, out towards the shops again, except when they come to the back of one of the stores, they turned through a gate, crossed a short yard past the privy, up to a door, and ended.

I paused at the fence, for here come that colored fellow with his cart again, and sure enough he looked about seventy and was leading a big mule. Negroes was great for talking like Lavender of what secrets is seen in eggs and so on, but I believe the reason why they knowed everything in those days was they was always trucking things through back alleys, cleaning up bedrooms and the like, and you can pick up a lot of dirt that way without even looking for it. He bid me the time of day and went creaking past, and then a black dog begun to growl on the other side of the alley and then hushed.

There was a minute when the alley was empty and quiet, and I took it to go through the gate on Mrs. P.'s trail. O.K., I reached the door as she had, but what now? It didn't have no keyhole and anyway probably opened into a dark hall. I put my ear against it and never heard a thing. Suppose I barged in and she was being fitted for a corset? I felt awful at the thought, but at the same time right excited. You have to recall I was fifteen years of age then and not the relic I am today. I am a dirty old man now but in that time I was only a filthy young boy, and I hope it is not so disgusting to you, for you must believe I was never before nor since in that much misery.

I certainly didn't barge in. Over to the side of the door was a big woodbox and beyond it a window onto the porch. A person my size could scrooch down next to the one and peer into the other, through a teeny crack in the shutters closed on it, and nobody using the alley were the wiser.

For all the things I noticed on the route here, it never struck me that I was at the back of the same building in which the soda-water place occupied the front. I saw that, if nothing else, when I staggered on out a couple minutes later and somehow drug myself back home.

What I seen through the crack was that proprietor and Mrs. Pendrake. They had their clothes on, but was pressed together. And just as I peeped in, he had bared his big teeth, pulled her high collar down a little, and bit her white neck. I would have broke in and killed him, but for her look of liking it immensely.

CHAPTER 11 *Hopeless*

THANKSGIVING TRANSPIRED during my time of bed-bound illness, and I missed it for that reason. So Christmas was the first white holiday I was to celebrate in more than five years. I had been looking forward to it back in the fall, but by the time it come, I had seen that episode through the shutters and it was ruined for me before it started, like everything else.

I passed that winter in a blur of pain, but apparently the breaking of my heart sort of fertilized my mind and I did real well at my studies. When I was over the pneumonia Mrs. Pendrake forgot she used to tutor me afternoons and went out more and more. So I got to staying later at the school, where we had a pretty, young teacher to replace the ugly old maid who retired or died or something. I don't want you to think I got a crush on this new woman. I was finished with that sort of thing for good: I don't mean love and I don't mean lust, I mean that half-witted captivity I had imposed on myself as regards Mrs. Pendrake, which come as a result of lack of decision. I had never been able to make up my mind whether she was my mother or my sweetheart, until I looked through the shutter and saw she was neither.

So if I stayed at school after hours it was because home had become hateful to me and I also took satisfaction in the company of this new teacher from the fact that I had no interest in her aside from what she could impart in the way of learning, for she was bright. Therefore I suppose it was inevitable that once she saw my immunity, so to speak, she got stuck on me, white women being nothing if not contrary. Her name was Helen Berry, and she was only about eighteen. She was real pretty, sort of plumpish with a pug nose. She'd smile at me in class, but when I was there alone with her she'd turn right shy if I looked her in the eye.

I could have kissed her any time I wanted. Reason I didn't was the Reverend had really got to me with that talk of sin—in a sort of backhanded way, through his wife getting her neck bit by that cake-eater. I was finished with golden chalices that might get turned into slop jars, just as I had stopped seeing that purple-titted painting. The way I accomplished that was to go right to the slop jars to begin with. By the time I turned sixteen, early in February, I was a regular customer at Mrs. Lizzie's.

Confessing I run to the whores was easy alongside of the next admission I got to make regarding my activities that winter, but there ain't no avoiding it if you want the whole truth. I become a small-sized version of that Kane what run the soda-water place. For one, I got to being a conscious dandy. I had earlier felt uneasy wearing them fancy clothes Mrs. P. had bought me, fur-trimmed and all, but now there was nothing I cherished more than ornate attire.

In them days kids wore jeans and stuff to school, but the way I got myself up you would have thought I was the headmaster except for my size: fawn-colored pants, dark sack coat, satin vest, and patent-leather shoes. It was all right with Miss Berry, who you know was stuck on me, and if you think I had any trouble with Luke English and his bunch you are wrong. Soon as I started to dress that way and put on the supercilious manner that went with it, that crowd began to suck up to me in the most shameless fashion, with Luke foremost among them.

Of course that meant the girls of the same age as well, and they got to inviting me to their birthday parties and such, to which I'd come with a smirk and make sarcastic remarks even to their parents as they officiated, and by God if I didn't hear more than one mother remark favorably on what a gentleman I was directly after I had to my mind insulted her.

So the winter passed, and Mrs. Pendrake I reckon continued to visit the back of the ice-cream parlor though I never followed her again, on the grounds my heart would never stand it. For I tell you I loved her. If anything, I loved her more than ever after looking through that shutter. I hated her, but I loved her for making me hate her. I was imitating Kane because she loved him. I was running to the whores because I loved her.

I love her still, for if you know anything about that kind of feeling, you know how close it is connected to hopelessness and thus is about the only thing in civilization that don't degenerate with time.

Spring came. It might have been April, for I recall a good deal of rain fell the night before, but the following day was clear and bright and the magnolia tree in the Pendrakes' front yard had sprung all its pink cups.

At around two in the afternoon a little scrawny fellow went into the soda-water place, drug that Kane outside to the street, and beat him half to death with a horsewhip.

No, it wasn't me. The man what did it was named John Weatherby, who owned a livery stable. He stood about five-five, was bald and forty, and had a sixteen-year-old daughter I knowed slightly. It turned out Kane had knowed this girl too, only in the carnal way, and had give her the start of a family of her very own.

Kane never tried to defend himself, just covered up his face—I reckon he didn't want his sneer spoiled—and took his hiding. I understand that frock coat of his was cut to ribbons. I didn't see the incident myself, but Luke English did and probably lied some in relating it. (Kane might have been yellow, but I can't see him going down on his knees and sobbing like a child.) I do know Kane shortly married the Weatherby girl, closed up his establishment, and moved to St. Louie. And then within another month or so, about the time she begun to swell, back she come, for he had give her the slip once in the big city.

"I believe that Kane would of screwed a snake if somebody'd held its head," Luke observed. "Though I never realized that about him while he was here, didjoo? I wonder who else's wives, mothers, sisters, and daughters he was—"

"Who cares," says I and changed the subject. Luke's mother and sisters was the ugliest women in town.

I hankered to see the effects the new development would have on Mrs. P. They wasn't visible, except she started staying home more in the afternoons again. She was sweetly sad as always, not I think because of this particular disappointment but rather at the general nature of living. I guess it didn't measure up to what that judge, her Pa, led her to expect, which wouldn't be the first time a lawyer give somebody a bum steer. Or maybe she did too much reading. She might have been happy with cross-eyes or buck teeth.

But the kind of fool I was, I went right back to my imaginary romance with her, forgot and forgave, read Mr. Pope again, and so on. I stopped visiting Mrs. Lizzie's. When the warm weather come, the Reverend suddenly grew aware of me as if I had been absent all winter, and allowed as how we should go fishing again. But by being vague about it until the notion passed from his mind, I managed to elude that. So it was perfect and the month of May. All my life since, May has retained the signification it acquired then though I never spent another in that fashion.

But along about the first of June, instead of reading on that afternoon, we walked down to the commercial district, Mrs. P. holding my arm, both of us real grand. She had decided I must have a new pair of boots. I already owned four or five, but she said the new bootmaker was an amazing craftsman in leather, hailing from Florence, Italy, and it was almost disgraceful not to wear the product of his hand, now such was available.

So we went to the shop, which was owned by a flabby-faced individual named Cushing, who rushed up as we entered and all but kissed the floor underneath Mrs. P. The Italian bootmaker was at his bench towards the back, a wiry, dark-complexioned fellow in his middle twenties. He wore a leather jerkin without sleeves and was hairy as an animal on the lower arms, and also I reckon the chest, for where the garment was open at the base of his neck was all curly black.

Cushing fetches forth a pair of Russia-leather slippers Mrs. Pendrake had ordered earlier, unbeknownst to me. They were cunning little red things, for she had tiny feet. Cushing come almost to the point of slaver here, a woman's foot in them days being thought almost unbearably sexy.

"I supervised the dainty work myself," he says. "You can't always trust that Eye-talian when it comes to ladies' items. You see this stitching, madam—"

Mrs. P. says: "Would you be so good as to deliver them to my house, Mr. Cushing?"

"Oh?" says he with a finger to the gold tooth of which he was real proud. "Very well, madam, I'll send the Eye-talian straight off."

"You must never do that, Mr. Cushing. I shall require Angelo to take this young gentleman's measurements for a pair of boots."

I figured Angelo would get a hard time when the old bastard got back, and I was sorry, for I liked that Italian right away if for no other reason than he was even more a foreigner in that town than me.

He come over from his workbench and took a pattern from my foot. It was then, looking up to smile at Mrs. Pendrake, I saw on her face the same expression she had worn for Kane.

The difference was that Angelo kept his head down mostly, covered with them tight black curls, and if he glanced at Mrs. P., his face was polite, innocent, and ignorant. Italians have the reputation for hot blood, but he didn't even seem to be lukewarm. Furthermore, he didn't have much English. He seemed to know two words: "lady" and "yes," which he pronounced his own way.

She said: "Angelo, I am very happy with these slippers. You have made them as if you held my foot while you worked."

He answered: "Yayss, leddy."

"But," said she.

He looked up under his thick eyebrows. "Leddy?"

"But I think I had rather they were done in blue. Don't you think blue would become me more?"

"Yayss?" he asked, all the while applying himself to the pattern of my hoof, and shortly had it done, for he was wondrously deft with his fingers.

I don't think he savvied a word she said, but she nevertheless went on about it and he nodded and said the usual and smiled empty and, making a little bow, went back to his bench, where he picked up a piece of hide and sliced out a sole freehand almost in no longer than it takes to tell it.

Towards Angelo I have never borne any ill will. It's hard to hate a man on the basis of the one short time you saw him, when he appeared far more interested in leather than he ever could be in Mrs. Pendrake. I was just worn out with the whole business.

So along about three o'clock next morning, with my lamp turned down low, I put on the most usable clothes I could find, got my money together—I had three-four dollars accumulated—put my scalping knife in my waistband, slipped down the stairs, and left forever.

Before I went, though, I wrote a little letter, for they had been all of them right nice to me in their fashion, and stuck it where it would be found.

DEAR REV. AND MRS. PENDRAKE,

I got to go off now, but it ain't your fault, for you been mighty kind. The trouble is I don't think I can ever be civilized like you two. For I can't get onto your ways, though I know they is the right ones. Please don't send after me. I promise never to reveal my connection with you so you won't be disgraced. Give my regards to Lucy and Lavender, who I am grateful towards for their many favors.

Believe me, your loving "son,"

JACK

Now you get the reason why I won't tell the name of that town, nor the faith of the Reverend's church, and as far as that goes, those people wasn't named "Pendrake."

It was partly on account of the promise I made in that note, but mostly because for all the things I done in my life, some of them fairly unrespectable, I never got so low as to speak ill of a lady in public. At least not so's you could recognize her. The type of fellow who would do that should be shot.

CHAPTER 12 *Going for Gold*

WHAT I HAD IN MIND on leaving the Pendrakes was of course returning to the Cheyenne. God knows I thought enough about it and kept telling myself I was basically an Indian, just as when among Indians I kept seeing how I was really white to the core.

But when I got to the river's edge that early morning of my departure, where I figured to take a boat across to the western shore and hit the emigrant trail, I suddenly lost my taste for that venture. I just couldn't see myself going back to a buffalo robe in Old Lodge Skins's tepee. I couldn't stand it at the Pendrakes' no more, but the answer to my problem didn't seem to be returning to savagery after that nine or ten months out of it. Being primitive ain't the easiest thing in the world to get used to if you know better. You get showed a more regular manner of obtaining your grub, for example, and it's pretty hard to return to a method that ain't guaranteed.

I reckon that was one consideration that changed my mind. I was too ignorant to reflect that I ate on schedule with the Pendrakes because I didn't have to provide the food myself. Then another thing was that in our town you heard a lot about St. Louie, and I figured so long as I was in the same state I ought to see that great city. I could always go west, and I oughtn't pass up a chance to take in the local sights while I was here.

So I went east to St. Louie, walking most of the route so as to save my money, which nevertheless had dwindled out by the time I reached the city and the rest of it went for my first meal there, for which they took fifty cents off me, prices being criminal high in St. Louie.

I ain't going into detail how I survived there, but it was barely. I sold my clothes, I cleaned outhouses, I begged, and I stole. Within a month after I stopped being Mrs. Pendrake's pampered son, I was a dirty old bum sleeping in the back of stables.

Don't ask me about the theatrical exhibitions they had in St. Louie or the fine stores or the great eating places or the luxurious boats that plied the Mississippi River, for my knowledge of them extended no further than the outside, where I'd stand as a ragged beggar, collecting very little, until rousted by the police constables.

But St. Louie was quite a center for the trade going west, and in time I had a bit of luck: got myself hired on as guide for a mule train of yardgoods and such heading for Santa Fe in New Mexico. Which took some lying, though of course I could back it up with my fluent Cheyenne. I had never been to Santa Fe, but I found out that from years of travel the trail was plainly marked, so figured to have no trouble in guiding along it. Anyway, them fellows what owned the train was dumb as hell and not hard to convince of anything unlikely. They hadn't never been west of St. Joe, but had raised all the money they could for this expedition, on which they expected to make a pile in one shot out of what they believed to be a bunch of stupid greasers. Their names was the Wilkerson Brothers.

What happened to change their plans was that the Comanche jumped us, killed both Wilkersons along with all the mule skinners, and stole the goods and burned the wagons. This disaster occurred along the Cimarron River after we had crossed the fifty mile of waterless plain from the Arkansas.

You notice I wasn't myself killed in this set-to. In fact, I wasn't even wounded. I just knowed how to handle myself, and when everybody else was down, didn't see no further reason to keep standing off fifty savages when all I had to do it with was one old muzzle-loader.

Well, there I was, within a barricade of cases of our trade goods, and the circle of screeching Comanche was drawing tighter, and you fire once from a muzzle-loader and then spend the next fifteen minutes recharging it: if you're faced with more than three of the enemy, they could almost have beat you to death with their hands before you found your ramrod. So I was forced to employ that weapon I carried on top of my neck. I remembered that invaluable story of Little Man again!

Down behind the barricade, I quick stripped off my shirt, made a ball of it about the size of my head, and jammed my felt hat onto it, with the brim down low, which is the way a man would wear it in the bright sun along the Cimarron. I had a jacket, too, and got back into it, pulling in my neck like a turtle and buttoning the garment right up over my head. The arms hung loose, with my own inside, and I slipped one hand up and held that shirt-head, wearing the hat, onto the jacket neck.

Up I rose, about six feet five to the crown of the hat, looking out of a peephole between the top jacket buttons, and started to walk towards the galloping ring of Snake People. All I had to rely on was their knowing the legend of Little Man the Great Cheyenne. And you can be sure that before they made up their minds, they kept firing arrows at me for a spell and one went through the limp arm of my jacket.

But directly they begun to slow down to a trot, then to a walk, still encircling but fascinated. Well sir, here goes, I thought; I'm going to shoot my wad. At that point I had passed the body of one of the Wilkersons, looking blank towards the sky and with two arrows in his chest. I pitched that fake head right off my fake shoulders. It hit the ground and rolled, but I had balled it tight and the hat never come off.

The Comanche stopped dead. I remember thinking: I've got you sons of bitches now, ain't I? Oh, ain't I? I had forgot Little Man's war song or I'd have sung it.

But I didn't have them by no means. A warrior suddenly rode over, picked up the shirt-head on the point of his short lance, looked at it and throwed it away, and then they took me captive.

Well, you can't call it a failure. Had I not done it, they would have killed me. And I learned a valuable lesson: Don't try to fool an Indian who has seen a lot of white men. The Comanche had been raiding the Santa Fe Trail for forty years.

They didn't treat me bad, and I reckon they intended to trade me off for guns or something, but having been put to herding their horses for them, one night I stole one and rode off. It was fast and hard travel, and before long he died on me and I continued to New Mexico on foot. It was the end of summer before I reached Taos, in the mountains north of Santa Fe. For quite a time I hadn't seen a town of any description, so I was rather cheered just to see the Pueblo Indians' dwellings there, though I never could get up much affection for that type of redskin, who was always farmers and lived clustered together like bats from time immemorial. With the whole world open to them, they settled down and raised little patches of beans. The Comanche used to raid them every once in a while and so did the Navaho and Apache. A wild Indian don't like a tame one.

There was a white town down the trail a piece from the Indian one, so I went on down there. I was sure a sight after those weeks in desert and mountain. I'd kneel down and drink from a pool with my eyes shut so as not see my ugly reflection.

So I can't blame a famous hero for what he done when I showed up at his front door. I saw this adobe house, see, built around one of them inner courtyards, and I figured this was where I might get a handout. So I goes onto the veranda, and the door was open for it was hot weather, and I calls into the cool, dark interior: "Anybody to home?"

A fellow about my size, short that is, with a sandy mustache and real bandylegs, appears from the shadows within and says: "Git on out of here, you hairy son of a whore."

And I did, for he was real mean-looking. Later some Mexican off whom I begged a couple tortillas told me that was Señor Kit Carson.

In a day or so I reached Santa Fe, down in its valley among the mountains, with its Mex women in their bright colors and naked shoulders, and Pueblo Indians sitting about selling their junk and a Ute or two in red blankets walking arrogant around, and Spanish cowboys in them tight pants slitted at the ankle, along with the more usual types you might see anywhere. That was quite a town for the time and place, but you would never have known it by one look. Most everybody lived in them adobe houses, which is no more than dried mud; consequently they seem a little childish at first, like some kids patty-caked them together. Even the Governors' Palace off the town square was of this construction. If St. Louie was your idea of a city, you wouldn't have thought much of Santa Fe, which one good rain would have turned into a hog wallow.

It was all right with me, though, and I did a lot better there than in St. Louie. I don't mean I got rich, nor tried to. I took up with a fat Mexican woman who sold chili con carne, tamales, and the like right on the street, also cooked them there over an open fire. She took pity on me for being so skinny, was how it started. Before long I had moved into her little 'dobe house, which we also shared with five or six of her kids, but her husband run off or been killed, she wasn't sure which. Sometimes she'd believe the first, in which case she'd threaten me with him coming back and knifing me; and sometimes the other, and would want me and her to go to the priest and get hitched.

Estrellita was always yelling and scolding, and occasionally would get sufficiently riled so as to threaten to knife me herself, but I discovered that was the Mexican temperament, and it was easy to get her in a good mood again by doing some romantic thing like calling her "my little chili pepper" or whatnot. Speaking of peppers, my stomach was ruined for years by that Spanish grub and it put more calluses on my tongue than I had on my hands during these months. For I didn't do no work. I just laid around all day in the shade, and then in the evening, when the air had cooled enough so that the effort of walking wouldn't upset me, I'd summon up enough energy to drag myself to a cantina and lay into glass after glass of pulque, which Estrellita give me the money to buy.

I was morally very low at this time, and just sixteen. I reckoned it run in the family, having seen my brother Bill, and didn't worry none. If you want to really relax sometime, just fall to rock bottom and you'll be a happy man. Most all troubles come from having standards.

I might have died of a bad liver, what with that diet, but I was saved by an old-timer I run into in that cantina. This fellow was about seventy, had a face of white hair, a speech defect which he claimed come from Apache torture when a lad, and professed to be a expert on locating gold. Everybody called him Crazy Charley, or Loco Carlos, depending on their lingo, and you can gather from that what they thought of his ability as a prospector.

The reason I took up with Charley, to the extent of buying him drinks with Estrellita's hard-earned money, was my natural weakness for people with a positive vision. He might have been a penniless old drunk, but there wasn't any getting away from it that he talked an excellent idea. After prospecting for fifty years, he claimed to have located the biggest lode of gold in the "organized world" (which is how he referred to it, for Charley always talked mighty grandiose), and just at that point the Ute stole his pack animals, to which was lashed all his tools, and trailing them he got lost in the desert without water, lost his mind for a time, wore out his boots, and walked all the way to Taos in his bare feet. In spite of these "horrendous misadventures," he remembered exactly where that gold was: in a region of Colorado between the Arkansas River and the South Platte.

Charley would take a sip of liquor, roll it around in his toothless mouth, swallow with his whiskers aflutter, and say: "If I had your pecuniary endowments, sonny, I'd buy a set of possibles and rambunculate northwards, coming back within six months as a man of means beyond the dreams of algebra." That is near as I can come to his style, and you must also realize that all the *s* sounds was slurred owing to that scar on his tongue. "Shunny" is actually what he called me. When he finished that drink, and if I wouldn't buy him no more, around the room he'd go and make such a nuisance of himself that the big Mex who owned the place would throw him out the door sooner or later, and when you'd leave, there he'd be, sleeping alongside the road with the pigs rooting nearby.

Then one day word reached Santa Fe that gold had been struck on Cherry Creek in Colorado, right in that area what Charley always talked about. From a bum he turned into quite a hero. He could have drunk free on it for some time, and immediately got all kinds of offers to head the expeditions that started to outfit at once. But soon as he was vindicated, Charley become uppity. "Go pound sand up the aperation of your hindquarters," he told them others. "It was Shunny here who give me refreshment, and it be him I'll make rich."

It wasn't until well into the fall of '58 that we got to Colorado after a wearing trip, for on the way we was raided by Apache and I took an arrow in my leg, fell down, and knocked myself out. When I come to, our horses and mules was gone and the cantina owner's cousins as well. "They go under?" I asked old Charley, who appeared all right himself, just setting there rubbing his toothless gums with a finger while his rheumy eyes was fixed on the horizon.

"Oh," says he, "I had to deliver them over to the Apache. It didn't enthrall me with pleasure to do it, but you and me would never reach the gold if I hadn't."

Like most of the border Indians, the Apache had a peculiar grudge against Mexicans. So as to be able to kill the three cousins in some excruciating manner, they had let me and Charley go. He was a treacherous old goat, I think you will agree. And while I should maybe have thanked him, the result was I got very little sleep thereafter, for now we had nobody extra to give away if the need occurred but me. And I was wounded, not serious but for a time I couldn't do no running.

We did not encounter any more Indians, but our gear was gone now and our guns, so all we could bring down in the way of game was rattlesnake, by club, which however wasn't the worst victual in the world providing you could knock it dead without prejudicing yourself.

Charley was supposed to know the territory, but had forgot it owing to his years of drinking. His memory could have come back, he said, with a drink of spirits, but we didn't have none of course. I myself would have settled for a drink of muddy water by the time we was wandering hopelessly in the Great Sand Dune area of southern Colorado. We would sure have died there had not that party trailing us come to our rescue.

You must have got the point by now: Charley was the world's worst prospector. He just didn't know his profession. That was a revelation to me. I had thought if a fellow practiced a trade, he would naturally be good at it. But that ain't true. He can be awful at it all his life.

In our condition at the time they found us, we couldn't very well refuse to let that party throw in with us, and we at last arrived at Cherry Creek just as winter set in. The rest of the world had got there before us, owing to newspaper accounts all across the country. There was about eighty cabins already built, and in case you don't know it that was the start of Denver, Colorado, though they called it Auraria for the first couple years.

I got no intention of going into detail on the luck we had at prospecting for gold. Near as I can gather, all gold strikes is about the same: somebody pans a little dust, has to shoot off his mouth about it, so that thousands of others come rushing to the place, no single individual gets much owing to the congestion, and then finally some big outfit buys up most of the claims and makes a business of it with the proper machinery. Those who come out best are them who service those what are looking for the gold: the fellows that set up stores and saloons, etc., for early in the game they can get whatever they charge and have their bundle made by the time the smoke clears.

The following spring and summer there was supposed to have been a hundred and fifty thousand come to Colorado along the Platte, the Arkansas, and the Smoky Hill rivers. That was the time of PIKE'S PEAK OR BUST painted on the sides of wagons, for a lot of them had to announce it in that stupid way, then two-thirds went on back home by the end of the year, at which time they printed BUSTED, BY GOD below the other slogan.

Me and that bunch of ours, we tried gold for a while, got us a claim, even built a sluiceway real scientific, for there was seven or eight of us, but it didn't pay off much. Oh, there was gold there, we got out seventy-eighty dollars' worth of dust in three months and only used up about a hundred dollars' worth of pick handles and shovels, and didn't have no time to hunt, so had to buy food that would have been cheaper at the finest hotel in St. Louie, and then most of the gold we derived from that effort was spent by Charley for whiskey and one of the Mexicans for whores, for you take the latter, they appear at every gold strike shortly after the first nugget is found.

But some of us was too shrewd to go on long at that sort of thing: I don't mean me, I never knew anything about business, but a couple of them fellows, John Bolt and Pedro Ramirez, they organized a general store shortly and set up a regular supply train down to Santa Fe and back for goods, and I was wagonmaster of it. We did all right and made a nice piece of money which was divided up amongst the three of us left from the original crowd, for a couple others was killed in saloon arguments and Charley disappeared. He turned out to have gone back to Santa Fe, where he hung around the cantina again talking of the old days in Colorado and mooched drinks, and slept with the hogs.

Even though that regular trip would have put me in the range of Estrellita again, that worked out all right for she had herself another man by the first time I come back down the trail. She also had herself a new kid—which might have been mine for all I know, but I was real irresponsible in them days, being only seventeen myself. If so, and if he's still alive, he'd be only about ninety-four today.

It was during this period that I bought myself a horse, an Indian pony in fact is what he was, and pinto, but I got him off some white fellows who come to Denver with a herd of them. I also procured my first handgun, a Colt's Dragoon, cap-and-bail, and I practiced with it on the run to Santa Fe till I was good enough to eat no man's dirt and stay alive, which ain't easy when you are my size: it must have been along in these years that I growed to five foot four and stopped forever. I got a pair of built-up boots made to my measure in Santa Fe that added two inches onto that, and I also wore a Mex sombrero with a high crown: it was black and trimmed with silver. In outline I was six foot tall, but quite a bit of that was air.

Not far from the white settlements in early Denver was a big camp of Arapaho, who as you know was close friends of the Cheyenne, and occasionally little parties of the Human Beings themselves would troop through the vicinity. I didn't see anybody I knew, but on the other hand I never looked very hard. I don't know why I should have had this disinclination, for I was white and doing what whites are supposed to, but the fact was that I felt kind of shameful as regards the Indians.

I would be feeling right good and then see a little band of redskins riding along and fall into melancholy. I could never remember how shabby Indians was until I saw some. Not because they was always poor; there was something awfully seedy about an Indian when he was by his lights dressed to the nines. Old Lodge Skins in his best turn-out looked like something the cat drug in by white standards. Now I never noticed this much till I had been to the Missouri settlements and back.

Our store was first in a tent and then as business grew, we built us a wooden structure, and in between the Santa Fe trips I'd be around there for a spell. Some of the Arapaho got to dropping by with skins to trade, and game if they had any extra. And that's when I noticed how much an Indian stunk. Get three of them indoors and you could hardly breathe for the aroma. We just couldn't tolerate their presence inside the wood building, so the Indian trade was carried on outside in an open shed. Their goods wasn't worth much anyway; by the time they got around to bringing in a haunch of fresh venison, it was half-spoiled and crawling with maggots, and the hides was poorly dressed and stiff as lumber.

After you had seen that soda fountain in Missouri, and them cunning boots that a fellow like Angelo could turn out, and Mrs. Pendrake in her hoop skirt with the understructure of whalebone, you just couldn't avoid noticing that Indians was crude, nasty, smelly, lousy, and ignorant. You know I was predisposed in their favor, and it wasn't easy for me to admit the truth. But I got to hating them now, which is why I felt shameful, so I never owned up to my partners that I had any more connection with redskins than the next white man. I didn't have too much to do with the retail workings of the store anyway, so it was easy to slip aside when the Arapaho showed up to trade.

The site of Denver was on their old hunting grounds, but they didn't cause trouble over it. In fact, I recall once in the early days a chief called Little Raven rode over from the Indian camp and gave a speech to an assemblage of white citizenry. Actually, he come twice: the first day his interpreter fell down drunk, so they had to postpone until the next morning, when the chief returned and give a long speech after the mode of Old Lodge Skins, which amused some people but burned up others, for they was anxious to get back to panning gold rather than listening to the wind of some dirty old Indian. Little Raven was a broad-faced, wide-built fellow, with big brass earrings and his hair hanging free. The gist of his remarks, after the lard was melted out, was as follows:

"The Arapaho welcome the white men to this place, which has belonged to the Arapaho since the time that . . ." (a long account of how much the spirits love the tribe, with various examples of history of the mythic variety).

"The Arapaho like white men and think of them as brothers" (an account of this, largely to do with getting free coffee with lots of sugar in it).

"The Arapaho are made happy to see the white men getting the yellow metal, if the yellow metal is what pleases them so much. Our mother the earth provides all things for all men, and each people has a part of the land which it calls home, a part which it has watered with its own blood. You white men are now camped upon such a place, and the Arapaho to whom it belongs welcome you in peace and friendship. They hope you do nothing bad. They also hope you will not stay too long."

They gave Little Raven a cigar, and a meal which he ate with a knife and fork, and then he went back to his camp. Not long after that the Arapaho warriors rode off west to fight the Ute, and in their absence a bunch of drunken miners went over to the Indian village and raped several women. The Arapaho made some angry talk when they got back, but never did anything concrete about it.

Now I had not heretofore been a great admirer of civilization, but I figured that was because I had no hand in building such of it as I had come in contact with. I didn't care much for Missouri, if you recall, couldn't see it made sense. It was different with Denver, which growed before your very eyes. There was a real town there by the following summer, for people kept arriving from across the plains and while not many of them struck significant gold, and others got busted, by God, and went on home, there was a good deal who stayed, too, and permanent buildings replaced canvas and a newspaper begun to publish, and it wasn't long before they stuck up a church—whose pastor, I might mention, I done my best to avoid along with the Indians, but in them days you had to have a church to make a real town.

So it didn't look like we was going to leave as soon as Little Raven hoped. Speaking for the person I had turned into, what with being a partner in business and making enough money to buy me bright clothes and take a turn with the Spanish girls in Santa Fe, I thought it swell that white enterprise was reclaiming the Indian wastes. You take the sorriest cabin, it was a triumph over the empty wilderness.

That was what I thought at that time, anyway.

During the next year or so, I would hear news from time to time of the Cheyenne, though I never sought it, for it was plumb through the lands of the southern part of the tribe that them gold-rushers had to pass coming from the east, and then those that was busted went trooping back through the same region on their way home. You can imagine what this movement would do to the buffalo herds on which the Indians depended for the necessities of life. There was also now a regular stagecoach line which followed the Republican River through this same country, and I think I have mentioned how a regular thing, with a schedule, will upset an Indian.

But with this provocation there was fewer incidents than you might think: for all his wildness, maybe because of it, a redskin is a patient cuss and always tolerant at first of anything unusual. The Cheyenne thought the people rushing west for gold was insane, and didn't bother them much for that reason. Once in a while the young men might steal a white person's horses, and it was standard practice when sighting a wagon drove by civilians for the Indians to come up and get coffee or tobacco, and they didn't so much beg for it as they had used to but sort of threatened. They did the latter because it seemed to work with white people better than expecting hospitality. But if the emigrants stood up to them, the Indians generally would not do them harm. One of the reasons for which being that the Cheyenne was never well armed. If they got hold of a few modern rifles, then they never had powder or lead. Even iron arrowheads wasn't easy for them to procure: they had to get the makings, a barrel hoop or whatnot, from the white man.

I mention these facts because of the rot you'd hear in Denver. Indians would never have been popular in that city unless they all decided to commit mass suicide, I reckon. Now I have told you I got a white taste for building a community where previous only "the savage and beast had aimlessly wandered," which is to quote from the old type of journalism, and as a result I found them local Arapaho uninspiring. But they wasn't doing any harm except to stink and carry lice—which was also true of a good many of the early white citizenry of Colorado, I might add. Still, there was always talk of wiping them out, and the way I remember is that this was less said by the prosperous than by them who had had no luck at finding gold. If you sold all your belongings to go West for fortune and ended up busted, why, it seemed like the fault of the Indians.

But to get back to my affairs: owing to rival commercial operations coming out of Missouri, Bolt, Ramirez, and me found ourselves getting undercut on prices, on account of goods cost more for us to buy in Santa Fe than they did in the eastern settlements, for much of them had to come overland from Missouri in the first place, and the trip down to New Mexico while shorter was more arduous owing to mountains, deserts, and lack of water than that across the plains. It was at this time that Bolt and Ramirez got the idea for me to make the journey to Westport, Missouri, what is now Kansas City, and come back with a pack train of supplies that would be more "competitively priced," as they put it, being both of them great for business.

I made the trip to Missouri alone, with a pack horse, without incident, carrying quite a bundle of money with which to buy goods. I figured to hire mule drivers in Westport for the return, and that's what I did, and got the supplies and animals and wagons, and we set out for Colorado within a couple weeks.

One day towards the end of August we was taking our noontime rest along a stretch of the Arkansas River in west Kansas that was treeless for miles, and I had crawled under a wagon for a bit of shade, laying there on a rolled saddle blanket and puffing at a short pipe I had lately took up as a vice. Maybe I had even started to nap, which would have been logical, when a sense of sudden quiet made itself known. I wasn't on unusually good terms with them skinners, who resented being hired by a kid, and had had to be fairly obvious about my Colt's Dragoon.

Well, now I got a suspicion they was about to jump me nonetheless, and it jerked me from my dream, gun in hand.

But what I saw from beneath the wagon was fringed leggings and a pair of moccasins with a little strip of blue and red beading across the instep and an interrupted band of white running from ankle to toe. I had once set and watched Shooting Star apply them beads, strung on sinew and stitched with a bone needle.

They belonged to Burns Red in the Sun, who must be wearing them at this moment though I could see him only as high as the waist from where I lay. He wasn't alone, but accompanied by some fifteen or twenty other pairs of moccasins. And there was something about them feet and legs that didn't look too friendly.

You may be interested to hear what it was. Well, from down that low I couldn't see the butts of anybody's weapons. Which meant they was holding them in a usable position.

CHAPTER 13 *Cheyenne Homecoming*

I WASN'T in no particular hurry to come on out of there; and when I did issue forth I did not care to do so at the feet of them Indians. As to the latter, I had no choice, however, for they was on the other side of the wagon also and at both ends.

So I crawled out and stood up soon as I cleared the edge of the wagon box, and it was sure enough the face of Burns Red in the Sun that I looked into. Painted heavily, it went without saying, and just as well for otherwise I should not have recognized him.

I oughtn't to omit to say that while I was rising, two other Indians seized my arms and lifted my pistol and knife. This bunch was not on a friendly mission. They continued to pinion me, and without making a fuss over it I was able to observe that my company of mule skinners stood or lay all around in various states of captivity, though it was not apparent that any struggle had took place.

Even with my credentials I found this a delicate moment. Burns Red was not being exactly quick to make me out. I had forgot, too, that if you encounter it of a sudden, face paint will scare hell out of you.

I had dropped my sombrero, so Burns had a fair shot at my features. I had got a year or so older since we had last been together and I had the beginnings of a mustache, though they wasn't enough to put off anybody.

Still, he was right cold when he spoke. His eyes showed unsympathetic out at me over vermilion cheeks and on either side of a nose with a white line down the bridge. He wore a full bonnet of eagle feathers tipped with down.

"Why," he asks, of course in Cheyenne, "did you steal my father's horse?"

It was then I noticed that nearby another Indian was holding the halter of that pinto I had bought in Denver. This man was an old acquaintance, Shadow That Comes in Sight, who had led my first raid against the Crow, you might recall, on which I had made that name for myself. However he was looking sullen at present.

"Brother," I says to Burns with some urgency, "don't you know me?"

You would have thought he might consider how I happened to speak fluent Cheyenne. Not him.

"You white men," he said in great disgust. "We took you in and fed you when you were hungry and lost because dreams of the yellow dust had made you crazy. Then you steal our horses. You are all very bad men, and we don't want to make a treaty with you."

The others roundabout muttered peevishly in agreement with them sentiments. I couldn't make head nor tail of his complaints, however, so I just explained where and how I had got the pony and said that regardless of that, he could have him on general principles, being my brother.

I had now used the word "brother" a couple times, and it was beginning to penetrate Burns's eagle feathers and the thick skull thereunder. So after denouncing white men some more and gesturing in an unpleasant way with his rifle—on which occasions them two holding my arms would give me a good agitating and the rest of the Indians would glower and mutter at my mule skinners, who though ordinarily the typical, uncouth, foul-mouthed swaggering bunch that follows that profession, was now paralyzed in fear— after a long time, during which I almost give up hope, for even though you've lived with Indians for five years they can be quite damaging to your peace of mind, he at last said in personal irritation, as contrasted with the racial charges he had been making:

"Why do you keep calling me 'brother'? I want you to stop doing that. I am not your brother. I am a Human Being."

And the swarthy fellow holding my right arm, who wore a belt full of scalps one of which was blond as corn and never come from no Pawnee, said: "I think we should kill him first and then talk." I did not know this man, but among the others I recognized Bird Bear and Lean Man and Rolling Bull, the latter restraining my left arm.

"Well," I says boldly, "it seems the Human Beings cannot be

trusted any more than the white men who did you wrong. Only two snows ago I was your brother, lived in Old Lodge Skins's tepee, hunted and fought with the Human Beings and on one occasion at least almost died for them. I suppose you will say with your tongue-that-goes-two-ways that you never heard of Little Big Man."

Burns Red in the Sun said: "He rode beside me at the Battle of the Long Knives, where the white men did not know how to fight. He was killed there after rubbing out many bluecoats. But the white men did not get his body. He turned into a swallow and flew away across the bluffs."

"I tell you," I cried, "that I am Little Big Man. How would I know about him otherwise?"

"All people know of him," said Burns Red in that stubborn red-skin manner. "He is a great hero of the Human Beings. Everybody knows the Human Beings, so everybody would know of him. I shall not talk of this further." He shifted his rifle to the left hand and put his right upon the handle of his scalping knife. "In addition to being a horse thief you are the biggest liar I have ever heard," he went on. "And also a fool. I tell you I saw *Little Big Man fall and turn into a bird*. Therefore you cannot be he. Besides, you are a white man. Little Big Man was a Human Being."

"Look at me," I said.

"Oh," said Burns Red, "Little Big Man may have had light skin, but that does not mean he was a white man. Besides, what you are showing me is you and not him."

Well, there you have it. There ain't nothing in the world, not the most intractable mule, that is so obdurate as a goddam Indian. I figured I was a goner at this point, especially since Burns said he was going to cut out my tongue for telling lies, at which that especially mean fellow on my right arm was considerably cheered. He was no more than a kid, about my age when I killed the Crow. I have said I didn't recognize him, but suddenly I did.

He was Dirt on the Nose, growed up some from that young boy to whom I had give a pony after the exploit in which I got my adult name.

Burns Red drawed his knife. I looked at Dirt on the Nose. Hell, it was worth a try.

I asked him: "You still have that black I gave you up on the Powder River?"

His ferocious look disappeared, and he answered: "No, the Pawnee stole him when we were camped at Old Woman Butte two snows ago."

"Did you hear that?" I asked Burns Red in the Sun.

His face went blank, insofar as you could say behind that paint.

"It is true," he said, "that there is a thing here that I do not understand."

I proceeded to rapid-fire a number of other detailed reminiscences at him, but he was not further impressed. He put away his knife, though. It was that particular about the horse that saved my life, or at least my tongue. People came and went in them days, but horses was serious.

So them Indians decided to take me to their camp and let the older men adjudicate the matter. I was no longer physically constrained, but neither had they reached the point of returning my weapons. They left a guard upon the mule skinners, who I told to accept this inconvenience in good grace; not that they had any choice.

The Cheyenne party had left its own horses in a basin half a mile off in the charge of two younger braves. Shadow continued to lead that pinto, but I figured it would not be my place to mount the animal at this time; and my extra horse was back at the wagons.

"What am I going to ride?" I asked Burns.

That was a real problem for the poor devil. Now that his stubbornness had been challenged on the matter of my identity, he didn't know quite what to think about anything.

He looked at me with his face all screwed up.

"There is a pain," he said, "between my ears." He reached back between the feathers of his bonnet and rubbed his scalp. It occurred to me then for the first time how dumb he was. As a boy I had thought Burns Red a brilliant fellow for his knowledge of the bow and arrow and riding, in which he trained me. I guess he knowed them things all right, but otherwise he was pretty stupid.

"I won't walk all the way," I said. "I can tell you that."

You could see he was kind of wistful that he hadn't been allowed to cut my tongue out, not because Burns was unusually cruel but rather because it would have kept this difficulty from arising.

"Ride behind me," said Dirt on the Nose, who trusted me about seven-eighths since mention of the horse I had give him. So I leaped up behind and took ahold of his belt, for I didn't dare to dig those

Spanish heels into the animal, and we moved off, going north for two hours, and fetching up along a tiny creek that for poverty of water didn't have its match.

There on the farther bank stood the tepees of Old Lodge Skins's little band, which seemed about the size it had always been, but Jesus God, I thought, had they always been so seedy? And it is a queer thing that the stench affected me more now than it had as a boy of ten, entering that first encampment with my sister Caroline. To tell you how powerful this general smell was, even when diffused through the air in the smart wind that was blowing at the time, it overcome for me the personal odor of Dirt on the Nose, who was right strong on the nostrils being I was close to him.

Up we go to the familiar tepee of the chief, which had been my home for five years, with its faded scratch-drawings and sewed-up places and tattered flaps. From the look of things I figured Old Lodge Skins must have been enduring another of his long runs of bad luck. The dirty kids come running and the barking dogs, and most of the adults in camp at the time was in cluster, for our party had returned as usual in bits and pieces, the firstcomers having apprised the other Indians of the matter at hand.

I begun to get nervous then, for though among Americans you tend to find people the less frightening the better you know them, the same wasn't true of Indians in my experience, with whom prolonged relations only led to the awareness that they was capable of anything. My knees had been steadier than when Dirt on the Nose and me dismounted.

Among a group of braves, I ducked in through the tepee entrance. Inside it was darker than of old, for no fire was lit and my eyes hadn't been accustomed for some time to coming into gloom out of burning sunshine. We turned to the right and paused for a minute, as was the proper manners, and the guttural voice of Old Lodge Skins come out of the twilight ahead.

"I wish you would go outside," he said to them Indians, "and let me talk to the white man alone."

They left and I went around the circle to where the old chief was setting. You might think it would have made more sense to cut straight across the diameter, but this was never done: a person traveled circumferentially in a lodge.

It was a while before my eyes was adjusted and I could make him out. Meanwhile he just set there quietly. I noticed he was bare-headed, and remembering how I had thrown away his loaned hat at the Solomon battle, I felt right bad about it. Now I was carrying my Mexican sombrero, which I had fetched along and worn on the ride. It was a real pretty thing with its band of silver medallions and embroidered brim.

"Grandfather," I said, "I brought you this present." And handed him the hat.

Now I had done my limit. If the Cheyenne was determined to put me to death as an impostor, there wasn't nothing more I could do about it.

"My son," said Old Lodge Skins, "to see you again causes my heart to soar like a hawk. Sit here beside me."

That was some relief. I took a seat upon the buffalo robe to his left, and he leaned over and embraced me. I tell you I was right touched by it. Then he took the sombrero, quickly cut out the crown with his knife, stuck a single eagle feather into that silver band, and put it on his head.

"Is this the same hat that I used to own?" he asked. "Which grew soft of skin and fatter?"

"No, Grandfather, it is another."

"We must smoke your return," he said, and went through the rigamarole of filling the pipe, lighting it, offering it to the four points of the compass and so on, so it was quite a while before I got a drag of that spicy mix of red-willow bark.

"I saw you in a dream," he said after a time. "You were drinking from a spring that came out of the long nose of an animal. I did not recognize the animal. Alongside this nose he grew two horns. The water that gushed from his nose was full of air."

I don't care if you believe me or not, but you might reflect that if I was going to make up something out of the whole cloth, it'd probably be more ambitious than that. What he was talking about was of course that elephant-head soda-water fountain in Kane's establishment. I can't explain it.

We set there maybe an hour before getting around to what was to me the important issue, but you can't rush things with an Indian.

Finally Old Lodge Skins said: "Do not be angry with Burns Red in the Sun and the others. They had unhappy experiences last year with some white men they found wandering, sick and hungry, in a place without water. These white men had lost their minds in the search for the yellow dust, and our people took pity on them, fed them and treated them for the illness of the mind, and then when they were well, these white men stole twenty-six of our horses and the rifle of Spotted Dog and ran away during the night."

Old Lodge Skins calmly dragged on the pipe and let the smoke waft from his mouth and nostrils.

"What particularly annoyed some of the Human Beings," he went on, "was that we had come down here to attend the peace conference at the fort of Bent, which the Father of the whites asked us to, and that is why we are dressed in our good clothing, and then Burns Red in the Sun and the others came upon your mule wagons and saw the pinto which had been among those stolen last year."

I took the pipe from him. "I don't understand why they did not recognize me."

"Yes," said Old Lodge Skins. "Do you want to eat?"

He never said anything lightly, so I knew I was supposed to take refreshment at this point by the etiquette and said yes, and in come Buffalo Wallow Woman who started the fire and boiled some puppy dog and served it up in bowls with the little paws sticking out over the rim as a mark of special distinction. Still, she kept her eyes down, and we never greeted each other, for Old Lodge Skins had not yet pronounced his O.K. of me to her. By time this was finished, it was nigh evening.

The chief wiped the grease off his mouth with the brim of the sombrero. This was not a case of slovenliness, however: after several meals, that piece of headgear would be so impregnated with fat that rain could never soak it.

He took up the conversation just where it had left off.

"I do not understand exactly what happened to you at the Battle of the Long Knives, at which the horse soldiers did not know how to fight properly," he said. "We all went away on account of the wrong medicine. But when the Human Beings collected again and you were not there in your own body, we saw a swallow who flew above us for a long time. It was natural to assume that was you. It was also pleasant to think so, for you were a man for whom the Human Beings felt honor and affection. Later I dreamed about the long-nosed animal that gave you a drink in the village of the whites, but I did not tell anybody because it might have meant bad luck for you to do that.

"Therefore," he said, "Burns Red in the Sun cannot be blamed for his ignorance." He got up from the robe and, indicating I should follow, went out in front of the tepee, where the whole camp had been waiting all this while. The sun was setting across the infinity of prairie to the west, in streaks of orange, vermilion, pink, and rose, and this light give a glow to all the colors on the people there.

Old Lodge Skins looked right smart in that sombrero. Standing there in his red blanket, with me alongside, he give quite a harangue, as you might expect. I won't go into it, except for the conclusion.

"I have thought and talked and smoked and eaten on this matter," he said. "And my decision is that Little Big Man has returned."

He went back into his lodge and the rest of the camp come and greeted me dear as I ever experienced, with embraces and compliments and every type of affectionate chatter, and I had to eat five or six times more and talk for hours, and I reckon I was affected by this, for I knowed nonetheless that I could never be an Indian again.

Well, I got filled in on what those people had done since that Solomon battle: just about what they had been doing from time immemorial, been up north as usual during most of the year and come down south for the tribal get-together both summers since. Hadn't had no more trouble with the soldiers, for they had kept out of their way. And it seemed they was still acceptable to the main tribe, which meant that Old Lodge Skins hadn't got his hands on anybody else's wife.

What an Indian chooses to characterize a whole twelvemonth is something like: "That was the time that Running Wolf broke his leg," or, "During the winter a cottonwood tree fell on Bird Bear's tepee." Insofar as they kept a mental diary, it was events of that sort that filled it up, and there might be no remark whatever of something real important. For example, that Solomon retreat was only mentioned to me by Burns Red and Old Lodge Skins; everybody else had forgot it soon as possible. If you'd have asked a Cheyenne what he did that summer that was notable, he might have said something like: "My chestnut won a race against Cut Belly's black."

As Old Lodge Skins had said, they was in this area now because of the peace-treaty conference called by the Government at Bent's Fort. The Indian Commissioner himself had promised to show up, so I gathered, and this impressed the chief no end. He expected to get another medal and maybe a new plug hat. Beyond that, however, he was undecided on the prospects.

One of the many meals of celebration give for me was in the tepee of Hump, who was still war chief and hadn't changed at all.

"Welcome, my friend," he says to me when we met. "You wouldn't by any chance have brought me a gift of powder and shot?" So I presented him the extra paper cartridges and percussion caps I carried for my Dragoon pistol, retaining only the loads already in the chambers. I could have been hanged for doing that if the Army found out, I reckon.

"Come and eat," says he. Old Lodge Skins was also invited, and Shadow That Comes in Sight, Burns Red, and several others of my old friends, and that is where we talked about the treaty.

"I do not know," said Old Lodge Skins after we finished the boiled buffalo tongue, "whether it is right for a Human Being to become a farmer, though Yellow Wolf had that idea, and he was a wise man."

Hump said: "Yellow Wolf was a great chief, but the white men put him under an evil spell or he would never have got that idea. He loafed around the forts too much."

"I want to speak now," said Shadow That Comes in Sight. "I think I would rather die than plant a potato."

Burns Red in the Sun was still sore about the dirty deal he got from them gold hunters. He said: "No matter what we do, the white men will cheat us. If we plant potatoes, they will steal them. If we try to hunt buffalo, they will scare the game away. If we fight, they will not make war properly." He didn't come to no conclusion, but fell into one of them depressed moods that stayed with him for the rest of the day and next morning, during which he set right there in Hump's tepee, never speaking nor drinking nor eating, and Hump's family let him alone, walking around him.

"That may be so," said Old Lodge Skins. "On the other hand, the white men are coming in ever greater numbers and building permanent dwelling places. If they do not find wood, they cut bricks from the earth or burrow into the ground like prairie dogs. Whatever else you can say about the white man, it must be admitted that *you cannot get rid of him*. He is in never-ending supply. There has always been only a limited number of Human Beings, because we are intended to be special and superior. Obviously not everybody can be a Human Being. To make this so, there must be a great many inferior people. To my mind, this is the function of white men in the world. Therefore we must survive, because without us the world would not make sense.

"But to survive if the white men drive away the buffalo will not be easy. Maybe we should try this farming. Other red men have done so. When I was a boy a people called Mandan farmed along the Big Muddy River. It is true that the Lakota were always attacking their villages and killed a lot of them. And then the Mandan caught smallpox from visiting white traders and died every one. There are no more Mandan." Old Lodge Skins raised his eyebrows. "Perhaps they were not a great people."

"I never heard of farmers who were," said Hump. He then asked me: "I suppose you have a lot of powder and lead in your wagons?"

I didn't answer, not wanting to get into that. Which was all right, for I was getting ready to make a speech myself. I ranked pretty high in these quarters, not because I was important enough to lead a wagon train—the Cheyenne didn't care about that, nor had they asked me how I spent the time since we had last seen one another— no, I was influential here because though I had apparently been killed on the Solomon's Fork, I had returned.

Here's what I was thinking: Old Lodge Skins had spent more than seventy years on the prairies and what did he have to show for it? Indians loved their land, but the peculiarity was that the most miserable cabin of a white man had a relation to the earth that no nomadic redskin could claim. One way of looking at it was that in any true connection, each thing being joined makes a mark on the other: a tree, say, is fastened to the earth, and vice versa. In Denver they was erecting buildings now with foundations: not only on the ground but in it; so that if one day the whites left that place again, it would still bear their brand for a long time. I never heard of a natural force that would tear cellar walls from the earth.

Maybe white men was more natural than Indians! was what I had got to thinking. Even prairie dogs had fixed villages. . . . Now I know that every living thing is neither more nor less of Nature than the next, but I was young then and them distinctions bothered me, what with the conflicting claims: Indians believing they was more "natural" than white men, and the latter insisting they themselves was more "human."

Whatever the judgment on that, I knowed right then that the Cheyenne way was finished as a mode of life. I saw this not in the present camp, but back in Denver; for truths are sometimes detected first in a place remote from the one to which they apply. Think of how if you was standing in China when gunpowder had been invented, you could have known that thousands of mile away stone castles and armor was finished.

So what I said in that speech of mine had practicality as its point of view. I stood up in Hump's tepee. I wore Burns Red's best red blanket. We had exchanged gifts, and he in his Indian way give me his finest possession.

"Brothers," I says, "when I sit among you, I think of the beautiful Powder River country where we did so many happy things when I was a boy. Do you recall the time Little Hawk was sleeping in his tepee and suddenly was awakened by the smell of beaver-gland perfume and raised the lodge cover and saw a Crow stealing his horse and killed him? And when Two Babies returned from his lone war trail against the Ute, after staying away a whole year, his belt full of scalps and singing the song an eagle had taught him as he lay wounded in a dry wash.

"Do you remember how lovely Cloud Peak looks with its cap of white and shoulders of purple and blue? And think of the clear, cold water of the Crazy Woman's Creek, which runs fresh all summer from the melting snows of the mountains. The forests full of lodgepoles and firewood, the elk with his great antlers, the bear in his coat of fur. . . .

"I think it is better up on the Powder River than it is here in this place.

"I know nothing of this treaty, but I do know that more and more white men will come through this place where we are now camped, because it is as the bird flies from a white village called Denver to a big white place called Missouri. I have been to both of these places and I know that neither will go away but will rather grow larger. It is my opinion that as they do, they and the land between will be less and less pretty to the eyes of a Human Being."

I took a breath; it ain't easy to get supernatural when you are out of practice. "I had a dream," I says, "after the Battle of the Long Knives. I flew above all this country and saw below me white men building square houses, but to the north, along the Powder River, I saw the great nation of Human Beings living happily, fighting the Crow and Mountain Snakes, killing buffalo and elk, and stealing horses."

Old Lodge Skins spoke: "I believe that I have heard wisdom," he said. "We had intended to talk of this treaty in support of our southern brothers. Black Kettle and White Antelope will go there, and they are great chiefs. I understand that the Arapaho, Kiowa, and Snake People will also talk. It is a very pretty sight to see all the tribes at a treaty conference with their countless ponies and in their best clothes. The Father of the whites gives presents to everybody. Just because you go to a treaty council, that does not mean you have to touch the pen.

"The Father wants to buy from the Human Beings and others the land where the yellow dust lies. Bent will be there and he is a good man who has married a woman of the Human Beings. I was willing to go and talk about farming because Black Kettle and White Antelope, who are wise men, have said the Human Beings must think about settling down.

"But dreams do not speak two ways, and there must be some reason why Little Big Man has been returned to us to tell of his vision."

I hadn't give him a new idea. Indians wasn't necessarily fools about what they should or shouldn't do. They sometimes just had reasons that a white would find difficult to understand. Old Lodge Skins was going to the council mainly to get another silver medal and to see the entertainments put on when all the tribes got together and showed off their prowess at riding and their best clothes so as to impress the Government representative. He might even have went so far as to sign the treaty without any intention of taking up farming as a result.

Now he had decided on my suggestion to forget about the whole thing and return to the north country. But I'll tell you something: he never did that because of my "dream"; he did it because he knowed damn well I was white and knew what I talked about as to the situation in Kansas and Colorado.

So did they all, and if you'll look again at the myth they had built around Little Big Man, you'll see what I mean. It hadn't aught to do with me personally, and insofar as I was to be identified with it, I had to live up to it rather than vice versa. If I did something that would not jibe with the legend, that meant I was not Little Big Man.

By this means Indians kept their concepts straight and their heroes untarnished, and did not have to lie. I guess it wouldn't work, though, for somebody who understood the principle of such things as money and the wheel.

After the talk in Hump's lodge, my other foster-brother Little Horse, dressed like a Cheyenne woman, come in and entertained us with very graceful singing and dancing. It did my heart good to see he made such a success of being a *heemaneh*.

I stayed the night in Old Lodge Skins's tepee. Next morning I met another old friend. I was coming back from a wash in the little creek when I saw an Indian who seemed to be either blind or deliberately walking through sagebushes and cactus on his route from one point to another. I decided after observation that it was the latter, for only by intent could he have found such a rugged course for himself. Eventually he reached the creek, where he proceeded to wash. But not with water, with earth from the bank.

I had recognized him straightway. It was Younger Bear. So when he had finished his curious ablutions, I went over to him. I didn't know whether he still considered himself my enemy or not. It seemed so long ago that I never even thought of it.

At my greeting he turned, not unfriendly, but instead of saying the Cheyenne hello, he says goodbye. Then, the way a person who has just took a bath will sit upon the bank to dry, he goes into the creek and sets down in the water. I guess it made sense, seeing how he had just washed with dirt. I realized he was doing everything backwards, and understood then what he had become.

Later I had this confirmed by Little Horse, who put aside his beadwork and left the crowd of women he hung out with ordinarily to chew the fat a spell with me.

"That is true," he says. "Younger Bear became a Contrary last year. He bought the Thunder Bow from White Contrary."

I have to explain. You know the ordinary Cheyenne is a warrior the peer of which is hard to find. But a Contrary carries it even farther. He is so much of a warrior that all of life apart from fighting, he does backwards. He don't walk on the trails, but rather through the bushes. He washes with earth and dries off in the water. If you ask him one thing, he does the opposite. He sleeps on the bare ground, preferably an uncomfortable bit of terrain and never on a bed. He cannot marry. He lives off by himself some distance from camp; and when he fights, he fights alone, not with the main body of Cheyenne. He carries the Thunder Bow into battle, which has a lancehead afixed to one end. When it is in his right hand, he may not retreat.

Well, there is a million other rules to it, I expect, and because it is so special, you'll only find one or two Contraries around any camp.

"Then," said Little Horse, "you remember Coyote. He was killed by the Pawnee. The Ute killed Red Dog. . . ." He went on with the news, which was fairly bloody. Then he said, looking somewhat arch: "I am thinking of moving into the lodge of Yellow Shield as his second wife."

I congratulated him and give him a little shaving mirror I carried on the trail, with which he was greatly pleased, and after we parted he sat for hours admiring his appearance in it.

But before that, I asked him about my old girl friend Nothing.

"That is who White Contrary married," he said. "She is big with child."

I saw her a little later, sitting before her lodge mashing up some berries. It was remarkable how that girl had changed in a couple of years. She would have been right fat even without the pregnant belly. Her nose had spread across her whole face, and I could not recall that she had had that greasy look in the old days. What had used to be shiny black hair now looked like the tail of a horse that had been rid through a thorn patch.

But the most remarkable change seemed to have taken place in her personality. When I come upon her she was bawling out a dog in as brawny a voice as I ever did hear, and then her husband come out of the tepee and she lit into him. Cheyenne women make fine wives, but sometimes they are also great scolds.

I reckon you might say the saber charge upon the Solomon's Fork saved me from having to listen to that for the rest of my life.

Well, after a bit they begun to strike that camp and prepare for the move north. Old Lodge Skins and me stood there and watched the women take down the tepees and make pony-drags of the lodge-poles and pack them full. He was wearing the sombrero, which owing to the difference in our head sizes sat a little high above his braids. Since that was really only a replacement of that plug hat of his that I had lost, I really hadn't give him anything yet, so now I felt there was nothing for it but to present him with my Colt's Dragoon pistol. On the one hand, it was little enough. On the other, that left me without a pony or a weapon of any description, without a hat, without a jacket—my own of which I give to Hump—and in return I had received a blanket, a stone pipe, a string of beads, and suchlike, with which to rejoin them unfriendly mule skinners and traverse the rest of the mileage to Denver.

"Grandfather," I says, "I cannot go with you to the Powder River."

"I have heard you," answers Old Lodge Skins, and that was all there was to it. He would never ask the reason.

Yet I couldn't leave it at that. Maybe it was myself I had to convince, for I noticed on this second day with the Cheyenne that they was already a little less unattractive to me. I was getting used to the smell of camp again. It was conceivable that in time I might have gone back to what I had been earlier.

Maybe not, but I felt the threat. The important thing was that I had been doing right well in Denver. I had got onto the idea of ambition. You can't make anything of yourself in the white world unless you grasp that concept. But there isn't even a way to express the idea in Cheyenne.

Now, Indian boys want to grow up into great warriors and some feel the call to be chiefs, but these is all *personal* goals, for a chief ain't got no power as we know it. He leads only by example. Take this move to the Powder River, Old Lodge Skins didn't order his people to go there. What he done was decide *he* would go, and Hump decided *he* would, and so on, and the other folks would follow along because they thought these men were wise—or might not if they thought they weren't. Burns Red had not yet made up his mind: he was still setting there on the site of Hump's late abode, and Hump's wives and daughters had took down the tepee right around him.

On the other hand, what I had been contemplating while leading that mule train back to Colorado was going into business for myself. I have said I had no head for commerce, but had got myself to believing you didn't need none to become a rich man in a brand-new place like Denver. Already there was a move on to make Colorado a Territory. In a few years if I made enough money I might even go for governor: I could read and write, which was more than half the current population along Cherry Creek could claim.

But how could I give an Indian like Old Lodge Skins the faintest glimmering of it?

I was helped at that moment by the appearance of Younger Bear, who was riding towards us. He sat his pony backwards, of course, facing the tail—which, however, made his backward commands to it and his movements of the bridle come out all right. He'd indicate "left," meaning "right," and since he was facing the rump, the sense was switched again so far as the pony went, and it done the correct thing.

"Why," I says, "did Younger Bear become a Contrary?"

As I relied upon the chief to do, he give the traditional reason: "Because he was afraid of the thunder and lightning."

"That's why I have to ride west with my mule wagons," I says. And, you know, there was a certain truth to the statement.

The way that treaty finally turned out, I was proud to have played a part in sending my friends out of harm. Black Kettle, White Antelope, and the other Southern Cheyenne and Arapaho who touched the pen got a reservation along the Arkansas in southeastern Colorado, a piace of no game, little water, and arid soil. A few years later, while peacefully camped on Sand Creek in that region, they was massacred by the Third Colorado Volunteer Cavalry.

CHAPTER 14 *We Get Jumped*

THE MASSACRE AT SAND CREEK took place in '64, late in the year. By then the Rebellion was finished out that way or it couldn't have happened at all, for the troops would have been otherwise occupied.

Speaking for myself, I turned into an indoor type of person after that trip to and from Missouri with the mules. I had got this idea of becoming a big-shot businessman and maybe going into politics. I had also begun to be suspicious of my so-called partners Bolt and Ramirez, who was supposed to split even with me, but how could I check on that if I was always out on the trail? To confirm this, you should have heard their protests when I says I was going to stay around the store from now on.

Well, I didn't understand much of account-keeping, so I never could prove what they had stole from me in the past, but my take increased noticeably from the time I stopped going on trips. And the next things I did was build me a house and get married!

I was about twenty at the time. The woman I married—girl, rather, she being eighteen—was a Swede, born in Sweden, come to this country a few years back with her folks and settled at Spirit Lake in Iowa, where her Ma and Pa was killed in the famous massacre carried out by an outlaw band of the Santee Sioux. That was five years before, so she was still small enough to hide in a potato cellar, which she did and survived. This girl was named Olga. At the time I married her, it would have took a larger cave to hide her: she was five nine if she stood an inch and had the weight to accompany it though not an ounce of fat. She was something larger than myself even when I wore my built-up boots.

Olga was real fair-complected, with hair so light and fine that even on a rainy day it looked like the sun was shining on her. She had come out to Denver with some folks who took her in after the trouble, in return for which they got an awful lot of work out of her: she cooked their meals, minded the children, did the cleaning, and chopped all the wood, while the woman laid around the cabin in a sour mood and the man was always trying to put his hand on Olga's bottom.

I took a fancy to her first time I ever seen that girl, not just because she was pretty, which she was, and that extra size made her twice as attractive for my money, but mainly for the reason that she was the best-natured person I ever knowed. It was just about impossible to rile that girl, and I always had a weakness for tolerant women. For example, she never had the slightest suspicion that that family had got at least a 300 per cent return on what little they done for her. After we was married, it was all I could do to keep her from going back to them every afternoon and doing their chores when she had finished with ours.

By the following year me and Olga had ourselves a kid and I got that house built I mentioned, a right nice dwelling place of all wood construction with a peaked roof and four rooms. It couldn't yet compare with the Pendrakes' residence but it was good for Denver. That baby Olga had was a boy and we named him Gustav after her Pa what was killed by the Santee, and even as an infant he looked exactly like a Swede with his corn-yellow hair and blue eyes.

My boyhood amongst the Cheyenne had give me this conviction I was shrewd, and not even that time in Missouri had altered it, for I reckon cleverness doesn't apply to love. But it does to business, and I thought I was being clever. We had not ever had a written agreement to our partnership. Bolt used to mention that every Saturday night when he figured up the week's take, subtracted the costs, and then divvied up what was left three ways, though after a while I observed that only I got a handful of cash on such occasions. Him and Ramirez preferred to let their money ride in the safe. When I commented on that, I was informed they "ploughed back their returns." Bolt was a great one for using phrases of this type to explain every peculiarity.

"Then what do you use for your everyday money?" I asked. Ramirez laughed with his strong white teeth, but Bolt said soberly: "Credit, of course. We got civilization here now, Jack, which runs not upon money as such but rather the *idea* of money. Take those

Indians that trade with us: they bring in an animal pelt and want for it something of equivalent value on the instant. It would never occur to them to set up an account with us, according to which they could draw supplies and other goods whenever they needed them, the retail price of these to be entered against their names to be defrayed by deposits of skins at a later time.

"By this means they could even out the highs and lows of their savage economy and live according to the same standard the year around, lean times and fat, paying back in periods of good hunting what they put on credit in bad."

Well, he had a lot more to say about the theory of business, and how him and Ramirez preferred to reinvest their shares in the store rather than walk about spending dollar by dollar. They had charge accounts at the barber shop and the saloon, etc., and as to most of their other needs, they took them from our own merchandise and entered a charge against themselves in the books, as opposed to my own practice of buying Olga some yardgoods, say, and putting the actual money for it in the cashbox, though I would of course take an owner's discount.

But now as to that other thing he would mention so often: that our partnership was founded on no more than a handshake. He was right proud of this, whereas to me it was a cause of some worry. I guess why he spoke of it so often was that I suggested with about the same frequency that we get legal papers drawed up.

However, by this tactic they succeeded only in raising my suspicions to the point where I had to put my foot down as I did with that sign, and we hired a lawyer and he made up the papers by which my third was certified. Or at least that's what I thought, for I studied them documents very carefully, being able to read as you know. But I reckon legality has a language all its own.

Olga was a great comfort to me, and one of the main reasons why she was is that she had never learned too much English, and I of course couldn't speak a word of Swede. Not being able to talk much to each other, we got along wonderful, and never exchanged a cross word.

That kid of ours, little Gus, he was a right cunning infant, and I took pleasure in rocking his cradle with my foot, while he burbled and goo-gooed and suchlike as tiny things do, and across the small room Olga set with her mending and would grin in that pink Swedish fashion if I looked towards her and ask if I wanted to eat, for she was like an Indian in that she expected everybody to be hungry at all times.

Then one day in the late fall of '64, Bolt and Ramirez suddenly blowed town, leaving me with all that credit of theirs to make good. For that is what our agreement done, I then discovered: give me sole legal responsibility for the business and all debts in its name, and I have already suggested to you that them fellows even put their haircuts and shaves on the company account.

Well, I had got myself into a tight spot owing to my "acumen," to use the Reverend Pendrake's term. Despite outward appearances to the contrary, the store had been failing for some time. What happened was that Bolt and Ramirez had cut prices to where the more we sold, the more we lost. I mean, the more we lost in *idea*, on account of they never actually paid out any money as I have said.

I did not hang around. Me and Olga, who I don't think ever quite understood the reason for it, and little Gus, we packed a carpet bag and caught the early stage next day, leaving house, business, and my ambitions towards respectability behind. I wasn't yet twenty-three years of age, and already I was financially ruined.

All the same, I felt a certain relief. I sure like to succeed, but you can't get away from the fact that failure gives you a great liberty. So as we bounced along the road south to Colorado City and Pueblo I was right calm of mind if not real merry like Olga. I think she believed we was on a holiday trip, for the time was about the middle of December of 1864, and the coach route turned east at the Arkansas River and if you stayed to the end of the line you'd find yourself at Fort Leavenworth in time for Christmas. I had bought tickets for the whole distance, which left me with only about enough money to buy meals and lodging at the station stops, though we was able to save a little on food at the first few because Olga brought with her a big basket full of grub.

I might have had some kind of idea to cross the Missouri at Leavenworth and go to that town where the Reverend Pendrake lived and hit him up for a loan. I say I might have. I might also have looked up that commanding officer at Leavenworth who promised to help me when a kid, and get into the Army. I didn't have no fixed scheme, that's for sure. I figured I had learned my lesson to take what come without trying to force it, and Olga and little Gus was a great comfort to me in that state of mind.

Gus was about two and we never cut his curly blond hair on account of it was so pretty, and his little eyes, blue as turquoise, took in everything there was to be noted. This was the first trip he had ever experienced and the bumpier the terrain, the better he liked it, just laughed and laughed when we was thrown around inside like beans in a gourd, for a stage ride in them days would loosen up all your teeth. He took after his Ma in every way, which was O.K. by me, for I wouldn't wish my own looks on anybody, or my personality for that matter.

What I haven't mentioned is that the Sand Creek massacre had took place two weeks earlier, when Colonel Chivington struck the Cheyenne and Arapaho camp at dawn and wiped it out, two-thirds of the kill being women and children.

Well, I wasn't at Sand Creek so don't feel I have a right to discuss it further even though what occurred there had a bearing on my future. For what happened was that in succeeding days the Cheyenne went to war along the whole frontier. But Colonel Chivington, we met him and his troops along the Arkansas downstream from Fort Lyon while he was still following up the remnants of the Sand Creek Indians.

The column drew up and a young lieutenant rode over, touched his hat to Olga who was looking from the coach window, and said to the driver up top: "The colonel's compliments to all on board. We have scoured the river downstream and can assure you it is secure to the limits of our jurisdiction."

The driver expressed relief at the news, which in turn pleased me, for at the last station all he could talk about was the possibility of running into hostiles, and while Olga wouldn't understand much of any other subject, let somebody mention Indians and she suddenly become fluent.

"You hear that?" I says, patting her hand, which might not have been as smooth as Mrs. Pendrake's, but it belonged to me.

She held little Gus to the window, telling him: "Luke, byootiful horze."

She didn't mean the lieutenant's animal, but rather a gigantic stallion at the head of the cavalry column fifty yards off. On top of this beast sat Chivington himself, who I had seen in Denver. In fact I had shook hands with him once, and mine was numb the remainder of the afternoon. God he was big, most of it going to chest though his head alone was as big as little Gus's whole body.

He seen us studying him, and sat his mount like a statue, and then he saluted with a big cleaver hand and shouted in his thundering preacher's voice: *"Oh how we have punished the devils!"*

So the troops went on west and we continued east, and I reckon it wasn't later than an hour from where we had met him that, just after fording a shallow creek and hauling up the slope beyond, me holding Gus partway through the window so he could watch the water drops still spinning off the rear wheels, I heard Olga make a whimper and turned and seen her pink face chalk up and her sky-blue eyes benighted.

Then I looked ahead, where some fifty riders had come into view on the northward bluffs: Indians, and nobody had to tell me they was Cheyenne. Little Gus saw them the next minute and begun to burble happily, clapping his small hands, and as I was giving him back to his Ma, they rode down upon us.

Well, we shortly gained the crest of the slope, moving thence onto the rolling prairie, and started to run through the clear winter's afternoon, the chill air streaming through the side curtains. I fetched out my pistol, but the range was still too great. The idiot riding guard up top, however, immediately went all to pieces and commenced to discharge his shotgun to no purpose, for the closest Indian was not within the quarter-mile, and when they finally come in near enough for the scatter-weapon, he had run out of shells.

Now the reason for a shotgun was that except by chance no man would ever hit a target with rifle or revolver from a moving stage-coach, for not only was he being flung about but so was his target. You can get some idea of the situation by throwing a dried pea at a jumping grasshopper while you are running at top speed. The only advantage was that the Indians did not find it no easier to pick off anybody in a coach. So long as we kept rolling the day was far from lost. Our animals wasn't fresh, but on the other hand that in itself meant the next station, where they would be changed, was within five-six mile.

But I hadn't reckoned on our fellow passengers. There was three, one a breezy type of drummer who had been with us since Colorado City and all along had been trying to peddle stuff to everybody else. He had a trunk strapped up top, but carried a little case on his lap and it is amazing the junk he could produce from it. Then there was a solid-built rancher of about fifty, who kept trying to get a conversation going on Chivington's victory and "whether it really had taken care of the Indian problem." Finally, at the last station a right mean-looking customer had got on without a word for nobody, and shoving the drummer out of the back right corner, sunk into it and shifted the butt of the big Colt's in his waistband so that he could take it after anybody who breathed in his direction. I tell you I wouldn't have suffered the son of a bitch to have dealt with me like that, but then he hadn't, so I never did nothing, for I wasn't related to the drummer.

Now we was under attack, though, I was grateful for the presence of this mean fellow. What with that panicky guard on top and the drummer who was unarmed and that rancher, by the name of Perch, who suggested we should stop and try to buy off the Cheyenne—for it turned out he had bought some land once from the friendly Osage and believed on that basis that every Indian had his price—in view of such companions, I took a quick liking to the other man, who I am going to call Black for the color of his big mustache, because I never did find out his name. He was real cool, just set there facing forward, never even looking back at our pursuers, in fact, but his pistol butt, shiny from use, stuck up ready when it'd be needed.

This latter appeared to be the case sooner than I had figured. We run for maybe half a mile along open prairie, keeping our distance, but then the Cheyenne ponies commenced rapidly to gain. I was facing backwards, in the front left corner of the coach, and when the leading Indian got within a hundred yards I leaned out and fired at him, for while there had been no point to wasting shell like the guard had, it was wise now that the range had shortened to let them know we was capable.

I come nowhere near that brave, but he swerved and rode to the other side of the coach. I says to Black: "You try him now, partner." But he responded in no fashion, just kept looking ahead real mean. And I thought, if we get out of this I'm going to see about you, boy, but there wasn't no time for suchlike now, so I let it go, and anyway the little drummer was jerking at my sleeve.

He says: "I got a combination gun oil and solvent right here what will take the lead fouling out'n any barrel." He pulls a little bottle from his case of wares and tells me to go ahead, take a sample cleaning with it free of charge, and if I liked it he would make me a good price on a pint.

You see what use my companions proved. I struck the bottle from his hand and the cork come out, with the contents spilling on Perch's boots, where I swear it immediately ate through the end of his toe, being pure acid I reckon, and he quick had to pull off the left one and pitch it out the window.

Well sir, what do you know but when the closest Indians come upon that boot, two of them reined in and dismounted to study it. That give me an idea, so I clumb outside, with one foot in the window, which ain't easy when a coach is running full tilt, and hailed the fellows outside. The driver didn't have no time to gab, and that guard put his shotgun on me as my head come level of the roof and I figure he would of blown my face off were it not he had spent his shells. He thought I was an Indian.

It took a while and a good bit of breath to be heard above his hysterics and the rush of the wind, but finally I got my plan across to him, and he crept back to where the baggage was strapped, opened it piece by piece, and begun flinging out the clothes and such therefrom. That drummer's trunk yielded the greatest variety: coats and suits and collars, bolts of cloth that rolled out in the wind and went sweeping back—one of them lashed across an Indian, streaming out on both sides, and he swathed the ends around him on the gallop, but then didn't have the nerve to keep on but stopped to get out his mirror. Well, the trunk had mirrors, too, but they broke in glitters as they struck the ground and so did the bottles of hair oil, but the tin dishes didn't, and when a Cheyenne would reach one, he'd halt and pick it up, but that ain't nothing to the effect created when the ladies' hats went sailing back. Them and the contents of our carpet bag which was opened next, is what ended that phase of the pursuit. When last I saw, before the coach dipped into descending ground, two Cheyenne was quarreling over Olga's ribbon-trimmed drawers, stretched from one horse to the other, and a half-dozen of them had got into the hats, which was all trimmed with furbelows and flounces.

Then a wheel come off the stage and we tore up two hundred yards of prairie before the animals could be halted, for that team was tired but panicky, and as soon as the driver unhitched them they run off, harnessed together.

The driver and me had some confab as to whether we should stand where we was or hike for it. We was located on the upland above the river, for the bottom had been too soft as this point to bear a vehicle. Across the Arkansas, very shallow in winter and thinly crusted with ice, lay a stretch of sand hills where we might be able to hold out till the failure of schedule was noted and troops come out from Fort Larned, though that might take a time for nobody got worried them days when a stage was up to a day late.

One thing sure, the Cheyenne would not be permanently distracted by them new possessions of theirs. They'd come along directly, though being we was in a shallow valley below them they would not yet have seen our accident.

Nobody was damaged in the wreck, for the coach didn't roll over, and maybe the slight shaking-up done some good to our little party, at least for Perch and the drummer, jostled them into reality so to speak. And Olga herself seemed less worried than when it had looked like we was getting away. Everybody piled out and I had had the talk with the driver, when I noticed that Black had not clumb from the coach, so I looked within, it leaning crazy, and there he was still in his corner, staring straight ahead out of that mean face, only his eyes was now filmed like a scummy pond. So I waved my hand in front of them without effect, and took the Colt's off of him and got the ammunition from his pocket and searched a little for his papers but couldn't waste much time at it and never found none.

I reckon he had died of heart failure sometime back, whether from fright or not nobody could say, and I didn't mention it to them others at that moment, for we was soon wading the Arkansas, getting our feet wet with chill water and no means of drying them, because at first we didn't dare to light a fire and then, when discovered, was too busy with other matters. It was shortly after getting into the sand hills on the south shore that we saw the Cheyenne clear the rise and ride down upon the abandoned stage, which they figured was still occupied, and circled it and whooped at it, and then they got down and pulled Black's body out, stripped him, throwed a lariat over his head and pulled him around the prairie back of a pony until he come apart. But I reckon he was beyond caring.

A good many of them was dressed in particles of female clothing: fancy hats, as I have said, and some corset covers, and the brave what finally won Olga's drawers had ripped them in two and wore each leg as a sleeve. The tin plates they had punctured with knives and run red ribbons through, tying them on their animals to clatter. Some was wound in yardgoods. Not all the hair-tonic bottles had busted, for I saw certain Indians drinking from them, and asked the drummer as to the contents. Since he couldn't sell them now, he told the truth for once: nought but colored water, and I says thank God for that.

Then they saw our trail across the river. We had thrown a line of defense along the highest sand hill, with Olga, Gus, and the drummer, who wasn't yellow but rather unarmed, down behind it. The driver had him a carbine and the guard luckily carried a pair of revolvers besides that useless shotgun. I give my pocket Remington to Perch and used the big Colt's I took off Black. The Cheyenne possessed only two-three rifles, probably in bad condition. If we organized our volleys for greatest effect, at a distance beyond arrow range, the Human Beings might take discouragement from it.

So to each of our boys I give a specific target among the leading riders as their animals crunched through the ice-rim of the stream, stepping gingerly there so as not to cut their feet, and then as they reached the free water and kicked into the gallop, we fired.

I wasn't familiar with my weapon, so shot too high and clipped the white end-plume off a brave's head-feather. But with my tiny pistol and sheer luck, Perch hit a horse's knee, likely chipping rather than breaking the bone, but it pitched its rider splashing, and in avoidance two more braves collided, and our driver splintered the bow in the hand of one and he dropped it as if hot.

This was enough to slow that flank of the charge and disaffect the general spirit, but two Indians was out for coup, so would have come on into the mouth of a cannon. Well, our driver was reloading our only long-range weapon, the guard was firing wild after his habit, and Perch had no more luck.

Twice I missed clean, by when the braves, keeping lateral of each other, one on a galloping pinto and one a black, splashing through the shallow Arkansas, was at a range of seventy yards and proceeding strong. I had my belly in the sand and my chin, too, and a few grains had got into my mouth and felt like little pimples under the tongue. The fellow on the paint commenced to howl his victory song, and I of course understood it and felt right strange, knowing he was in the Cheyenne frenzy and wouldn't be stopped short of being blasted out of life.

Forty yards, and my target had now cleared the water and was quirting his animal up our sand slope. I then missed with my last round, but the driver had got his carbine loaded now and with it hit the Cheyenne dead in the midsection, a fine, difficult shot even so close, and over the pony's tail he went in a flutter of the flounces on the lady's hat he wore but which I had not marked till then, tumbling almost back to the river, losing the hat, losing his song, and never got up though he was still alive at twilight when it had got so quiet we could hear his gasping breath.

I don't recall what become of the other: turned back, maybe, his medicine gone bad. There was two more charges before twilight and in these the whole bunch participated. There are more pleasant experiences than lying on cold sand with fifty screaming Cheyenne heading towards you. But we turned them back, wounding a few in the process, though the second time before retiring they got Perch in the shoulder with an arrow.

As the sun fell the Indians lined the other bank, no longer yelling taunts or waving spears; they was bored with that aspect of the quarrel so far as that day went. We could expect a resumption by first light, next morning. Meanwhile they stared quietly across, and then some started fires as the light waned, for it was right cold and getting more so. Then they all wrapped themselves in blankets and ate pemmican from their rawhide parfleches.

There we sat as darkness worked in and the wind rose, and it grew too cold to snow. Perch had got his shoulder wound and his foot was froze on account of having to discard one boot and then wade the river. I reckoned he'd lose that hoof, but at the moment he refused crude surgery, claiming the pain was equalized to a standoff by that from his shoulder. He was a tougher old bird than I had took him for.

The driver had brung along a big canteen, so we had sufficient water at least for the night. But no grub. Nor could we make a fire with nought to burn in them barren hills of sand. However, everybody wore their heavy winter clothes, and the hollow behind our ridge was protection against the wind and so we all went down into it after the dark become impenetrable, taking turns as single sentry up top.

I have mentioned that Olga calmed down soon as the wheel come off the stage and our situation turned critical. She continued in that wise, and bandaged Perch's shoulder with strips off her petticoat and tried to chafe the blood back into his frozen foot. And that guard, skinny, long-nosed, nervous fellow who fired wild and in between the charges he jerked and sniffed and scratched his body like he was lousy, well, when he come into the hollow Olga went and wiped his forehead which despite the cold was welling sweat, and then he says God bless you, missus, and goes to sleep directly like a child.

I mean to say she was a good woman and a useful one. And little Gus, when the guns popped the first time, delighting him marvelous, he wanted to fire one himself and towards that end crawled up the embankment but Olga caught him. Then he lost interest in the conflict and played by himself in the hollow, making cunning little scratches in the sand. I was right proud of them two and also concerned for them, and decided if I was to save their lives I must take a chance.

I aimed to go for Larned, a trip of maybe forty mile, but within the next ten of it there was a stage station where, unless the Cheyenne had wiped it out, I could get me a horse. I had ought to be back with the Army by nightfall the following day. Our people could hold out that long, for sure.

The others agreed with this, though that plucky little drummer wanted to go instead, for he claimed to be useless as a fighter, and the driver wanted the guard to go, on the same ground, but I knew I had the best experience for it and held out.

I shook hands all around and then kissed Olga. Little Gus was sleeping in her arms, and I didn't want to wake him up, so just pressed my lips to his chubby cheek, then pulled the wool cap closer around it though he felt warm as a glowing coal in the chill night, sturdy lad that he was.

"You'll be all right, my girl," I says to Olga.

"Ay vait here," says she, patting the sand, and I believed her for she was right substantial, so it was in nothing like a hopeless mood that I give my weapons to the drummer and set forth through the utter dark, wading to the north shore down about a mile, then pulling on my boots and hiking it to the stage station. Where all was well, except that coming in the middle of the night like that I nearly got myself shot. There was only three fellows there, not enough to take back and drive off fifty Cheyenne and anyway one was dead drunk and the others so yellow when they heard hostiles was near, they run into a dugout in the ground and pulled sod over themselves, but I obtained a horse, nearly killed it riding to the fort, presented my story to the commanding officer, he mounted a column without too much delay, I took a fresh animal, and back we rode. Made good time, too, for the Army.

It was an hour before sunset when we topped a swell of ground that, with borrowed field glasses, give me a view on our abandoned stagecoach. The Cheyenne was gone from around it. Nor could I see anyone across on the sand hills, but they would be lying low over there, for at our distance we could not have been distinguished by them from more Indians.

That's what I kept telling myself, anyway, as we trotted nearer, and then I broke for the far shore, lashing the tired cavalry mount through the soft bottomland that had thawed in the day's sun, and into the water, and as he floundered with exhaustion gaining the opposite bank, I leaped from him and run, hallooing, up the bluff.

The first I come upon was the drummer. A procession of ants had already reached his eyes though he couldn't have been dead above a few hours. Three arrows was in him, and his head naked and raw. Nearby lay the driver in a similar situation, his right hand also gone; for he was a good shot, and the Cheyenne had so acknowledged that fact.

The guard was badly sliced, but Perch not at all, he with the bandaged shoulder and frozen foot being spoiled, so to speak, for trophy-taking, and bald besides.

They had somehow been overrun. The driver might have got rubbed out, and then the rest of them went to pieces. I don't know. I was fair numb as I descended into the hollow, but no Olga and no little Gus did I find there. Nor any place else in that region. The Cheyenne had carried off my family.

CHAPTER 15 *Union Pacific*

I AIN'T GOING into the details of the hopeless trailing we did next day, for after their fashion the Cheyenne broke into many little elements and there was no way of knowing which included Olga and Gus. It was just as well, for had we got close with the troops, them Indians would likely have killed my wife and child out of pure spite.

As it stood, they might offer them for ransom sometime later on. If the Cheyenne hadn't killed them at the Arkansas, they weren't about to do it after they had gone to the trouble of kidnaping. I was fairly sure of that, though you can't count on a savage to have his practical interest constantly in mind. If they got beat in some encounter with the whites, or if some brave got drunk— Well, there wasn't any future in speculations of that type, which left me with nothing to do.

At the time, I only thought: Them bastards have my wife and kid. I reckon I might even have held a grudge against Old Lodge Skins, were he not up on the Powder River.

Of course, now I realize that him and his band would have been my best means of tracing the location of my family and buying them back. Provided I could have found that chief without being killed while looking for him—you couldn't telegraph an Indian or write him a letter. Well, the point is I never tried. I went on back to Fort Larned with the troops and hired on as a scout for a while, but there wasn't any more trouble along the Arkansas. The attack on our stage had been an isolated circumstance. The real action took place up along the Platte, where the Cheyenne had smoked the pipe of war with the Sioux and Arapaho, and together in a force of a thousand warriors raided the town of Julesburg in early January, plundering the stores there. For a month they terrorized the South

Platte, destroying ranches and stage stations, ripping the telegraph lines, and capturing wagon trains. Then in February they hit Julesburg again, and having sacked it once more, burned it to the ground.

In the spring the hostiles moved north into the Black Hills, and then on to the Powder. The Army went up there in summer and got more or less whipped in a series of engagements and then was caught in an early-autumn storm that killed most of their animals and come back, ragged and barefoot, making it only because Frank North and his Pawnee Scouts found them and led them in. The following year the Sioux and Cheyenne run Colonel Carrington out of the north country and made the Army vacate the forts he had built to protect the route to the gold mines of Montana.

I am working my stomach up to admitting here that instead of looking seriously for Olga and little Gus, I become a drunk. That's a hard confession to make about yourself, and I have never done it before, but it is true. I lost my guts. I had got whipped at everything so far, and a habit of that kind can mark a man. When we patrolled the Arkansas the next few months and never found no hostiles, I was relieved, for I had got to thinking my family would be safer if the Indians they was with kept eluding or beating the Army. Maybe when things settled down, I could get me some negotiable items, blankets, beads, and such, wander among the tribes as a trader, and find Olga in that fashion.

Meanwhile I was drinking, and the more I drank, the less I saw about Indians in general and the Cheyenne in particular that I approved of. I won't go into that, which was an elaboration of the feelings I had commenced to get in Denver. I'll just say that now it no longer seemed stupid for me to hear somebody say what we ought to do was exterminate every one of them. For all I know, I may even have been the fellow who shouted that sentiment at the top of his voice, for I always heard it after I had got towards the bottom of the jug, and sometimes I'd be sitting all by myself along the stockade wall.

I had almost rather do it over again than to recount my ensuing wanders during the summer of '65, for when I wasn't drunk I was suffering the aftereffects, which is worse. I wended eastwards, and Kansas was building up now with the War over, and there was ranches and even towns where it was buffalo range before, and one wagon train had its nose at the arse of the next, and wherever you'll find white men, you'll find whiskey.

Now I didn't have no money to use in a saloon, and I wasn't in no condition to render service around a camp, like hunting, say, for I hadn't a gun and couldn't have steadied my hand if I had. I might have got me a drink or two out of sheer hospitality, but could hardly have consumed the volume of liquor I nowadays needed without some form of recompense to them who poured it.

So that accounts for how and why I become a buffoon. I mean, I would come into a wagon train at their evening stop, or up to a ranch house, or into a saloon if in town, and say: "How'd you fellers like some entertainment? You buy, and I'll provide."

There was a lot of curiosity in them days, and somebody'd always agree to the deal and set 'em up, and I would pack in enough rotgut to stop the tremor that got to running through my frame whenever I was empty, and then make a public spectacle of myself. I'd sing and dance, getting my talent from the drink, for I had no natural gift in those directions, being born hoarse and then the firewater roughed up my palate further, and I reckon it must have sounded like a raven announcing to the rest of his pack that he had just spotted some juicy carrion a-rotting on the prairie.

One of the songs I croaked out I had learned down in Santa Fe, which concerned a little mule, and I can dimly recall singing it once in a saloon in Omaha, Nebraska, and some of the boys there was mule skinners and they makes up from some belts and junk a mock pack saddle and puts it on my back and I trotted around on all fours on the floor while they booted my rump, and a specially mean type of soul fetched forth his long-lashed whip and I believe was ready to take skin from my hindquarters with it when another fellow stepped up to him and said: "I'll take that off'n you."

"You will like hell," says the other.

I had collapsed on the floor at the moment and was watching them through my bloodshot eyes: I never really cared whether I was to be flogged or not. I couldn't even recall at that point as to how I had reached Omaha, or why. I say this because if anybody had ever asked for a good beating, I did.

"All right then, you blue-arsed, buffalo-balled, piss-drinking skunk, then I'll knock your f——— teeth out," says my savior, and proceeded to do just that, with a mighty blow that swung from southeast to southwest, catching the whip-man where his big mouth hung, and his front choppers spewed out like a handful of corn amid a torrent of blood.

His friends carried him out directly, and the rest of the crowd was whistling and yelling: "Goddam, you *are* the hairy one, a real two-tit wonder," etc. None of this meant nothing to me. Then the victor in that little scene leans over, uncinches the pack saddle from my belly, picks me up like a child, throws me over his shoulder as if I was a folded serape, and hikes on out of there.

The next thing I knowed is that I had been dropped into a horse trough outside, and that every time I tried to come up, a big hand pushed my head back into the water. So I figured, O.K. then I'll drown if that's what you want, for I didn't have no will of my own any more. But when I was all set to draw a lungful of brackish water, I was suddenly pulled out again by my tormentor, clouted in the back two or three times, put up onto his shoulder again, hauled up a narrow stair, into a room, and throwed onto a brass bed.

Then I got my first good look at this stranger, for he took off his hat and his long red hair fell out of where it had been poked into the crown. Only it wasn't a man but a woman. And she come then and set beside me on the bed.

And says: "I don't know why I done this, little feller, but I go for you real strong. No sooner than I seed you crawling the floor, it come over me. I'm helpless for you, honey, worthless polecat that you are, and I a-goin' to love you. You're my own little man," and so on.

I says: "Hold on there, Caroline. Don't you recognize your brother Jack?" I had to say it several times, my voice being weak, before it took effect on her, for as she said she was real heavy for this mistaken idea of hern.

But at last her mouth fell open and she almost lost the plug of baccy she was chawing, and then said: "Oh my God." Then: "You son of a bitch!" And then a few more choice oaths, for few could curse like my sister.

And finally she starts to cry and kisses and hugs me like kin, and fetches some water in a tin basin and washes off my filthy face and recognizes me for sure, and goes through it all again.

Well, I was glad to see old Caroline and even gladder to have someone care for me a bit, but after them months of dissipation and shame I didn't have much energy and my mind was weak, so I soon fell to sleep.

Next day I felt real horrible and required whiskey merely to sustain the breath of life itself, but Caroline wouldn't allow me any, soaked me instead for hours in a tin tub they had in that house. All day and the next she soaked me, pouring in fresh kettles of boiling water whenever the tub got bearable to my hide, and when I finally emerged from this treatment I might have had the poison sweated from me but it took along with it the rest of my juice as well, and I had the rubber legs of a foal.

Caroline hadn't changed much. Her features had coarsened up some, and she chewed tobacco always, which did not benefit her teeth; and though she washed regular as most, the smell of mule was right noticeable in her presence, for that was what she did for a living: drove a team, hauling out of Omaha for the Union Pacific Railroad, then a-building along the River Platte.

While I was still weak she related the story of her intervening experiences between the time she left me in Old Lodge Skins's tepee and the present date. These I gather was varied and characterized by violent ups and downs, for I think you have the correct idea by now that Caroline was romantic as they come and thus ever being disappointed.

She had gone on farther west, been to San Francisco itself. That was where she had tried to hire on as seaman on a ship, but the crew thereof, they was quicker than the Cheyenne to discover her gender, and pitched her into the bay. I don't know why Caroline could never get it through her thick head that the way to attract men was not to do what they did, but rather—no, I do know: she thought she was ugly, that's why. Only she wasn't. She wasn't beautiful by a long shot, but she was nowhere near hideous, just had a strong cast of feature.

Well, she had got a better idea when the Civil War started and went East for that and took up nursing the wounded, at which I believe she must have been right good with her qualities of muscle and stamina added to a real feminine nature underneath. She sure liked men, that Caroline, no mistake about that; in fact, her troubles could be traced to the fervor of that taste. In time she fell in love with a man she met in a military hospital near Washington, D.C., which shows you how far east she ranged. He was not a casualty but rather a male nurse who worked alongside her, a real cultivated person who went so far as to write poetry in his spare time. According to Caroline, he was shy but she felt sure he returned her feeling, for he give her some of his writings and it was full of burning passion and though he never come right out and admitted it to her face, she knowed she was the one he meant, and together they bathed and bandaged them poor devils, and the very suffering around them cemented their love for one another, etc.

I see no need to go through the whole story, for the point is that when this fellow got to where he saw Caroline was in great sympathy with him, he confessed he was in love with a curly-headed little drummer boy what had got his rosy shoulder barked by a Minie ball. It had never occurred to that sister of mine to question why some big healthy man would be volunteering to carry bedpans when he could have been out fighting. I remember this individual's name, but I ain't going to mention it, for he got quite a reputation in later times for his robustious verse, some fellow told me once, and I wouldn't want to sully no one's pleasure in it, in case it's still being read at this late date.

So much for Caroline, who had then brought her broken heart out West again and took up mule-skinning. She wasn't embarrassed at all about mistaking me at first for a potential lover, having been hardened by her various troubles in that area. I reckon she figured now that the only way she would ever get a man was to carry him off as she did me.

I asked if she had ever in her travels run across any of the rest of our family.

"No, I never," she says, throwing her boot across her knee and spitting a thin stream of tobacco juice into a spittoon the landlady furnished her with, "though I heerd from a soldier in the hospital that he served with a Bill Crabb who died a hero at Fredericksburg, and I reckon that was our little brother, God rest his soul."

Nothing to my mind was less likely than that Bill had straightened out from what I saw him as in '58, but I didn't mention that to her. Also, at present I was hardly in a position to cast aspersions on another man.

And the next thing Caroline says was: "Tell me about yourself, Jack, and how it was you went bad."

That was putting it on the line. So I related my story, and I'll say this for Caroline, she had never paid much attention to me as a little kid and even deserted me there among the Indians, but she realized after a while now that I done a few things worthy of her attention and give it freely. And it is strange that though she made a mess of her own affairs, it was her attitude towards my calamity that pulled me out of that hopelessness I had fell into.

For when I told her about the capture of Olga and little Gus, she says, quite merciless: "You best forget about them, Jack. They have shorely been kilt long since."

"Don't talk like that, Caroline."

"I was just saying what it appears you already decided for yourself, Jack old boy," my sister states, making another use of the spittoon. "You should know how Indins act, if you lived with them as long as you claim to. And then I take it you ain't forgot the way they butchered Pa and misused me and our Ma. I for one have never got over that experience. You was probably too young at the time to recall how attractive I used to be as a young gal afore my maidenhood was brutally stole by them dirty beasts. I still have nightmares upon the subject."

I reckon Caroline believed this, for it give an excuse for her failures at love; just as my brother Bill took from his own version a motive for becoming what I had seen him. Lest you think I am being too hard on my family, I might say that they wasn't the only ones who found Indians right useful in them days for explaining every type of flop.

And there was I, in the same situation. My wife and child had indeed been captured by the savages, and it was certainly possible they had been killed. But it never give me no excuse to throw over my manhood, and no matter how many misadventures you suffer, you ain't a genuine and absolute failure until that occurs.

But I had lost my old free ways during them years of respectability in Denver, and it was the wildness of that experience on the Arkansas which had unmanned me.

"Oh, they mightn't have *kilt* your woman," Caroline goes on. "They maybe just—"

Funny how members of your own family, even when you haven't been specially close to them, can drive the knife home with perfect accuracy. In this case, though, it was more complicated: if you recall, I always figured Caroline had been disappointed that the Indians had not offered her violence. Sight unseen, she was jealous of Olga on several counts: for being married, for having had a kid, for likely being raped; these in addition to the natural disapproval felt by a sister for the woman who has got her brother.

All of which produced a change in Caroline's attitude. She

stopped the reclamation procedure that had begun to straighten me out—baths, solid food, and so on—and brought in a jug of whiskey and encouraged me to drown my sorrows in it.

She found me more satisfying as a derelict, I expect. My sister really had the same type of taste as them men who was entertained by the spectacle of my degradation. The Cheyenne would have been depressed to see a fellow tribesman gone to rot; they would have believed it reflected discredit upon all Human Beings. On the contrary, an American just loves to see another who ain't worth a damn. And my sister proved no exception.

Well, I get a grand pleasure out of disproving expectations. I reckon I would of died of drink had I not encountered my sister; and had she continued trying to reform me, it might have hastened the process. But from the time she took an active interest in assisting my ruin, with an eye I reckon to looking after me the rest of my life, fishing me out of saloons, beating up my tormentors, etc.— from that moment on, I never took another drink. At least not during that phase of my career.

I don't mean I got up the next minute and become a normal person. It took a couple weeks before I could walk with any kind of vigor, and a month or so before I could resume a man's work, for I ain't kidding when I say I had hit bottom. For quite a spell my hand quavered when held tightly by the other, and there was hours at a time when my vision was like looking under water. On into the fall, I still thought I'd pass out from the effect of the midday sun.

The latter comes to mind because towards the end of summer I took me a job. Same as Caroline, driving a team of mules, though she tried hard to keep me from it, going so far as to tell the contractor what hired us that I was an irrepressible alcoholic, and therefore he watched me close and I had to do twice the work of anyone else.

The only reason I had the job at all was that they needed every man they could get for the building of the U.P., which had took such a while to start up that they was in a big hurry now. It was supposed to begin in '63, but first steel wasn't laid till the summer I'm talking about, '65, and by October only ten miles had been completed. However, what happened during that winter was the effects of the War being over took hold and Government money was forthcoming, so that by the following April end-of-track lay at North Bend and by July, another eighty-ninety miles on, at Chapman.

For hard labor they used a lot of Irishmen who had emigrated to America, but there was also a number of War veterans who done this work, and they really hit a stride in '66, laying two-three miles of steel a day, with big sweaty devils pounding spikes like carpet tacks, and others meanwhile setting ties in place further on and running up new rails. And right behind them an engine, puffing and roaring. Its sparks was setting fire now and again to what was left of the prairie grass after that human herd had trampled it, and the buffalo had long since took off for other parts.

At the end-of-track the honkytonkers set up shop in tents and moved right along with the railroad, offering drink, gambling, and harlots, and there was purveyors and traders, and even preachers, and soldiers and some Indians, friendlies, who would come up and trade an item or two or sell their womenfolk or just stare, and if you never seen an Indian stare you have missed a real phenomenon, for it might go on all day. I recall seeing a Pawnee study the locomotive smokestack for hours, and after a while I couldn't forbear from asking him, in the signs, what he figured it was for.

He says: "First I thought it was a big gun for the shooting of birds, but then I saw that it scared the birds away before they could fly over it. Next I thought it was a big kettle for cooking soup, but then I saw the white men eating in another place. Fighting Bear looked at this thing and believes it is for making whiskey, because all the white men are drunk every night."

He stopped then and looked baffled, so I figured I would set him straight, but no sooner than I fixed to start in than he says: "Will you give me some tobacco?" I cut him off the end of a plug, which he took and then dug his heels into his scrubby pony and galloped off from where he had been standing three-four hours. Maybe that's what he had in mind from the beginning.

Me and Caroline kept at regular work by hiring onto the different outfits that was grading the roadbed as the U.P. proceeded westwards. Local contractors would sign up to grade a mile or two and they was always ready to hire any wagon and team they could get, for they had to work ahead of the track-laying and that was going so speedily that you was always in danger of being run down by the oncoming steel. I never got over how fast they built that railroad along where me and my family had trudged with oxen only a dozen years before. It was frightening.

Me and Caroline had started out just as drivers, working for them who owned the teams, but at Lone Tree we acquired mules and a wagon of our own. We pooled what we had made so far, and Caroline had a few shekels in an old sock that she thought of as her dowry if a chance ever came for such, but the aggregate was not near enough for our purpose, so we had to take on a partner to make up the price. This fellow's name was Frank Delight. I don't know whether he was born with that handle, but it was appropriate enough for his present trade. He run two of them portable pleasure-tents what followed the railroad to service the track workers: one was a saloon where you could drink the poorest whiskey ever made —I had stopped indulging, but could gauge the quality of his goods by taking a deep breath as I walked outside—the other was a travel-ing whorehouse. Both establishments was extremely profitable ow-ing to their convenience. You take a man who has laid steel all day, he ain't in the mood at night to look far for his drink and sport.

The way we met Frank was that Caroline had some friends among his women, who she had met washing clothes down at the river. These harlots believed it a great shame that a girl should have to work so hard driving mules and was always after my sister to join their profession, which is practiced laying down. On her side, Caro-line developed an enormous zeal to straighten out them whores, and since she didn't have no success at it, Frank didn't mind her none. In fact, she got to where he found her right amusing, and would set up the drinks just to hear her denounce him for a procurer.

When he found we could use a hand in buying our team, Frank offered his in exchange for a percentage of our earnings, mostly as a favor to Caroline, I believe, though he never passed up a chance to make an extra dollar. I had been kind of sour on partners after Bolt and Ramirez, but Frank wasn't a bad sort of fellow, and I handled the money.

So across Nebraska we proceeded during '66, slowed some by the winter, but by April '67, end-of-track lay at Paxton, which wasn't but fifty mile from the northeast corner of Colorado, where the line would drop southwards to touch Julesburg in that Territory, and then back north to cross the rest of Nebraska and into Wyo-ming.

That was when, as the weather warmed, we begun to meet the Cheyenne and the Sioux. They stole our animals at night and harried the workers by day, coming always in small parties that hit and ran, and did a deal of damage but never really slowed the progress of them steel parallels. It must have been mighty disheartening, now that I think of it, for them to come back next day and find the railroad three miles further on, and three the next and the next until the continent was cut in two. Of course they never got everybody together at once for a full-scale assault that might have made some real effect. But then, had they so done, I guess it would only have meant that the U.S. Army would have got real serious about wiping them out and so brought on all at once the ruination they was this way falling into by degrees. They had lost Colorado, and now this strange machine come roaring and smoking across Nebraska, leaving a permanent trail of metal. I believe I have said earlier that the railroad cut the continental buffalo herd in half, for them beasts would not cross a track even while no train was on it, and the Indians knowed this by now.

As for me, I had figured the hostiles would show up once we got into their region, and that was exactly why I had taken my present line of work: it looked like the most effective means by which I could make contact with the Cheyenne and trace the whereabouts of my wife and child. I had studied that out back in Omaha during my time of convalescence.

No, the idea I had was to let the Cheyenne come to me, so to speak, and therefore for two years I had drove them mules conscientiously and ate my grub at end of day and put up with Caroline, who never really got more sensible, and bedded down early in my little tent, waiting, just waiting for this time to come.

I don't know whether anybody has ever pointed out the patience you need if you live a life of violence. It ain't the action that takes the guts, but the minutes, hours, days, even months of interval between encounters. When the Indians finally did begin to hit the railroad, they seemed to avoid my immediate area of it and strike the grading parties further west or the track layers to the east. And though they run off stock, they never come near my mules, which I would tether close to my tent and then lay awake much of the night with a coiled lariat in my hand. Capture is what I intended for the brave what come close, not slaughter. I didn't want his scalp, but rather the return of Olga and Gus, and needed to be in a bargaining position. But as I say, wherever I was the Cheyenne struck elsewhere; that's what I mean about needing patience.

It had got well into the summer when I finally received my chance. End-of-track lay just beyond the old stage station at Lodgepole, and my work at present was with the graders on west of that, but I had gone down to Julesburg upon an errand and was about to start back when an engine stopped for water at the tank there and I saw it was pulling several freight cars loaded with Frank North and his Pawnee Scouts, who the Government had hired as protection against the hostiles.

"What's a-going on, Frank?" says I, for I knowed him.

And he answers: "The Cheyenne have caused some trouble down at Plum Creek and we're moving there to fight them."

"All right if I come along?"

He allowed it was a free country, so I clumb on. I was armed with a .56-caliber Ballard rifle, along with a percussion Remington .44 in my belt. There wasn't time for to go get my saddle horse, which was being newly shoed at the blacksmith's, for that engine pulled away while the tank was still gushing water. I asked North if he could mount me, and he said the Pawnee might have an extra pony but that would take a special kind of horseman.

I just laughed to myself. I hadn't told nobody thereabout of my years among the Cheyenne, who for obvious reasons weren't none too popular a tribe at this point, and in them days people was suspicious of you if you spent any length of time with hostile Indians and come back alive.

While we was larruping down the track, a Pawnee staggered over to the corner of the car where I was sitting—I don't mean he was drunk: that ride was so rough you practically had to crawl when you wanted to move—and commences to peer at me. Now the Pawnee used to fight white men along the Santa Fe trail, but they turned friendly after the traffic got too heavy to deal with, and also they was hereditary enemies of the Sioux and Cheyenne, so made common cause with the Americans sometime back. A Pawnee shaved his head on either side, leaving no hair but a high-standing scalp-lock, which you call a roach. Everybody has his own taste in Indians, and I didn't care much for the way they looked. This was natural enough considering my upbringing. You recall how I had warred against them when a young fellow among the Cheyenne.

Well, this brave studies me for a spell, then moves over to North and converses in Pawnee. He had to shout, for the train noise was awful, but I couldn't gather a word, not knowing the lingo.

Then Frank cups his hand at his mouth and says to me: "He claims he fought against you once on the Niobrara River, when you were a Cheyenne. . . . Don't laugh or you will hurt his feelings."

The warning wasn't necessary: I wasn't amused, for undoubtedly this sharp-eyed Indian was telling the truth. I remembered once that some Pawnee had raided our pony herd in broad daylight along that river, which we called the Surprise, and we Human Beings went after them. One Pawnee's horse was hit, throwing him onto the prairie, and being closest, I sought to ride him down, but he kept me off with a rapid fire of arrows until a comrade come back and he swung upon the pony's rump and yelling the Pawnee victory cry they made their escape untouched through a blizzard of our shafts and musket balls, in despite of our fast-running pursuit though we got the rest of the party and took their hair.

This man must have been one of them two which got away though what startled me was that he could recognize me these years later without paint and in American clothes. Well, I didn't say no more till we reached the Plum Creek station and left the cars. I let North think it was a joke, for I didn't want to explain, but while he and another white officer was going over the situation there, I went to that Pawnee and says, in the signs: "You had big medicine that day."

This Indian's name was Mad Bear. He says, without expression: "You were a Cheyenne then. Now you are a white man." And then give the signs for "I don't understand."

"That is a long story," I replies. "But the Cheyenne since then have stole my white wife and child, and I am going to fight them with you, and I don't want that anything bad should stand between my heart and yours." To which I adds, it being an Indian idea: "Everything changes except the earth."

"And now the earth does too," he signals, pointing to the railroad. He went on: "I believe you, but not because of what you tell me, for you look like a liar. I believe you because Pawnee Chief" (which was to say, Frank North) "says you are only a fool who drives a wagon. He asked me to protect you if we get into a fight."

Before telling what happened when we had that fight, I ought to say first what the Cheyenne done at Plum Creek, for it was quite a success for them and never done before nor since to my knowledge. They derailed a whole freight train! Somehow they pried out the spikes and bent a rail up into the air, then give it a twist so when the next engine come along, why off it tumbled and the cars followed suit. I don't know where them Indians had got so clever. Earlier there had been reports of Cheyenne braves who rode alongside trains and tried to lasso them, and this was believable, for a savage Indian wouldn't have no sense of mass or magnitude when it come to a hunk of metal that big: and he would take the fact that a white man run it to signify that a red man could as well rope it.

We stayed at Plum Creek a couple days, and the Pawnee patrolled the country roundabout, finding it altogether clear of hostiles. North and his officers had just about decided to return to the end-of-track when a force of Cheyenne appeared on the south bank, coming back, I reckon, as an Indian will, to the place of their prior victory: remember they had hit Julesburg twice.

The Pawnee howled their war cries and headed for the bridge near the old stage station, which was too small to accommodate their whole force, so a good many went into the water and forded the stream, but coming up the other shore their horses stuck in the mud, so the scouts dismounted and footed it up the bank. This movement confused the Cheyenne, who had not expected resistance where before they had it so easy, and when the Pawnee delivered a murderous fire from their Spencer repeating carbines, making a half-dozen kills, the Human Beings turned and run for it despite their advantage of number.

I rode with North across the bridge. As I have suggested he had a low opinion of me, but when the action started he didn't have time to take a mind of what I was doing and once we reached the other bank I galloped free on the borrowed Pawnee pony. It was a liberating feeling once again to have such a mount. I hadn't rode pad saddle for many a year, but once you have been trained to the Indian style of riding you don't forget it no more than you disremember to swim if dumped into the water after years away.

There we went, pounding along, us few whites and forty Pawnee, with maybe a hundred and fifty Cheyenne in full flight across a mile of prairie, with the roar of hoofs and Pawnee yells and the frequent crack of them Spencers, the Human Beings loosing a few futile arrows but mainly running in disorder.

The ground slowly ascended towards a line of hills. Now and again a Cheyenne dropped from his pony and a Pawnee sprang off to deal him the death-stroke if he still breathed, and lift his scalp. I hadn't fired yet and never intended to except in self-defense, but that Pawnee, Mad Bear, kept lateral and eyed me, his roach blown flat from the rush of wind, so at length I squeezed one off from my Ballard, purposefully aiming midway between the two nearest Cheyenne. But I had little practice at firing from a running horse up to then, on account of not having had a gun in my pony days, and by a quirk of chance cut off a flying braid from the farther man. It was entwined with blue ribbon, for I saw it on the ground as I thundered over, and indeed it looked queer there.

Now we was reaching the slopes, and higher on could see the Cheyenne women and children with their camp baggage on the pony drags. They was fleeing too, but hardly so fast as the overtake, so their warriors flowed around them and turned and rode back against us, but the Pawnee broke the charge with their rapid-firing carbines. Then the Cheyenne dismounted, give their ponies to the women and children, who abandoned the baggage and run for it behind the barrier of their menfolk walking backwards.

They managed the retreat as well as Indians could with no discipline and no strategy, and was no longer in rout though steadily losing men. Seventeen Cheyenne was killed that afternoon and countless wounded, and it seemed for an hour or so that the whole band might be rubbed out by nightfall, for as usual they owned few rifles, and the Pawnee continued between charges to pour a fire from beyond arrow range and drop them one by one.

Then we outflanked them, being they was afoot and with their fleeing village spread across the hills and into the valleys between, and despite what North could do to prevent it, his men killed a few noncombatants, for the Pawnee medicine was great that day and fed by fresh blood, and to an Indian an enemy is fair game of whatever sex or size. I saw a Cheyenne woman get shot off her horse. She was fat and for some reason looked familiar to me, and I rode alongside while the Pawnee put his knife above her ear and carved. For a second I thought it was my foster-mother Buffalo Wallow Woman —but no it wasn't, and I galloped on.

However, it did give me a start, for this fight was another thing from the trouble in which Olga and Gus was carried off. I got no satisfaction in running with the Pawnee: having been raised to hate them. I felt right uneasy about the whole business and sure didn't like shooting at Cheyenne who was defending their families. And suppose this very band was holding Olga and Gus: soon I'd find their bodies with the skulls busted in. I had been a fool to board that train at Julesburg.

Thinking in this negative fashion I continued to ride and before I knowed it had got separated from the Pawnee now charging the right of the Cheyenne line, which was ever falling back though stubbornly. I was on the left and descending the valley behind the first range of hills. Ahead of me and widely dispersed, the Cheyenne women and children was quirting their ponies, here and there pursued by Pawnee riders.

It was right dry, and clouds of dust climbed to meet those of gunsmoke, and then the wind spread the mixture as a thin fog across the country, filtering the sunlight, and the colors looked intense as they do at a certain hour of evening. I was about half a mile now from the concentrated fire, so that it popped rather than blasted or snapped to my ear.

To make these observations and to rest my frothing pony, I had pulled him up at the lip of a deep ravine. Bad place to halt during a fight, and being an Indian mount he knowed it, and strained to move on, tired as he was. And then he give a deep sigh and sunk beneath me, like I was sitting on a big bag of grain that had a small puncture out of which the grains leaked steadily. But I leaped free before he was all the way down, being horseman enough to realize he had took an arrow in his belly. Though I hadn't heard its flight nor felt its entry.

There was a Cheyenne in the ravine. I lay just back of the margin thereof, waiting for him to appear, my horse gasping out its life nearby, and not another sound. I put my hat onto the muzzle of the Ballard and stuck it just over the rim, and *thungg!* come an arrow into the brim, passing through feathers and all, and in descending almost hit me though its power was spent. Then before I could withdraw my weapon, he had seized the barrel end with a grip so mighty that had I retained hold I should have been drug into the gulch atop him. I am a small man. I let go and lost my rifle, though managed to discharge it before my hand was tore from out the trigger guard, the ball puffing up the sand on the far bank, not hurting him except for the shock of passage, from which his brown fingers jumped as though burnt. Then the stock upended and slid out of view.

Well, it was single-shot and wouldn't do him no good unless he carried a supply of .56 rimfires. So I pulled my pistol and hurled myself to the brink and had he been still up on the bank where he seized my rifle I'd of killed him straightway, but he had already slid to the bottom with the Ballard at his knees all fouled with sand and empty, and he knowed it and was out of arrows, and drawed his knife, and, standing up, began to sing of death.

I recognized this man. It was Shadow That Comes in Sight. I wish he done as much for me, for as I started down the bank, he come to meet me with unfriendly intent and that edged weapon.

CHAPTER 16 *My Indian Wife*

"HOLD ON, BROTHER," I cried in Cheyenne. "Let us talk." And then, with my attention so strenuously fixed upon him, I tripped on that steep slope I was negotiating and plunged directly towards him, my pistol firing inadvertently as my hands clenched.

He held up his knife, with his left fingers gripping the right-hand wrist, so as to give added support for the impact. Which is to say, I was about to be impaled just below the arch of my rib-cage. My accidental shot had gone into the air.

Well, I was only falling six feet, but the time consumed by any type of action is relative, and I recall hanging motionless there in space like the subject in a photograph or artist's rendering. Shadow wore two eagle feathers, aslant one from the other. There was beads of sweat upon his brown shoulders. He wore a choker of horizontal porcupine quills divided by vertical lines of blue beads; and between his left bicep and elbow cavity, a copper armlet; between his legs a dirty breechclout of red flannel. The black points of his narrow-lidded eyes was fixed on the target of my upper belly, and his legs was braced for the collision. Vermilion was the predominant color of his face paint, with an overlay of yellow bolts of lightning.

Almost at my leisure I floated down upon the point of the knife, and when I struck it and thought sort of lackadaisically that I was sure disemboweled, time speeded up again, and I was tumbling over him at great speed and still unwounded, for without willing it I had somehow altered my style of fall and took the blade in my shirt between arm and ribs. It seemed warm there from the close call, from the threat unsatisfied; had I been cut, I would have felt nothing; that is the peculiarity of knifeplay. Well, roll we did through the sand and scrub brush, and he was a powerful Indian though fifty year old. I had lost my pistol, but he kept his knife. Still I sought to talk, but his thumb was into my throat box so far as almost to break through the floor of my mouth. Being small and limber I kneed him frequent in the lower belly, but his iron ballocks sustained these blows without effect, and I missed my chops at the paralyzing neck-cord below the left ear.

Soon I was pinned between his thighs, like steel pincers from forty years of pony riding, and now I yearned for the knife to plunge and free me from that compression which had caught me on an exhale and my vision was turning black.

He lifted high the blade, a Green River butcher weapon without a guard, and I won't forget its slightest property. And then a little hole sprung beneath his chin, and blood begun to burble out of it. He swallowed twice, like to get rid of a little bone that got stuck in his throat. Only then did I hear the shot. His shoulder jerked as though pushed from behind: another shot. He dropped the knife and leaned towards me, the fluid running from his neck, yet his eyes was still open. Then I pushed him in the chest and back he went all the way, bending like rubber at the waist, for his legs was yet locked about my ribs and killing me, and locking my hands together into a kind of sledge, I smote him at the navel: *spang!* his thigh-grip loosened like a toy when you hit its spring.

Then down leaped that Pawnee Mad Bear from the bank above and putting the muzzle of his Spencer an inch from Shadow's fore-head, he gave him a third shot and a middle eye, and shortly ripped away his hair, which parted with a *whap.* He smirked at me, tore away Shadow's breechclout and wiped the scalp upon the dead man's private parts, saying something victorious in Pawnee.

He had saved my life, sure enough, but I reckon I knew how Younger Bear had felt when I did the same for him them many years before: I wasn't grateful. Shadow That Comes in Sight had took me on my first raid, having ever been like an older brother or uncle. I was right fond of him. What caught me in the heart now was not that he had been killed, for we all will be sometime. Nor that it had been violent, for as a Human Being he would not have died another way. Nor even that in an involved fashion I had been the instrument of his loss. No, the sadness of it was that Shadow had never known who I was. He had fought me as an enemy. Well, that's why I was there, wasn't I, to fight the Cheyenne?

Goddam but he had powerful legs. I still could barely breathe. I got up and watched Mad Bear climb the bank and shortly reappear at its brink on his pony, smugly shake his rifle, and trot away. He hadn't even commented on the loss of my horse, which had been borrowed from him.

I had not had time to wonder how Shadow happened to be down in this draw in the first place, but now, moving slow for I was mighty sore, as I scratched out a shallow grave for him with his own knife and covered him over, I considered there might be other Human Beings somewhere below among the brush and if they wanted to shoot me in the back, they was welcome to do so. I'd rather that than meet them face to face and see my old friends and brothers.

But I had just got the tip of his long nose covered over with sand when I heard a rustling in the bushes down a ways, and it is queer how my instincts for self-preservation arose without my conscious will, and I seized my fallen revolver and blowed and worked the action clean and replaced all the caps. This in an instant, and then snaked along the bottom of the draw. The brush was trembling, but whatever it could be was staying within. I lurked a moment, then parted the twigs and crept through pistol first, with my face just behind the hammer. I was looking into a clearing just big enough for one person, and that person lay upon her back. She was an Indian woman with her skirt pulled up and her bare legs stretched apart and between them she was giving birth.

The tiny brown head was already emerged, eyes closed and looking a mite peevish at its entry into reality, and now the little shoulders squeezed through. There was never a sound except where that one straining knee was scraping the brush, which I had heard. She watched what went on and bit from time to time into a wad of her buckskin collar; maybe her eyes winced out a drop of moisture, but there was no more commotion than that. She had been there all the while, and that was the occasion for Shadow's presence and why he fought so hard.

Cheyenne women at such a time always go off by themselves into the brush, and when it is done, come out with the infant and return to work as usual. The only difference here was that she went into labor in the middle of a battle. But the little fellow had to come when he was ready.

I was embarrassed for a variety of reasons, giving birth being an occasion of unusual modesty for a Cheyenne, so much so that I reckon this woman would take Shadow's death less heavily than my observation of her. Yet I was fascinated, for within half a mile from the soles of my upturned feet the firing had not abated, nor the yells concerning the great day for the Pawnee. . . . Out of her come the little cleft behind of the infant, tightly pinched together. She strained some more, and then the rest of him emerged smooth as a fish onto the blue blanket spread beneath, and she set up, bit off the cord, tied the baby's end against his tiny belly, and slapped him into wakefulness, to which he come like a real Cheyenne: with a little start but almost no noise. I expected he already knowed a cry would bring the enemy down on his tribe, so he forbore from loose utterance, and always would. That was also the first and last slap he would ever get from his own kind, while moving into a life that otherwise would know every type of mayhem.

I backed on out of there and went down to the sand heap under which lay Shadow. In a minute she come out of the brush, walking strong and vigorous and matter-of-fact, the child's head a-peeping from the blanket at her bosom. Eying me, she then went for her belted knife and I reckon might have been a tough customer with it in spite of her newborn. Only I put my revolver forward, which would seem brutal did you not understand by now that a Cheyenne, man or woman, has got a terrible thick skull when it comes to hearing white men.

"Now," I says, "I am going to shoot you and your child if you don't listen. Shadow That Comes in Sight was killed by the Pawnee. That was the shot you heard, and then you heard him ride away. If you are related to Shadow then maybe you have heard of Little Big Man, which is what I was called when I lived with Old Lodge Skins's band. I was a friend of the Cheyenne until they stole my wife and son. That is why I am here now. I am going to take you along with me and trade you for them."

She studies me through them dark eyes and says: "All right."

"I don't like to do this," I says, "with your newborn and all, but I have no choice."

"All right," she answers and sets down, opens her dress under the arm, and puts the infant to feed.

"Look," says I, "we had better get to open ground. A Pawnee might come upon us here unawares and kill you before I could explain."

"He must eat first," she tells me quietly and sets solid.

So I kept my watch upon the rim of the draw during the ensuing conversation. I didn't know this woman—girl, rather, too young at the time I lived among them to take my notice, if she had been there. I figured her for Shadow's wife, which accounted for his guarding, but it turned out she was rather one of them young daughters I have mentioned him training, way back, to control her giggle at his funny stories.

"Your husband been rubbed out?"

"By white men," she says without apparent passion. She was a winsome Indian, when I noticed, having a plump face like a berry and large eyes in a slightly Chinee slant and with a sheen across the underlying tear-sacs; fine though short brow beneath the vermilion parting of her hair. Her shining braids was intertwined with otter-skin, and she wore bright beads, with brass circles in her earlobes.

I started to ask Where, instead of Who, for she probably wouldn't have told his name, when I heard the pounding of at least three riders on the plain above: unshoed horses, signifying Indians but whether Pawnee or Cheyenne I couldn't say, and so far as that went, I disliked the approach of either in equal measure. Not speaking Pawnee, I might not get time to use the signs afore they had shot down this woman. If it was Cheyenne, well, that is obvious.

I mention this because you might question what I did next: grabbed that girl and hastened her back into the brush, the infant still at her pap, and crouched there with her, holding her still though she made no resistance.

The Pawnee arrived, for so they were as I could tell from their talk, and apparently inspected the ravine bottom from above but did not come down. Shortly they rode off, after I believe, from the sound, one had voided his water right from the saddle down the bank.

Yet me and the girl stayed where we was for some time, and it came to me that sitting on her heels she leaned her firm body back against me, taking support from it, and unwittingly in clutching her I had got through the side-lacings of the nursing dress and that unoccupied left breast of hers, weighty with milk, lay against my hand. Now I gently cupped it, I don't know why, for I surely wasn't lustful in that circumstance. But me and her and the little fellow, who had now went to sleep with his tiny mouth still quavering upon the protruded nipple, we was a kind of family. I had protected them like a father should, and like I had failed to with Olga and little Gus.

She leaned her head back and placed her warm cheek against my forehead. She smelled of suck, that sweet-sourish fragrance, and then of all them Cheyenne things I knowed of old: fire, earth, grease, blood, sweat, and utter savagery.

She says: "Now I believe you. You are Little Big Man, and I will be your wife now to replace the one you lost, and this is your son." She puts him into my arms, and he wakes briefly up and I'll swear, small as he was, grins at me with them beady black eyes. I felt right queer.

She says: "I think we had better be going. They will probably collect at Spring Creek."

"Who?"

"Our people," she answers as if that went without saying. "The Pawnee had great medicine today, but next time we will beat them and cut off their peckers, and their women will sleep alone and weep all night."

I was still holding the baby.

"You have a beautiful son," she says, looking at both of us in admiration, then takes him back. "Do you have any baggage for me to carry?"

I was still sort of stunned and didn't reply, so she fixes the baby inside her bosom, cinches her belt so as to secure his legs, then crawls up the bank to where my dead horse was laying, takes off the blanket from it and the pad saddle and my coat which I had took off and tied behind, and slides back down. She looked disappointed that that was all she had to tote.

"The wolves will eat my father tonight," she says. "We should put him on a burial scaffold, but there is no timber here and it is too far to carry him to where there are trees."

Then she steps back so I can take the lead as a man should. I guess it wasn't until that moment that I gathered her intent.

"We can't go back to the tribe," I says.

"Do you think the white men will let you have a Human Being wife?" she asks. She had a point there, though exaggerated. It wouldn't be a crime, but it would sure seem odd to Frank North were I to come back from that fight with a family I had suddenly acquired from the enemy. I could of course present this woman and child as legitimate captives, only then they'd be let in for considerable abuse from the Pawnee and later be turned over to the Army at some fort, to be held for exchange with whites taken by the Cheyenne. This was what I had had in mind earlier on, with an idea to control the trade and reclaim Olga and Gus. But right now, at a fairly outlandish moment, I got realistic. I had never received one word that my white family was still alive, and I had checked the forts along the Arkansas. And those along the Platte while working on the railroad.

Truth was, I had just about decided they was dead without admitting it.

I says: "In the mood they're in at the moment, the Cheyenne will shoot me on sight."

My woman answered: "I will be with you."

So that is how I rejoined the Human Beings. I didn't have no regrets, leaving behind only my horse with the blacksmith in Julesburg and my share in our little hauling business. As to my sister Caroline, I ought to say that just before I had went down to Julesburg, she told me Frank Delight, the whoremaster and saloonkeeper, had asked her hand in matrimony, and she was inclined to entertain the proposition favorably.

I won't detail our route down the ravine to an intersecting one and then on, coming out behind a hill that obscured us from the Pawnee, no more of which we encountered. And continued mile upon mile of rise and fall, during which night overtook us, and that woman arranged some brush and roofed it with blankets and we slept therein, cheek-by-jowl against the chill you usually get at night upon the prairie, where the wind blows all the time.

The next day we reached Spring Creek and along it found a gathering of the tribe, with remnants like us still coming in. As I expected, I had a close call or two with some of the young Dog Soldiers, but my woman drove them off me like she said she would, for she had a fierce tongue and concentrated purpose.

Old Lodge Skins had got a new tepee since last I seen him, but I recognized his shield hanging before the entranceway.

"Wait here, woman," I says, and she did as told, and I went within.

"Grandfather," I says.

"My son," he greets me, as if I had seen him last two minutes ago. "You want to eat?" He had the most equable temperament I ever knowed in a man.

He looked the same to me when I could make him out, except his eyes stayed closed. I figured he was dreaming, and sure enough he proceeded to paint a verbal picture of the incidents in that ravine.

"I saw you were returning to us," says he. "There was nothing you could have done for Shadow That Comes in Sight. He knew he would die today and told me so. Our medicine was no good against the many-firing rifles. Perhaps we should not have gone again to the iron road, but the young men wished to destroy another fire-wagon if they could catch one. It is very amusing to see the great thing come snorting and puffing with a spray of sparks as though it would eat up the world, I am told, then it hits the road which we have bent into the air and topples off onto its back, still steaming and blowing, and dies with a big sizzle."

Next to him I took a seat and we smoked then, of course. And observing that through all this procedure he had not opened his eyes, I decided at length he could not and had the bad manners, maybe, to inquire.

"It is true that I am blind," he admits, "though the rifle ball did not strike my eyes but rather passed through the back of my neck, cutting the tunnel through which the vision travels to the heart. Look," he said, opening his lids, "my eyes still see, but they keep it all within themselves, and it is useless because my heart does not receive it."

His eyes did look bright enough. I reckon it was the nerve which had been cut or stunned in some manner.

"Where did that happen, Grandfather?" I handed him back the long pipe.

He looked some embarrassed, and the smoke stayed inside him a great time before it come gushing from his mouth and nose.

"Sand Creek," he finally says.

And I groaned: "Ah, no!"

"I remember your advice," he says, "but we did not go up to the Powder River, after all. Instead we went to the treaty council. I shall tell you how it was. Hump had never attended a conference, and it was one of his needs to own a silver medal like my own. And then our young men said: 'Why shouldn't we get presents from the white men for talking to them? We are always in the north, and these Southern Cheyenne get everything.' I must admit," Old Lodge Skins goes on, "that I did not myself mind having a new red blanket.

"So that is why we turned around and came back, and we

touched the pen with the white men sent by their Father, and Hump received his medal and the young men their new pipe-hatchets, knives, and looking-glasses, and then we were going to the Powder River, but the soldier chief said: 'You must stay in this place. That is what you agreed to do when you touched the pen.' But I tell you I did not understand that. However, I know very little about treaties, so I believed the soldier chief was right, and we stayed, though that country was very ugly, with no water and no game. And then the soldiers attacked the village where we were camping with Black Kettle, and they rubbed out a great many of us, and that is where I was hit in the neck and became blind."

Then I feared the worst and asked after Buffalo Wallow Woman.

"She was rubbed out at Sand Creek," says Old Lodge Skins. "And White Cow Woman too. And Burns Red in the Sun and his wife Shooting Star. And Hump and High Wolf and Cut Nose and Bird Bear."

"My brother Burns Red in the Sun."

"Yes, and his wife and children. And many more, whom I will name only if you intend to mourn them, although that was several winters ago and now they will have reached the Other Side where the water is sweet, the buffalo abundant, and where there are no white men."

The latter designation he pronounced nowadays in a special way: not exactly hatefully, for Old Lodge Skins was too much a man to sit about and revile his enemies. That was for a loser, like the Rebs what lost the Civil War. And he wasn't a loser. He wasn't a winner, maybe, but neither was he a failure. You couldn't call the Cheyenne flops unless they had had a railroad engine of their own which never worked as well as the U.P.'s or had invented a gun that didn't shoot straight.

Just to check my impression, I asks him: "Do you hate the Americans?"

"No," he says, closing up his gleaming though dead eyes. "But now I understand them. I no longer believe they are fools or crazy. I know now that they do not drive away the buffalo by mistake or accidentally set fire to the prairie with their fire-wagon or rub out Human Beings because of a misunderstanding. No, they *want* to do these things, and they succeed in doing them. They are a powerful people." He took something from his beaded belt at that point and, stroking it, said: "The Human Beings believe that everything is alive: not only men and animals but also water and earth and stones and also the dead and things from them like this hair. The person from whom this hair came is bald on the Other Side, because I now own this scalp. This is the *way things are*.

"But white men believe that everything is dead: stones, earth, animals, and people, even their own people. And if, in spite of that, things persist in trying to live, white men will rub them out.

"That," he concludes, "is the difference between white men and Human Beings."

Then I looked close at the scalp he stroked, which was of the silkiest blonde. For a moment I was sure it come from Olga's dear head, and reckoned also he had little Gus's fine skull-cover someplace among his filthy effects, the stinking old savage, living out his life of murder, rapine, and squalor, and I almost knifed him before I collected myself and realized the hair was honeyer than my Swedish wife's.

I mention this because it shows how a person's passion can reverse on the instant he is reminded of his own loss. I had just been moved by Sand Creek, and the next minute was ready to kill him.

Now, Old Lodge Skins took cognizance of my state though blind.

"Have you," he asks, "a great sorrow or is it only bitterness?"

So I told him, and he never heard of the incident in which Olga and Gus was taken. He could not have lied. I have said that it is amazing what and how Indians know about events far distant from them; but likewise there are things they do not hear. In that era the capturing of white women and children was commonplace. A Cheyenne of one band might not know of those took by another, unless they camped together.

Then Old Lodge Skins said: "Our young men are angry nowadays. Many times they have not the patience to wait to ransom or exchange prisoners, but will become crazy with rage and rub them out. But was that not the voice of Sunshine I just heard outside my tepee? She is the widow of Little Shield, who was killed two moons ago, but now she will be your new wife and give you a new son, so that you have what you had before and better, for of course a woman of the Human Beings is superior to any other kind."

He wasn't being heartless, just making the best of likelihoods, as an Indian had to do in the sort of life he lived. His own two wives was massacred, and so he had mourned them for the proper time and then got himself replacements. These last had come and gone in the tepee while we talked: young women, sisters again, probably fifty year below the chief in age, but by God if they didn't both look pregnant to me.

"All right," I said. "But I tell you this, that if I find my first woman and my son again, I will take them back from whatever man is keeping them. And if they have been rubbed out, I will kill whoever did it."

"Of course," said Old Lodge Skins, for there wasn't nothing an Indian could better understand than revenge, and he would have scorned me only if I had not wanted it.

There couldn't have been a worse era for running with the Cheyenne. They was being chased throughout the whole frontier, and whenever they eluded their pursuers, would commit some new outrage against the whites. So I would be on the one hand a renegade to join them, in danger from the whole of my own race. On the other hand, I was under a constant threat from the Cheyenne themselves, for to many of them the very sight of a white face was the occasion for mayhem. I reckon the only thing that saved me was Old Lodge Skins's band had collected apart from the main force of Chief Turkey Leg, who had commanded the fight at the railroad, so I was most of the time among the group in which I was reared and where the Little Big Man legend still had some power. My woman Sunshine was good protection, and of course Old Lodge Skins too. But there were braves who had growed up since I left the tribe, like young Cut Belly, who one day raided a stage station and come back with a jug of whiskey and says to me:

"I want you to go out on the prairie and hide, because though I do not wish to kill you now, I will when I am drunk. I'm sorry for this, because I am told you are a good man, but that is what will happen."

Now the best way to get killed was to let a young fellow like that give you orders, so I says: "I think it is you who had better go out on the prairie for your drinking, because the way I am is that something comes over me when I see a drunk, and I have to shoot him, even if he is my brother. I can't help it; that's just how I am."

He took my advice in that instance, and I survived other such threats, but can't say I was ever popular, which hurt when I recalled my boyhood up along the Powder River as Little Big Man, but I was grown up now and that always involves disappointments. I was real lucky just in that I had still kept my hair. I lived from day to day, and there is a certain sweetness in that style of life, even when you have a long-range purpose as I did, for I was letting it come to me rather than chase it, and knowing it *would* come, I could live otherwise without apparent point, like an Indian, and eat roast hump when we found buffalo and draw in my slack belly when we didn't, and lay under a cottonwood and watch my woman Sunshine at hard labor with that little fellow sleeping in the cradleboard lashed to her back. His name was Frog Lying on a Hillside, for we had passed such in fleeing that afternoon of the railroad fight and the tiny child seemed to wake up then and nod at it, and both me and Sunshine believed it was right to let a boy pick his own name.

When we had reached the Indian camp, Sunshine had to mourn for her dead father and though she was quite good at that, weeping and wailing with a horrible din, she had to knock it off whenever she was feeding Frog, and she also never felt free to tear her hair or cut herself up with him on her back. So her kin helped out, all through one night and the next as well, for Shadow had been a man of high repute and it was extra terrible that he didn't have a scaffold to protect his carcass from the wolves. So these women howled and moaned until they gasped for air, the way a child does what has cried himself hysteric—I mean a white kid; little Indians don't do that.

Take Frog now, tied up into his cradleboard, with his little head like a brown bean; when he wasn't sleeping or eating, them sharp black eyes was studying everything within short range and never took displeasure. He reminded me frequently of little Gus, for my boy had had the even temperament of his own Ma, but there was a difference no less marked. Gus was ever delighted in my pocket watch, which I'd hang before him to produce its tick, like everybody does with babies and they is fascinated. Not Frog. It didn't make him sorry, for nothing did that, but he just cared nought for it: looked through and listened past it, you might say.

Or maybe what did not interest him was the person holding it. Talk as Sunshine did and Old Lodge Skins too of him being my son, Frog himself was not fooled. He didn't hate me; I was simply to him a kind of device that picked him up on occasion and embraced him, or swung him high into the air and let him down again, and he liked the motion and the contact but acknowledged in it nothing personal.

Then again, maybe the deficiency was mine, for though I liked him, I had had no hand in making him and could see no future for us as boy and Pa, no matter whether I ever found Gus and Olga again or not. The Cheyenne was finished. They knowed it, and I knowed, and little Frog was born into that knowledge. The best I could of done in acting like a father would have been to carry him off to Omaha or Denver and put him in a school. Make him white, bring him up to live in a permanent square house and get up every day and go to work by schedule. But you have seen what he thought of that instrument to measure time.

However, I couldn't have asked for a more ardent wife than Sunshine. That woman was utterly devoted to me, so much so—and I hate to say this, but it was true—that she commenced to bore me. I reckon the circumstances of our meeting had to do with the respective attitudes of us both. She saw it as a perculiarly touching thing that I had showed up in her hour of grievous need—though she exaggerated that: she was tough enough to have had that baby and escaped by herself—whereas to me she had started out as a burden, which while I freely assumed it there in that ravine as an emergency measure, seemed to gain weight as we lived in the camp.

I have to explain, for as you know the Cheyenne male never does what the white world understands as labor. When not hunting I spent most of my time on the flat of my back beneath a tree or, failing that, in the shade of a tepee. I gambled a little with the other braves and occasionally raced my pony which had been give to me by Old Lodge Skins, but was somewhat leery about winning on account of I didn't want trouble with the losers. I did not join no war or raiding parties, for nowadays they was always against white men. You might see mine as an impossible position to maintain, but if so you don't know Indians, whom you can live among on almost any terms but those of outright enmity, and I expect you could even survive the latter situation as long as you had one loyal defender. I had two: the chief and my wife. Sometimes an overwrought young man would come in with a fresh white scalp and offer to insult me with it, but I'd either handle him like I did Cut Belly or look right through him as if he was glass, depending on the situation and my judgment of his character. Or if Sunshine was around, she'd light into him so rough I'd usually end up secretly on his side, for she had a right sharp tongue and I don't remember as I have said that whereas Cheyenne maidens was shy and soft-spoken, the married women was just the reverse and specialized in themes that in civilization was more common to the saloon than to where ladies gathered. They had license to talk this way, I guess, because in practice they was so respectable. You seldom saw a cut-nosed woman among the Human Beings—did I mention that a Plains Indian clipped off the end of his wife's nose if she dallied with another man?

Well sir, I suppose a bachelor is at a peculiar disadvantage up against a respectable married woman everywhere in the world, and Sunshine would cast reflection on the young fellow's potency and speculate unfavorably on the quality of his endowments, etc., with the other women laughing nearby, maybe including some young girl he had a crush on, and away he'd slink, poor devil, having arrived a hero and departed a buffoon.

Now, as if it wasn't bad enough to be defended by a woman in that style, next Sunshine would get to boasting about me. First it was how I saved her from the Pawnee, and that story growed from what had really happened, us cowering in that bush, to my standing off five or six of them and dropping three. She wasn't a liar: I reckon that somehow that is what she saw through the distorting spectacles of her recollection. Then of course if she could be vocal about another man's sexual abilities of which she knowed nothing, think of what she might do with the man on whom she stood as the local authority: I become a champion stud.

And I tell you it embarrassed me to be so characterized, but you know how it is, a person is sometimes the victim of his own vanity, so I fair killed myself trying to live up to my reputation, during the nights under our buffalo robe. Jesus, there was mornings when I couldn't stand up straight, feeling like I had been kicked by a horse into the small of my back. I guess it ain't right to tell this, for Sunshine was my wife and though a man can talk endlessly of his adulteries and fornications, the subject is in bad taste when it concerns respectable mating, I don't know why.

The only way I finally got off the hook was that Sunshine one day turned up pregnant. That must have been about late March of '68, figuring on the basis of what happened nine months after; otherwise I'd never have had any idea of the time, for by then I had been with the Cheyenne for three seasons and fallen back into the style of dating things by the northward flight of the wild geese, for example, which meant the oncoming of spring, as did the appearance of hair on the unborn calves taken out of buffalo cows we killed.

During all this time we ranged mainly between the Arkansas and the Platte, which is now southern Nebraska and northern Kansas, and there was another railroad building in the latter state: the Kansas Pacific, along the Smoky Hill River, which had been good buffalo country, and so the game grew scarcer and we ate more roots than meat. And the troops was after us, and the Pawnee, but by the superior generalship of Old Lodge Skins, blind though he was, as a village we eluded them all, though our small raiding parties had many a small-scale brush.

Our band continued to live apart from the other Cheyenne, though we'd run into some of them from time to time, and when we would I'd inquire after Olga and Gus. Which was a ticklish business, my being white, and maybe I didn't always hear the truth. Anyway, it availed me nothing except more close calls, for some of these outfits held other white captives and did not want me snooping around their tepees.

Nor was Old Lodge Skins a deal of help in this matter. His blindness cut down his horny behavior—he couldn't eye no more fat wenches—but it had strengthened his intention to go his own way. What happened in the fall of '67 was that the Government signed another treaty with the Southern Cheyenne, Arapaho, Kiowa, and Comanche, by which the Indians agreed to stay down in western Oklahoma, then known as the Nations. A runner found our camp and delivered an invite to Old Lodge Skins, but the chief had had enough of treaties after Sand Creek and wouldn't attend the conference. Nor did he purpose to abide by that agreement.

"I will not live in that bad place," he told me, referring to the western Nations. "The grass is poor there, and the water is bitter. And it is properly the country of the Snake People, who I know are our friends now, but they copulate with horses and that makes them strange to me. Also the People of the Rasp Fiddle"—Apache—"come there, and they are brave but extremely ugly, being short and bowlegged and not at all handsome like the Human Beings. A long time ago when we used to fight them, I captured an Apache woman but it was like lying with a cactus, so I sent her back to her people with some presents, which was a great insult. . . ."

"They tell me Black Kettle attended this conference. I am only too familiar with the kind of treaties to which he touches the pen. I was at Sand Creek with him and lost my family, my friends, and my vision. Without eyes I see more clearly than he."

Now it might have been to my own interest to want to stay down south, and even urge him to join the main body of the Southern Cheyenne, for if my own family was yet alive, that is where they would probably be. But I couldn't, just couldn't. I had a weakness where that old Indian was concerned.

So what I says was: "I can't understand why you don't go up to the Powder River. If you had done that when I first suggested it, you wouldn't have been at Sand Creek."

"I shall tell you why," says Old Lodge Skins. "I prefer it in the Powder River country. I was born there, on the Rosebud Creek. Indeed, my medicine works only half-strength when I come below the Shell River," which is what he called the Platte. "But the Americans, other than a few trappers, do not care about that country. So long as the Human Beings stay there, they will not be bothered by the white men."

"That is exactly my point," says I, wondering whether the old devil had lost his wits as well as his sight.

"Yes," he said, "and I, chief of the greatest warriors on the face of the earth, I should avoid danger like the rabbit? I should let them drive me from this land where I have killed buffalo and Pawnee for eighty summers? A Human Being has always gone wherever he wished, and if someone tried to stop him, he rubbed them out or was killed by them. If I were so cowardly, my people would never respect me. There are many fine young men in this band, and they no longer have the doubts that our warriors had in the earlier days. They have decided to fight the white men wherever they can find them, and rip up those iron rails and drive away the fire wagons. Once that is done, they will kill all the remaining Americans, so that we can hunt again without being bothered and make war on the Pawnee."

"Grandfather," I says, "do you honestly believe that can be done?"

"My son," says Old Lodge Skins, "if it cannot, then the sun will shine upon a good day to die."

The Beecher Island fight took place, in which five or six hundred Cheyenne cornered fifty white scouts on a sandbar in the middle of the Arickaree Fork and besieged them there for nine days. But the whites was again armed with the Spencer repeaters and held off every charge, killing a good many Indians, among them the great Cheyenne warrior, Roman Nose. Then the cavalry came.

I wasn't there, but our young men were, and they returned to camp full of weariness and defeat. I stayed inside the lodge for a time so as to avoid incidents, but I would not have had to, the way they was feeling. The Cheyenne still didn't have no firearms worth the name, and it must make a man feel pretty bad to have the advantage in number but still be beat by the other fellow on account of his superior armament. I had long since buried that pistol of mine and generally kept the Ballard out of sight: no sense in adding to the ill feeling.

So what them Indians got to doing now was trying to lick the problem from the other end and dream up some medicine to make themselves impervious to bullets. One fellow seemed to have made it, for he had been shot at Beecher's Island through the chest and did some hocus-pocus over the wound and it closed up without unfortunate effect, and he took the name Bullet Proof. So he fixed up several other braves with his medicine and a couple of weeks after the Island fight, they went against the cavalry. Out of seven Human Beings using that medicine, two was immediately rubbed out and Bullet Proof brought them back to camp and tried to raise them from the dead. One twitched his leg a little, stopped, and neither got up. Bullet Proof then admitted his failure.

I reckon it was because of such events that Old Lodge Skins and even his fierce young men had to limit their ambition to mere survival, and after a time we found ourselves with the village of Black Kettle, who the white men in afterdays sometimes called the great Indian statesman, I guess because he was always signing treaties to keep the peace and give away more of the Cheyenne hunting grounds to the railroads and ranchers.

Anyway, that's how I happened to be at the Battle of the Washita. And as usual, on the side that lost.

CHAPTER 17 *In the Valley of the Washita*

WE JOINED BLACK KETTLE at the end of the big summer buffalo hunt in which all the tribe in the area come together, and then moved on down into the Nations, across the Canadian River, past the Antelope Hills, and onto the Washita, in that reservation what had been assigned to the Cheyenne by the treaty of Medicine Lodge. There was several camps there, strung along the river for about ten mile, more Cheyenne below us and Arapaho, Kiowa, Comanche, and some Apache too. The Indians figured to winter in that valley, which was well timbered with cottonwood.

It was nice, right nice, and Old Lodge Skins had been exaggerating in his bleak description. He still claimed the water was bitter, but I couldn't taste it. However I didn't chide him none, for he was outranked in this gathering, what with Black Kettle and Chief Little Raven of the Arapaho and Satanta, the famous cutthroat Kiowa who painted himself red to the waist and went about tooting a brass bugle. And they none of them paid much heed to Old Lodge Skins, being he had boycotted the Medicine Lodge council and was poor and had such a small band. There is a snobbery among all people who run things, white or Indian.

So my old chief set by himself most of the time and continued to dream and once in a while he would orate, but didn't draw much of an audience these days, for his young men got to blaming him for not going to that council on account of the other Indians was boasting of the presents they had received for so doing and of the big show of riding the various tribes had put on for the Government commissioners, and a redskin hates to pass up a display or demonstration. Back in the old days when I was a kid we had camped near some Sioux on the Surprise River and one summer day they begun to yell and fire their pieces, and believing they was attacked we fell out to help them, but discovered they was only celebrating. Hump asked why and they said they didn't know, but the soldiers over at Fort Laramie was doing it and the Sioux wouldn't be found wanting in the celebration department. So Hump said he guessed the Human Beings better then, too, and all day we hollered and hooted and wasted ammunition. I figured out later it had been the Fourth of July.

You might have wondered what become of the two Indians who figured in my youth among the Cheyenne but seemed to have disappeared by this second residence: my enemy Younger Bear the Contrary and Little Horse, who was a *heemaneh*.

They had not been killed neither one, for I had asked after them and learned they was running with other bands, I expect so as to get companionship from others of their own kinds, Old Lodge Skins's camp being too small to accommodate more than one apiece of them exotic professions. A Contrary must get mighty lonely, having to talk in reverse to all the standard people, and though a *heemaneh* hangs out a lot with the women, gossiping and sewing and all, he probably yearns for the company of others who understand his point of view.

I missed both of them fellows, for a like reason. I didn't have no friends at all, other than Old Lodge Skins, and no private, personal enemies. There was plenty of surliness towards me, as I have said, and no more than I had learned to more or less walk unobtrusive past the young men of Old Lodge Skins's band, we joined the enormous gathering around Black Kettle and the run-ins started all over again, for though the Cheyenne was officially supposed to be at peace now, they didn't figure it to apply to white men and was still raiding the ranches and farms as long as the weather continued good, so they'd ride back in and see me and go for their weapons even in the middle of our village. It wasn't *me* them young braves disliked, but the skin I wore. That's my point about Younger Bear, who knowed me very well as personal enemies always do; and I realized, now that he wasn't around no more, that I had taken a good deal of satisfaction from his enmity, which was particular and special, since we had growed up together.

As to Little Horse, the pressure was off him because of his way of life and he was ever pleasurable company, good for a song or dance or light conversation, not having to worry constantly about his manhood and medicine as a Cheyenne warrior always did. So far as *heemanehs* go, I'll take an Indian one every time, for he knows his place in life, unlike the white variety.

Little Horse and Younger Bear: I met both of them fellows in that great camp down on the Washita River, and I'm going to tell you about it.

Late November was the time of year, the river skinned with ice and a foot of snow in the valley that would warm some in the day and then freeze into a crust at night, so if you got outside of the beaten-down floor of the campground you'd crash and crunch like a herd of buffalo and maybe cut your ankles into the bargain. Indians was still coming in from all points to this their winter quarters: war parties as well as whole villages with women, children, horse herds, and dogs. After they was settled, I'd always nose around for white faces, and having had so many unpleasant encounters with testy braves, I had got to painting myself as I done at the battle of Solomon's Fork years ago and traded a couple of Sunshine's dressed deerskins to a medicine man for one of them buffalo-head hats complete with horns, to hide my ginger hair. Only I didn't use colored paint, but rather dead black made from charcoal and grease. Otherwise, my settlement clothes having worn out anyway, I wore leggings and a blue blanket. People still knew I was white, but I think thought better of me for having gone Indian as much as humanly possible.

Well sir, on this day of which I speak, a village had come in and settled on the river about a mile below us near the big horseshoe bend of the Washita, where the water was maybe eight foot deep right off the bank, which the ones who knew the place was telling the new people in case they'd want to take that cold bath the Cheyenne go in for of a morning. By God, some of them did, plunged right in while the women was setting up the lodges and swum in that chill with the fragments of ice keeping them company. That's when I happened along and made out Younger Bear in the middle of the stream. He had a funny mode of swimming: on alternate strokes his head would rise from the water to the flanges of his nose, his eyes staying shut as the wash streamed down over them, and since he wasn't breathing through his mouth, the effect was as though a corpse was floating up off the bottom.

While watching him, I heard myself being greeted in a voice that was too melodious for either a Cheyenne brave or a grown woman, but like a young girl's, and I turned and there was Little Horse. He wore the most beautiful dress of white antelope skin, with an eight-inch fringe, that I ever seen. The bosom was magnificently stitched with glass beads of every hue and even in that cold winter sun give the impression of how the Northern Lights might look if illuminating the Grand Canyon. And he wore a half-dozen bracelets and a string of beads so long they should have tripped him, and his ear-lobes was stretched like melting taffy by the weight of the great copper disks he carried there.

The manner in which he approached me, I figured he was trying to pick me up, so I says quick who I was.

And he says: "Oh yes, I know you," and giggles, which I guess by now had become his habit, so while it got upon my nerves, I tried not show it for old times' sake.

We held a little reunion there on the riverbank among the trampled snow, and of course he never asked me what I was doing here, for that would have been impolite between two fellows raised together, but I did have to submit to an embrace that was more sisterly than brotherly.

"You left your father's band?" I asks after I got out of his clutches.

"That's right," says he, toying with his beads. "That was after Sand Creek. My father told me to. He said his medicine was bad and had brought misfortune to the rest of his family and that he didn't want anything to happen to me because I was too pretty. Still, I would not have gone even so, were it not that Younger Bear"—he pointed towards the water—"left us after Sand Creek. He had an accident there. You know that a Contrary may not sit or lie upon a bed but sleeps always upon the bare earth. Well, the night before we were attacked, Younger Bear, without waking, in a dream, arose from the ground, arranged a robe into a bed, and lay down upon it and spent the rest of the night in that fashion. To his horror he found himself there in the morning. The softness of the buffalo robe had taken all his Contrary power from him, so when the fight came he was weak as a baby, and I had to help him run away from the soldiers up the dry bed of the stream and hide."

"I am sorry for that," I says, and sincerely enough, for the enmity between me and Younger Bear had always gone in only the one direction, though he sometimes annoyed me.

But Little Horse, typical of a *heemaneh* I suppose, passed it off fairly negligent. "Oh," says he, "he got over it. We joined the band of Red-Winged Woodpecker, and Younger Bear sold his Thunder Bow and Contrary power to someone else, which freed him to get married."

At that moment the subject of these remarks come in out of the Washita, shivering off the water before it could freeze on him, and since Little Horse broke off our talk to dry Younger Bear with a red blanket and help him into his clothes, I got the idea who had participated in that wedding.

So when the Bear was all dressed and looked at me, I couldn't forbear from needling him a little, for though nobody among the Cheyenne ever condemns a *heemaneh*, it is O.K. to rib the fellow he lives with.

So I says: "I have just been talking to your lovely wife."

"All right," he says, smiling without malignance, I thought, and squeezing a quart of water out of each of his braids. "Now come and meet the other one."

He exchanged the wet blanket for a dry one from Little Horse, swathed himself in it, and led the way among the lodges, through the crowds of dogs, and pointing to one sharp-faced animal that had a good deal of coyote in him, I expect, he told Little Horse to cook it for the guest, so the Horse popped it in the head with a club from his beaded belt and carried its limp yellow body by the hind legs along with that wet blanket, and we come to a shabby tepee and went through its entranceway.

A goodly fire was blazing in the center and over it hung the usual black pot being stirred by the usual stout woman, except her face was white beneath the dirt and her hair blonde for all the sooted grease. It was Olga.

Younger Bear turns to me and shows what I took to be an evil sneer at the time, but now I realize it was mainly pure pride, for he had no idea that his female wife and me was related other than by race alone.

"We will smoke," he says, "and then we will eat."

Olga looks awful as to her person, wearing a dirty buckskin dress and leggings and old moccasins gone almost to rags. The Bear might have took his regular bath irrespective of the temperature, but I believe Olga abstained according to the same schedule. I said before I seen her blonde hair, but actually it was greenish, and the tail of an uncurried horse was less tangled.

Now, I had left all my weapons back at my own lodge, so as to display my peaceful intentions to any hostile braves I might encounter, and Younger Bear was a great husky fellow more than six foot tall and we was right in the middle of an encampment no doubt full of his friends. I didn't think of these matters. All I seen was my dear, sweet wife degraded into a slave for this damnable savage, and my fingers curled into murderous claws and I would have been upon the Bear and tore out his throat in the next second . . . had not Olga looked up right then and sounded off in a voice that for sheer raucousness took the cake from Caroline, or Nothing that time I heard her bawling out her man, or any other female white or red who ever tormented my eardrums.

"Maybe you can tell me what we're going to eat, you good-for-nothing loafer, you!" she howls. "I can't remember the last time you brought in any game. Why, Little Horse here is more of a man than you." The latter had stayed outside to prepare that dog, and now he come in with the bleeding hunks of its flesh, his dress arms pulled back so as not to soil them, and he tries to calm her down, but Olga continues to Younger Bear: "I think you should change clothes with Little Horse, except that you are too stupid and awkward to be a *heemaneh!* And who is this foolish beggar you have brought here to steal what little food we have, none of which you provided? Tell him to do his buffalo dance elsewhere."

Younger Bear scowls and says: "Unless you want a beating, woman, you will shut your mouth."

"You know who'll get the beating," snarls Olga. "I'll break a club against your lazy spine." She brushes back her hair, leaving a long smear across her forehead, and spits contemptuously in the fire. Then she takes them hunks of dog from Little Horse and hurls them into the pot with a splash of blood and boiling water, some of which hits the Horse and he shrieks in horror that his dress is stained, and Olga says: "I'm sorry, dear," and takes him outside to look at the spots in the daylight.

You might have thought Younger Bear was shamed in front of me, but he didn't show it. He shrugs and lights his pipe. "Usually," he says, "this woman is gentle as a dove. I think she acts this way just to show off for the guest, for I am a good provider. Did I not bring in that dog just now? I am also a wonderful lover, for I stored up my force for several years as a Contrary, when it was not permitted to have a woman, and now . . ."

Well, he went on boasting for a time, and lying, and I'll tell you his degeneration was awe-inspiring. How many times have I said that the Cheyenne spurned both these indulgences, and here this Indian had taken them up like a saloon bum.

Not that I thought of that at the time—no, I was still paralytic from seeing Olga. She wasn't a victim, that much was clear, but her whole personality had changed. You remember how amiable she was when married to me, even to the point of meekness. She never in those years learned much of the English language, yet here she was already fluent in abusive Cheyenne. Maybe her Swedish throat took more naturally to another harsh tongue, but what about that fear of Indians she had had since the massacre of her family by the Santee Sioux?

My God, but it was strange, and in the pondering of it I forgot for a time about Little Gus, when suddenly in he runs, dressed like a savage and with his fair hair in braids. He must have been about the age of five now and he was a robust lad, his sturdy little body half-naked despite the cold. He had a bow and took it to Younger Bear.

"Father," says he, "the string is broken. Please make me a new one, because I need it for our war."

The Bear smiled real fond at Gus, though he chided him: "It is not the way of the Human Beings to interrupt the smoking of a guest." But he pulled the lacing from his own quiver hanging from a lodgepole and stretched a new bowstring of it.

At last I found my tongue and asked Gus, the child of my own loins, "Who are you fighting? The Pawnee?"

My voice must have sounded strained, but he didn't take enough notice of me that it mattered. He was still breathing hard from his running, and as a kid will be, was absolutely occupied with that momentary need of his. So he grabs the bow from Younger Bear, which had now been repaired, and answers while en route to the outside.

"No, not Pawnee," he says in his high, fierce voice in that guttural language. "White men!"

"I wish you would come back here and show the proper respect for the guest," said Younger Bear, but rather weakly, I thought, and before he had got it all out, my Gus had rejoined his playmates. You could hear them whooping. He figured himself for a pure-bred Indian.

I didn't know what Olga thought, and having seen her in action I didn't want to find out. It was the goddamnedest thing I ever seen or heard of. The Kiowa, down in their camp, had a white woman who was used as the lowliest slave. I didn't have much protection in that village, so hadn't stayed longer than to determine that she wasn't my wife, but had seen the poor thing and her baby of eighteen months and she was a miserable sight.

But the only distress hereabout was in Younger Bear's countenance when Olga lighted into him. Now that we was alone he starts to boast of how he paid ten ponies for her to the Southern Cheyenne brave what captured her upon the Arkansas. The usual price for an Indian girl, paid to her father, was only three or four animals.

You might think I was sitting there gritting my teeth. I wasn't. I felt as if in a dream, and says right calm: "That boy has pale skin."

"And hair like the morning sun," says Younger Bear. "His name is Medicine Standing Up, only we usually call him Potbelly. I think he will become the most powerful war chief of the Human Beings. You know the great Crazy Horse of the Oglala has light skin and fair hair, and he cannot be hit with a bullet."

"You made this child?" I took a drag on the stone pipe and handed it back to him. I expected him to say he had, in the mood he was in then, but he looked into the fire for a time through half-closed lids and then replied: "No, his father was the same medicine bird that came to me at Sand Creek and said: 'Stop being a Contrary! Run away! Do not care what people think. You have a greater destiny than fighting these bluecoats today. You must marry a woman with pale hair and rear my son!' So that is what I did."

Well, Olga and Little Horse come in again and cooked that dog and served him up, and my ex-wife bawled Younger Bear out from time to time and give me no more notice than she had before, and I reckon if Little Horse had told her anything about me, it was some fantastic story that would never remind her of Jack Crabb.

Somehow I ate enough to be polite and when done even extended the return invite that manners called for.

I says: "I am married to the daughter of Shadow That Comes in Sight, who you know was a great warrior." I had some pride, too, and it had begun to get me that this Indian was bragging about having my white wife in his tepee. Though I wasn't angry at him, really, and if I hated him, it wasn't in the fashion that I had imagined I would hate the man what held Olga. For he wasn't detaining her: that much was clear. And though she seemed in a foul mood, it was the kind a female finds strangely satisfying. She had something on him; had found out probably, I guess from Little Horse, that he had showed the white feather at Sand Creek and was never going to let him forget it.

I hadn't seen this side of Olga when we was married, thank the good Lord, though I realized now that I might have, had she known about that business flop I suffered in Denver. But she hadn't. She never knew about anything in them days but keeping house and tending to Gus. She hardly knowed any English, I believe that's why. But by Jesus how she had took to Cheyenne life! After cooking that dog, she had went out and worked alongside and bantered with them other Indian women and beyond her skin and hair you'd never been able to distinguish amongst them.

I be damned! Excuse my cursing. It's just that it was a wonder to me and I don't know how to express the measure of it. I wasn't sad and I wasn't mad. I wasn't even embarrassed, though I might have been if I hadn't been wearing that buffalo hat and face paint. For it was Jack Crabb who had lost his wife, not Little Big Man; that was the way to look at it. You might think I should have been dying for the details of the final moments in which that little group of whites was overrun by the Indians down on the Arkansas and Olga and Gus was carried off; I should have wanted to discover from Younger Bear the name of the brave what had sold them to him, and go kill that Indian to protect my honor.

But none of that occurred to me at this time. No, seeing my wife and boy in Younger Bear's tepee, both of whom was apparently prospering in their own style, I was impelled rather to make that announcement of my own marriage to Sunshine. I done more: I boasted that, because her father was dead and she didn't have no brothers, I didn't pay nobody a single horse for her.

Now like most braggarts, Younger Bear couldn't stand to hear nobody else steal his thunder. He commenced to pout and chewed forever upon the same fragment of gristle. His eyes had got more Oriental as he grew older, and now they almost disappeared beneath the bulge of his low forehead and the underlying tear-sacs traced in paint that hadn't been altogether washed off by his bath. I had had a feeling all along on this visit that he didn't recognize me—that is, of course he knowed I was white though dressed like a Cheyenne, but did not connect me with his boyhood. The only other time I had seen him since the old days had been that once when he was a Contrary, lost in his backwards scheme.

Well sir, he don't say a thing now until we finish off our chuck and wipe our hands upon our garments and go outside, and there is Olga and some other women fleshing a fresh hide that is staked down upon a spot from which they have swept the snow—her big bottom is pointed towards me, and I would never have recognized it, for back in the old days Olga was robust but never portly. And little Gus runs by, ducking an imaginary bullet fired from a stick-gun by a brown playmate who he must have euchred into impersonating a white enemy. Only a son of mine could have pulled off such a trick, and damn me, that incident touched me more than anything so far. That was the closest I come to calling him, saying: "I'm your Pa, boy. Don't you recall your old Daddy?"

But of course I never, for it wasn't the place nor the time, and how in hell would I ever explain the get-up I was wearing to a five-year-old. I'm telling the truth here, and the truth is always made up of little particulars which sound ridiculous when repeated. But I'm prepared to say that maybe I didn't take back my wife and boy because I was wearing them buffalo horns, when everything was said and done.

Well, I took leave of Younger Bear and renewed the invite to come and eat at my lodge the next day and went so far in a bravado intended to cover up the emotion I felt on seeing Gus as to add: "And bring the whole family!"

The Bear suddenly come from his coma and says to me, very keenly: "You have decided to stay." So he did recall me.

"I never thanked you," he says, "for bringing extra food to me while I was being taken as a prisoner to the fort. I want to do that now."

I was afraid he would next start in on that old business about owing me a life, so I fixed to leave, but he says: "Wait. I want to apologize for the rudeness of my wife. She is a good woman, but she just cannot stand to be in the presence of white men, because they killed her father and mother. . . .

"Listen," he says, "on the way here we crossed a fresh trail made by white soldiers. I think they are looking for this village, though the chiefs touched the pen and we are at peace."

Younger Bear had the peculiar ability always to remind me of my proper race. I should have been armed against him, but I never was. When no issue was made of it, I'd generally be pro-Indian; and also if Old Lodge Skins or Sunshine was registering the complaint, maybe because they were sort of my kin. But the Bear always drew my blood on this subject.

"Maybe," says I, "they are trailing the big war party that has just come in from raids on peaceful ranches along the Smoky Hill River. Or they could be looking for that white woman and child held by the Kiowa."

He set his jaw real stubborn. "I don't know about those things. I am not a Kiowa but a Human Being. I have not been raiding along the Smoky Hill River. Yet I suppose if a soldier sees me he will shoot at me all the same."

He was right enough in that, and I for one didn't know how to explain it. However, I resented his unstated suggestion that it was *my* fault. And there I guess you have the issue between me and Younger Bear. If to a soldier one Indian was the same as another, no matter if they belonged to altogether different tribes, so to the Bear I was responsible for what all other white men did, even though I was at present living in this village and dressed as a savage.

I went back to my own tepee. Now I haven't mentioned yet that while Sunshine's father was dead and she didn't have brothers, she did have three sisters, and they lived with us. One of them was also a widow and had two little kids. I was the only grown man in the establishment and had to hunt for the whole bunch. In return, them women done all the other work, and I reckon I could also have laid with them had I a mind to, though I never did with anybody but Sunshine, on account of until she got pregnant she alone exhausted me, and so far as since then was concerned, I might be a bit of a prude, but keeping a harem was never to my taste.

As I lay on my buffalo robe and looked at the swell of Sunshine's pregnant belly, all I could think of was how Olga might at this very moment be carrying the seed of that savage in her. She was forever soiled. I could leave my lodge at any time, go back to civilization, take a bath, and be white again. Not her. The *Cheyenne* was inside her. Indians sure made me sick. I could hardly breathe for the smell inside my own home, where them sloppy women I supported stirred up the muck we was going to eat for supper. We didn't have no fresh meat, on account of instead of hunting that afternoon I had set and ate dog prepared by my natural wife in the tepee of her unnatural husband.

While I was in this poisonous mood, little Frog toddled over and handed me the tiny wooden horse I had carved for him. He was

now about the age of Gus when captured. I handed the toy back to
him. He just looked real solemn at me and then at it, and put it
down very careful on my bed and goes away. That was the first
indication I got of the atmosphere inside the lodge, but then I
noticed the women was all unusually quiet and the children of my
widowed sister-in-law, a boy and a girl, who I might joke with or
tell stories to before the meal was served, were keeping to their own
area.

Sunshine served me up a bowl of roots mashed up with some
berries. These ingredients had been gathered the previous summer
and saved in a dried version. It was like taking a mouthful of mud.

"Where's that cow haunch I brought in yesterday?" I asks in bad
temper.

She looks scared but corrects me. "That was three days ago."

"If I say it was yesterday, that's when it was, unless you're looking for a beating, woman."

She quickly begs my pardon, saying: "You are right, yesterday. I
am a stupid person and—"

"Oh, shut up," I says. "There are too many mouths to feed
around here. That's why I can't ever keep us in meat. Why don't
your sisters get married?" The women all put their heads down. I
coughed to free my windpipe from a swallow of that sludge.

"If you think I am going to lay with you," I addressed them
generally, "you are crazy."

One of them come over to Sunshine and whispered in her ear, and
then my woman says: "My sister will go out to trade her beaded
dress for meat, if you will wait."

I happened to know of the one that made this offer, that the shirt
was the sole item among her possessions for which she could have
got any more than a dried bone. And it wasn't much itself, being
stained and patched and there was places where the beads had fell
off. We wasn't a rich family, I can tell you that, having only one
man in the place, and that man me, who never did no raiding of the
settlements, and we didn't have association with the traders, who I
wouldn't have wanted to see me anyhow, and I didn't own any
horses apart from the pony give me by Old Lodge Skins.

"No," I says now. "I am not hungry." I was some ashamed, but
ashamed to show it. I knowed why none of them had got married, too.
Because they was living in the tepee of a white man, and the Chey-

enne braves would not come and hang about such a door and play their medicine flutes in courtship. Especially since, as the years had gone on, there was an ever greater surplus of females in the tribe, owing to so many men having been killed. I had put a curse on them girls, I reckon. But whose idea had it been to take Sunshine for a wife? Not mine.

"I am sorry you are angry with me," says Sunshine now. She had put in a full day's labor, including the chopping of firewood and then drug a great load of it on a buffalo robe for a quarter mile to our lodge. She was all ready to have that kid any time now. When the moment came, she would throw down her hatchet, retire behind a tree, and have it in the snow, and then chop the rest of her quota and bring back both child and cottonwood logs.

"Sit down here and eat," I says. "I'm not angry with you."

Which she did, shoveling in that mush with a big horn spoon, and the rest of them likewise, with a sound like an army tramping through a swamp. If I hadn't been a fool at business back in Denver, by now I could have been setting in my own big house, dining off porcelain and silver and sent me to England for a baldheaded butler wearing a swallowtail coat. If my Pa hadn't been crazy, God knows what I would have been. I guess everybody toys with ideas like them.

When Sunshine was finished and had picked off her dress the bits of grub what slipped off the spoon, and also some from the earthern floor, for she was still bothered—they all was, even though my mood had sweetened—when she done that and took her bowl and mine to go clean them, she hesitated and says in a low tone:

"When will you kill him?"

"Who?" I asks, getting irritated all over again, for I knew very well what she meant, and remembered my earlier aim though I didn't wish to, which accounted for my annoyance. "You just better," I says, "keep out of what doesn't concern you."

Sunshine squats and smooths out that buffalo robe next to mine. "I'll make a nice bed for her," she says, "and give her my best red blanket. And the white boy can sleep next to our nephew Spotted Pony, if he likes it there."

I says evenly: "The white woman with Younger Bear is not my wife and the boy is not my son. My family was killed upon the Arkansas River." I reached for a bow that was hanging from a lodgepole behind me, which I used to hunt when saving powder and lead. And I says: "If I hear any more talk about the matter from you, old woman, I'll give you a beating that you won't forget."

Sunshine had took on considerable flesh with her pregnancy—though even so she was slimmer than Olga—and showed a real moon-face as she now grinned. And directly the rest of the women and the kids cheered up, though I had spoke softly and they was eating loud, and they commenced to chatter and laugh like they did normally, for it was ordinarily a happy lodge.

See, they had all thought I would rub out Younger Bear and take Olga and Gus back and that accounted for my earlier meanness: that I was working myself up for the killing, and I don't wonder they figured I might not have stopped with the Bear but murdered them all as well, for Cheyenne women knowed where high passion could lead a man.

Well, they could set their minds to rest, for Little Big Man was not a-going to make any trouble for anybody. On the other hand, I was more or less obliged to honor my invite to entertain Younger Bear and his family on the morrow. After that, I was done with the matter. I had no intention of getting in thick with Mr. & Mrs. Bear and going on exchanging dinners one after the other. I didn't expect Olga, the way she changed, ever to find out the true state of affairs —for I'd be wearing that buffalo hat and black facial paint, and she never would be looking for me—but one of the Indians no doubt would smell it, for they was keen about such matters. Not Younger Bear, in his stupidity and conceit, but Little Horse, probably, or one of my own women. Or maybe Gus, and that would kill me.

So I figured to run off right after dinner on the following day and go back to the railroad. I had now got what I rejoined the Cheyenne to find, such as it was.

That was the state of mind in which after a while I pulled a number of animal skins and dirty blankets over me and tried to sleep. The women and children had also retired, but the fire was banked with enough logs to keep it burning all the night, otherwise we would have froze even within our multiple wrappings, for frigid air entered between the door-lacings and from beneath the lodge skin. Occasionally I could hear my pony stamp against the cold outside. I had picketed him near the entrance rather than meadowed with the rest of the herd. Being he was my sole animal at this time, I couldn't afford to have no Pawnee run him off; though I had not heard of any in the area.

As to the report of a soldiers' trail by Younger Bear, I took that to be some more of his foolishness. We was down here now on the reservation assigned to the Cheyenne at the Medicine Lodge council, so why should they be after us? I mean Old Lodge Skins's band. If they looked for anybody, it would be that war party that had come in to the villages downriver. But the whole business was unlikely in this weather. Nobody fought in the winter, least of all the U.S. Army, whose big horses could never negotiate that crusted snow.

I thought about a lot of stuff like that, for I couldn't get to sleep. I might have determined to be done with the matter of Olga and Gus, but it was far from done with me. The veins in my temples was throbbing, and my groin was giving me trouble. I mean it felt as if I was pursing up there, like a dried apple. After a time it occurred to me that I was feeling lust in a different form from any I had hitherto knowed, especially while with the Indians. I have told you it was Sunshine who was ardent, rather than yours truly. Well, now I reached over for her, completely forgetting her present condition.

What I touched was the summit of her big belly, through the robes, and she was awake right smart, getting out her hand and rubbing mine.

She says: "Wunhai's feelings are hurt by what you said."

That was the sister what offered to sell her beaded dress for meat. Her name meant "Burns"; maybe she had singed her finger when a girl or something. She was right comely and the youngest of Shadow's offspring, a couple years beneath Sunshine and favoring her as to the eyes and glossy hair but slim as a willow wand. When I thought of it she recalled for me my old girl friend Nothing before she got married and turned fat and ill-tempered; poor Nothing was another killed at Sand Creek.

Anyway, I had up to now regarded Wunhai as a sister-in-law, white fashion, never having adapted the Cheyenne view of such things. What Sunshine meant had hurt Wunhai's feelings was that statement I had made earlier to the effect that I would not lay with any of them other women.

I patted Sunshine's belly and withdrew my hand. As usual, my trouble lay in deciding whether I was finally white or Indian. If the former, I had ought to go to sleep: Olga's having went savage was her problem, not mine. On the other hand, I commenced to realize the responsibility I had for Sunshine's sisters: it wasn't enough to support them. On account of me they was old maids. I had ought to do something, for they was a good bunch of women. Maybe I was being hypocritical, I don't know; you figure it out. Next I remember, I had rose and slipped through the fireglow halfway around the circle of the tepee and was kneeling by Wunhai's robe. Her eyes gleamed through the shadow I threw across her.

"I'm sorry for what I said," says I.

She says: "I hear you." And opens up her covers on that side and I enters thereunder, against her slight brown body, which happened to be naked and burning hot after my chilly journey without my breechclout. There was a sweet girl. It turned out she had never knowed a man before, being a real fine example of the high morals of the Human Beings, but her instincts was sound. My oh my. I reckon she was about eighteen years of age and very lithe.

Well, I won't hazard a guess on how long I was engaged in discharging my brother-in-lawly duty, but it was a spell, and finally come a point when little Wunhai had received sufficient apology to drop off to sleep in my arms. O.K., I climbed out and tucked her in, experiencing an odd sensation when a cold draft flushed through my loins. I reckon I shivered, and another sister-in-law of mine who slept nearby sat up and beckoned to me.

When I come to her she whispered: "Shall I put more wood upon the fire?"

"It's all right," says I, quaking away, for I had got up a sweat beneath Wunhai's robes and it now felt as if it was turning to ice.

"Well," she said, "you better get in here before you freeze."

This girl's name was Digging Bear, and she was a few years older than Sunshine, maybe about twenty-three or four, very wide across the horizontal centerline of her face, an effect that was made more so by her sometimes wearing the braids behind her ears. She had positive features but handsome and was firm as a mare. She wore her dress in bed but had it lifted by the time I joined her. She was the only sister shorter than me; still she was right powerful of muscle. Having admitted me to the field of battle, as it were, she made me struggle over the outcome, and for a long time thereafter, the calves of my legs bore bruises where she had dug in with her heels as if riding a pony upside down.

Afterward she wanted to talk: "I heard that white woman with Younger Bear is ugly and has a funny smell. I knew that she could not be your wife. Nobody but a coward like him would keep a woman of that type." Etc., etc.; she was the malicious sister, but I'll tell you that a nasty streak ain't the worst quality for a woman in bed. Adds a touch of seasoning. The best kind of war pony always has some meanness in him and so escapes being hitched to a travois.

I was a bit hung over by the time I pulled away from Digging Bear, and having been recharged by her own comments, she was clutching at me for another go.

"Stay here," she whispered. "Corn Woman is too tired."

This referred to the remaining sister, the widow. I swear I had not thought of her until then. She was the biggest, the plumpest, the oldest, being maybe twenty-eight, with them two kids on adjoining robes.

"So am I tired," I tells Digging Bear. "And you should be too. Go to sleep." But I could feel her watching me as I went back to my bed alongside Sunshine, and I had to lay there awhile in pretense before her head disappeared beneath the covers and I could steal out again and over to Corn Woman.

Yes, tired I was and sore, but whatever had sent me on those rounds was not extinguished while one sister remained. Whatever, Corn Woman was sleeping when I got there, and I didn't go through no eeremony, just flung back her robe and got inside. She clasped me without rightly awakening: she had had a husband and two kids, and this wasn't no novelty as with Wunhai nor a fierce exercise like with Digging Bear, but as natural as eating a meal. She was warm and soft, and I found her mighty soothing for a skinny, nervous fellow like myself.

Who was best? None of your business. I maybe said too much already, for I cannot impress upon you too earnestly that my activities that night were by Cheyenne standards the opposite of loose morals. These was all my wives, and I was doing my duty towards them.

I could hardly walk when that was done, but a great calm had descended upon me. I still wasn't sleepy, but no bitterness nor unresolved problems kept me awake. I put on my breechclout and leggings again—I had worn my shirt through all of it—wrapped a blanket around me, and went outdoors.

It hurt some to breathe deep, so cold and merciless clean was the air. A dog yapped a mile away, in Younger Bear's village: you could hear it perfect. The moon had set by now and all was dead black, for the dawn would soon rise. I had consumed the night in delivering my masculine services. There could be no doubt that I had once and for all turned 100 per cent Cheyenne insofar as that was possible by the actions of body. I might have planted a new human being or two by that night's work, and I never thought about how they would be little breeds, growing up into a world fast turning uncongenial even to fullbloods. No, all seemed right to me at that moment. It was one of the few times I felt: this is the way things are and should be. I had medicine then, that's the only word for it. *I knew where the center of the world was.* A remarkable feeling, in which time turns in a circle, and he who stands at the core has power over everything that takes the form of line and angle and square. Like Old Lodge Skins drawing in them antelope within the little circle of his band, but concentric around them was all other Cheyenne, present and past, living and ghost, for the Mystery is continuous.

It was a grand moment, and into it, out of the night, stepped Sunshine. I smelled rather than seen her, for the blackness was absolute.

"You cannot sleep?" I asked, believing she had come from the tepee.

"I was in the woods," she said, and took my arms and put between them a tiny parcel in a blanket. It felt like a warm coal, but was a newborn child. She had gone out and had it while I was bedding with her sisters. "Another son for you," she said. "He will be a great speaker. Did you not hear his powerful cry?"

But of course, with them sisters, I had not been listening. I had not knowed she had even left the lodge.

"I hope our enemies are far away," she said, "for when he came to life he had great lungs."

Well, this was no break in my medicine feeling but rather a richening of it. I held the little fellow to me and Sunshine leaned her head upon my shoulder, and then this thing happened. A burning golden ball appeared on the dark horizon, and as it slowly clumb into the sky, it changed through marvelous colors, vermilion to yellow to emerald green, turquoise to intense blue, then into purple and indigo and bright again, like a moving peephole through the roof of the world onto the great rainbow outside down which the chiefs ride in ceremonial array in the Other Life. Finally, when it got well up, there was a moment of mother-of-pearl and then the colors burned off into full radiant white.

"That is his name," said Sunshine. "Morning Star."

I handed my son back to her and she went into the lodge to feed him.

As it happened, another person was also provided with a name by that heavenly display, which he was watching at this same moment from behind the hills overlooking the valley of the Washita. I reckon he took it as a favorable portent of the fate what had made him a general at the age of twenty-three. And maybe he was right, for in a few moments now he would ride to the greatest victory he ever knowed.

In later years his Crow Indian scouts would call him Son of the Morning Star. His real name was George Armstrong Custer.

CHAPTER 18 *The Big Medicine of Long Hair*

FIRST LIGHT COME OUT of the east not long afterward. I was still out of doors and full of wonder, so much so that I was actually considering to go break the ice on the river and take me a Cheyenne plunge. But my pony, tethered near, was stirring for a morning drink. Actually—you won't believe this—he looked at me out of his big clear eyes and said: "Father, take me down to the water." I don't mean he spoke in words, but he said it. Then he said: "We are in for a big fight." To hell with what you believe. He said it. I was there.

I said: "Oh, you hear the crashing of the snow crust up the valley. That is just the horse herd of your brothers and cousins."

"No," said my pony, stubbornly shaking his head as I undid the halter from the picket pin. His breath and mine was steaming great clouds in the cold.

"Come," said I, "I'll show you." I mounted him and started out of the cottonwood grove which the camp was in among. My own tepee stood near the edge with no timber close enough to fall on it in case of storm, so we rode only forty yards to the open bottom-land of the valley and looked up the meadow where the herd was. At that moment I heard a distant shot behind me, from the hills on the far side of the village. Reason I didn't turn, though, was that straight ahead, galloping in a line that stretched across the snow-whitened bottom, come a great body of animals. But you can be fooled by the morning air and all the more when crystalline, which magnifies, so that at distance a man will seem a horse, a horse a buffalo. Allowing for this effect, I seen that charge as our pony herd in stampede, set off by Pawnee raiders. With a purpose to go get my gun, I wheeled; and as I did, a whole brass band commenced to play, trumpets, flutes, and drums. I thought I had lost my mind. It was an Irish tune called "Garry Owen," what I had heard the post band at Leavenworth play in Sunday concert. At the first strains, my pony reared and throwed me. "I told you," he screamed and bolted crazy towards the oncoming charge, going maybe fifty feet before his front legs broke at the knees and he plunged into the snow, skidding in a long trace of red.

He had been hit in the neck while I was still mounted, for that whole line had begun to fire upon the first notes. I was drenched with his blood. From about three foot above ground the air seemed solid with whining lead. Yet I got up and run untouched towards my tepee. I might have been yelling but couldn't tell owing to the music. I couldn't even hear the hoofbeats or the carbine fire, just that band blare.

Digging Bear was coming out of the lodge door, carrying my piece and a leathern pouch of ammunition. Ten yards still away, she throwed me the rifle and swung her arm back to hurl the pouch, but a little black hole sprung in her broad temple, like a fly had lit there, and she set down dead in the snow. A dozen more slugs snapped through the lodge cover behind her, and when I run inside, I seen young Wunhai had gathered half of them into that warm brown breast I had fondled several hours before, her deerskin bosom all bitten up.

Sunshine sat in the rear, Morning Star at her nipple.

"Down, down!" I shouts. "Lie flat." She curled around the baby, and I covered her over with buffalo robes. I went to do the same for Frog Lying on a Hillside and Corn Woman and her children, but they were gone from the tepee.

By time I got to the door again, the bluecoats was so close they fired beyond our lodge into those in the timber behind. To leave by that egress would have put me under their hoofs, so with my knife I slashed a rent in the back and slipped through it. Indians was coming out everywhere, some not getting far before they went under, others diving behind cottonwoods and subsequently delivering a return fire, mainly arrows, but the targets was bad and their own folk running between.

The cavalry pounded in among the lodges now, the band still playing out in the open valley where they rested. That music was driving me batty. I belly-flopped behind a tree. I had not yet fired my piece, but not because of delicacy. No, I would have dropped them troopers without mercy had I the wherewithal to do it: they was ravaging my home, had killed two of my women, and because of them my dearest wife and newborn boy lay in uttermost jeopardy. At such a time you see no like betwixt yourself and enemy, be he your brother by blood or usage.

But my gun was empty. Around the lodge I kept it unloaded in case them children got to tinkering. The ammunition rested in that pouch under Digging Bear's body, some fifty yards of galloping cavalry from where I lay.

Some Cheyenne had went to the river, leaped in, and was using the high bank as fortification behind which they covered the retreat down the center of the icy stream by a large body of women and children. I thought I saw Corn Woman and her young among them, but the gun smoke was thick now and closed across about that time, and when it cleared a trooper's horse was shot under him and fell into my line of vision. I was distracted by the sight of them saddle-bags, where the cavalrymen generally packed their extra ammunition. I run towards it, but before I got there the animal clumb to its feet and galloped away riderless. Just stunned, I reckon. But the trooper was hurt worse. He lay with his left boot at a strange angle from his upper leg. He was a young fellow, hardly beyond a boy, with a newly started mustache. Him and me, our eyes met, and a blaze come into his as they was windows in back of which somebody just fired a torch, but it was dying caused it and not recognition, for the next instant his head pitched forward showing the back of the skull busted open like an orange. And the Cheyenne who did it, using a wooden war club embedded with a triangular blade of rusty iron, took the lad's carbine and cartridge belt and dashed for the river, whooping, but got his own as he leaped the bank, belched blood as he hit the water, and sank in frothing commotion.

Already the troops had passed into the lower reaches of the village, the noise suddenly half-distant as if from a fight in the room next door. I had a mind to go back to my lodge and fetch the cartridges from underneath Digging Bear, but knew the soldiers would soon reverse for the clean-up and my activity might bring them down on where Sunshine was hid, so I run among the other tepees, and that was when I saw the stout body of Black Kettle, sprawled near his lodge door. He had signed his last treaty. Sand Creek and now this. His wife lay nearby, still dying.

Old Lodge Skins, I thought: I must get to him. He'd be helpless now, with no sons and blind. So I doubled back, for his tepee was near my own, and on the way I passed numerous dead Indians and almost got shot by a wounded brave I didn't know, but he went under before he could stretch the bowstring. The incident brought my appearance to mind. I hadn't cleaned the black paint from my face of the day before—it keeps your nose and cheeks warm in winter—but some of it must have been scraped away in this or that activity since. Aside from that, my hair was wholly exposed. Well, I didn't know what to do about it at the moment.

I plunged in through the entranceway of Old Lodge Skins's tepee. Sure enough, he was still there. But he was not abandoned. Them two young wives of his was trying to get him to flee. The one had a baby strapped to her back. The other was especially wrought up, and automatically went for me with her butcher knife, though she used to see me often.

I held her off on the muzzle of my empty gun, and says: "You women run for it. I'll help Grandfather."

"Kill me then, too," cries Tassel Woman, who had that knife.

"Get on out, you fool!" I yells, and stepping to the side, fetches her a swat in the ample hindquarters with the stock of the Ballard. "Go down to the river."

That shook some sense into her, and the other with the baby said: "I believe you"; and they left.

"My son," Old Lodge Skins remarked, quite casually. "Sit down beside me and we will smoke."

Would you believe it? That old man set there upon his buffalo robe and commenced to fill his pipe.

"Grandfather, have you lost your wits? The bluecoats are wiping us out. We have only the time of a bird flight to get under the riverbank before they turn back."

"Black Kettle is dead," said he. "I know it. I am blind and cannot fight. Yet neither will I run. If it is my day to die, I want to do it here, within a circle."

Well, I could see from the set of his leathery old jaw that talk from me would never stir him.

I says: "All right, I will light the pipe." He stuck his head forward, I grabbed away the pipe stem with my left hand, and with my right fist I hit him full force upon the chin. My hand was perfectly stunned, I couldn't unclench it. Old Lodge Skins, however, setting there like a rock, appeared undamaged.

"You are worried too much, my son," he said. "Your hand slips upon the pipe. Give me the brand. I will light it myself. Then we shall smoke, and your worry will lift and fly away like the little buffalo bird."

I didn't think I'd ever regain the use of my right hand, so I brought him a glowing coal in my left. By now the shooting outside was coming back in our direction. What I had intended to do with that blow, you see, was to knock him unconscious and carry him to the river. I now considered cold-cocking him with my rifle butt, but it was likely his head was even harder than his jaw, besides being padded with that coarse, thick hair.

He puffed on the pipe and offered the usual smoke clouds to East and West, etc. By God, I thought, he is sticking to it, he is an Indian to the core. You know how you think about foreigners, savages, and so on, that in an emergency they'll be just like yourself, even to talking English. But it was me who had to become Cheyenne here.

I got the eloquence of desperation. "The river is part of the great circle of the waters of the earth," I says in the highest, squeakiest voice I could imagine, in mimicry of the falsetto of classic Cheyenne oratory. It seemed to work: Old Lodge Skins come alert and put down his pipe.

"The sacred waters flow through the body of the earth as the blood runs within a man and the sap within a tree. All things are joined in this great current. O White Buffalo Spirit, hear me! Lead your children to safety by the river!"

I don't want you to think I was mocking anything at this point. Get into a battle and see how derisive you feel. No, I felt the call then. It might have been an instinct for preaching inherited from my Pa, but I was right exalted.

Not so much so, however, that I failed to see Old Lodge Skins picking up a huge old muzzle-loader from where it had laid beside him. My God, I thought, he's going to shoot me for trying to save him, the crazy old galoot.

Then I heard a noise at the door and turned, and a soldier crouched there, thrusting in a pistol and trying to see through the dim light.

"*Barroooom!*" I never heard a louder report than that made by Old Lodge Skins's piece. It must have been double-charged to make such a noise, spitting fire and smoke halfway across the tepee circle, and when the ball hit that soldier boy he was flung out the door like an empty suit of clothes.

The chief set up from where he had laid back with the five-foot barrel between his moccasin toes. He had sighted on sound.

"Go get his hair, my son," said he. "Then we will talk some more about the river. Maybe I will go there."

"It's probably too late already," I says. "Now they will come like coyotes to a rotting carcass. I won't argue with you any more."

I took an arm and pulled him to his feet. He never resisted in the slightest. I reckon he had decided to go: otherwise I'd never of moved him, I'm sure of that. I slit the tepee cover with my knife and prepared to lead him out.

"Wait," he said. "I must take my medicine bundle." This was a sloppy parcel about three foot long and wrapped in tattered skins. Its contents was secret, but I had once peeked into that of a deceased Cheyenne before they put it with him on the burial scaffold, and what his contained was a handful of feathers, the foot of an owl, a deer-bone whistle, the dried pecker of a buffalo, and suchlike trash: but he undoubtedly believed his strength was tied up in this junk, and who was I to say him nay. So with Old Lodge Skins. I got his bundle from a pile of apparent refuse behind his bed.

Then we started out again.

"Wait," the old man said. "My war bonnet." He never wore this item since I knowed him, because I think I have said that Cheyenne chiefs did not go in for display: they was generally the plainest of the men you'd see. He kept his in a round rawhide case hanging from a tepee pole.

"Perhaps you would like to see it?" he asks. "It is very beautiful and a reminder to me of my fighting days as a young man." He actually starts to undo the case.

"Some other time, Grandfather," says I, hanging it on my shoulder by its leathern string.

About that time, a number of carbines begin to pour lead into the tepee; it sounded like we was in a beehive. But do we leave? No, Old Lodge Skins has first to get his sacred bow and quiver of arrows, and then a special blanket, and of course his powder horn and shot bag, and his pipe and tobacco case. I am loaded down with this crap, and the United States Cavalry is blowing out the front of the lodge.

I commence to curse in English and howl in Cheyenne, and try to push him through the slit I cut, but no use, he stands embedded like a tree and puts on the rest of his jewelry: bracelets, bear-claw necklace, breastplate of tiny bones, and the lot.

Now the soldiers set fire to the face of the lodge. I guess that's when I might have started to cry. I didn't care about being killed no more, would indeed have welcomed death, I think, if I could have got the suspense over. I say crying; it might have been laughter. Whatever, it was hysterical.

"Come, my son," he says. "We cannot stay in this tepee all day. The soldiers are about to burn it down."

So after all that, it is him who leads me out, my legs like tubes of sand. Now of course not even the cavalry was so dumb as to assault only the tepee door. They was around back, too. We stepped directly into the reception of three troopers, and they fired point-blank, so close I don't know why our hair didn't burn from the flash.

All I can testify to is that they missed, and while the fearsome reports was still reverberating through my tortured eardrums, I heard Old Lodge Skins say: "Pay no attention to them, my son. I have now seen that it is not our day to die."

If you have any sense, you won't believe the following account of how we gained the river. I don't, myself. But then you have to find another way to explain it, for here I am today and therefore I must have survived the Battle of the Washita in 1868.

Old Lodge Skins give me his rifle and he lifted that medicine bundle up before him in his two hands and started to sing. I saw then that the eyes of them troopers was not focused upon us, and we walked right past them while they fired again into the rip we had come out of. I heard one of them say: "We got them all, boys. Let's have a look." But another believed they should give it a few more rounds, so they went on pouring lead into that empty tepee.

The chief walked slowly on, in a dead line for the river, singing and holding high his medicine bundle. The soldiers was everywhere among the village now, mostly afoot but some still mounted, but neither kind made no difference to us. We walked right through them without incurring their interest of eye or ear, though the chief's voice was loud, ranging from the heavy guttural to the piping falsetto, and in appearance we must have been a novelty, even in a Cheyenne camp: first, Old Lodge Skins, his blind eyes shut, and then me, with black-streaked face and sandy hair, leggings and blanket, and carrying all that rubbish and two empty rifles.

Now we approached the rear of a line of skirmishers firing at the Indians defending the riverbank, the whole action having moved downstream some from where I had first seen them, as the Cheyenne retreated slowly along. The main party of women and children was gone from sight, though some stragglers waded here and there in the cold Washita.

Well, he had kept it up so far, and I didn't know why we wasn't seen and shot down except maybe because the sheer audacity of the stunt made us invisible to the soldiers, but would he march through them skirmishers and into the crossfire?

He would and did, and we went untouched though, as if in accompaniment to his song, I heard much whistling of lead about my ears. But one thing happened: the Indians stopped shooting till we reached the bank. *They* saw us all right, and I think their so doing is the only thing that kept me from being permanently warped by that experience. That, and the shock of jumping waist-deep into the frigid water, which felt like I had been skinned from toe to belly-button.

Once me and Old Lodge Skins was in the Washita, the other Indians pushed us downstream after the women and children. Someone said: "Leave the river at the big bend, where the depth is over the head from shore to shore."

I reckon they took me for the chief's personal nurse in his blindness. I was reluctant to go, what with Sunshine and Morning Star still hiding beneath the robes in our tepee, so far as I knew. But I couldn't do no good for them. The soldiers now had complete possession of the village and was already herding together such women and children as had neither resisted nor run. They'd no doubt soon find my two and add them to the captives, and all I'd accomplish by making an attempt at this time to liberate them would be to get myself executed as a renegade, if not shot down before my identification was established.

So off we waded, the chief and myself, and now I led him rather than vice versa as it had been this far, for he had come out of his medicine spell on entering the water and was a blind old man—which I guess given his character was typical now that the worst of the danger was temporarily gone. He was his best when confronting a menace. Keeping under the bank we was out of the line of fire, and made good progress, though after a time in that freezing element my body felt like stone.

We waded for about three-quarters of a mile when we overtook the women and children what had gone on before, they being slowed by the smaller kids, some of whom was in up to the neck. I dropped that junk I carried for Old Lodge Skins, including both our rifles, and seizing one little boy, put him upon my shoulders. In this fashion we did another good mile to the horseshoe bend, and then all left the water to avoid that deep section, with a purpose to cut across the intervening tongue of land and re-enter the river below.

The air was ferocious upon my wet clothes. I swung that boy to the earth and he rejoined his mother and her other children, but we hadn't got much farther when that woman set down and begun to tear strips from her dress and bind them about the feet of her offspring, which I reckon was about to freeze off though the kids had not made a sound.

That was when a party of cavalry rode up on our rear. I realized later that this was the detail commanded by Major Joel Elliot, who Custer sent downstream to strike a large concentration of Cheyenne on the south shore, below our family group. We had three armed braves with us, traveling as guards, and a man called Little Rock who had a muzzle-loader stopped and shot a horse from under a trooper, and the instant after, himself fell dead from the answering fire.

The women and children hastened to get back into the river, and I must say I went along with them. There was a moment there when Little Rock fell that I thought I should go pick up his gun and perform a manly role, but another of the remaining two braves beat me to it.

Well, the women and children was almost all into the water, below the bend, and me and Old Lodge Skins was just climbing down the steep bank to join them when a man shouts down from above: "You can come back. We have surrounded them."

So I push Old Lodge Skins up again, and he is seemingly lighter to move than when we was on the downslope.

He says, right lively, handing me his medicine bundle, "Give me my rifle. I want to rub out some soldiers before the young men get them all."

"I left it over there," I says and takes that opportunity to slip away. There was plenty of women around to help him from now on, and a great body of Cheyenne was running up from the south, while others had got between the cavalry detachment and the river, driving them into the tall grass of the rising ground towards the bluffs.

The trooper unhorsed by Little Rock's shot had earlier dropped off to take captive the woman who was binding her children's feet. She had delayed till he was surrounded. Now I saw the rush that overwhelmed him, and when the Indians cleared away, he was stripped naked and lay red upon the trampled snow.

Elliot's command dismounted and let go their horses, which run wildly down the valley and the soldiers lay in the high grass, where they was concealed except for the smoke of their carbines. They kept up a steady fire, but it was panicky and unaimed, most of it straight up into the winter sky, and when the Indians saw that, they didn't bother to creep up no more but those that was mounted rode right in and commenced killing them like chickens, and the women and children come up to watch. The fight lasted maybe twenty minutes, and at the end all you could see was the swarm of Cheyenne backs as they bent to take coup and butcher.

I don't know if you ever seen carnage in winter. It ain't pretty at no season, but in the cold the blood soon freezes and a body stiffens up before you know it. If you wait too long, you have to break its limbs to get its shirt off.

I mention this not to be ghoulish but to list my motive in hastening into the grass: I needed one of them uniforms. There was forty-fifty Indians and only fifteen bodies to be shared among them. I had a bit of luck: I run into Younger Bear, on his knees and at work with a knife. I realized now that he had been one of the two or three braves who had first rode in among the soldiers. He was wearing a big war bonnet that I hadn't recognized. His left shirt sleeve was reddened and drops of blood was dripping from the fringe onto the nose and lips of the corpse he was scalping. He was also sweating profusely, for I guess his knife was dull and that left arm didn't have no strength to pull the hair away as the skin was severed.

However, he was quite calm as to mood. He noticed my leggings alongside him and said without looking up: "You pull while I cut."

So I did. I knelt and took hold of them light-brown, rather fine-textured locks of the dead white man. I think he was right young. His mouth was strained open as if in a silent cry. I endeavored not to study him, for he might have been somebody I once knowed, and there wasn't anything personal in what I was doing. So at length his skull cover come free, and I was obliged to Younger Bear for taking it quickly from me.

"I saw you charge in to take coup before," I says. "That was brave."

The Bear wiped the sweat from his brow and left a great smear of blood in its place. He sighed and shrugged, but he was pleased. He handed me his knife and said, as you might to a guest sitting before a roast turkey: "Go on and take something for yourself. There is a pretty ring on his left hand."

"Well," says I, "I could use the shirt and pants."

Younger Bear makes a gesture as if to say it's on the house, and I got the uniform off that soldier and his boots, and later I found his hat nearby. I bundled that stuff under my arm, and the Bear went back to work. The soldier now lay in his wool underwear. He had unbeknownst to himself done me a favor, and I thought I would try to return it though he might never know that either.

I said to the Bear: "You had better get your arm tied up before you bleed to death."

He looked like he noticed it for the first time, poked the muscle and winced.

"Come," I said, "where's your pony?" Then I saw his horse over a ways, and who should be patiently holding its bridle but Olga. And there also with her was little Gus, watching the other Indians milling about with their gory trophies, and he had a tiny wooden knife and was wielding it in imaginary scalping procedure. I reckon he would have liked to do a little real cutting with it, but Olga was restraining him with her other arm, I'll say that much for her.

The Bear took a minute more to do something which I surely didn't watch and then got up.

"All right," he said. "I'll go and you can have the rest of him. Thank you for your help." He puts out his hand to me, and I took it—and kept it, for it wasn't his, but rather the right hand of that soldier, which he had severed and stuck into his sleeve, drawing his own arm up.

"Hahaha!" he laughed. "Good joke!" He was still laughing as he went over to Olga, carrying the scalp and trailing that suit of long underwear like a whole human skin.

Now I had to put on that uniform, a ticklish proposition, for soon as it was on my back I'd be alien to the Indians, but I could not get back to the village dressed otherwise. My purpose of course was to go find Sunshine and the baby. They would be prisoners by now. Wearing the blue clothes, I could get access to them, and in the disorganization of battle we could make off to the hills. Nobody would question a soldier herding along an Indian woman with a baby on her back.

Having finished their butchery in the tall grass, the Cheyenne started to move downstream again. I saw blind Old Lodge Skins among them, being led by a woman—no, it was Little Horse, who was after all his own son. That was as it should be. I done my job and had my own to look after.

The firing had died away except for scattered flurries throughout the valley, and the smoke rising above the camp was now black from burning lodges. Our people was heading for the other villages along the lower Washita. I doubted that the soldiers intended to press on in that direction, for it was afternoon now, and on the bluffs across the river I could see a body of mounted Indians which I reckon had come up from the downstream camps to oppose their progress. There was fifteen hundred lodges in that valley, of which only a little more than fifty stood in Black Kettle and Old Lodge Skins's village. But these other camps was strung out over ten mile and discontinuous one from the next. I believe it was at the Washita that the Indians learned a lesson in villaging, for eight years later on the Little Bighorn they didn't leave no space between their tepee circles to let Custer through.

George Armstrong Custer. I had never heard of him by this time in my life though I understand he had got a name for himself in the Rebellion. Here's something maybe you didn't realize: Indians almost never knowed who it was attacked them until the battle was done, and sometimes not even then. Look at what had happened to me so far upon this day: I had seen only two soldiers close up: one had been that trooper what fired into Old Lodge Skins's tepee; and the other, Younger Bear's victim. We had been charged at dawn by whites, dressed in blue. Nobody knew who led them, nor cared. Later, if another treaty council was held, the soldier-chief would likely be there, and say as an opening statement to the Cheyenne: "You remember how I beat you on the Washita." Which would be the first time the Indians had this information.

Afterwards they'd call that man not by his white name but by a peculiarity of his appearance on this occasion, like in later years General Crook was Three Stars; General Miles, Bear Coat; and General Terry was called by some The Other One, I guess because they run out of names.

When they got to know Custer, the Cheyenne and their allies named him Long Hair, but I believe 99 per cent of the individuals within the tribe would not have recognized him in parade gear at the head of his troops; and not even the chiefs he counciled with would have knowed him with his hair cut. This time will come.

Right now, there I was trailing along behind my Indian comrades as they proceeded downriver at the Washita. Custer I never heard of, but the brass badge on that dead trooper's campaign hat told me his outfit was Company G, Seventh Cavalry. Suppose I run into other fellows from the same company? I undid it from the felt and throwed it aside. Then with my knife I tore a hole where the badge had been, as if a bullet had blown it out.

But I had yet to get into the uniform, though the other Indians what stripped the soldiers had put on articles of their loot, here a brave in a sergeant's jacket, there a little kid wearing the gray-flannel Army shirt like a dress, and maybe a woman in a piece of wool underwear over her deerskins.

At last we come to where the ground swelled and I set down as if to tighten my moccasin lacings until the last of the Cheyenne had disappeared over the rise. Then crawled two hundred yards through the grass-matted snow, stood up, took my bearings, saw a clear route to the riverbank and took it, plunging once more into the icy Washita, which rose to my chin at this point. It was all I could do to keep that uniform above the stream, but it was still dry when I reached the other side, and for warmth alone I was glad to exchange it for them buckskins which would freeze stiff between each step.

I also remembered to scrub the black from my face; what I missed would look natural enough as the soot of battle. As you might suppose, the clothing was all too big. Now, trousers and shirts was worn voluminous in the Army, but the cavalry jacket was cut snug. I'd just have to leave this one unbuttoned to cover up the situation, despite the cold. My feet had room to tour independently within the boots, and the hat was pretty loose even with a stuffed headband.

But I was ready, and stuck my head out of the brush patch which I had used as dressing room. I found myself looking directly at a

Cheyenne brave some twenty yards on, who sent an arrow towards me before I could blink. It seemed to travel quite slow through the atmosphere, the only difficulty being that my dodge was of similar character, as if immersed in a barrel of molasses. The triangular iron head, with its razor edges, had an affection for my nose and followed wherever I pointed that feature. I mean, it seemed so. It seemed as if I was somersaulting over and over, and the educated arrow followed every convolution, a spare half inch from my beak. Actually, whatever happened was over in an instant, the arrow had disappeared, the Cheyenne was face down and dead, and a cavalry corporal rode up with a smoking weapon.

"My God," he said, "what a place to take a dump." Which is what he figured I had been doing in them bushes and what could I do but grin at him. "Git on," he said, pointing to his horse's hindquarters. "Don't it hurt?"

Then I saw from the corner of my eye that the arrow was lodged in my hatbrim, as close across my right temple as it could have been without tearing skin. From the trooper's angle, feathers fore and head aft, it must have looked as though my skull was spitted. I throwed it away and mounted behind him and we went back to the village.

Now we got in among the tepees at the lower end of camp, and this soldier, he trotted up to a little group of blue-dressed figures, we dismounted, and he saluted a man.

"Sir," he says, "I scouted the—"

"Just a moment," interrupts the officer what he has addressed and turns to me. I am standing there apart, getting my bearings, for troops is going hither and yon, looting tepees, herding Cheyenne women and children together into one party, driving captive ponies. I hardly knowed the place where I had lived some weeks.

"Soldier," orders this officer, "come here." I seen he meant me, so went to him. He was a right good-looking fellow, tall and well-proportioned, and I recall the collars of his blue-flannel shirt was embroidered with two gold stars on each point. He had a yellow mustache and his fair hair was so long in back, its curls barely cleared his shoulders.

His eyes was icy-blue, and under brows so pale you could see them only by their bushiness. He says in a voice like a rasp across the grain of a board, "Button that jacket!"

I proceeds to do it.

He says: "Consider yourself under arrest. Give your name to the sergeant of the guard."

Now that trooper who picked me up does me another favor. "If the general pleases," that soldier says, "I found this man in the brush and had to kill an Injun to get him clear. He was hit in the head by an arrer, poor devil, and is out of his mind, I believe."

I didn't need no further cue. I laid my head on the side and sort of goggled my eyes, letting my tongue flap loose.

A spasm of impatience run over the general's face. "Well, get him out of here," he said. "This is a field headquarters, not the laboratory of an alienist."

"Now," said my benefactor, "if the general will hear the report of my scout—"

"No, I do not intend to," responded the officer. "It cannot have much value if instead of observing the enemy's dispositions, you were rescuing lunatics." He jerks his back to us, and says to them others: "I have decided to shoot the captured ponies."

One of them officers was a heavy-set, fatherly-looking man with a full head of white hair showing below his hat. I seen him gazing at me with a trace of amusement, as if he knowed the deal. But now he gets disturbed at what the general said and starts to protest.

"There are eight hundred ponies in that herd," he says. "Had we not better save our ammunition for—"

"I have decided to shoot them," says the general, "and do not require your suggestions upon the matter, Benteen."

Benteen gives him a long look of undisguised scorn. Then he says in his benevolent way to the corporal, who was still standing with me alongside him: "You had better collect a detail of fifteen men and go and execute all of our four-legged prisoners. If you run out of ammunition, you might go over on the bluffs and borrow some from the Cheyenne."

The corporal salutes him, and so do I, and I swear he winks at me. The general never saw it, though, for he was striding vigorously up and down in his smart boots, ordering things of various officers and men, and one of them is the director of the band, I guess, for shortly that group begins to play.

When we had gone on a ways by foot, the corporal says: "I'd think you would of knowed better than to let Hard Ass Custer catch you with your jacket open. He is a real son of a bitch, ain't he? Goddam, I'd pay the Cheyenne what put a bullet in his brass heart."

I said, "But that Benteen ain't bad."

"Ain't bad?" exclaimed the corporal, right angry at my under-statement. "I know fellows in his company would whip you for saying less than that he is the best officer who ever rode in the U.S. Goddam Cavalry."

"That's what I meant," says I. Actually, at this point I was trying to find a chance to slip away from him and get to where the prisoners had been collected.

"You see how he looked at Custer? He don't give a damn for him, I'll tell you that. You can't fight rank, but you don't have to put your nose up in it, either, and the Colonel won't. He's right worried now over Major Elliot. Hard Ass won't send out a patrol to look for him. That was what I was really doing out there when I run into you. You see anything of him?"

"Not me," I says. That was when I realized it was probably Elliot and his command that the Cheyenne had wiped out and butchered in the grass across the river. I had been wise to throw away the badge from my hat.

"Benteen and Elliot served together in the War," he says. "Well, we have to get shooting them horses. And you best find you a carbine if you can and praise your luck that Custer didn't notice you'd lost yours. He'd of spread-eagled you in the snow."

"I left it with my bunky," says I, for I had learned the lingo when I was with the soldiers after the Solomon battle. "I'll go fetch it."

"All right, and then you get back on the double, for I got my eye on you," he says, assuming the style of a noncom now he had work to do. That's how it goes with rank, among the whites; I had forgot how quick relations can change.

Soon as I got some men and horses between him and me, I headed for the prisoner's corral, which I found to be several tepees they had let to stand near the center of the camp, into which the women and children had been collected. I could hear them singing that doleful death dirge of the Cheyenne as I approached. These lodges was of course ringed by a guard of soldiers, and I looked for some diffi-culty in gaining access there, for I wouldn't want to tell my purpose in so doing.

In addition I never wanted to get caught again by anybody and put on special duty. My late uneasiness as a white man among Indians was nothing beside the feeling I had now, slogging along in the enormous boots, with only my ears holding up that hat, and the jacket stood away from my body as if it was an empty hogshead.

But then I remembered Old Lodge Skins's stunt in walking through that crossfire, which by the way was the only time I could recall his medicine working against the whites. He had kept up his assurance, that's why; and I reckon being blind had helped; he wasn't distracted by anything he saw. Well, I didn't close my eyes but I did put myself in a state of concentration: I swelled up to fill that uniform, somehow, and I walked hard and smart up to a sergeant standing at the door of one of them tepees.

"General Custer sent me to interrogate the prisoners," I said.

"All right," he responds, and steps aside. But then before I could enter, he grabs my elbow and puts his mustache into my ear.

"Listen," he says, "you say a word for me with one of them young squaws and I'll make it worth your while. I mean, being you speak Indian, it wouldn't be no chore. Tell her after dark to come and whistle out the flap, and I'll give her a present." He slaps my shoulder, and I go within.

That lodge was packed solid with Cheyenne women and children, too crowded for anyone to sit down. They stood looking at me, with their blankets drawn close and a good many of the wives had undone their braids so their hair would hang free to be torn out in mourning. Some had scratched long rents down their cheeks for the same reason, and the wailing, rise-and-fall of the death songs did not diminish for my arrival. But when the smaller children saw my uniform, they grasped their mothers' legs and buried their little brown heads in the blankets.

One old woman was crying in high-pitched shrieks that at length would exhaust her air and then she would gasp and cry in a different tone on the in-breath till her lungs was filled and back to the positive weep. After a minute or so of this, during which I had not spoken, she breaks off and says to me: "Go away and let us die of sorrow."

It turned out that this sentiment, while it may have been sincere enough in the long view, had also the particular aim of ascertaining whether I could understand the language. For no sooner had I indicated that I did, she hangs upon the sleeve of my jacket and wails again, but alternates it with the following.

"I am the sister of Black Kettle. I told him we would be punished if he did not stop our young men from raiding the whites. But he would not listen to me. 'Shut your mouth, you foolish woman,' he would say. Well, was I not right? Black Kettle is dead, and all our warriors, and we helpless ones will be put to death by the soldiers. I told him it was bad to make war on the white people, who have always been our friends. They are wonderful people, good and kind, and I can understand why they punished the wicked Human Beings. But we helpless ones could do nothing, and now I suppose must suffer for our bad men."

"Shut your mouth, you foolish woman," I says. I knowed her, she was called Red Hair though hers was gray, and frankly I never heard before that she was sister to the chief. I won't say that was a lie, but if it wasn't, it was the only particle of truth in her whole harangue. I'm not blaming her, see, for it was a good line to take and I believe she used it a little later on General Custer himself with some success, but I had better fish to fry.

Quicklike, she stops her weeping and says: "Would you like a beautiful young girl to bring the moon and stars into your lodge tonight?"

All this while of course I had been surveying the faces roundabout, but I did not see Sunshine.

"Now, they aren't going to kill you," I says, "so you can stop working your tongue two ways. If you weren't busy lying, you would see who I am. You know I'm not a soldier. I have just come back from helping get the rest of our people safely downriver, and am dressed like this so I may pass among the bluecoats."

The old hag squints cunningly at me. "Certainly, I know who you are. I just believed you had become a traitor." This is a free translation. What she actually said was she thought that at the sight of the white man's meat I had become their dog.

"I am looking for my wife and child, old woman, and I want to find them before they grow to such an age as yours, when the mind shrivels, falls into dust, and blows out the earholes in the night wind."

She was beginning to enjoy this exchange, the way harpies of that sort do, and come back at me with doubts about my manhood, etc., as if we was bantering in the midst of normal Indian life a thousand mile from the U.S. Cavalry, for them Cheyenne women were tough and got more so with age. She was a hard-bitten old bitch, and give her a knife she would have slit that horny sergeant from belly-button to breastbone if she thought she could have got away with it. As it was, I reckon she might function as procuress for him. She'd last as long as she could, and I take my hat off to her.

However, she never knowed what become of Sunshine, and I looked through them other prisoner-tepees with the same result, and then, with a terrible apprehension clawing into my vitals, I went to the upper end of the village where my lodge had been. But nothing was there save the ashes of our fire, a strip or two of deerskin, some buffalo hair, and the like. The soldiers had drug down all the tepees and burned them, with all therein that was left after looting, in one great blaze upon the Washita banks, the smoke from which I had seen earlier. By now that bonfire was down to a steaming heap of gray and black, and the snow melted off roundabout in a great circle of yellow.

In the meadow, they had started to shoot eight hundred ponies, and that was a mess, for some of the fellows on the killing detail must have got excited by the rearing, coughing, bleeding animals trying to kick each other's guts out as the lead seared within them, and pretty soon the bullets commenced to fly through the camp, and cursing consternation come from the troops on the other side. I reckon they griped to Custer, for I saw him ride by with an officer trying to talk to his stiff back, but as usual he wasn't listening, and what he did when he reached the herd was to dispatch a few of the ponies himself with his sidearm, I guess to show them the right way.

The band was still playing. Next place I went was to where they was digging a burial trench for the Indians what had died in camp: the bodies lined up side by side, still dressed except for the smaller articles that made souvenirs: necklaces and such. Very few of them was scalped, and I didn't see no mutilations at all. That should be said: this wasn't Sand Creek, and these troops was Regulars, not Volunteers; professional fighting men are always less bloody than amateurs.

I seen Black Kettle again; his silver medal was gone. And then I seen young Wunhai, and I seen Digging Bear. . . . Seventy-eighty bodies there might have been, and I expect more in the brush and timber which they wasn't bothering about, and then the Indians from downriver might have recovered some others.

Corn Woman and her children and little Frog, they must have escaped down the Washita; they wasn't here. But what of Sunshine and Morning Star? Thank God, I couldn't find them among these dead; on the other hand, when I went to help Old Lodge Skins, they had been still under the buffalo robes. Had they gone into the river at a later time, I would have seen them when myself below the horseshoe bend.

I left that burial place before they lowered Wunhai and Digging Bear and shoveled earth upon them. I recall feeling disorderly at the time, like if I had stayed, I would have thrown myself into the trench alongside. Wunhai looked like a dead wren, but Digging Bear had not died easy as I had thought ———— I don't want to talk of it, I had been fond of them women. They was maybe just Indians, but they had been mine and small use I was to them.

I searched the timber and I searched the brush, and I found three bodies but none of them was Sunshine, and I wandered so far as to come below the bluffs and the Cheyenne watching there seen me and started down, and I had to run for it. There was sufficient of them up there to retake the village, especially while the troops was shooting ponies, burning property, herding prisoners, and all, but Custer knowed how to put Indians on the defensive. It was winter, and he burned up their robes. They lived by their riding, and he killed their horses. He held captive fifty of their women and children. They watched him helpless.

Now they was afraid he would go after the camps along the lower Washita, and he knowed they was, so had determined to move in that direction and by posing as a menace to the downstream villages he would keep them too worried to counterattack. This I found out later. At the moment, back in the timber, I heard the bugles sounding assembly call. I reckon it wasn't no more than a half hour afterward that the whole regiment commenced to march downriver, carrying with them the captives on ponies saved for that purpose from the massacre of the herd, and naturally the band was blaring.

I never come from concealment either to cheer them off or see what they was doing. Easy enough to follow the latter by ear. Take a river valley hardened by winter, you can hear a gunshot about five mile away: think of the distance a brass band will carry. The Cheyenne had left the bluffs in a panic to get to their families. Custer had the knack, all right. Everything he done said to all other living creatures: *I win and you lose.*

Well, when it sounded like the rear guard had reached the horseshoe bend, I returned to where our camp had been. Before leaving, the army had also pulled down the tepees where the captives was held and put them to the torch. These was still burning. The dead bodies of eight hundred horses lay in the meadow, here and there a hoof still jerking. Owing to the cold, they had not yet gone ripe enough to attract the carrion-feeders, though I seen three coyotes lurking a half mile up the valley and a raven or two high in the cottonwoods. The raw wind of late afternoon lifted black fragments from the refuse pile on the riverbank.

Custer had also shot such dogs as didn't run with the fleeing Indians, and them little bodies was strewn about amidst spent shells and arrows and the other litter. Considerable blood had spattered upon snow and earth, and when in shadow it froze bright red, soaking in and browning only where in sunlight.

Of the several hundred souls that occupied the place of late, I alone stayed quick. I set down upon the cold bank of the Washita. Though the river had earlier known some blood, them red bursts and filaments never last long in a flowing stream but join the mix and move on, and someplace a thousand miles away a fellow will drink himself some water and unbeknownst imbibe a particle of somebody else's juice of life. The sun was falling behind a blue ridge of smoke fringed with gold, like a sash hung across the western sky. You might have said that Custer flew his personal colors even on the horizon.

I wasn't setting there in self-pity, mind you, nor anger. I was just trying to figure it out. Circumstances seemed to disintegrate upon me shortly after I had got settled in them. I was twenty-six years of age, yet as I could recall, this here was the first time I could ever locate the source of my troubles in one individual.

I would have lived in that camp on the Washita throughout the winter, and when the new grass come up in the spring we would have broken the treaty and moved north, got us buffalo and Pawnee en route, and maybe run one of them antelope surrounds again if Old Lodge Skins was up to it and if the railroad hadn't scared away all the game, and so on up to the Powder River for some good fights with the Crow, and bear hunts and lodgepole-cutting in the Bighorn Mountains. All the while I'd have had them four women tending to my every little wish.

I seen General Custer as responsible for my loss. And I didn't yet know how nor where I would do it, but I decided to kill that son of a bitch.

CHAPTER 19 *To the Pacific and Back*

WHAT BECOME OF SUNSHINE? If I couldn't find her body she must have got away; probably waited till the cavalry had swept past the lodge, then slipped out and made it to the bluffs. She was a resourceful and resolute woman, and better than me at that sort of endeavor.

An Indian was more suited in mind and spirit for taking this type of beating than me. Here was I, aiming to kill Custer on the one hand; and on the other, I also decided I could never again live with the Cheyenne, for the simple reason that I couldn't afford to undergo another massacre on the losing end.

Darkness fell while I was still setting there on the banks of the Washita, plotting murder. It had got monstrous cold, and me covered only with a flannel shirt and cavalry jacket. The troopers had looted every blanket and robe in the village, beyond what they burned, for they had left their overcoats and haversacks back where they started their charge that morning, and the Cheyenne had circled round and got that stuff. Talk of having no weapon—I must first find some protection for my own hide or the weather would do me in before I put a blade in Custer's.

So I went to what was left of them lodges where the captives had been gathered. Luckily, a little hunk of one tepee skin had not been altogether burned. So I beat out where it was still smoldering and wrapped myself in it. Buffalo hide it was, with the hair scraped off, so afforded none too great a warmth. And not only was it cold in that place, but the moon come out and shone across that field of pony corpses, and now the coyotes had got to them and I also saw the big ghostly shapes of the gray wolf, a nasty creature, and the noise of them fangs tearing at limp flesh and the growls and whines was quite unpleasant.

I just had to start a fire, for the sight of so much carrion gives a wolf the confidence to take on something living. I was scraping among the ashes of the tepees, trying to find a coal still burning, when I heard the sound of horses coming from downriver. Custer had carried out his bluff, you see, threatening the villages in that direction so the Indians would strike them and run without hitting him; then he turned and come back.

Wolves, coyotes, and me melted away. I don't know where the vermin went: I retired into the brush, and more listened to than watched the column troop through the razed village. Then, after the rear guard had passed, I fell in a quarter-mile behind and followed them at this interval some hours up the valley of the Washita to where they finally made camp. Oh, but it was a cold and barren march for me, the desolation adding to the temperature. My only solace was that them troops dwelt in a similar predicament as to the weather. But they had comrades in misery, whereas my recent partners was dead or dispersed.

Soon they lighted great bonfires which illuminated the riverbottom. Well, I could just as soon cut Custer's throat after I singed my shanks a little, I thought. Indeed, without so doing it wasn't likely I could lift my knife for the shivering. So I snuck through the picket line and pushed up close through the throng about one blaze.

Some soldier wrapped in an Indian blanket says: "You ain't got a chaw?" I shook my head. The reflection of the flames flickered in his blear-eyes. He says: "Wasn't that a brilliant idea of Hard Ass's to leave the packs and overcoats behind? I reckon he'll get another medal for that."

A fellow on my other side says: "I don't doubt he kept his own overcoat and a side of bacon which his striker is frying up at this minute."

"Custer's luck, hey boys?" This come from the blear-eyed fellow, and someone else said hush or Hard Ass would hear him.

"Screw him," says Blear Eyes. "What's he gonna do, put me on half rations?"

The other soldier says: "He'll have a hole dug right through the snow and throw you in it, boy."

"He will?" I asks, trying to seem a natural part of this group.

"Will he? You must be a recruit or you'd know he done the very thing on the campaign a year ago last summer. Ask Gilbert," nodding at a long, thin soldier with a crooked nose and a growth of whiskers who was rubbing his skinny hands towards the fire. This man says: "Yeah, we was in the field and he never had no guard-house. Some of us boys showed up late for call, so he had this hole dug in the ground, thirty foot square, maybe fifteen deep, and throwed us in, then put boards acrost it. Fierce hot it was under the sun, and there was too many of us to lay down all at once."

"Then Hard Ass himself goes over the hill to see his old lady," Blear Eyes says. "Runs right off an Indian campaign. And you know all that happened to him? Suspended from command for one year, and he goes back to Michigan and spends it fishing."

Gilbert says: "I don't condemn the bastard for running back to his woman, much as I hate him, for there's a pretty piece of fluff."

"That right?" says I. I was fair warmed now and beginning to plot my course.

"Oh my yes. You ain't never seen Miz Custer? I tell you when you do you'll howl and lay down and lick the dirt, boy, and go to bed next night with Rosy Palm and her five sisters. That's the difference between a general and a private. Hey, who's for going over to the prisoners and getting us an old squaw?"

The conversation degenerated from that point on, as you might expect if you know anything about an army, and I edged off and proceeded across the campground. If I was going to assassinate Custer, I first had to locate him without arousing suspicion, which was not easy, since six or seven hundred soldiers was present and I was not tall enough to see over anybody's head.

The Cheyenne captives had an area and a couple small fires to themselves, and they was now so many silent blanket-rolls upon the earth, the children wrapped right in with their mothers: nothing keeps a redskin from his sleep. Down a ways beyond that, their ponies was herded, with a wide separation between them and the cavalry horses, who the Indian animals make nervous.

I made quite a scout of that bivouac, which was spread out and well lighted by the enormous cottonwood fires; and with the men cold and tired and hungry, what a slaughter could have been managed by fifty Indians. But the tribe had been whipped and then tricked, and anyway they never fought at night. Custer could just as well have pulled in his guards. Only one active enemy lurked in that area.

That was me, and by a process of elimination I found him at last. The officers had their fire at the base of a little knoll, but the

General wasn't there, he was by himself on top of the slight eminence. He had his own little blaze, and was seated on the ground alongside it, writing by its yellow light. Occasionally his striker, that is the orderly who done his servant-work, would come up and put a new log on the flames, which he had got from a detail of poor devils who was kept cutting wood in the timber all night and hauling it into camp.

So on one of their trips in with a load, I joined these last and helped them stack logs, which they did not question, and watched for Custer's striker to come over for a supply, which he finally done just before my back was broke.

"How's the General?" I says. Now I must explain that the type of fellow who takes that job has got the personality to suit it. He helps his master dress, serves his master's food, and digs his master's latrine, and for all I know wipes his master's behind. But sucking up to one man satisfies his appetite, and to all others he is extra-snotty.

"Don't you worry about that," says he. "Just give me two of them middle-sized logs."

"I was thinking he must be plumb wore out."

He give a sneering laugh. "You will never see the time when the General can't run any man in this outfit into the ground. He only went into camp now on account of the likes of you. He don't need no sleep nor food. Whipping one tribe of Indians only gives him the taste for another."

I says: "I seen he was writing something."

"Yes," says the striker. "That would be a letter to his Lady. He writes her most every day." There wasn't no postal boxes on the plains at that time, so when Custer mailed them letters he had to send some scout through a couple hundred mile of savage wilderness. I had yet to hear a thing about that man that didn't gall me like a cactus burr.

But just about the time I thought I had got this worm's confidence, he suddenly stops and squints suspiciously.

"Say, have you got an eye on my job?"

"Not me," I hastens to say. "No sir, I admit I am too dumb for it. But I tell you, I am right fascinated by heroes. I guess that's because I am kind of yellow myself. I near pissed my pants on that charge this morning, and the only thing that kept me going was the sight of the General up there ahead, his hair streaming in the wind and his arm waving us on." I put this watery, worshipful look on my face, and he swallowed it.

"Well," he says, "you want to carry this wood for me? I reckon it's O.K. if you come along to the bottom of the hill, where you can look up at him. And that's a favor I wouldn't give to any of the rest of these scum."

"Listen," says I, gritting my teeth with another feeling than that which he took it for, "it's worth a month's pay to me to actually go on up and put the wood on the fire near that noble individual."

He was first scandalized at this suggestion, but after a good bit of talk and my signing an IOU, with a false name, to hand him over thirteen dollars at the next payday, which is what a private earned per month, I gained the privilege of carrying the wood alone to the top of the hill, sticking it into the fire, and coming immediately back thereafter.

We set out for the knoll, and upon reaching the bottom of it, he stayed there and I mounted the slope with my two logs. Them griping soldiers had been wrong: Custer wasn't wearing no overcoat, and he had even laid his hat beside him and loosened the top of his shirt. Of course he was right close to the warm fire. His hair and mustache was golden in the light. He never looked up from the paper, supported upon an order book, which he was covering with line after line of fluent script, occasionally dipping his pen into a little ink bottle, then flinging the excess drops hissing into the flames.

I poked a log into the embers, with my back towards the striker at the foot of the slope, so he wouldn't see my other hand go beneath the jacket to the hilt of my knife. Some sparks went up the pink smoke stream towards the open black heavens. Custer did not raise his head, for to do so he would have had to change the angle at which his noble profile took the light. He was posing here quite as much as he had done when striding about the Cheyenne camp that morning. Then he was "General in the Field"; now, "Soldier at the End of Day."

It's funny how a man with Custer's personality could influence that of his would-be murderer, but I was seeing myself in various illustrations: knife raised over unsuspecting general, him with his halo of golden locks, me with teeth bared, and so on through a series that ended with "Assassin at Bay."

Who knows how much time I wasted on them childish visions. If you set out to kill, leave your imagination at home. Reality should suffice, at least if you're white.

For what happened now was that Custer spoke.

Still scratching away with his nib, his eyes to the paper, he says: "I'll take a cup of coffee now."

Maybe I simply lost my guts at that moment; maybe I never did have the stomach to slaughter a man in cold blood, but what I have always thought to be the case was that the *trust* in Custer's voice saved his life at that moment and so changed the course of history. Call me coward, but I wasn't able to slit the throat of a man while he was writing to his wife and fixing to drink coffee.

So the assassin answers slavishly: "Yes, sir," and goes down the knoll to where that striker is waiting.

"Get up there on the double," I says. "The General wants you to give him a bath."

I don't believe I have to take you along every inch of my route when leaving the Seventh Cavalry—for I did leave them that very night, in the dead of winter, and struck out alone across the wilderness. I had to. I had not given up my resolution. I was going to kill Custer sometime, but first I had to get away from him for a while. Nor could I stand to be in the proximity of them captive Cheyenne. And going downriver to the still free Indians was equally unthinkable. I had had it, right up to here.

I was going back to the settlements and get me some money, I didn't care how or where, and buy a frock coat, a brocaded vest, and a pearl-handled revolver. And dressed like that on one fine day, I would encounter General Custer a-strolling with his Lady through the streets of some town, Topeka, say, or Kansas City, for I knowed he liked his cities—oh, I found out more about him than I have said: he liked fine restaurants and theatricals, knew New York City, even, like the palm of his hand; so said his striker.

"My compliments to your Lady, sir," I would say, and then beg a private word with him, and we would step aside while his pretty Mrs. stood there simpering under her parasol. Then, "Sir," I would say, "you are a son of a bitch." And of course as a gentleman he would demand satisfaction, so the next scene was upon the prairie at dawn, our backs together, take ten paces forward, turn, and fire, then him upon the ground, a spreading red stain coming through his embroidered buttonholes. "Sir," he says to me with his dying breath, "you are the better man."

Then I'd dig a cold root out of the frozen ground with a pointy stick and gnaw on it, or pack more leaves as insulation between my shirt and jacket, and trudge on. I soon lost track of time. In fact, I went right out of my head and don't know why I survived at all. I seen nothing but a mass of white, like I was in the middle of a desert of cotton. It was snow of course, blizzards, but I don't recall it as cold, for I had got to the condition where I was more affected by textures than temperature, and it was all I could do to refrain from laying right down and going to sleep forever.

I guess I finally give in to the urge. I had been moving almost due east, having struck the Cimarron and stayed on it: in delirium you will follow almost anything that seems to know where it's going. So what I was doing was to cross Indian Territory horizontally rather than proceeding north to Kansas which I had intended, and I reckon I had reached the edge of the Creek Nation when I just flopped down in a white prairie that looked like one big bed.

When I woke up, I was in the log-cabin home of Creek Indians. The man of the family had come across me while hunting and brung me in, and these kindly folk, him and his wife and several youngsters, they nursed and fed me, and give me clothes to replace that blue uniform now in shreds. The Creek was Georgia redskins who was whipped by Andy Jackson, and not long afterward, the Government forced them out of their native country to go and live west of Arkansas, same as they did the Choctaw, Cherokee, and others. But these tribes was right civilized, had them log cabins, wore white type of clothes, did farming, and before the war they had even kept Negro slaves of their own.

I stayed with them Creek until the spring of '69. After I recovered, I done some hunting to pay my keep, and I helped out with the spring planting, and while I was sure glad to lend them people a hand, I proved to myself I was like a Cheyenne when it came to farming.

Actually, though, that civilized life in the eastern Nations was more dangerous than you might think from a look at them peaceful little farms thereabout. That Creek family, seeing my blue uniform, took me for a deserter, a common type in the Nations. And liked me for it, because they had old cause against the Army from the time of Jackson, and then during the War most of the Creek had been Reb sympathizers, which is a laugh considering how they had been kicked out of Georgia, but what they liked about the South was slavery. Anyway, when the War was done, the Federal Government punished them, and the Choctaw, Cherokee, etc., by taking away the western half of Indian Territory, which had earlier belonged to them tribes, and making it into reservations for such as the Cheyenne. From which followed in natural progression the Battle of the Washita.

What I started to say, though, was that there was considerable Army deserters in the eastern Nations, along with freed slaves who now didn't have no work, and former Reb soldiers in a similar situation, and Indians what had gone bad, also fugitives from justice back in the States, bully-boys, cutthroats, and just plain rotten fellows. There was in addition every sort of breed in them parts: some being part white, Negro, and Indian all at the same time, with the worst traits of each.

I said it was dangerous living in that part of the country even though you kept to your cabin and cornfield, for gangs of the foregoing was always riding about and murdering people. It was a specially good place to practice that profession, for there wasn't any local law to speak of. Generally, if you rubbed out a person you hadn't nobody to get after you but a Federal marshal out of Fort Smith or Van Buren over in Arkansas, where the court was, and they wasn't active much at this time because the court people had all been Rebel and thus got the boot with the war. A saying went "There ain't no Sunday west of St. Louie and no God west of Fort Smith."

Now the center for the rough element was a town in the eastern Creek Nation called Mooskokee, which was where I proceeded upon leaving that family what had befriended me, with a view to getting the stage there and so travel up to Kansas and thence take the Union Pacific out to end-of-track, find Caroline and Frank Delight and cash in my third of our hauling business, for as I have said I needed money. In any event, I could always borrow a bundle off of Frank, for he would now be my brother-in-law.

I walked it to Mooskokee, about forty mile. I didn't have a cent for stage fare, but over my shoulders I was toting a pack of raccoon skins that I expected to sell once in town, for they make a serviceable cap. Indeed I was wearing one. Well sir, I had reached what I took to be the outlying suburbs, a long muddy hog wallow, lined with ramshackle sties, and I saw an old colored man there, looking for his pigs, and says: "Uncle, could you direct me to the city of Mooskokee?"

He scratches through the sweat-rag on his head and answers: "You has already got almost clear through it."

"I was just a-looking for the stage line."

"The station," he says, "is up the street and around the corner. But if I was you I'd hold off going there at present, for it is in the process of getting robbed, I do believe."

Sure enough, no sooner had he spoke than a volley of shots sounded from where he pointed and directly a body of men on horseback come tearing around the corner and galloped towards us and would have run us down had we not rolled into a slough alongside the road. I don't know what was their hurry, for they had nobody chasing them. Somebody had shot the sheriff yesterday, my acquaintance pointed out as we drug ourselves from the mud.

I thanked him and went down to the stage station, which I figured was safe enough now. The agent was lying in a pool of gore, and great holes gaped in the thin board walls where a fellow had been mighty free with a shotgun. Well, I was standing just inside what was left of the place, thinking how it didn't make much difference to me, on account of I didn't have the price of a ticket yet anyway, when I heard the noise of horses outside and in busts three very nasty-looking customers, bristling with firearms.

These fellows glare at me with their red eyes and then take in that body of the dead agent, and the one who seemed their leader says to the others: "Told you we was goin' to be late. Now this no-good bastard has done beat us."

Then he says to me with hurt pride: "We got the one before, and we would of beat you here this evenin' hadn't we been occupied down the road a piece with the stage itself. We robbed it and we burned it and we kilt the driver, we kilt the guard, we kilt the passengers, but one of them was a gal, and so we all _____ her before we kilt her."

As I say, I never had the price of a fare, anyway. What concerned me at the moment, however, was my lack of a gun, which these skunks would soon notice and then I would join the stiff on the floor. I had to make the most of my time while they was still jealously admiring how they thought I had rubbed out the agent.

"My boys won't like that," I says. "They was fixing to get that stage themselves, and I reckon have found it by now and turned back and will want to meet them who stole their thunder."

"How many boys you got?" says the leader. If he ever would introduce a drop of water to his face, he might have come out fairly good-looking. He was a breed of Indian and white, with fairish hair and thin features but walnut-colored skin. Another was almost black, with straight raven hair gathered in a knot behind. The third looked pure white but was the ugliest mortal I ever seen: had a bad eye, and an old knife cut that when healing had lifted his lip on the right side so you could see his teeth there even when he wasn't grinning or snarling though it seemed as if he always was.

"Nineteen or twenty," says I, and turned away right insolent, upon which I knowed they would make up their mind to shoot me in the back or knuckle under. It turned out they was bluffed, for the leader commences to boast.

"I guess you have heerd of me," he says; "Johnny Jump? I got me quite a rep hereabout for murder and mayhem. Ain't no marshal ever laid a hand on me, though many have tried. Just last month I blowed the head off one come out of Van Buren. This yeer's my cousin, Jim Smoker"—pointing to the black-faced fellow— "and the other we call Cockeye. He ain't got no tongue. Had it shot or tore out. Can't talk, but my God he is mean."

I says: "I never heard of you small-time trash. We're from St. Louie by way of Texas and have just stopped off in this mudhole to get tobacco money. And then on to Kansas, where we figure to cut and shoot and rob and violate from one side of the state to the other."

Cockeye grunts some and slobbers out of his cut lip. Jim Smoker goes on outside and in a minute I hear him firing his rifle and look out and see he is taking target practice at the curly tail of a wandering hog.

"My cousin," says Johnny Jump, "ain't got all his buttons, but he is real useful at killin' and stealin'. I was a-thinking maybe us fellows could join your boys. I would shore like to rob and murder and the rest of what you said up in Kansas." He looked like a kid who was begging his Daddy to take him fishing, his eyes bright and wistful. There was something real innocent about Johnny Jump, even likable, I don't know why. Maybe it was the Indian in him.

In at last reluctantly agreeing to admit him and his boys to my nonexistent gang, I did not intend to travel in their company any further than was necessary. I told them I was to rendezvous with my bunch twenty miles north. They could come along at their own risk.

I pretended my horse had strayed somewheres, so Johnny Jump lent me an extra animal they had took from the stage. I still didn't have no gun, though. We rode till twilight, and then I pointed at a grove of trees and said that was the place my boys would be or come to later, and so we stopped and built a fire and ate some bacon and beans from a bag of loot they had, for as they went about the countryside this bunch would kill anyone they met and take whatever he was carrying. In fact, we had passed a little farm on this trip, and I only had kept them from pillaging it by promises of the mayhem we all would wreak after collecting the rest of my boys.

I didn't notice that Jim Smoker had dropped behind, for he rode always in back anyway, but he was gone when we went into the grove and only showed up later while we was feeding. He wore a different hat and carried two bottles of whiskey and led another horse behind his, to which was lashed all manner of booty: bags of sugar and corn, blankets, coal-oil lamps, and even a little footstool.

Johnny Jump spoke to him in Creek and then laughs hee-haw. "My cousin just had to drap by that place we went past back a piece. He cain't resist a thang, being a chile at heart."

I was sorry for the poor folk what had lived on that farm, but I guess they was out of pain now, and the way it turned out, the ill wind that blowed them a sudden death saved my life. For I couldn't have kept up the pretense of meeting my gang beyond the following morning and would have gone under for sure. But what happened instead was that Johnny Jump and Jim Smoker shared them bottles of whiskey, and after Johnny got a bellyful of liquor he commenced to turn sentimental. It seemed he was a poet in addition to an outlaw, and setting there beside the fire, with tears running down his cheeks to mingle with the whiskey leaking over his chin, he recited verse of his own composition.

> The darlin' love of all my life,
> In women I never had no other,
> The sweetest thang in this vale of strife,
> Was always my dear Mother.

And now she is in heaven
Where the angels play them harps,
For in years it is six or seven
Since I laid away her carpse. . . .

There was ten or twenty more stanzas to it, which I don't remember no more, and when he gets through he lets out a great howl of agony and picks up his rifle and shoots Jim Smoker between the eyes. Then he gives Cockeye a couple in the spine where he lays sleeping, and finally empties the rest of the magazine of his sixteen-shot Henry into the blanket roll topped by the coonskin cap which I had earlier arranged to represent myself.

After which he lays back and goes peaceful to sleep. I come back from behind the tree where I had watched all this, picked up the Henry he had dropped, got me the two best Colt's in the bunch and all the horses, and left, heading north. I considered putting a bullet into Johnny Jump's head and so do a lot of his future victims a favor, but in addition to my dislike for cold-blooded murder, I had developed a soft spot for him. It might have been on account of that poetry.

The next couple years I spent in transit, mainly looking for Caroline and Frank Delight, so as to get some money from them, for as I have said, I couldn't go kill Custer as broke as I was. What I had not known when down in the Nations was that the U.P. had reached Utah and linked up with the Central Pacific around the time I left the Creek family with whom I spent the winter of '69. The railroad was done building, that is, having spanned the continent. But with the proceeds from selling Johnny Jump's little horse herd, which I had drove to Topeka without further incident, I rode the coaches on out west from Omaha, anyway, figuring my relations might have settled their saloon business in one of the towns that had sprung up along the line.

At every station I inquired for Caroline and Frank, with no result, but I had always wanted to take a look at San Francisco anyway, so rode on out there, by when I was sure glad to get off the railroad for a spell. That transcontinental road was a wonder of civilization no doubt, but what with stopovers I had been riding them lurching cars for a week and had swallowed an awful lot of smoke and ashes as they blowed in the open windows, and every now and again a live spark would start a little fire in the green plush seat-upholstery or someone's clothes. However, they said the train went twenty-five miles an hour, and I don't doubt it.

I wasn't in San Francisco long before I run out of my money, for everything was terrible expensive. You couldn't get a decent meal for less than fifty cents. And I don't know why, but them hills the town was built on commenced to depress my spirits: you feel great upon the summit, but then you always have to come down sometime and when you do, it's like you been demoted. I had lived too long on the flat.

Nor could I locate Caroline and her husband, though I must have traipsed through every cheap saloon and bawdy house in the place, and that took me several months, for that town wouldn't take a back seat to none in the disrespectful entertainments. When my money was gone I got work in a livery stable, forking hay, shoveling manure, and the like. It was all I could get at the time. Then one day a fellow come in from the south of California and I heard him say they was a-looking for wagon drivers down there, to haul freight from San Pedro to Prescott, Arizona, and would pay good money for it.

It was the spring of '70 when I reached Pedro and found the man who had the hauling business. At first he doubted a man of my size and figure could handle that employment.

"This is a hairy job, my friend," he says. "If the desert don't get you, the Apache will, and if not him, then the outlaws. The Salton Sink is a hundred mile of fiery hell where you feed your animals in the harness and keep moving lest you shrivel in your tracks. You got twenty days to make four hundred and fifty mile, and I don't want my mules kilt doing it."

Suffice it to say I convinced him to take me on, and he says: "I'll take a chance on you. Couple years back I hired a boy of seventeen and he turned out fine, though he *was* big for his years."

That's the kind of thing you have to put up with if you're my size. But the reason I mention this is he said the boy was called Wyatt Earp. First I ever heard the name, but I remembered it because of its unusual sound, sort of like a belch.

The boss wasn't exaggerating none about the hairiness of that run, and during the time I was making it we encountered all the obstacles he listed, but thinking it over, I'll take heat, sand, Apache, or bandits in preference to ten mules every time. What I found toughest to manage was to refrain from getting a club and beating them animals to death. I drove mules in the grading of the U.P., but that beast's character worsens with the kind of terrain he has to cover. Though as I guess can be said of a lot of humans, his very nastiness is what pulls him through.

Same goes for me. I stuck at it throughout most of '70 and never got no sweeter in the process. But I earned good money, and then went back to San Francisco in the winter, bought me a fine outfit of clothes and a Smith & Wesson revolver of the model called "American" that had just come out, a beautiful .44-caliber weapon.

Then I bought me a first-class ticket on the U.P. to Omaha for one hundred dollars and two dollars a day for a sleeper on top of that, for I was going back to kill George Armstrong Custer in style.

CHAPTER 20 *Wild Bill Hickok*

I REACHED KANSAS CITY in the spring of '71, which had growed considerably since I had knowed it as Westport, and if you recall, Fort Leavenworth was nearby. No sooner had I hit town when I found that none other than the Seventh Cavalry itself had wintered there, General Custer commanding. He was often to be seen over in K.C., at his tailor's, at restaurants, and at theatrical performances, being extremely fond of the last, as might be supposed from his character. His Lady was ever by his side, and she was so pretty it was said both men and women turned around when she passed by. Of course, the General was right comely himself.

The man who told me the foregoing had long blond curly locks falling to his shoulders and a silken mustache of the same hue, was above six foot in height, slim in the waist and broad as to chest, and in clothing a remarkable dandy. He wore a black frock coat with velvet facings on the lapels, an embroidered vest, turn-down collar with a black string tie, and topped it off with a silk hat.

No, he wasn't Custer, but blonder, curlier, warmer blue of eye, and his face was softer, with a hooking nose and short chin. He was James Butler Hickok, so-called Wild Bill after he rubbed out the man who named him Duck Bill.

But back to Custer, for whom Wild Bill had scouted on the Kansas campaign a year before the Washita. He knowed him well, and liked him and vice versa, and had a harmless crush on his wife and let her believe much exaggeration concerning himself, which Custer also believed, and so everyone was friends, as big, pretty, handsome, and powerful people always are. For everything goes their way, until some wretched, crosseyed, broken-nosed bum shoots them in the back, as Jack McCall did to Hickok in Deadwood in '76, only two months after the Indians did in the other Long Hair.

However, that was five years into the future, and here we was on Market Square in K.C., and I was fully intending to find Custer before the week was out and do my duty. Let me say about Market Square that it was the hangout for buffalo hunters in the summer when the hides run poor, and scouts would come there when off a campaign, and mule drivers between trips, and it was where you'd go for news if you was my type of case rather than read the papers.

And that is how I met Wild Bill, who was one of the centers of attraction thereabout, having already got his reputation a year or two before as marshal of Hays City, Kansas.

During the day, Hickok generally set on a bench outside of the police station where his friend Tom Speers, the marshal in K.C., encouraged the frontier types to congregate partly because he knew and liked most of them, but also I believe because it tended to keep them out of trouble. They could palaver with one another and even hold target matches without bothering the respectable element in the better part of town, and being that Speers and his deputies was around, real fights was rare.

Not that celebrated gun-handlers ever fought each other much, anyway. Anybody who specializes in violence has the greatest respect for another such expert.

Now, as to my revenge against Custer. Well, you can go to the history books and read how he died fighting Indians on June 25, 1876, so you know I never killed him in Kansas City. If he had been a nobody, I could have kept up the suspense till the last minute, whereas the way it stands I got to admit it was near the first of April when I reached K.C., and the Seventh Regiment had been recalled from the plains in March, Custer going back East. I had missed him by a few days!

You might wonder why I did not follow him. After all, it wasn't that he had gone to China. I already come across the western half of the country expressly to shoot him down. The image of that deed was what I had been living on for two years, ever since my vow on the banks of the Washita.

All I can say is that there was something about the Missouri River that took my drive away. Old Lodge Skins felt the same about the Platte, and look what happened to him when below it: Sand Creek and the Washita. I hoped he had now learned to rely on his instincts rather than his pride, and gone up north to stay.

In my case, I stopped right there in Kansas City, where the Missouri takes its big bend for the run to St. Louie. I looked at its muddly swirl and thought: Well, Custer's anyway gone off the prairies; that's the important thing. Maybe it was me who scared him off, in a spiritual or medicine sense, for it was right queer the coincidence of our comings and goings. Anyhow, I didn't go East. I had a funny idea of that part of the country: I figured it to be cityfied from St. Louie right on to the Atlantic Ocean, and mainly slums at that, filled with poor foreigners from Europe who had pasty faces and licked the boots of powerful, glittering people like Custer. I would be at a peculiar disadvantage there.

In Kansas City I was not far from the place where the Pendrakes had lived thirteen years before, and probably were still residing, for people in their situation maintain it forever, and I thought about going over there and just riding down the street once and be done with it, but didn't have the stomach for even that much. I tell you this, I was still in love with Mrs. Pendrake as ardently as I had ever been, after all them years and battles and wives. That was the real tragedy of my life, as opposed to the various inconveniencies.

The subject came to mind now because with the news of Custer's departure I felt more let down, despondent, and bereft than at any time since I had left Missouri years before, and naturally, in such a mood, thought of Mrs. P. was inevitable.

Well, if Custer ever come West again, I would kill him. I swore to that, but rather mechanically, for I didn't have no hopes he would.

The central plains was all cleaned up now of hostiles. The summer after the Washita battle, troops under General Carr whipped the Cheyenne Dog Soldier band at Summit Springs, killing their chief, Tall Bull. That was the end of the Human Beings in Kansas and Colorado.

So what did I do? Well, I met Wild Bill Hickok, and knowing him become almost a profession in itself for a while. I had inquired around about Custer, and a fellow pointed out Wild Bill as having been sometime scout for the General. I had never heard of Hickok at that time, but he was the celebrity of Market Square, and I recall that when I come up to him for the first time he was showing to some other fellows a pair of ivory-handled revolvers he had been give by a U.S. Senator he guided on a prairie tour.

I pushed amidst the throng and says: "You Hickok?" He had been pointed out to me as such, but I had to say something for openers.

"I am," says this tall, lithe man with the long fair hair and gives me but a fleeting glance from his sky-blue eyes, and then lifts the pistol in his right hand and fires the entire cylinder faster than you could count the shots, at a sign upon the wall of a saloon a hundred yards and at a slant across the square.

This incident later went down in history, I understand—without any mention of my part—but standing there at the time, I was not impressed. I was intent on finding out about Custer, and the flowing hair of this specimen made me think he was another of the same ilk.

So when he had exhausted them five shots, I says impatiently: "Well, Hickok, if you can spare the time, I'll have a word with you."

He throws the fresh gun from his left hand into the right, while at the same time and in the same fashion transferring the emptied revolver from his right hand to his left. This maneuver was called the border shift, and constituted a neat-looking trick as both pistols traveled through the air for a second.

Following which Hickok fired five more shots at that sign, and then the whole bunch walked on across the square to see how good he did. One of them at the back of the crowd comes over to me and says: "I reckon you must know Wild Bill purty well, to bother him at a time like this."

"Don't know him a-tall," says I, "and don't know as I want to. What makes him so important?"

This fellow says: "You never heard how he took care of the McCanles gang ten year ago at the Rock Crick stage station down in Jefferson County? There was six of them, I believe, and they come for Wild Bill, and he took three with his pistols, two with his bowie, and just beat the other to death with a gunstock."

I immediately reduced that by half in my mind, for I had been on the frontier from the age of ten on and knew a thing as to how fights are conducted. When you run into a story of more than three against one and one winning, then you have heard a lie. I found out later I was right in this case: Wild Bill killed only McCanles and two of his partners, and all from ambush.

"Yes sir," this fellow goes on, who belonged to the same type as Custer's striker, "that is what he done. And over in Hays City when he was marshal he had a run-in with Tom Custer, the General's brother, who he locked up when drunk and disorderly, and Tom come back with two soldiers to put a head on him, and Wild Bill knifed one and shot the other."

Now this interested me, so I asked how he got Custer's brother, with knife or gun.

"It was the soldiers he killed, not Tom."

That figured.

Hickok and the others now returned from looking at the saloon sign, and this suck-up who had been talking to me, he asked what happened and another man says: "He put all ten inside the hole of the O, by God!" And everybody was whistling and gasping at the wonder of it—well, not exactly everybody, for there was other scouts and gun-handlers around, people like Jack Gallagher, Billy Dixon, Old Man Keeler, and more who was well known in them days, and they looked thoughtful so as not to display jealousy. As elsewhere in life, there are specialists on one hand, and the audience on the other.

I steps up to Wild Bill again and says: "If you can spare the time—"

He is feeling good what with his performance and the adulation rising from it, and I guess it might have irritated him that I should be totally occupied with my own matters, and he says quite negligent to one of them men at his elbow: "Run him off."

So that fellow comes towards me with a contemptuous look on his ugly, hairy face, and he is right large, but then he stops abruptly. For my S & W .44 is on a dead line to where his belly sagged over his belt.

"Pull in your horns," Hickok tells him with a guffaw. "That little bastard has got the drop on you. . . . Come on," he says to me, "put aside your popgun and I'll buy you a drink."

So Wild Bill and me went over to the saloon and passed under the sign where he had put ten shots in the hole of the O at a hundred yards, and I glanced up at it and saw he sure enough had. Inside, we got us our whiskies and then he found the farthermost corner from the door and put his chair in the angle of it and pulled his frock coat back on either side to expose the handles of the pistols stuck into his waistband, and all the while we was there he was eying every individual who came and went without it making any difference in his attention to our talk, except once when the bartender dropped a glass, at which Hickok automatically responded like a cat, coming half out of the chair.

So that was where he told me about Custer's going East and all, and the stuff I related earlier.

"Why did you want to know about the General?" he asked, but of course I never told him of my true interest but some lie about hiring on as a scout, and then to cover up whatever emotion I might have showed, I says: "I understand you had some trouble with his brother Tom."

"Well," he says, "that is all over."

Now this is a good example of a point I want to make. Wild Bill Hickok was never himself a braggart. He didn't have to be. Others did it for him. When I say he was responsible for a ton of crap, I don't mean he ever spoke a word in his own behalf. He never said he put a head on Tom Custer, nor wiped out the McCanles gang, nor would he ever mention them ten shots inside the O. But others would be doing it incessantly, and blowing up the statistics and lengthening the yardage and diminishing the target. Until about thirty year ago, I was still meeting people who claimed to have been on Market Square that day when Wild Bill put ten shots one on top of another into the point of an *i* at two hundred yards.

It was just after this that the bartender dropped the glass and Hickok come out of his chair, hands ready at his gun butts.

When he sat back again, I says: "What are you so nervous about?"

"Getting killed," says he, as simply as that, and takes a sip of his red-eye. And then he looks at me, a little amusement crinkling his blue eyes, and says: "Maybe you figure to do it."

That just made me laugh, and I says: "It was you who asked me to have a drink."

"Look," says he, "tell me straight, was it Tom Custer who sent you here? For as far as it goes with me, that is over and done with. But if he wants to start it up again, he ought not to send a fellow around carrying a S & W American in a tight calfskin holster. I tell you that for your own good, friend."

I was insulted, being proud of that new piece of mine, and I also took it hard that I would be considered as working for anybody named Custer.

"Look yourself, Hickok," I says. "I ain't no man's flunky. If I got any killing to do, it'll be for myself and no other. If you want to fight, we'll drop the guns and I'll take you on bare-knuckle though you be big as a horse."

"Settle down," he says. "I didn't mean to hurt your feelings. Let me buy you another." He called the bartender, but that individual had gone into a storeroom in back and couldn't hear him, so Wild Bill asks me would I mind fetching the bottle?

Still sore, I says: "Are you lame?"

He answers apologetically: "I don't want to get shot in the back." Hastening to add: "I don't mean by you. I believe you, friend. But I don't know about these others."

Meaning the ten or twelve harmless persons who shared the saloon with us at the moment. It wasn't crowded, being the middle of the afternoon. There was a table of four, playing cards; another couple or three men was down towards the lower right of the bar. And I recall a person dead drunk at a table in the middle of the place. His head and shoulders was flat limp on the tabletop in a pool of spilled whiskey, sort of like a piece of harness dropped in some standing rainwater.

So I felt a contempt for this Wild Bill, thinking he was either batty or yellow if he couldn't walk across a peaceful room. Then it occurred to me that he might be putting on an act for my benefit. Maybe he was waiting for me to turn my back on him so he could drill me.

This is a good example of the suspiciousness which warps the minds of gunfighters. I had fell into it right quick, just being in Wild Bill's proximity. You feel like your whole body is one live nerve. At that moment one of them cardplayers, having just won a pot, let out a holler of triumph, and *both* Hickok and myself come out of our chairs, going for our iron—and he had been right about that tight calfskin holster of mine, which fitted the piece like a glove: the faster you pulled at it, the more it gripped the revolver.

I says: "Now you got me doing it."

"I never," says Hickok, "have held by a holster." Now that he seen my deficiency I reckon he finally did trust me. "Always carry my weapons in the waist. You have to get a tailor to make a real smooth band there, no excess stitching nor suspender buttons, and of course your vest ought to be cut so its points don't interfere. And," he goes on, "see how I had my coat designed so it swings away on the sides."

"The only thing," I says, "is I wonder that sometimes when walking, your guns just don't slip on through and run down your trouser legs."

"Ah," says he, "you open the loading gate and catch it onto your pants-tops."

He was warming up to me through this technical talk, a man generally being fascinated by his own specialty and the tools for it. Bill proceeded to lecture me on the merits of the various means of toting a pistol: silk sash, shoulder holster, hideout rig inside the vest, derringer harness along the underside of the arm, back pockets lined with leather, and so on. He even claimed to know a fellow who carried a small pistol in his crotch, and when cornered he would request to take a leak before dying, open his fly, and fire. The trouble was onetime he got overhasty and shot off his male parts.

I learned an awful lot that afternoon. I had thought I was pretty handy with a gun before reaching K.C., but I was awful raw alongside of Wild Bill Hickok. Of course, I could see he was a fanatic. You had to be, to get so absorbed in talk of holsters and cartridge loads and barrel length and filing down the sear to make a hairtrigger and the technique of tying back the trigger and earing the hammer to fire, etc., etc. He had forgot about that drink and even his suspicions and commenced to call me "partner" and "hoss," rather than that sinister "friend."

I got tired after a bit and reminded him we was going to wet our whistles again, and started up, but he says: "Sit down, old hoss, I'll get them." And makes for the bar, despite the fact that the saloon-keeper had sometime since returned from the storeroom and could have fetched the bottle over.

One thing that amused me: Wild Bill carried that silk hat of his with him rather than leave it behind. I figured this was the last bit of suspicion he held towards me, that maybe I would swipe that article. Or maybe it was just that he didn't want to forget and sit upon it when he come back.

Now he had got within six feet of the bar and was already in the process of giving his order, when that drunk I have mentioned at the middle table suddenly reared up, revealing a pistol at the end of the arm that had been crumpled under him, thrusts it purposefully in the direction of Hickok's tall, broad back, and pulls the trigger. I would estimate the range as fifteen feet. Now this was quick. I mean if you had sneezed you would never have knowed anything happened, for in the next instant the "drunk" was sprawled once again in exactly the same position he had just emerged from, the difference being that blood was leaking out of a small hole between his eyes, adding to that pool of liquor.

He had fired all right, only his bullet went into the ceiling, for in the time between his rearing up and pulling the trigger, Wild Bill had seen him in the mirror back of the bar, turned, flipped his silk hat into the left hand, revealing the pistol he had carried under it in his right, and killed the man. Then he put the hat upon his head, went over, and inspected the corpse. The other fellows gathered around, and shortly in come Marshal Tom Speers, and Speers says: "Know him, Bill?"

"No," says Hickok, expelling the empty cartridge and replacing it with a new load. Then he shrugs, gets that bottle from the bar, and joins me again.

Somebody says: "That's Strawhan's brother."

Now I was some agitated by this event, being no stranger to violence but not having looked for it here. I gulped the drink Hickok poured me with his calm hand, and coughed, and says: "The name mean anything to you?"

He shrugs again, sips his whiskey, and his eyes is heavy as though he is going to fall asleep. Finally he answers: "I recall a man of that name in Hays."

"Have trouble with him?"

"I killed him," he says. "Now then, about that S & W you carry. It is a handsome weapon, but the shells have a bad habit of erupting and jamming the chambers. I'd lay the piece aside and get me something else: a Colt's, with the Thuer conversion. . . ."

Meanwhile, Speers had got two fellows to drag the body out and he says to Wild Bill: "Drop by the station later when you have a minute."

I reckon the marshal had to make a report. Hickok gives him a little wave of the hand—the left one, of course. I should have known something was up when I seen him carrying that hat in his right, which he reserved absolutely for his gun. Pointing, gesturing, scratching, going for money—think of everything you do with your right hand: he did none of these, but kept it totally free at all times. The one exception was shaking hands, in which case he barely touched your fingers before whipping his back.

Not that afternoon, but later on I asked Wild Bill if he had really suspected that apparent drunk or if he always crossed a room gun in hand.

"I did, indeed," he answered. "I suspect any man whose gun hand is out of sight, be he even dead. I am wrong ninety-nine times out of a hundred; but I am right once in that same space, which pays me for my trouble."

Hickok was a marvelous observer of anything which pertained to killing. He noticed now how I had been shaken by the incident, though otherwise I don't think he would have recognized me if I had gone off to the outhouse and come back. He was like an Indian in his single-mindedness. For example, he never reacted at all to the quality of the whiskey we was drinking, which was fairly rotten. And later I come to realize that he had talked about General and Mrs. Custer in that apparently interested way only because he suspected me of being out to get him and playing for time. Actually he did not care anything about them or anybody else as persons.

But he could be considerate, if it fell within the area of his obsession. So now he says to me: "It is always harder on a man to watch trouble than to be in it. Best thing for you to do now is go get yourself a woman. Come on, I'll show you the best place in town."

He had to stop first at a restaurant and eat a big steak, because he said it was funny, but trouble give him an appetite, but other than for those two references, I never heard Wild Bill mention the shooting of Strawhan's brother, though in the street and at the restaurant, various individuals who had heard about it congratulated him and others got out of his path in a marked way.

This place he took me to was a dancehall, though by the time we got there it was early evening, for he ate that steak slow and with great relish and afterwards had some pie, and it took so long that I come back to normal, for after all, killing was no novelty to me. So I had some baked ham, for the steak looked mighty tough. The ham was no better, I might add, and I complained to the management, but Hickok seemed to find the grub just perfect.

Then we went to the dancehall, and as I say it was early, with us being the first customers and the girls come straggling out of a door at the back, yawning and stretching for I figure they had just got up after sleeping the day. At the entrance there was a sign reading: PLEASE CHECK YOUR FIREARMS, and when we walked past it, a big man in a striped shirt come out and states: "Sorry, fellows, that means what it says."

Wild Bill just looks at him with his clear blue eyes and says in his quiet voice: "Is Dolly around?"

"You'll have to check them weapons," says the other. And then, I guess because he allowed Wild Bill was an imposing-looking fellow, he explains: "They'll be all right with me. You see, I put one of these here tags on each piece and write on it who it belongs to." He goes into his vest pocket undoubtedly to get that tag and pencil, and knowing Wild Bill's principles, I thought oh my God, there goes another one!

However, just at that moment, a big woman appears from the office. In her forties, heavy-set with a great high bosom, to show the grand divide of which her red satin dress, embroidered with black beading, had been cut low. She had a wealth of black hair piled upon her head and a faint mustache of the same color.

She cries "Billy!" in her bass voice, comes over and hugs Hickok, pushing the breastwork into his waistcoat and planting a fiery kiss on his cheek. Then she tells the bouncer: "Mr. Hickok has the privilege."

"Hickok!" says he and his face goes to pieces and he makes himself scarce. Which shows you how a reputation worked. That man was a bouncer by trade and done a good job: I later seen him beat up three rough and drunken buffalo hunters with only the help of a middle-sized club. But soon as he heard that magic name, he was beat so far as facing the individual who owned it.

"Who's your cute little short-armed pal?" the woman asks Bill, and he gets my name for the first time and tells her.

Then Dolly grabs me, smothering my face in her spongy cleavage, and damn if she don't slide her hands around onto my posteriors and grind and bump her treelike thighs against me. I don't say it wasn't somewhat interesting, for she was quite a bit of woman, though it was also rather disquieting as if an aunt got fresh with you, and in addition I had my pride to think of, so I pushed her off.

"Ooo," says she, making a coy thing of her heavy lips, "he's a spunky little fox, ain't he now?"

Hickok says, laughing: "You got a nice girl for him? He's nervous, you see." So she calls the women over, and they was a good deal better-grade than you could find on west of there until you got to San Francisco. One or two was right pretty, even, and all was fairly clean-looking and showed no old knife-scars or bad pock-marks. Dolly run a first-rate place, I'll say that for her.

I looked them over, and some made lewd remarks to me while others acted standoffish and even cold, for as a group they had to appeal to all tastes, but the one I chose wasn't either forward nor snotty. She was kind of sad and wistful-looking, in figure short and slight, with dull reddish-brown hair that appeared to have been set to curl but come out rather wispy. Some faint freckles showed in the tender skin underneath her eyes. She wore a red dress that exposed her shoulders and her legs to the knee, and the heels of her slippers was run over so she stood slightly bowlegged.

Don't sound spicy-looking, do she? Well, she wasn't. But neither was I in need of a whore at that point. That was Hickok's idea and not mine; and I'll tell you when a fellow like him suggests something, you take it under consideration, especially when you have just seen him shoot down a man with such little ceremony.

So not feeling any desire, I chose this here girl as the least desirable when it come to the fleshly, and we danced some to the pounding of a baldheaded man on a tinny piano, who was addressed like all such as the "Professor." I ain't much of a dancer, and you wasn't supposed to be in a place like that, where your partner would shove out her belly and roll it against yours for a minute and then drag you off down the back hall and into her little cubicle or crib from which the expression "crib-girl" derived.

Now that's what this little gal done hardly had the music commenced, come grinding into me, only she didn't have no stomach worth the name, and was instead raking me with her sharp hipbones, and being I was skinny too, the last thing it brought to mind was lust. So I pushes her away, meanwhile trying to jig a little in my heavy boots, for the Professor was beating out a lively tune, but she takes this action as indicating that I was raring to head for the crib, and wearily, mechanically, yet with positive force, pulls me down the hall.

Her cubicle had an iron bed in it and a rickety chair that would have collapsed had there been space to do so, for its width consumed the distance between bed and wall, and as to the length of the room, you can gather that from the fact that its door had to swing out into the hall.

She lit a coal-oil lamp on a bracket, and I set upon the bed, being there was no place further to go, and in one movement she shucks her dress, hangs it on a hook, and mother-naked, takes a seat upon my knee.

Now I had knowed she was right young, but not until this moment did I realize to what degree. Her flat little bosom, her slender flanks and bony knees: she wasn't just skinny, she was hardly more than a child, which condition her facial rouge had misrepresented.

I asked how old she was.

"Twenty," says she.

I leaned back to put some distance between our heads. "Go on," I says.

"Well, eighteen, then." She lays further into me and begins to work at my collar.

So I dumps her off and stands up, which a wider man could not have managed, and I don't see how a man of Hickok's length could have stood erect under that low ceiling.

I guess she was worried I was about to leave, so she assured me in consternation that she knowed how to do everything and anything, and never had a complaint yet.

I says: "All I require at the moment is the truth about your years. I can't use nothing more at this time, on account of I believe I picked up a dose the other day, but I'll be glad to give you the dollar anyway."

"Dollar?" she cries indignantly, and all thoughts I had of her basically innocent and wistful ways had to change. "You cheap bastard, it costs five times that to let your pants down in this house."

"Well," I says, "damn me if I would pay five dollars to top the Queen of Russia." I was amused by her anger. Them freckles lit up and her hair went redder. She reminded me of someone. "No, indeed," I goes on, "let alone some skinny kid of fourteen."

"I'll be seventeen any day now," she says. "And you get on out of here with your dollar or I'll call Harry and have him throw you out."

I was took by something in this little gal. Still not lust, for I have always preferred them seasoned and sturdy for that purpose. I guess I just liked her spunk.

I says: "All right, I'm good for the fare. But I'll tell you what I want for it. I just want to sit here long enough so my friend will think I had a good time. You'll get your money and not have to work for it."

That was O.K. by her when she saw I meant it and creased her little paw with the cash. In fact, I reckon she liked it a whole lot better: there wasn't much opportunity in them days to make five dollars by setting.

Now since she had revealed her cockiness once, she didn't go back to that drab, melancholy style no more, which was merely a role. I have said they tried to offer all types at this place. I reckon she appealed to the hombre who liked to imagine he was laying some little overworked servant girl, maybe an orphan to boot, under the back stairs.

In her true character she was right impudent. She could have put her clothes on now, but she didn't, just lay back with her hands behind her head and her knees raised in the glare of the kerosene light, and says: "Say, you ain't got a cigar?"

"Smoke, too, do you?" says I. "My, ain't you the rough one." I was needling her for the fun of it. I had to kill some time and didn't know what else to do. I set down again on the foot of the bed, where there was ample room, for she lay along the length of it but was small and besides had her knees lifted. "I expected," I says, "to find the K.C. gals more refined and ladylike."

Well, her green eyes looked as if they started to flash, then suddenly she flung an arm across them and her thin chest commences to quake with sobs. Shortly I felt terrible, and I gathered her up in my arms, setting her on my lap again, and she cried against my shoulder, clutching into me as if it was her last hope upon earth.

"Now, now," I says, giving her a fatherly kiss into the tangled red curls on the top of her head and patting her bare, bumpy spine, "you tell your troubles to Uncle Jack."

She snuffles into my neck a bit, and then tells me the following.

"I was born and bred in Salt Lake City to one of the most respectable families there, my Ma being married at fifteen to a famous Mormon leader. You would know the name right off if I was to tell it. Now, outside folks have a funny idea about Mormons on account of the number of wives they take, but I tell you that is the reason why you won't find a den of iniquity like this in Salt Lake. My Ma was my Pa's eleventh wife, and you take us girls here at Dolly's, why, we fight amongst ourselves all the time, but my mothers never did exchange a harsh word with one another. I had fifteen sisters and twenty-one brothers, and we lived in a house that was like a hotel. All we did was work and pray from early in the morning until night.

"Up to the age of fourteen, I guess there wasn't a purer girl on earth than myself, for I regarded the human body as the holy temple of God and wouldn't have dared to profane my mind with other than a wholesome thought. I had grown right pretty by then. One day my mothers sent me over next door to borrow some sugar. Now the people that lived there was another Mormon elder named Woodbine and he had only six wives and ten children, and as it happened all the women and younguns was out working in the fields at this moment, only the elder was to home, a man of fifty with a big black beard.

" 'Amelia, isn't it?' he says as he lets me in. 'What a pretty girl you have become. The sugar is I believe in the pantry.' So he goes along with me there, and says: 'I believe it is on the high shelf. I'll lift you up.' Which he does with his huge hands, and that's all that happened then, except that when he put me down he was purple in the face and breathing hard though I couldn't have weighed much.

"But a day or so later, my Pa calls me into his presence and informs me that Elder Woodbine would like to take me as his seventh wife. It wasn't no good to protest, for my Pa had decided on it and I didn't dare to cross him, so what I done is run away that very night.

"Well," she says, sobbing at the thought of it, "there have been many times after when I regretted my foolishness, for in these two year since I have seen little but the worst side of the Gentiles, many of them just as whisker-faced as the Elder Woodbine and as old, and some with bodies furry as a bear; whereas instead of a device of pleasure to any man who comes down the road I would have been an honored Mormon wife."

It could have happened, I reckon, though it was the typical story you could get out of any whore: they always stemmed from good families, by their account. I don't say I swallowed the entirety of it. The mention of Salt Lake and Mormons, in themselves, would not have take my especial note, though you may recall my Pa's aim away back to head for Utah, which is why I fell in with the Cheyenne and had all the subsequent adventures.

But while this here Amelia was setting on my lap, jaybird-naked, I noticed a tiny mole she had in the hollow at the base of her neck. Now the peculiarity of this was that my sister Sue Ann, who was thirteen when I last seen her, had a similar mole in that exact spot. I said before that this little harlot reminded me of somebody. But other than for the blemish, it wasn't my sister, who was fairer and different of feature.

"Say," I says to Amelia, "I might have some kin in Salt Lake. The last time I seen them, years ago, they intended to go there and become Mormons. You might have heard of them if they made it."

She pulls her head up and looks at me straight. For all that crying, her eyes was utter dry, but she had succeeded in rubbing away much of the powder and rouge on the lapels of my black coat. She was basically as freckled as me, underneath it all; and her hair was quite reddish.

"What did you say was the name?" she asks, with a shrewd squint.

"I never," I says, "but if you want to know, it was Crabb. It would be my Ma and my sister Sue Ann, who I reckon might now be more than—well, thirty years of age, and then Margaret, a little younger—"

"Sue Ann," cries Amelia. "That's my mother's name!" She laughs and shakes her hair and starts to cry again, clutching me about the neck.

That was when I finally figured out who she resembled: Myself.

"Then you *are* my Uncle Jack!" she says.

"Here now," says I, "you better get your dress back on."

CHAPTER 21 *My Niece Amelia*

I RECKON of all the things that ever happened, this give me the greatest turn, meeting my niece under them conditions. Suppose I had— My flesh crawled to think of it. Would have had to blow my brains out, I expect, for damn me if I ever been a degenerate.

Now the more I looked at her, the more obvious was the relationship: I never cared for the way my beak turned up as if someone pushed me in the face when I was small and it moldable, but you know, I saw the same type of nose on this girl-niece of mine and it looked right cunning. I had a real kin-feeling for her, I expect, right from the first, which is why I picked her from the lineup and also why she did not attract me in the fleshly way.

That is the positive side of the situation. The negative is that she was a whore. There was no getting away from that fact, and it give me a deal of shame. I didn't know what to do, so said again: "Get on them clothes." Kindly though, like an uncle, and I reached her dress down from the hook and turned my back while she put it on.

Then I was suddenly embarrassed by my presence in this type of place. Funny, ain't it, that I should apologize to her? I says: "Amelia, I just want you to know I come here only as a favor to that other fellow."

"Mr. Hickok?" she asks. "Yes, he is always hereabout."

I says: "I am going to take you away from all this. Beginning this very minute, you ain't a crib-girl no more. Why, in a week you will have forgot all your unfortunate experiences, and in six months you'll be a fine lady."

For I did suddenly get this idea, standing right there. All my life I had yearned for a bit of class, and I purposed to achieve it in this niece of mine. I was going to put her into one of them schools run by a maiden lady. I had my little roll to start on, and then, from what I gathered from the talk of them who hunted buffalo, there was wealth to be made in that profession. Two to three thousand dollars in a single season from September to March, which most of them would bring here to K.C. and spend over the summer on whiskey and women. Not me. I had an aim, the reclamation of Amelia. I had lost two families in violent circumstances; now I had found the beginnings of another in a house of ill fame.

First, though, we had to get out of that house. I expected some trouble about that, and took my gun out of its holster and put it into my waistband like Hickok had advised. But then I thought, little Amelia might get hit if there is gunplay. Better to buy out. Which is something you can do anywhere among white people.

So I went for my roll—and could not find it, though I had just earlier paid her that five dollars. I was sure I had kept it in my vest.

"Amelia," I says, "did you see where I put my money?"

Now I have been talking here exclusively about my own reactions. That's because my niece was apparently thrown into a state of shock by the revelation of our kinship. She had got dumbly into her dress and then stood primping her hair with her fingers, and when I briefly indicated my intention to take her out of there, had received it with a vague smile involving only the mouth. But now she gets a keen expression again and says: "I expect it might have fell out and rolled under the bed."

So I gets down to take a look, and she pushes the door open quick and offers to run through it, but her old uncle proved more dexterous than she figured. I got her ankle and held on.

"I guess," I says, "it'll take you a while to straighten out. Now cough up that roll of mine or I'll have to shake it out of you."

She takes it from her hair. She had lifted it while telling the story of her Mormon years and clutching me, during which time she was going through my pockets. I wasn't angry, considering the associations she had had for two years, poor kid.

We went up a back staircase to her room, and it was hardly an improvement on the crib, and she gathered together a few sorry possessions, powder and stuff, and put it into a cardboard suitcase, and I made her get into a more seemly outfit than that whore dress, and with my hand firmly under her arm, I steered her down and out to the front, in the course of which we passed through the hall again, and now noises come from all the cubicles and the dance floor was crowded with a gathering of men, drunk and disorderly, so that you could see the point in lifting their firearms on the way in, else they'd all killed one another in short order. This was when I seen that big bouncer Harry beating the heads of them three buffalo hunters and pitching them into the street.

Well sir, I pulled Amelia through and into that office near the front door. Dolly was still there though Wild Bill wasn't. I always remember she was rebraiding the lash of a rawhide riding quirt as we come in. If she swings it at me or Amelia, says I to myself, I'll put five soft-nosed bullets in her, woman or not.

She looks up, smiles with her mustache, and says: " Enjoy yourself, Short Arm? Whyn't you go take another, be a sport. Billy won't be out for a while yet."

"Looky here, Dolly," I says, "I'm a-taking this kid along." I was ashamed to tell of our relationship. I just said: "Don't try and stop me."

She tied a knot at the end of that quirt and swung it against her palm. Then says: "Why should I do that? This is Liberty Hall, hoss." And chuckles hoarsely and in her grand swagger leaves the room and passes through the dancehall crowd towards the rear, them drunks falling away on either side of her as when a big ship comes into the harbor at San Francisco and the smaller craft make way.

I took Amelia to the hotel where I was staying, and the desk clerk started to grin with his bad teeth but I cut him off short by renting her a room next to mine on the second floor, and we went upstairs and I turned down her bed for her, sniffed at the pitcher on the dresser to see if the water was fresh, give her a flannel nightshirt of my own, for she didn't have no decent sleeping garment, and kissed her goodnight on the forehead.

She had gone through all this right docile, without a word; not, I expect, having yet recovered from the surprise of finding her kin.

I was too excited to sleep much that night. "Amelia Crabb" is what I had wrote down on that hotel register. I didn't know her Mormon name and did not want to. Nor was I really curious to hear more about her earlier life—not even about her Ma, my sister Sue Ann. I had been too long away from them people of my regular family. It kind of depressed me to think of their life in Salt Lake among the Latter-day Saints, being so foreign to all I knowed. I had asked Amelia, on the way to the hotel, about my own Ma, her granny, and she said she didn't recall her, so I reckoned she died somehow. I don't mean I was without feeling, but all I had was now centered in this young girl, and more as to what she would become than what she was at present. Somebody to take care of. And I was going to do a better job than I had in the past. I hadn't no Indians to worry about here, nor no U.S. Army. I could handle anybody else, even Wild Bill Hickok if it come to that.

Next day, pretty late, for Amelia had got into the habit in that whorehouse of sleeping through most of the light, we went out and got some clothes and in a dress what buttoned up to the throat and with her face washed clean you'd never have taken that girl for anything but the gentlest-born. She was right pale, but then that made her look all the more respectable, for a lady in them days never let the sun touch her skin.

Then I realized we hadn't ought to stay at that hotel, which was not buggy or anything, but it was in the rougher part of town, flanked by a couple of saloons, and there was uncouth fellows sitting around the front, spitting tobacco juice all over the floor, and some of them might have knowed Amelia from Dolly's. So by God if I didn't go to the swellest place in K.C., with fancy gaslights and plush furniture in the lobby and flunkies in gold-braided outfits, and hire us a combination of connecting bedrooms with a nice parlor between. Must have cost seven-eight dollars a day or more. I don't recall. I do remember the management was right snooty, but I threw money around like seed and their attitude changed directly.

Amelia herself didn't do me no harm there, for it is amazing how she took to the new life. I suppose that Mormon upbringing hadn't been so bad, as a foundation, and then her natural spirit added the rest, along with what she got from ladies'-fashion papers I bought her and the studying she did of the high class of women who resided in the hostelry: Senators' wives and daughters, and those of Army generals and leaders of commerce. She developed a walk that looked like she was on tiny wheels beneath her long skirts, and when she took a cup of tea her dainty hand was raised like a bird in flight.

And pretty, right pretty she proved to be, with that turned-up nose and little mouth, and her hair was bright as a fall leaf when it had been washed a couple times and set by a professional hairdresser. The men around the hotel was fascinated by her, but discreet and respectable, not gawking nor licking their lips and such, like the kind of louts I always hung out with heretofore.

Well, this was costing me a plenty and within a few days I had peeled so many bills off my roll that it was down to the size of my little finger, with the hotel account still unpaid and growing by the hour, for Amelia was continually ordering things to be sent up to our rooms. And that was as it should be, for I wanted to keep her in seclusion until the genteel way of life become a habit that replaced whoring in the way she thought of herself.

I had been to several schools so far without finding the right one, for various reasons: at some, the withered spinsters in charge looked at me over their pointy noses and says they was full for the next five years; and I'll tell you this, there was others who reminded me of Dolly.

But I had to get more dinero somewhere. Now the only thing I could figure doing to raise it was to go back over in the Market Square area again and play poker. Them buffalo hunters had real big games every night, generally starting after twelve o'clock, when they returned from the theaters and dance halls, and running into the morning. When I say big, I mean with luck you might walk away from the table at about four-thirty A.M. with two-three hundred dollars. This time was good from my point of view: I could see Amelia safely to bed and then slip out, play all night, get back in before she arose, and nobody the wiser. For I didn't want her to know her uncle was gambling: that was the sort of life from which I had sworn to protect her.

The first night I was over to Market Square, I run into Wild Bill Hickok. He was sitting in his favorite corner of that saloon where he shot Strawhan's brother, and when I entered, he waved me over. He was with some others in a poker game and had just won a big pot.

"Hoss," he says to me, "I have missed you. I never took you for the type of man who would run off with a crib-girl."

I did not like this reference to Amelia, but to protest against it effectively I would have had to admit she was my kin, and I didn't want to do that.

"Yes sir," he goes on, "if you are as mighty a poker player as you are a lover, I'd take it kindly if you would sit in. You," he points at the man directly across the table, "give him your chair."

This man looks miserable, but ain't slow about complying. Now of all people I did not want to play against Wild Bill. For I neglected to say earlier that I intended to cheat. I know there are people who take dishonesty at cards as one of the nastiest sins in the world. I don't admire it greatly myself, but figured my cause was sufficient to justify it in this circumstance. I guess that's what everybody says about every type of unscrupulosity employed by himself, but I ain't preaching morality here, I'm merely recording history, and what happened at that time was I proposed to cheat my opponents to the hilt. Except I never expected to be in a game with Wild Bill Hickok.

So I played honest for a couple hours and by two o'clock in the morning I was down to my last five dollars. Now I took hold of myself and reflected that little Amelia was all I had in the world. Either I got the money to make a proper woman of her, or we was back where we started, in which case it didn't matter if I was shot by Wild Bill. I saw I never had a choice in the matter.

Now, Frank Delight who had a crush on Caroline and was a master of games of chance, had showed me several devices that put the odds on the side of the man what employed them. I really had not practiced enough to manage the ace-up-the-sleeve, which the expert can make to appear more swiftly than the eye can follow; and the same weakness applied to the fake shuffle, in my hands. So what I done was to use the mirror-ring. This is an ordinary finger ring that has a good flat surface on it somewhere, highly polished, which will reflect the markings on the cards as you deal them face-down. So that you know what your opponents are holding and can play accordingly.

I had purchased a brass ring and filed down a plane surface for about a quarter-inch on the underside of its good wide band and buffed her up, and she was small enough not to be detected, yet adequate to transmit the information. I hadn't dared to use it so far, but now when the deal came to me I rubbed my palms on my coat as if to dry off the sweat but in reality polishing up the tiny looking-glass on the inside of my left hand, and started in.

Directly, Wild Bill's winnings started to dwindle, and I reckon it was five-thirty in the morning when he finally pushed over the last of his pile and with a funny smile says: "Well, friend, if you are as good a lover as you are a gambler . . ." His voice trails off and he gets up and strides out the saloon door into the morning, showing his back all the way, so you could see he was right upset.

I haven't mentioned them two other slobs we played with, being they was the kind who figured it a privilege to be beat by Wild Bill. There was a number of flunkies around there who took turns losing to him every night. Now as I was putting away my win—it turned out to be a little over a hundred dollars—these men smirked at me and then each other.

And the one says: "I recall the late Hank French. He also won from Wild Bill at poker."

I just sneered at them and went out from the nightlong stink of smoke and liquor into the pure morning. You had to keep your face in them days, and it is just as well they was behind me when I seen Hickok waiting in the street outside, his silk hat cocked forward, his golden hair streaming over his shoulders, his fine white hands hooked by the thumbs into his lower vest pockets, with them two pearl handles a-jutting out of both hips. Down the street come a man trundling a handcart, and across the square someone was saddling a mule which was blowing out its belly as they always do so the cinch straps would be loose, and the owner was fixing to kick him in it.

Well sir, I thought, here's where I get it after all these years of close calls, for Hickok was going to drill me for cheating him, and Amelia would return to whoring, and I had failed again.

But I would not back down to Wild Bill even though in this instance he was right. I don't know why: I was afraid of him, yet at the same time his presence was a challenge to me.

So I stepped out through the swinging doors onto the porch and says: "You waiting on me?"

He gives me that famous level look for one long, breathless moment, and then he suddenly relaxes and says: "Come on, hoss, let's get some breakfast."

It was over our steak and eggs and fried potatoes that Wild Bill says: "Anybody who plays poker as well as you ought to learn to handle a gun." I don't know whether he meant it sarcastic or not, nor did I understand his motive in offering to give me his expert instruction free of charge. But I accepted, and that's what we got to doing every morning after them games: me and Wild Bill would eat and then we'd ride to the edge of town and we'd shoot. And I found that though I had carried a revolver for years and had used it upon occasion, in comparison with Hickok I knowed very little of the weapon.

He talked more of the technical specifics of pistols, holsters, cartridges, etc., but we spent most of our time practicing marksmanship and the fast draw. I gathered that, before he took me along, he come there anyway by himself, for like a fine piano player a gunfighter had to rehearse continually lest he lose the precise touch. Here's the exercises Wild Bill used to keep his hand in: driving a cork through the neck of a bottle and splitting a bullet on the edge of a dime, both at a range of forty-fifty feet, starting with the guns in his pants. I would hold a silver dollar chest-high, drop it, and before it struck the earth he'd have drawed, fired, and hit the dime so that the soft-lead .45 slug was cut in two equal parts.

Maybe the first thirty times I tried this, I even missed the length of the board in which the dime was embedded, or tore up the prairie on either side, front and back, of the bottle. But then I got to where I was missing only by about six inches, and consistently to the right of the target, so I adjusted my technique to pull left, and made my first score one morning after we had been going out there only a week. This was with the dime; later I shot the cork through the bottle, too, an easier accomplishment.

But I couldn't get the sense of merely being the fastest draw or the best shot, with no further purpose to it. Take Wild Bill, the only thing he was suited to be was a peace officer, patrolling the streets of a cowtown in hopes someone would offer him resistance so that he could use his guns on them. He couldn't even be an outlaw, for suchlike had to be more interested in robbing than gunplay—or in the case of Johnny Jump and his gang, murder and mayhem. Something concrete, that is. But gunfighting was all idea when you got down to it, devoted to testing the proposition: *I'm a better man than you.* It might have been fair, for size and weight did not enter, and a midget was on the same terms as a giant, when they both held Colt's. But the question was, what did you establish when you found the better man?

That's what I got to thinking about, for no sooner had I developed my proficiency than Hickok says: "Of course, firing at bottles is the least part of it. It's the man-to-man encounter that proves everything. I've known champion shots who froze when going against men who hardly knew a butt from a muzzle, and died."

I was playing poker every night, all night, and needless to say I was winning with my mirror-ring. Now I was not such a fool as to get recklessly overbearing about it. After that first session, I held my earnings down, twenty dollars one night, thirty the next, maybe falling back on the next to as little as fifteen; and if I'd get as high as fifty, then I'd balance it some by maybe losing five-six dollars the following night. In the aggregate I was making a good income, but not so conspicuous as to rouse serious suspicion, though of course any success at a game of chance is apt to be suspect to them off whom it is gained. But I was deft with my ring, and if my opponents looked for anything, it was the obvious tricks like palming cards or stacking the deck, of which I was utterly innocent.

Then I'd take them shooting lessons and afterward go back to our hotel and find little Amelia just arising from her slumbers at around eight o'clock, and I'd pretend I just got up myself and we'd take our morning coffee brought by the help to the sitting room between our bedchambers. It was real nice, and she didn't seem in the least bored by this new life, as I feared she might be, and I could afford the bills, so the shank of the morning would find us visiting the expensive ladies' shops where she'd buy more dresses and shoes and hats, and then in the afternoon we'd rent a carriage and ride about or stroll through the parks, and in the early evening we'd take in the genteeler entertainments: piano or violin recitals, dramatic readings, and the like.

In between all this, and the meals we ate, I tried to catch a few winks of sleep; but I didn't need much in that period. I was twenty-nine years of age, and in the prime of life; had somebody to straighten out, and someone to cheat; was an acquaintance of Wild Bill Hickok; made money, ate and dressed to the hilt.

But the main thing was my fondness for Amelia. I'd have done anything for that girl. She was developing into such a lady that shortly I believe I could have took her back to Dolly's and nobody would ever have recognized her. It was not just her fine clothes, but she had picked up, from them magazine pictures and watching the respectable women in the better places of K.C. where I took her, the most elegant way of carrying herself. She had a longish, willowy neck to begin with, and now she held her head, with that great pile of red hair cunningly arranged with pins of shell and amber, above it like a wonderful bird's nest upon a marble pillar.

"Uncle Jack," she would say, coming to the door of her room as we was fixing to go out, "would you prefer I wore the paletot or the basque or the sacque this evening?" These was all types of women's coats of that day. Now I didn't know one from the next, but since I was flattered to be asked, I'd make a choice and she would don it, for her major delight lay in pleasing me. Now you have that attitude on her part, and then you have mine: I found pleasing everything she did, for it was all graceful and sensitive, and her voice, which had been right tinny when at Dolly's, had turned as pretty as the sound of a spring bubbling out among ferns. I got an immense joy out of just seeing her eat a plate of food. I'll tell you how refined she was: you couldn't see her teeth when she chewed, and she was so quiet about spooning up a bowl of soup that if your eyes was closed you'd never know what she was up to.

All this she had worked out on her own, for them ain't the kind of things you can teach a person, and God knows I am hardly an instructor in deportment. But my experience with Mrs. Pendrake had give me at least this: I know class when I see it, and insofar as was within my power I could encourage Amelia when she headed in the right direction, which meant I had to maintain that flow of money, which in turn kept me cheating at cards.

Which brings me back to Wild Bill. I didn't want to play against him, and some evenings managed to elude his company. But he'd come looking for me from saloon to saloon, and when he caught up, would run one of the three other fellows out of their chair, take it, and proceed to lose. It was strange, too strange for my stomach, and I got to not using the mirror-ring after he set down—while making the most of it before he showed up, so the evening would still show a profit.

Now what that ring done, it never gave me better cards than the next, but rather the knowledge of what hands the other fellows held and then only when I was dealer; it was not nearly so dishonest as palming an ace, say; a certain skill was still required, and pure luck determined what cards a man would get from the deal. I can't say my luck either improved or worsened when using the ring. But here's the oddity, whenever Bill set down and I refrained from employing the tiny mirror—played square, that is, my luck commenced to run extreme and fantastic. Flushes, straights, three of a kind, pairs: they flowed to me as if by magic.

Bill played doggedly on. And always we went to breakfast afterwards and then out to our range; and other than that queer look that come over him when I took my first pot of the evening and never left it till I walked from the saloon to meet him in the street outside —for he continued to leave first—he did not display anything that could be termed bad feeling, suspicion, spite, or envy.

As to the shooting lessons, I figure they served him as an exercise in pride, reminding me directly after every poker session that, whereas he had lost, he was pre-eminent in the more serious game of chance in which the stakes is life and death—for though we was shooting at dimes and corks, you could not overlook their similar diameter to that of the human eye.

However, I believe that when Wild Bill Hickok faced a man he looked at his opponent's eye as if it was a cork.

I was getting real good with my weapon against them inanimate objects, and I was fast. Though speed itself was of lesser concern than accuracy, for as Bill said what mattered was putting your bullet where you wanted it to go. He had seen a fast man fire three shots before a slow man got off one; but the three missed, whereas the laggard's struck the quick man dead center.

'Course, he says, there's where the personality come in; whether fast or slow, there was one perfect shot for each occasion, and you killed or died according to how close you come to achieving it. Once arriving at your decision to fire upon a man, your mind become a blank, and your will, your body, and your pistol merged into one instrument with a single job. It was as if the gun growed out of your hand, your finger spat lead and smoke. Indeed, that was the technique of aiming: like you was pointing to make emphasis in a argument. On such an occasion the ordinary person is naturally accurate: notice next time, he says, when you are in a verbal quarrel; if your opponent's finger was a gun, you'd be dead.

One morning we set up twin boards with dimes protruding from slots in them, and both me and Wild Bill went back twenty paces and fired. We both split our bullets perfect on the dimes' edge, and the two shots sounded as one explosion.

"Hoss," says Hickok, looking down at me over his hooked nose and blond handlebars, "I have taught you all that can be learned out here. The rest is to be had only from a target that shoots back."

"That must have been luck," I says. I meant it. He could have repeated that performance all day; whereas I knowed I couldn't have done it more than say twice out of five: you can tell that about yourself. I also had the definite feeling he had not used all the speed of which he was capable.

"I don't believe in luck," he answers, and his voice was like the cracking of a whiplash. But he drops the subject then and appeared his old self on the ride back to town.

Wild Bill Hickok had devoted friends and sworn enemies. Mention his name anywhere in Kansas during the '70's and you could get a sharp reaction on one side or the other, and there might have been more men killed in arguments about him than he himself ever sent under. There was some people, I suppose out of envy, who even insisted he was a second-rate shot as well as a coward, and of course that greater number who had him doing impossible feats.

So in the face of all that I submit this experience of mine with the man in Kansas City in '71. It wasn't everything he done that period by a long shot; he even played poker with others and won. But I'm saying what I knowed of him personally. When I weigh all the pros and cons he comes out even.

He learned me about the precision handling of a revolver. However, had I never met him it was likely I could have got on right well without that specialty, which was not the necessity you might imagine for surviving in the West. Take the incident with Strawhan's brother: if Wild Bill had not been expert at gunfighting he would have got killed; but if he had not been a gunfighter, Strawhan's brother would not have been after him in the first place. So what did Hickok actually do for me? Show me how to save my life? No, rather he give me a new means by which to risk it.

I felt a curious relief when them lessons had ended, and somehow I got to believing that I wouldn't see him no more across the poker table, either. Nor did I for a night or two, and a fellow told me Hickok had been offered the marshal's job in Abilene, which was one of them new towns on the railroad to which the Texas men drove up their cattle for shipment East and when they got there the cowboys collected their pay and went wild till they was broke, drinking and whoring and shooting, and not long before had killed the then marshal, Bear River Tom Smith, who had enforced the law with his fists. So now Abilene wanted to hire a gunfighter.

"Reckon he'll take it?" I asked.

"Sure do," said that fellow. "He ain't killed nobody since Strawhan's brother."

This was a typical opinion about Hickok: that he enjoyed sending people under. So many of them who admired him liked this idea, for in any white population there is a vast number of individuals who have murder in their hearts but consider themselves too weak to take up its practice themselves, so they substitute a man like Hickok. A Cheyenne enjoyed killing, but not Wild Bill: he was indifferent to it. He had barely looked at the corpse of Strawhan's brother except to check whether it would draw on him again. In fact, I don't think Hickok enjoyed anything. Life to him consisted of doing what was necessary, endlessly measuring his performance against that single perfect shot for each occasion. He was what you call an idealist.

Well, it appeared a day or so later that my assumption he had left town was erroneous, for we had just started up our nightly poker session when Hickok's big form swung into the saloon, and he stepped aside so his back would not be in a direct line with the door while he sized the place up as was his custom. He wore a new outfit; no longer the frock coat, but a beautiful soft deerskin shirt that fell to his knees, trimmed at the collar and cuffs with fur and a four-inch fringe hung from the hem. At his waist was tied a sash of red silk, with fringed tassels dangling from the knot. Into this, above both hips, his ivory-handled sixguns was thrust butts forward.

I knowed he was looking for me; there weren't no point in trying to hide, so I give him a holler, and he come and set in, and of course I won all night as usual, perfectly honest, not using my ring, and along about dawn he called me for a hundred dollars and showed an ace full house.

At which I says: "I got two pairs."

It was unusual to see Wild Bill grin, but he did now and tugged at the end of his sweeping mustaches, and he says: "Well, I finally did it."

And I says: "Two pairs of queens."

However, he just kept smiling as he pushed the money over, more than I ever took off him in the past at one setting, and he even bantered a bit with the other men, and then followed them out. I don't know why I had toyed with him like that: it was mean to let him think for a moment he had at last beat me. But it had been instinctive on my part. I ain't the first or last man to needle an individual who presents his weakness so obviously.

Well, I left the saloon myself finally, last man in the place, and the barkeep yawns and bid me goodnight, and I get to the porch and there of course is Wild Bill standing in the street at a range of twenty paces. It struck me that had been the distance in our gun practice, for when you have trained so much, your eyes gauges them things automatic.

I says: "You want to go to breakfast, Bill?"

He says: "No."

I comes down into the street, and he backs up for the same distance, hands hanging loose at his sides.

I says: "Something wrong?"

He says: "You have been cheating me."

"No, I ain't," says I. "Maybe that first night we played, but never since. And I'll refund what I won then."

"Don't go for that pocket," he says.

"You can see my gun," I points out, "here in the belt."

"I think you have a hide-out derringer in that vest."

"I swear I have not, Bill." I'll tell you a funny thing: I wasn't scared now, whereas I believe he was. I wasn't, because I had no intention of shooting it out with Wild Bill. As to him, he could hardly worry much about our respective talents at gun-handling; he was scared of some treachery or other, especially now that I had admitted cheating him that once. Few men of that time would ever admit anything even when caught in the act.

"Go for it if you want," he says.

"I don't want," I says.

"God damn it," says he, "I taught you everything I know. You saw you were as good as me. It's fair, ain't it?"

I never answered.

"Well, ain't it?" he repeats, sort of pleading. "Look here, hoss, nobody cheats Wild Bill Hickok. If you wanted money, all you had to do was ask."

"I said I never cheated you but once."

"Then," he says, "you are also a liar, hoss. And nobody lies to Wild Bill Hickok."

Now there was two things to note about this colloquy. One was that he referred to himself like he was an institution: personally, he didn't care so much about these supposed outrages of mine, but he could not let the noble firm of Wild Bill Hickok, Inc., be loosely dealt with. You know, like you're supposed to say "Your Honor" not to the person setting up there, but to the office of judge.

Secondly, he was getting gradually more abusive, adding "liar" to "cheat," both of them shootable insults in the West at that time though they seemed to have lost their force as the years have went on. I reckoned he would eventually get to "son of a bitch," the ultimate, except for "horse thief," which wasn't appropriate here.

If you was called any of them names in public, you was expected to do something about it. However, lucky for me there wasn't yet another soul along the street to hear my degradation in the fresh light of the rising sun. Them other fellows from the card game had gone on, and the barkeep left the saloon by the back door on the alley.

But somebody might show at any moment; and before they did, I had to decide on whether to choose quick death or lingering shame. I think I have made it clear that I didn't like to draw on Wild Bill. However, I wouldn't want my backing down to be general knowledge. If it so became, my poker playing was at an end. Not only would everybody soon know I had been cheating, but would take me for a coward who from then on could be pushed around with impunity. It was really the last-named that mattered, for cheating was no rarity at that time. Everybody tried it, but I was just cleverer than most. Hickok himself would occasionally sneak looks at the discard in a poker game, what they called the "deadwood." You couldn't tell what a man was holding by that means, but you could learn a good deal by seeing what he throwed away. Therefore the practice was frowned on to the degree that if you was caught at it, you could get your head blown off. Except that Hickok usually played cards with men who was afraid of him.

So he didn't stand on no firmer moral ground than me, and in addition, he was talking about fairness, but he had no idea of how I cheated him, was prosecuting me for murder without a corpus delicti. I tell this so you won't have too hard an opinion of me when you hear what followed.

The next moment, I seen a wagon coming way up the street, as yet too far for the man driving it likely to realize what we was about, but he would within another hundred yards. I had moved my position so it lay due west of Wild Bill, which meant the rising sun was just above his head and consequently shining at my eyes. Ordinarily, I would have reached to pull down the brim of my planter's hat, but facing a man like Hickok you don't make the most innocent move.

So I commenced to squint. "You claim I am a cheat, do you?" I asks.

"That is right," says he.

"And a liar?"

"Yes you are."

I says: "I want to lower my hatbrim against the sun. I'm a-going to use my left hand."

"Make it real slow," he says, and hooks his thumbs into that red sash just forward of the white gun-butts on both sides.

My left hand crawled upwards like a caterpillar on a wall, caught the brim, and depressed it an inch. Then I turned my palm forward and flung open my fingers.

At the same time I went for my gun with my right hand. For a particle of a second I didn't know what Wild Bill was doing; if you remember, he had trained me to concentrate on myself at the instant of action. So I didn't rightly see him draw, but I sure saw the muzzle of his Colt's spit lead and smoke directly at me.

CHAPTER 22 *Bunco and Buffalo*

I SURELY WOULD HAVE BEEN KILLED had I not employed a trick.

I caught the sun in my mirror-ring and reflected its glare into Hickok's eyes, then dived to the ground. Though momentarily blinded, he drew as efficiently as always and sent two shots a-roaring through the space occupied by my head a scant instant before. But he couldn't see nothing but green spots for a time, I reckon, for he next lowered his sixguns and stood there blinking. He looked right pathetic, now that I think of it, for all his six foot of dressed deerskin, trimmed with fur.

I laid quite safe there in the street, under his fire, but I daren't speak a word on account of he could then have sighted on the sound of my voice. I had my own pistol out, and could have killed the great Wild Bill at that point and gone down in history for it.

Well, the moment of silence wasn't any longer in reality than the moment of gunfire, and then Bill says: "All right, hoss, you whipped me again. Blast away." I don't answer. He says: "I tell you you better fire, because in a second I'm going to kill you if you don't."

That fellow with the wagon had pulled to the side of the street and crawled under his vehicle, still several blocks distant. But two shots wasn't enough to wake anybody out of bed in them days, especially that early of a morning, so we as yet did not have no other audience so far as I knowed.

"You trying to play me for a fool?" says Bill, right exasperated, and he sent three more hunks of lead blowing through the air that I had lately vacated, then does that so-called border switch, the flying transfer of his guns. And his vision cleared some by now, so I guess he could make out I was laying on the ground, and he come over and prodded me with his boot and says: "Oh, I got you anyway," taking me for dead and wounded. I laid there with my eyes closed.

Then he says: "I'm sorry, hoss. But it was fair, wasn't it? I taught you, didn't I? And now I'm going to carry you over to the doc, and if you are dead I'll buy you a nice funeral."

I figured by now he would have put away his gun, so as he bent over to pick me up, I come to life and shoved my pistol into his nose.

"Are you satisfied?" I asks. "I could have killed you ten times by now."

Living his type of life, he didn't have much energy to spare for astonishment. He squinted and backed up with his hands in the air. Then he let them down slowly and laughed a huge guffaw.

"Hoss," he says, "you are the trickiest little devil I have ever run across. You know there are a couple of hundred men who would give all they owned to get a clear shot at Wild Bill Hickok, and you throw it away."

He was laughing, but I reckon somewhere deep he was actually offended, such was his idea of himself. He would rather I had killed him than take pains to show I was basically indifferent to the fact of his existence so long as I could protect my own hide.

He tried one more thing to pry from me an admission that I was fascinated by him. He says: "I guess you can go about now saying how you put a head on Wild Bill Hickok."

I says: "I'll never mention it." And I have kept my word from that day to this. I wasn't going to give him no free advertisement of any kind. That was the trouble with them long-haired darlings like him and Custer: people talked about them too much.

His mustache drooped in disappointment, but he laughed again to keep up the hearty front, and he says: "I'm going over to Abilene to be the marshal. If you ever get over that way, hoss, why I'll be proud to buy you a drink. But damn if I'll ever play poker with you again."

He shakes with me. I don't know that I have mentioned that his hands was right small for a man his size, and his feet as well—as little as my own, almost. Then he turned and walked away down the street, straight as a die and certainly not swaying, yet with that hair hanging down his back and the long buckskin tunic descending almost to his knees like a dress, I was reminded of a real tall girl.

I stayed in Kansas City all the summer of '71 and continued to earn my and Amelia's living at the poker table and continued to cheat and was finally caught a time or two at it and shot once in the calf of the leg by a fellow, but it wasn't permanently damaging, being only a derringer, and on another occasion a man took a knife after me, and I had to shoot him in the hand.

Anyway, after a few such incidents, I commenced to get a bad reputation. It got more difficult to find people to play cards with, and once I did have a game, I was watched close. If I played with any of them other able practitioners of the violent arts that was in K.C. that summer—Jack Gallagher, say, or Billy Dixon—you can be damn certain I kept my nose clean: for the more you know about gunfighting, the more respect you have for those to whom it is a specialty.

Little Amelia's spending grew to wondrous proportions. I come back to the hotel one day and found a grand piano, made of mahogany, in our parlor-room, and along with it some elderly German gentleman with a beard and eyeglasses, come from St. Louie along with the instrument to tune it and give lessons in the playing thereof. Not only did I owe for the piano and the shipping costs, but also for this individual's wages and his room and board—so far as he was concerned, in perpetuity, I suppose, for though in time Amelia might learn to play unassisted, the instrument would need tuning for the rest of its life.

I never did figure out whether or not he was a confidence man, but he seemed a real German all right, and sure knowed his music, except it was hard as the devil to get the bastard to play any piece as such and not just the scales over and over, in the course of which he'd get out his set of tuning forks and monkey about with the wires and hammers.

The whole bill was well into four figures, though I don't recall the precise sum, for I blacked out when I saw it. However, when I recovered from the shock, I was really kind of proud of Amelia for her initiative. Seems she had just got the address of the piano manufacturer, sent them a letter on the stationery of the hotel saying send your best model, and by God if they never, without even a deposit, upriver from St. Louie along with that German. Lucky for me, he didn't care nothing for the nature of his accommodations, being a pure fanatic for his music, so I had him bunk down on a cot in the corner of my bedroom, and that was all right with him, and he lived on sausage and rye bread, when he remembered to eat at all, so I saved a little that way.

I must say though that Amelia never did learn to play the piano well. That was the one thing she did awkward, and the result wasn't much more tuneful than had a cat got to walking on the keys. Used to drive the professor crazy, and he'd storm and yell and tear his beard, and once I recall when she was attacking a particular exercise for the ninety-ninth time and making the same mistake at every instance, the German cried like a baby.

After a couple months, Amelia come to me and says: "Uncle Jack, do you mind if I send the piano away? It has grown to be a dreadful bore." That's the way she talked now, sort of like an English person, with her mouth made small and sending the words through her nose. Sure classy it was.

And of course I agreed, for I wanted her to be happy, so I bought the German a return passage, a loaf of bread, and a hunk of cheese, and I hired some brawny fellows to take the piano out and crate it up and put it upon a riverboat back to St. Louie. But as it happened that boat got into a race with another craft, which they was always doing in them days, and fired up so high its boilers blowed and the son of a bitch burned right down to the waterline, the piano with it. I still owed something like $930 on that instrument, and was the frequent recipient of threatening correspondence on the subject, followed by duns wearing derby hats and carrying various types of documentation: dispossess papers and all, and when they found there wasn't nothing to reclaim, they believed I ought to be imprisoned for it, but a lawyer I hired worked out some arrangement by which I would pay them fifty dollars a week for the rest of my life, so they eased off, and the lawyer charged me only two hundred dollars for his services.

And this at a time when I couldn't get nobody to play poker with me. The hotel bill was run way up high again, the dress shops was sending statements around, and I owed the hairdresser, the livery stable, and two restaurants. Then too, Amelia was stuck on this idea of gaining musical accomplishment, so the next thing we had to replace that German and his piano was a huge woman with a chest on her that would have made Dolly look tubercular. She taught singing and claimed to be Italian, late of the opera in a place called Milano, according to her story: Signorina Carmella. She could sing all right, so it might have been true. Under a full head of steam she would crack every tumbler in our rooms, and when she tackled the scales we'd get complaints from guests as far away as the fourth floor rear.

So it was just as well she was drunk most of the time, for then she'd drop her bulk on the sofa and stay right quiet while giving the beat to Amelia with a fat finger stacked with cheap rings and after a while hiccup once or twice and fall dead asleep. Then I had my choice of leaving her to sleep it off, which might take hours—for which I was charged at the rate of three dollars per—or waking her up, at which moment she would clutch at me under the illusion I was some intimate acquaintance of hers called Vincenzo. This amused Amelia no end.

As to my niece's talent for singing, however, I am afraid it proved in no respect superior to her gift at the piano, though Signorina Carmella, unlike that German, would have been the last to admit it, I reckon with her fees in mind. It was funny to me that with such a melodious speaking voice as Amelia had developed, she would sing like a crow rather than a lark; but I guess there ain't no connection. I didn't think the worse of her for it. I even approved of her indomitable ambition to be musical, but when she and the Signorina announced that they figured she was ready to hire a hall and give a recital, well, I didn't want my dear little relative to be mobbed by a crowd of irate ticket buyers after she got out one song, but I knowed that would sure happen unless we could scratch up an audience of deaf persons. So, for the first time, I says no.

Amelia didn't cry or scream about it, she just quietly fell ill, wouldn't eat nothing for several days, and when I come into her room, give me a sad sweet smile, her wan little hands lying still upon the coverlet, and I seen she would probably die before her time unless I relented, for she had that romantic Crabb streak in her. So at length I says O.K. and rented a hall from some lodge, had programs printed, and got some boys to go about the respectable part of town giving away tickets, for it was no use trying to sell them, and the night of the recital, I loaded up a double-barreled shotgun and took a conspicuous seat down front in case of trouble.

But I hadn't had to worry, for only six people come, and Amelia was so nervous she hardly noticed the audience, and the Signorina, who accompanied her upon a harmonium, had belted the vino a good deal beforehand and fell off the stool a couple times and we had more difficulty in propping her upright than with any protests from the crowd.

As I recall it, it only cost me five dollars to get a favorable review printed in next day's newspaper, for journalists in them days was notoriously underpaid. However, that was the only bargain I got: I owed for the hall, the rented harmonium, the printer, and of course the Signorina for her services and the piano stool she broke.

But little Amelia sure got satisfaction from her concert and bought ten or twenty copies of the paper with that commendatory notice and made sure everybody around the hotel knew it was her; so I had no regrets though my financial obligations was growing to a magnitude not far this side of gigantic. Whereas my expectations was nil, so far as poker went, for it had now reached late August and them buffalo hunters was a-leaving for the range to start their new season, so soon there wasn't anybody left in K.C. to get up a game with, even provided that they would have played with me, which many was now disinclined to, anyhow.

Now what I intended to do was to hunt buffalo myself, for in one season from September to March a good man could clear two-three thousand dollars in hides, but to do that you had to go into it like a real business, which meant you must have a stake to start on. You needed a big Sharps buffalo rifle with a supply of heavy-caliber ammunition, a wagon and animals to pull it, and then you required a man to do the skinning, for no self-respecting hunter would touch a knife to the beasts he shot, I don't know why: just snobbery, I reckon, but that's the way it was. It might sound funny, but buffalo hunters considered themselves a type of aristocracy. Anyway, I just name the barest essentials. Most of the well-known hunters carried along a team of ten or twelve men, including wagon drivers, cook, fellow to tend the stock, etc., and an arsenal of weapons, on account of when you fired that Sharps a number of times its barrel would overheat, and you couldn't wait for it to cool while the herd might get the smell of blood and stampede.

Suffice it to say my problem was solved by running into a man called Allardyce T. Meriweather, in one of the drinking establishments of Kansas City, whence I had repaired one afternoon to ponder over a beaker of the grape. Just thinking of him brings to mind his type of phraseology.

A man steps up to me while I am standing at the brass rail, and intones the following.

"Sir," he says, "I know you will pardon my forwardness when I say that as the only two gentlemen among this clientele of ruffians, it is my opinion that we should make common cause."

"Pardon?" I says.

"Exactly," says he, and introduces himself.

"Crabb," he says when he has my handle. "Is that of the Philadelphia, New York, or Boston branch of the family?"

Now I thought he was one of them Eastern swells come out West for his weak lungs or whatnot, which a tour of the prairies was supposed to correct; and right then, bothered about money as I was, it annoyed me that this here cake-eater could roam around at his ease, all expenses paid, whereas I was denied a dishonest living, so I says to him: "Philadelphia." What the hell did I care whether he believed me?

"Ah," he says. "My acquaintance, I fear, was with the New York and Boston lines." I haven't yet said what he looked like: well, he was the middle-size facing you, but in profile he was developing quite the potgut. He was clean-shaven with a blue jaw and a flabby mouth, and he wore or carried a deal of gewgaws: diamond stickpin, lapel flower, watch chain with dependent ornamentation, gold-headed cane, doeskin gloves, and the like. I reckon he was around my age.

"Which was your university?" he says. "Harvard or Yale?"

"The former," says I.

He says: "Mine was the latter, but I had a host of acquaintance, nay, friends of the bosom, up at Cambridge in the early sixties, which must have been your years there. Did you know Montgomery Brear or William W. Whipple or Bartley "Doc" Platt, all of the Indian Pudding Club? Or Chester "Chet" Larkin; he was a Musk Ox. Or Mansard Fitch, who belonged to the Kangaroos?"

"No, I never," I says. "I was an Antelope."

"Well, sir," says he, "let me shake your hand again on that. I don't require a further bona fide. I expect every gentleman in the organized world knows of the exclusivity of the Antelopes. It is no wonder then, sir, that I was able to pick you out of the crowd: breeding will tell."

He goes on in that vein for a time and we had another drink and while I was some amused to have put one over on him, I tired of his yapping finally and was fixing to leave, when he says: "Sir, I have no recourse but to hurl myself upon your mercy. I find myself in a desperate condition. Alas, I have not your moral fiber. I am a bending reed, sir, and I fear the grand old firm of Meriweather, bankers, to which I shall one day fall heir, will find in me a pillar of sand.

"In short, sir, I have in two weeks squandered, in games of chance, the five thousand dollars my father put into my pocket for the first month's expenses of my Western jaunt. I dare not wire him for more. I appeal to you as a fellow gentleman among the rabble. Twenty dollars, Mr. Crabb, a mere pittance to you, but it would save my life.

"In exchange, you will have my note, Jack, signed with the name of Meriweather, good as the coin of the realm, and you may hold my stickpin as security."

I couldn't have been less sympathetic, but mention of that jewel caused my heart to warm real sudden: it was big as an acorn, and I reckon twenty dollars wouldn't have paid for the box it come in.

So I could scratch up that much, and got my wallet out before he changed his mind.

"God bless you," he says when he took the bills and handed over the stickpin. "May we meet someday under more fortunate circumstances."

He was so relieved that he left the saloon directly, without giving me the IOU, which was all right by me, for that made it a sale: a half-pound of diamond for twenty dollars. I would not scruple to sell it soon as I could find a customer, and pocket the difference.

I paid the bartender then, and in the exchange I dropped the stickpin upon the floor and that gem shattered into sufficient splinters to prove it pure glass.

I run out the door and spied that thieving skunk dashing down the street and after not a long chase, I being fleet of foot whereas he was not as quick of leg as of mind, I backed him against a wall and shoved my pistol into his breastbone.

He was sweating from the exertion and gulping air through his slack mouth, but in a right casual tone he says: "Sir, you have called my bluff."

"And I might blow out your eye," I says. But then I laughed, for I have always liked people of spirit, and I took back my twenty and put away my weapon. "Bunco artist born and bred," I says.

"Well," says he, "that is perhaps an overstatement. I was absolutely square until the age of twelve."

"What strikes me," I says then, "is that you have made a poor thing of it. Now that I look you over, I see your arse is almost out of your pants, your cuffs is chawed as if the dogs have been set on you many a time, and don't I notice a hole in the upper of your shoe where you have inked your ankle so it won't show?"

"I have seen better days," Allardyce says, with hurt pride. "But surely my present run of ill fortune is transitory. You must admit my techniques are beyond reproach. You bought the pin readily enough."

"True," says I. "It was just by accident I dropped it; otherwise you'd have got away."

He sighs deeply and says: "If it is convenient, I'd just as soon we went straightway to the police station. It distresses me to mull over my failures."

"I was thinking, Allardyce," I says, "I ain't really lost by this experience, and there's nothing that pleases me so little as to see a man's liberty took away. I don't hold by jails. I believe in shooting a man or letting him go scot-free. Right now I stand in want of big money, but I need a scheme. Dreaming up the latter would seem to be your specialty."

You could see the self-esteem come back into him as I talked. He tilted his hat and manipulated his cane, and somehow the shabbiness become invisible again. Allardyce was a real good actor, and could have made his fortune in the theaters.

"Sir," he says, slapping them doeskin gloves into his left palm and extending his right hand to me, "I am your man."

What Allardyce suggested was pulling the brooch trick. All I had to do was go to a certain jewelry shop and buy a brooch he had already sized up.

"What will that cost?" I asks, and he says, oh, a matter of three hundred dollars, and brushes his silk-faced lapels in such a supercilious fashion that the ordinary person would never have noticed how worn they was.

"If I had three hundred," I says, "I wouldn't have to work a bunco."

"My dear Jack," says Allardyce, "in an exercise of this type you must set all your standards in proportion to the sum you intend to gain. Our aim here is two thousand dollars; therefore, to obtain three hundred in working capital is but a minor matter. Among my gifts you will find a facility for pocket-picking. I can gather the amount we need in one evening—and I anticipate your question: why, if I am so deft at this art, do I not habitually make my living from it? Why, for example, did I not filch your wallet rather than vend you the stickpin?

"Ah!" he says, "therein lies the moral crux of the matter. A man has a sense of himself, a definition. I am a swindler, Jack, and I must observe the code of my profession or I cannot live with myself. I may pick pockets only in the interest of a bunco scheme; otherwise my fingers would lose their cunning, I would soon be nabbed, and imagine my shame in being hailed before the bar of justice as a petty sneakthief."

Allardyce was a philosophical crook, and I felt he might easily while away a couple months in sheer musing on the subject, but I was impatient for cash, so told him to get into motion, and he did and in a day or two turned up with that three hundred dollars all right, which I reckon proved his devotion to the ideal, for he could easy have drunk it up or otherwise squandered it. But once you accepted the fact that he was crooked, he was square, if you get my meaning.

Now here's where my part come in. I took the money and went to a very high-class jewelry shop named Kaller & Co., where I bought that brooch which he had described to me, and there was no mistaking it: being a heart formed of rubies within a wreath of gold, and in the middle of the heart was a little diamond. They was asking four hundred, but when I offered them three, take or leave it, they took. This also established that I was right casual about the purchase. Doubtless they figured me for a rancher with some free money he was spending on a whore who took his fancy, which was not unusual in K.C.

Next day Allardyce went around to the shop and pretends to throw a fit when he finds that brooch has been sold. Oh, he must have carried this off to perfection, for as I say he was a born actor and I would have loved to see it, but we wasn't supposed to have any connection with each other. Allardyce posed as a visiting swell from the East. He had seen the gewgaw in Kaller's window, he said, and determined to buy it for his sweetheart, but had had to wait until his monthly five thousand come in from his father the well-known banker, etc. Now having rushed to the store with the wherewithal, he felt Kaller's had stabbed him in the back in disposing of that pretty.

Old Kaller, bald-headed and in his high-winged collar, took personal charge. "But, sir," he says, "we had no idea that you were interested in the piece. If only—" But Allardyce cut him off and went into a tantrum, in the course of which he refused to look at any other jewelry, threatened to discontinue his trade at Kaller's— though he had never set foot in there before—and demanded they get him a duplicate of that missing brooch. "It was one of a kind, you know," says shrewd old Kaller, "but let me telegraph New York. Perhaps we might persuade the craftsman to do just one more for such an ardent admirer of his work."

When Allardyce heard "New York," he threw another fit, and the personnel was fanning him and fetching him water, and he finally makes it known that he intends to leave K.C. next day for San Francisco where his lovely girl lives, and that brooch or a duplicate of it will be worth twice, no, three times the asking price if they can put it into his hands before he boards the noon train.

Kaller almost swallows his cravat. "Ah well," he croaks, "it might just be possible, it might just. We were asking," he says, the crafty old goat, "we were asking, I believe, a thousand dollars." He pops his eyes at Allardyce as if about to suffer a seizure.

And negligent as could be, Allardyce says: "Then I'll pay you three thousand. But enough of these petty delays, my man, you had better get cracking. Your deadline is noon tomorrow. Until then you can reach me at the Excelsior Hotel." And presenting one of his cards, he leaves the shop.

I had made my own hotel known to Kaller in the course of making my purchase, so the next thing that jeweler does is run over to see me. Not wanting to involve little Amelia in the sordid affair, I let him into my bedroom and closed the door. She was taking one of her singing lessons with Signorina Carmella, anyway, in the parlor, and that screeching did not serve to soothe old Kaller's nerve none.

"A terrible thing has happened, my dear Mr. Crabb," he says. "That brooch had already been purchased by another and paid for in full, I fear, to one of my associates, although I was in ignorance of the transaction. I wonder whether I might refund your money and take it along. A terrible inconvenience, I know, and I mean to make it up to you, dear sir. Please accept any other piece of jewelry at ten per cent discount."

I was grinning to myself at a memory of what Allardyce had told me of the bunco philosophy: that in any swindle there was two crooks, both victim and victimizer, and that you couldn't never work a confidence scheme on a square man. Then, however, he went on to say that in all his travels he had never met an individual of the latter type. But look at old Kaller: he was out to make $2700, in return for which he'd allow me a twenty-buck deduction.

So I didn't feel no sympathy for him. I said it was out of the question, that my darling little niece in the next room, the famous concert artist, had fell in love with that pretty and I'd rather cut my throat than take it away from her now; that the sale was proper legal and not my lookout if he run an inefficient business.

Well, at length he got to offering me more, and I says money meant nothing in this circumstance, so he increased the sum by degrees, and my only worry is that the old devil would in his desperation get a heart attack and die on my carpet before he got to two thousand, which is what Allardyce and I had decided on as a reasonable amount, for if Kaller's profit got cut down much more than that he might smell a rodent.

He reached the destination in about two hours, and I says: "Mr. Kaller, you got yourself a deal. I can't stand to see a human being in misery."

He had the cash with him, and when he pulled out his roll I regretted not having gone to twenty-five hundred, for it looked like he had brought along that much, but hell, even so, it wasn't bad for my first time out. I had made a hundred times ten for a couple hours' work. Later I met Allardyce at a saloon and we split the take down the middle.

"I registered at the Excelsior," he says, "and left word at the desk for Kaller that I had changed my plans and gone on a hunting trip out west of Topeka, returning in a week, at which time I trusted he and I could do business. That," he says, "will cover my leisurely escape from town."

"Where are you going, Allardyce?" I asks, because he led an interesting way of life.

"Oh, St. Louis, I suppose. I'm clean there. And what about yourself, Jack? I would advise your leaving Kansas City. It is true that Kaller has nothing on you, but he will soon get the picture and I imagine might cause you discomfort. What about coming along with me? I think you have a real talent for bunco."

He didn't know about Amelia, you see, for I had kept him away from my hotel. After all, he was a crook.

"That might well be," I says. "But I believe my real calling lays outdoors. I'm heading down to the buffalo country for the winter hunt."

Allardyce stuck out his hand. "It has been a pleasure, Jack."

"I'm real proud, Allardyce," says I, "and I wish you the best in whatever mischief you next take up."

That was the last I saw of him, standing there in that lowdown saloon, ordering a bottle of champagne, so anxious to begin the high life he couldn't wait to get to where he could rightly practice it. I had the feeling he would be broke again within a day or so, for what he liked about bunco was the acting required rather than the money gained. What a professional he was! And a real nice fellow who helped me out in K.C.

I give a pittance to my creditors to show good faith and to quiet their baying for a spell, and I laid down an advance payment on a girls' boarding school that I finally found for Amelia—it was a snob place where the students lived in, with a headmistress so stuck up she could hardly say a word.

Now I know that with the normal dirtiness of mind in which a person picks up someone else's reminiscences, you are expecting to find sooner or later that Amelia went back to her earlier ways. People just hate to see others reform. I just have to disappoint you. There wasn't no force on earth that could have kept Amelia from becoming a fine lady now she had got a taste of it. To give an example, if while eating in a restaurant she dropped her fork, she wouldn't lean over and pick it off the floor, not her. That's what servitors was for, she said. And it got so she applied the same principle to everything she done, so that if in our rooms she let a book slip from her lap to the carpet, why, she'd yank the bellpull for one of them boys in his monkey suit to run upstairs, pick up the volume, and hand it to her.

Now the only thing that worried me was she might resist being put into Miss Wamsley's Academy for Young Ladies, which would seem right austere after that luxurious summer in the hotel, with the German, Signorina Carmella, and all, but my apprehensions proved false, for Miss Wamsley come out of England, or maybe just Boston, anyway she said stuff like "hoff" for "half," and that was something new for Amelia to take up, and after our first trip over there to get registered, I says to my niece: "You won't miss the Signorina?" And she says: "Don't make me loff."

I didn't put the query as to whether she would miss Uncle Jack. I did not expect she would, but had no desire to hear either a lie or a painful truth. I was not so big a fool as to fail to realize that the more she become what I wanted her to be, the less thrilled she would be by my presence.

So I felt the time would never be riper for me to go buffalo hunting, freeing Amelia from association with me and also making more money with which to support her in style. I would not be back till the following spring; then maybe I would just look in at the school every other Sunday, when visitors could come for tea, and try to remember to remove the spoon before sipping. I didn't have no other long-range plans at the moment.

After paying in advance for a half-year of that school, along with pocket money for Amelia, I didn't have much money left again, but was able to get most of the necessary gear and supplies on credit from an outfitter, and hired me a skinner, who would not have to be paid till we come back in the spring and sold our hides. I done this at Caldwell, Kansas, which was headquarters at that time for the buffalo business. As to K.C., I had blown town in the middle of the night, leaving all my bills behind, including the hotel account. So far as I know, I owe them yet.

The buffalo range stretched from southern Nebraska down to the Colorado River in Texas. Before the railroads, it run all the way up into Canada in an unbroken sweep, the great herds moving north as the year warmed, then returning south when the first snows commenced to fall up that way.

Now when I say, as I have on occasion, that the continental herd was cut in two by the Union Pacific, I don't mean there wasn't plenty of animals left south of the tracks, nor north either. Indeed, there was at least ten million buffalo in 1871, for that is how many was killed on the southern plains from that year up to '75. Ten million in five years. And I helped in that extermination to the fullest degree of my personal energy, for the simple reason that the more hides a person brought in, the more money he made. The main use of them hides when tanned was to be cut into belting for the operation of machinery. But they also made shoes of them, and harness and lap robes.

When you was a hide hunter you didn't have no facilities nor time to deal with the flesh of the creatures you shot, other than to take an occasional tongue or hump for your own supper; so most of it was just left where the animal fell, and ate by the wolves or rotted in the sun. In later days someone discovered the bones made good fertilizer, so they come and collected them by the wagonload, ground them into powder, and farmers spread it about their acres.

That still leaves the matter of the meat, and you can't escape the fact that there was awful waste in that area, whereas Indians generally consumed in one form or another every inch of a buffalo from his ears to the hoofs, including even the male part, from which they boiled up a glue. Yet, as you know from my story, Indians was frequently hungry long before the buffalo had been eliminated, and even more so before the white man made his appearance, prior to which they never had the horse from which to hunt, nor the gun with which to shoot a buffalo at long range while afoot.

You got to consider them things before you get to blaming us hunters, the way I see it. We was just trying to make a living, and all we cared about was the market price of hides. Sometimes you get the idea from accounts of this enterprise, wrote by men who wasn't there, that the great army of hunters went out to exterminate every bison on the continent so as to clean up the range for cattle grazing, or to whip the Indians by destroying their source of wild food. These things happened, of course, but it wasn't by our plan. We was just a bunch of fellows carrying Sharps rifles, and if you ever topped a rise and seen a gigantic ocean of sheer buffalo covering maybe twenty miles, you couldn't believe the day would come when a few thousand of us had caused them millions to vanish utterly.

Still, having said that, I admit it now seems a pity. But we done it, and here's how: in late August and early September, the hunters would go up to Nebraska, make contact with the herds and follow them southwards down to Texas as it growed colder, killing as they went, and the hunt would generally extend until March of the next year. Then in spring the hunters closed up operations and went to K.C. as we have seen, for their vacation, while the buffalo was shedding on their summer plod back north.

You didn't use a horse in this type of hunting. You moved by foot as close as you could get to one of the little bunches that a herd divided into while grazing, you set up your crossed-stick shooting rest, laid the long barrel of the Sharps into it, and picked off animals one by one around the edge of the bunch. Now, done right, you could get away with this for quite a spell before the buffalo got wise, for they never cared about the sounds of firing nor did the others worry when their comrades dropped roundabout. The only thing that spooked them was the smell of blood.

If the wind stayed favorable, you could drop upwards of thirty animals with the remainder still grazing quietly, but much beyond that number and one bull would get a whiff of blood and stir and paw the ground, and then another animal smelled it and would bellow, which panicked the bunch and so on to the whole herd spread across five square mile of prairie, and within a minute or so you saw the tails of a monstrous stampede. Or, as happened once in a while, for there might well be other hunters a-working the far side of the same herd, the stampede would come in your direction and you'd see a remarkable horizon of horns just before you was trampled to death.

But usually that never happened, and when the herd was gone, your skinner would come up with the wagon, which had been kept back until then, and get to work on the fallen animals: cut a few slits, lash a rope around the gathered neck-skin, hitch the other end to a horse and lead him away, peeling off the whole hide. Back at camp the skins was pegged out to cure and stacked when that was done to await the buyers, who sent wagons around from time to time to all the hunting parties.

Well sir, that is about the size of what occupied me in the winter of 1871-72, and me and my skinner ended up the season down below the Canadian River, in the Texas Panhandle. In late March we come back up to Caldwell and tallied up with the hide buyers and received around six thousand dollars for that winter's work, which meant I alone killed over twenty-five hundred buffalo my first time out. Old hands like Billy Dixon and Old Man Keeler done better than that.

Still, it seemed like there hadn't been a dent made in the buffalo population. Near Prairie Dog Creek below the Canadian, me and the skinner come up over a rise and seen the entire world carpeted with brown hair. I reckon you could see twenty-five mile across the prairie, for the day was clear. Now, sweeping your extended arm from left to right across the horizon, you would have pointed, in so doing, at a million buffalo.

At Caldwell me and my partner split the take, and after settling up my obligations with the outfitters, I still had several thousand dollars, and I headed back to Kansas City to see how Amelia was making out.

Before I get to that, though, I ought to mention a kind of coincidence that I experienced. Remember that fellow with the funny name what had preceded me as mule driver on the run from San Pedro to Prescott, Arizona? Wyatt Earp? Well, I had a run-in with him down on the buffalo range, and I'm going to tell you about it.

WE WAS DOWN on the Salt Fork of the Arkansas River at the time. At night after the day's shooting, the buffalo hunters in the area would collect at one of the larger camps for sociable drinking and poker. The source of liquor was the peddlers who come out with wagonloads of barrels. No place was too remote for them fellows. There was a good many spots on the prairie where you might have died for want of water, but you could get a drink of whiskey most everywhere.

One evening me and the skinner rode over to a nearby camp to get us a blast, and who did I see tending the whiskey wagon but my brother Bill. One thing about him, he had found a trade at an early age and stuck to it. Maybe you recall what a rotten-looking man he had already been away back in '57 when I encountered him selling rotgut to the Indians. Well, having sunk so far so soon, he didn't degenerate much further during the next fifteen years. His teeth was all gone, but otherwise he looked the same to me: utterly filthy, of course, and as I come near he was telling his customers how he knowed John Wilkes Booth, who hadn't been killed a-tall but was living at that very moment in El Paso, Texas, where he kept a general store.

Having heard from Bill's own lips of how he dosed his goods, I decided to teetotal that evening, but couldn't have talked the skinner out of his cup without revealing the kinship, which I hadn't no interest in doing, so he went and ordered. As it happened, Bill was way down to the bottom of the present barrel, and had to tip it over so as to fill the dipper. In so doing he pointed its mouth towards the firelight, and I saw my skinner peer within and then stare at Bill.

"Hold on," he says. "What's them lumps at the bottom?"

Bill says: "That's just the mother. You know, like on vinegar."

The skinner shoves him away and tips the barrel over and a half-dozen objects slide out along with the trickle of the remaining whiskey, and alongside the campfire their identity was not long in doubt.

"You are a mother _____," says the skinner. "Them is rattle-snake heads!"

Bill makes a toothless grin. "Well, all right," he says.

Now the fellows all begin to get riled and threaten to break into the rest of his stock, so he admits there ain't a barrel of whiskey on board that don't have six snake heads inside it. That news causes some of them who been drinking to go off into the bushes and heave, and the remainder get out their lariats and look for a convenient limb on which to elevate my brother, but a tall, skinny young hombre pushes his way among the crowd and says to Bill: "You hitch up and get out of here and don't come back."

"They don't hurt none," says Bill in whining indignation. "They just put the old be-Jesus into the stuff. The boys like the bite of my goods."

"Get out," says the skinny fellow. "And you men step aside and let him do it." And by God, if they didn't; I don't know why, for he didn't look special to me, but he had some of the assurance of Custer and Hickok, if not the long hair.

The skinner rejoined me and says: "Did you ever see the like of that?" Meaning my brother, and being under some strain, I just belched. The sight of them snake heads had got to me, though I never touched a drop of the rotgut.

The skinny fellow walked quickly to me and staring coldly from under his straight black eyebrows, says: "You have an objection?"

I allowed I did not, but I also requested he state a reason why in the goddam hell he thought I might.

"You just spoke my name," he says.

"I don't know your name," says I.

"It," he says, "is Earp."

"Oh," I says, laughing, "what I done was belch."

He knocked me down.

Well sir, I arose directly with gun in hand, but Earp strode away, giving me the choice of ventilating his back or agreeing with him that the incident was closed. But damn if I was going to let him set the terms, so I throws some spectacular abuse at him in front of them other hunters, and he turns and comes back.

"Draw, you goddam Belch you," says I, for in that measured stride he had come within ten feet of me and his weapon was still holstered, his hands swinging freely as he walked. But onward he come, and I found it impossible to raise my gun and shoot him down until he went for his, but he never. Finally, having reached a range of one foot, he detained my right wrist with the wiry fingers of his left hand, drew his pistol, and struck me over the head with its heavy barrel. I was cold-cocked for fair.

This was the technique called "buffaloing," and it was Wyatt Earp's favorite when he became a marshal later on. In all his violent life, he only killed two or three men, but he buffaloed several thousand. I guess he was the meanest man I ever run across. In a similar circumstance, Wild Bill would have killed his opponent. Not Earp, he was too mean. To draw on you meant he considered you a worthy antagonist; but he didn't; he thought most other people was too inferior to kill, so he would just crack their skulls. I don't know how it worked, but when he looked at you as if you was garbage, you might not have agreed with him, but you had sufficient doubt to stay your gun hand a minute, and by then he had cold-cocked you.

I returned to K.C. in the spring of '72 as I have said, got a haircut and a twenty-five-cent bath at the barbershop, and having donned my city clothes from a trunk I kept in storage, went over to Amelia's school.

That prune-faced headmistress could not have been kindlier.

"Ah," she said, pouring me a dinky little cup of tea, "we were so concerned that you would not get back to us in time from your scientific expedition."

I was aching to see my niece and what further refinements she had acquired over the winter, but figured I had ought to play along with Miss Elizabeth Wamsley, especially when sitting in the parlor of her Academy for Young Ladies, with a potted plant sticking its leaves into my ear and a crocheted doily under both arms and another back of my head to catch the bear grease.

"I trust," Miss Wamsley said, "that you collected many rare fossils for deposit in our Eastern museums."

You can see what little Amelia's version of my buffalo hunting must have been.

"You must tell me about it," Miss W. went on. "But first, I do think we should dispose of certain matters which, though crass, are pressing. Indeed," she said, showing her long front teeth in a supposed smile, "aren't they usually one and the same? . . . Now of course you understand, dear Mr. Crabb, that when a student withdraws after completing more than two weeks of a given term, no refund of fees is granted."

I swallowed all my tea in one gulp, so that it wouldn't make too much of a mess in case I dropped the cup and saucer.

"Amelia has run off," I says, and my heart turned to bone.

Miss Elizabeth Wamsley give a high titter that sounded like somebody was ripping a silk shawl.

"Not in the least, my dear Mr. Crabb! Our dear Amelia is to be married. We had no earlier means of apprising you, no telegraph or postal address by which one could reach your far-flung desert and mesa."

"Who to?" I asks. I reckon if I had been elsewhere than that stuffy parlor with its stink of dried flowers, I should have followed up the query with a fervent threat to kill him. I had just naturally assumed that anybody who might want to marry Amelia, or say he did, would be some low-life skunk. You see, in spite of my frequent mention of how much class she had developed, in the bottom of my mind was the memory of pulling her from the gutter, and a conviction that if left to her own devices she would return there.

Miss Wamsley says: "Modest as we habitually are here, Mr. Crabb, I do think that in this case we might be permitted to suggest our satisfaction at Amelia's engagement. Wamsley Academy alumnae are mistresses of some of the finest houses in our Nation, and ____"

"Who to?" I asks again, for I didn't realize she was delaying so as to build up the effect, rather than soften the blow.

I swear to you she then mentions the name of a state senator, and says it was his son, a young lawyer in K.C., who Miss Wamsley had hired to represent the Academy in a matter of nonpayment of tuition—here she give me a meaningful look—in the course of which business he come to the school, saw Amelia, and "his heart was pierced by Cupid's bolt," according to my informant. The courtship took place over the winter, and the marriage was set for May.

That was why Miss Wamsley was a-worried about the fees: her semester run to June. The money I had laid down the last fall covered only the first term. So far in '72 Miss W. had carried Amelia on credit, though of course she knowed a celebrated explorer like myself was good for it.

I paid her forthwith a handsome sum. I was ashamed of my quick and erroneous judgment on Amelia, but the rapid rise of that little gal made me dizzy. A respectable marriage was what I had dreamed of for her, but coming this soon had caught me unawares.

The old crow cleared out soon as she got her cash, and sent for Amelia, who was taking her needlework class or some such. My niece give me a kiss upon the cheek and I was sure relieved I had had it shaved just prior. For if anybody come close to the gentility of Mrs. Pendrake, it was her. And mind you, Miss Wamsley had them Academy girls dress right severe in dark-colored clothing and covered from chin to ankle, without paint or powder or jewelry, and most of the students I seen didn't have no more distinction than a flock of sparrows. They was drab. Not Amelia. In the same circumstances, she looked exactly supreme.

She set beside me on the sofa, with her hands in her lap and her chin at a graceful angle, and said: "I trust your trip was gratifying."

"Miss Wamsley," said I, "has told me you was getting married." A little spark come into her eye, and I quick added: "I don't have no objection." Then I said: "I reckon you are in love."

Amelia first looks proudly down her nose, and then she suddenly goes into a knowing expression: not tough or cynical, but simply realistic.

Putting aside her formerly lofty tone, she says: "You never really believed I was your niece by blood? Because if you did, I would honestly feel awful."

You know how you can go along in life for years without facing essential matters of this type. Absolute definitions generally make a person feel worse. I've known heavy drinkers who have survived for years merely by not admitting they was confirmed drunkards. I expect you thought back a ways when I commenced my association with Amelia that I believed in our blood-relationship on mighty flimsy evidence; that a girl in her position would say anything a customer wanted to hear; that playing the role of my niece was a hell of a lot easier profession that the one from which I had reclaimed her.

These considerations was not unknown to me. But look here: the kind of life I had lived, I had earned a right to say who was or wasn't my kin. Every real family I had ever possessed had been tore away from me by disaster. I got to figuring the natural relationships was jinxed for me, and when little Amelia offered herself, I accepted forthwith and believed the privilege was all mine.

"I mean," she says, "I knew you were getting your fun out of it and so was I, but I have this chance now to become respectable, and who knows when it would come again?" She takes my hand, and she says: "I'd like it real fine if you could give me away. My mother ran off with a drummer when I was twelve, and my father drank himself to death a couple years later. That was in Saint Joe, and then I came downriver. A fellow that came into Dolly's used to tell me about the Mormons; which is how I know about their ways." She smiled; I reckon you could say she somehow preserved a innocent quality that was genuine.

Well sir, after I got used to the idea, I was right proud. I felt forlorn in that I would soon lose the company of my "niece," but the satisfaction that I had significantly altered her fate brought me back almost even again. If respectability was always denied me personally, at least in this instance I was able to arrange it, so to speak, for another. That's about as high as a white man can aspire.

"Amelia," I says, "you don't have to have blood-ties to get a family feeling about a person. I am connected in natural brotherhood to a man who is so low as to drop snake heads in the whiskey he sells, and I do not give a damn for him if you will pardon the expression. Most of the people I have really cared about in this world, I have elected to the position. I have a belief that a man's real relatives are scattered throughout the universe, and seldom if ever belong to his immediate kin.

"So you are my niece in the only fashion that means anything. And because I love you as such, I am not a-going to give you away. You had better go as an orphan to this wedding, which is the truth, anyway."

She really did protest, which made me feel good for I reckon she wouldn't have wanted me there had she not had some fondness for me, but I stayed firm. I seen now that my old dream of getting her well married and then dropping around to the house of a Sunday to take dinner with her and her husband would not work. I could never keep up the pose of explorer or fossil-hunter or whatever the tale she'd handed the senator's son as regards her "uncle." However, after a time I did realize that it would be humiliating to have nobody stand up for her, considering the wedding was to be a social affair attended by the better class of K.C. So I promised to provide a man.

I appealed to Signorina, and by George it turned out she was living with just the right sort of fellow at this time: a decayed-gentleman type, about fifty year of age with gray sideburns and a spiky goatee. He was also an alcoholic, but swore he could walk down a church aisle without staggering when supported by the money I give him.

I also bought Amelia the finest wedding outfit, along with a complete wardrobe for the time after; and such money as I then had left, I presented to her as dowry. She never said a word of thanks. She had never expressed the sentiment of gratitude at any time during our association, for she knowed it was always a square deal for me. Maybe it is not the worst training for a woman to put in a season as a harlot.

I watched the wedding from the choir loft, and seen for the first time the young fellow she was marrying, and he wasn't much. He was built tall and flabby and wore eyeglasses at the age of twenty-five. His Pa was a stocky man with a hard jaw and iron-gray hair. It was easy to see that Amelia was taking over from the old man as the supply of force for that boy.

Signorina Carmella's lover worked out real fine in his role. He walked so straight up the aisle, with Amelia on his arm, that there might have been steel scaffolding beneath his tailcoat. Carmella, on the other hand, never got to the ceremony. That pair lived according to some kind of rule by which at any given time one of them lay stinking drunk at home. Today was her turn.

But Dolly come, and watched from up in the loft with me. She got right overwrought at seeing how one of her girls had made it, and cried all through the service, though I never seen no tear-streaks on her powder and paint when she was done. After the newlyweds had gone out the church door and various swells was crowding around their carriage throwing rice in that husband's nearsighted face, Amelia looking slightly sarcastic, Dolly leans her bosom against my elbow and says: "That was a sight to remember. Come on now to my place, Short Arm, and have one on the house. Maybe you'll find another niece."

We kept to the rear of the crowd so as not to embarrass Amelia, and then the carriage drove off, and that was the last I seen of that little gal forever. But damn if I didn't, along in 1885 or –6, read in a newspaper that Grover Cleveland had put her husband in the Cabinet! So she worked out real successful, the only family I ever had that did, and that is why I have told you the story.

I went buffalo hunting during the next couple winters, and summers I wandered about the Kansas cowtowns, playing poker and I also got to dealing faro, a popular game of the time. As to buffalo, by God if you couldn't notice already by the season of '72–'73 that the herds had commenced to dwindle. There was still hundreds of thousand, but not millions. Plenty, but not infinite. If you seen one of them railhead collection points where the skins was brung in, you'd appreciate why. What looked like a new block of buildings from out on the prairie, was in actuality stacks of hides awaiting to be loaded on the freight cars. And down on the range, you never encountered no more of them immense herds me and the skinner come across that time in '71. No, that was a wondrous sight never to be repeated on this continent.

But if the buffalo had started to fail because he was wild, his tame cousin the steer was gaining. Up the Chisholm Trail from Texas the cattle herds was drove, through the Nations and into Kansas, to the new towns that had sprung up as the railroads came. Now almost every year in the early '70's another place was in fashion, commencing with Abilene and then Ellsworth, Wichita, and Dodge City. Everyone wanted the herds, for the cowboys was paid off after they had delivered their animals to the railside stock pens, and of course not having seen a woman in some months nor any other feature of civilized life, they would blow their rolls on the local amusements.

So it was profitable for the business people, and the cowboys was encouraged to enjoy themselves to the hilt, except when you tell that to such men they are inclined to take it literal, for they been eating dust for weeks and enduring foul weather and stampedes—a loud sneeze in dead of night will panic a herd of cattle—and maybe also rustlers and Indians. So you let a cowboy see a slogan like the one a certain town had posted on the trail in: EVERYTHING GOES IN WICHITA, why, he'll get crazy drunk the first minute he sets foot on Douglas Avenue and in the next he will have drawed his gun and started to discharge it recklessly.

Well, I had my run-ins with cowboys and bear yet the scars to prove it, and I was in Wichita a couple times in the years that everything "went" there, except that after a time they hired my old friend Wyatt Earp to see it never went too far, and when I seen him in action, busting skulls with his gun barrel, I'll tell you I thought better of the Texans.

I guess you get my point that during these years I never belonged to no particular faction. I might not have been all that old, but I got to thinking of myself as being a holdover from an earlier era, before the railroads and steers and gunfighters and main streets full of gambling halls and dry-goods stores. I was only in my early thirties at this time, so maybe it was mere sentiment. Whatever, the years had got to passing without a worthwhile mark upon them, and all I see when looking back is a blur of poker hands and whiskey fumes and occasionally the muzzle of a weapon, and I always survived that emergency in one style or another, and though I won at cards more often than I lost, I was at the same time ever broke. I believe now that I was actually expecting to be killed. I even got to where I was setting with my back to the door.

I mean I did that once, and I was promptly shot through the shoulder from behind, by a man I never saw. It was in Dodge City, and I never did find out who done it. That was the most hateful town on the face of the earth. Everybody there hated everyone else, buffalo hunters hated mule skinners, both hated cowboys, gamblers hated anyone who played against them, and all joined in detestation of the soldiers from the fort nearby.

All you had to do to make an enemy in Dodge was to be seen by another human being: he immediately loathed your guts. Look into the sky and predict rain, and you could get a fight out of it. So when I got it in the back, I was not surprised. He was a bad shot, incidentally, for the slug missed the bone. After six or eight months the stiffness was gone except when it rained. By that time I had left Dodge, though, and I didn't try very hard to determine the identity of the near-assassin. I would only have been interested could I have got enough dynamite to blow the whole place sky-high. For I was no exception to the rule: I hated everyone there.

My last buffalo-hunting season was the winter of 1874-75, and we spent a good deal more time looking for herds than shooting them. I cleared only about $350 from fall to spring—to give you an idea of how slim was the pickings. Then, not long after I got the skins into Dodge, I was shot in the back as aforesaid.

I headed north when I was fit to travel and went all the way to

Wyoming without seeing a wild Indian. Instead, I run across plenty of homesteaders, who built themselves houses out of sod and planted wheat and corn, and they was real friendly and sometimes had young daughters they wanted to marry off, so I was well received and they shared with me what food they had—which come in right handy, for you didn't see no game any more on the central plains.

It was nicer inside them houses than you would have thought, for the ladies tied cloth against the ceiling to catch the dust that fell, and the sod was so thick that it would endure a rainstorm without letting in a drop. The trouble come next day when the water at last penetrated; then it and mud dripped down for most a week. Of course, it rained very seldom—which was good for the houses, but death on crops. And then the summer of '74 billions of grasshoppers descended on the plains in a great blanket stretching from Arkansas to Canada, and ate up not only what grew in the fields but also harness and covered-wagon tops and a Union Pacific train was stalled at Kearney, Nebraska, by a three-foot drift of them insects. When the grasshoppers left, after two weeks, it was as if nothing had yet been planted, all being gnawed right down to the ground. Now I have mentioned how difficult it often was for an Indian to get his three squares a day, but there was also considerable risk to being a white homesteader, at least in them days.

Well sir, sodbusting never held no attraction for yours truly, that's for sure. I kept on moving north, and I'll tell you why. Once again, it was curiously connected with the activities of George Armstrong Custer. Who by the way I was not looking to assassinate no more; no, unless I get revenge within a reasonable length of time after the offense is committed, I can't keep up an active hatred for anybody. I reckon that's a weakness of my character. I mean, I missed him in Kansas City in '71, and then I got involved in reclaiming Amelia, and what with one thing another, eight years had went by since Washita. I guess most of us have got a sort of statute of limitations within our hearts; unless a man is a lunatic, violent feelings taper off after a while.

So though it was unlikely that Custer would ever become my personal hero, I had lost my former desire to do him in. I did not think about him at all, and when, in the summer of 1874 I heard he come back to the plains and led a column into the Black Hills to map that region, it never interested me none.

But as it happened, some scientists he carried along on that expedition found certain deposits in the area, and the journalists got hold of the report and spread it across the country:

GOLD!
The Land of Promise—Stirring
News from the Black
Hills.

The Glittering Treasure Found at Last
A Belt of Gold Territory
Thirty Miles Wide.

The Precious Dust Found in the
Grass under the Horses' Feet
—Excitement Among
The Troops.

It Can be Reached in Six Days—Expeditions
Forming All Along the Frontier.

The Black Hills had been guaranteed to the Sioux in the treaty of '68 after they run out the Army and burned down the forts along the Bozeman Trail, and it was a mighty nice piece of property, heavily forested and containing bear and elk. *Pa Sapa* is what the Lakota called it, the "sacred hills," for the Indians considered as divine any piece of ground that grew so much wood and animals. A white man on finding such a place that held everything he needed would move in and use it to the hilt. But not a redskin; he restrained himself.

I had been there once as a boy. Beforehand, Old Lodge Skins prayed a good deal and had a vision in which we would get six elk, two bear, and twenty-seven tepee poles, so that is exactly what we took from the Black Hills and nothing more, and left its dark-blue forests and silver streams as quiet as we found them. At that time we would not have known what to do with gold if we come across it.

But I had since changed remarkably. So that is why I now proceeded up towards Dakota Territory: I wanted some of that gold. I hadn't got much of it in the Colorado rush of '58, but I was white man enough to try again.

I wasn't trailing Custer no more, nor was I looking for Indians. But I sure found them both.

CHAPTER 24 *Caroline*

IT WAS THE SPRING of '76 when I reached the town of Cheyenne, in southern Wyoming, which was a stop on the Union Pacific and an outfitting place for the Black Hills gold rush.

Owing to the treaty with the Sioux, white men was supposed to keep out of the Hills altogether, no matter what their purpose; and the Army would turn back any expeditions they caught trying to enter. But there was a real difficulty in policing such an expanse of ground with only a few regiments. You might say any would-be miner who was kept away from the diggings by the U.S. Army wasn't trying. For all they'd do if they found him was to say no. He wasn't arrested or nothing, and once beyond the next rise, he could circle around the troops and continue towards his original aim.

However, even this much harassing caused popular peevishment back in the settlements. It was like the Colorado rush again: progress versus savagery; the Army should go in and wipe out the Indians rather than prohibit fellow whites from making a pile. For the Sioux had not sat still for the invasion, though they did not start seriously killing right away. They actually turned back some of the early-comers without sending them under, which I think showed remarkable patience.

I had no sooner got to Cheyenne—the Wyoming town, not the tribe; there wasn't no Human Beings there; if they had been, they would have been shot on sight—than I come across two fellows having a terrific fight on the main street. So, being I never had no business that couldn't wait, I went to watch them, and who did I make out on the losing end of it but my sister Caroline.

Now that was too much for me, seeing some bastard beat up my sister, though his reasons might have been of the best and though he was smaller than her, so I was fixing to drop him as soon as they drawed apart a little and I could get in a fair shot. So when he hit Caroline a mighty blow upon the jaw and she chewed dirt, I went for my brand-new Colt's Peacemaker, but before I could raise it a fellow alongside me in the crowd says: "Well sir, I reckon that proves which is the real one."

A curious comment and lucky it was, for it kept me from murder. I asks: "Real what?"

"Real Calamity Jane," says he, then lets out some tobacco juice to fall between his boots. "Them two bitches is fighting over'n it. That there big redhead was claiming the title up at the bar, and then t'other come in and called her and they went for each other."

I put my gun away and looked at Caroline's opponent a-standing there with her fists cocked over my sister's recumbent body, and I saw the ugliest woman in the world, and she was cursing at the moment and I'll tell you her prowess at that art was such as to make Caroline's foulest mouth, as I recall it, sound like hymn singing.

Calamity Jane: I had heard the name around but never run into the specimen before. She had a face like a potato and was built sort of dumpy, and when she seen that Caroline was down for good, she prodded her with a boot, spat onto the street, and picking up the sombrero what had fell off in the fight and clapping it back upon her man's haircut, she swaggered into the saloon.

You remember that time Caroline rescued me from drink by dunking me in a horse trough? Well, she was too big for me to return the favor, so I just filled the crown of my hat with water from the same and flang it into her face. Upon which she woke up, snarling: "Where's that whore? I'll kill her!"

I set back upon my heels. I said: "You been whipped, Caroline, and I believe you richly deserved it if you was pretending to be Calamity Jane. What did you want to do that for?"

Well, it took a minute or two for her to gather herself and realize who I was, but she was still too upset to express much affection for her brother, so I helped her up and she was all right though bruised and with a purplish eye and a cut lip and a bald patch where some of her hair had been tore out at the roots and the lobe of her one ear had been bit almost clear through. But I found a Doc and he dosed some liniment on her and it looked like she would live, so we went to a restaurant and she eat a steak as big as my back and about five pound of potatoes fried in grease.

"Now," says I as she was subsequently picking her back teeth—most of the front ones was missing—"now," I says, "you want to talk about it?"

"Well," says Caroline, "if you was any kind of brother, you'd go and shoot that bitch."

"Maybe I will," I says, "if I could know what she done to you other than whip you in a fair fight though smaller and with a shorter reach."

"I ain't in condition a-tall, Jack," Caroline says, pouring some coffee down her hatch. "I'm feeling real poorly, and 'spect to die."

Now you can't take a person serious on that subject when you just seen her devour an enormous hunk of steer.

But Caroline went on: "I don't mean sick of body, but of soul."

She takes another drink of coffee and wipes her mouth on her shirt sleeve. "I reckon a person of your cold temperament would find it hard to understand how another might die of love, Jack, but I'll thank you not to sneer at it."

Instead of replying to that, I says: "Caroline, what ever became of your intended, Frank Delight? I recall you was supposed to get hitched to him back in '67."

"Well I never," says she, "if I correctly remember the man after all these years. You mean that honky-tonker who followed the U.P.? He turned out real bad, Jack. I believe that was when you run off and left your defenseless sister all alone, and this Frank, if that was his name, soon as you was gone, he made lewd and unseemly advances towards me and I had to cold-cock him myself, seeing I never had no brother to protect me. Where'd you go?" she asks, and then adds: "Major North told me you showed the yellow streak at that fight with the Indians and turned tail and run away."

Caroline was one of them people who utter three failures of judgment for every two words they speak, and by trying to correct them, you only succeed in presenting further occasion on which to exercise their vice, so I kept my remarks to the minimum.

"So after that," says she, "I couldn't very well stay around the U.P., so I went to Californy and Oregon and Arizona and Santy Fee and Texas, I been to Texas a couple times, and Virginia City, and Ioway. I been many places, Jack, and done more than a few things, but I have kept out of the gutter."

"But," I says, "what is this stuff about Calamity Jane? I understand you was pretending to be her."

Caroline gets a sheepish look and wipes her mouth again, all the way to the nose, upon the cuff of her man's checked shirt.

"Because," I goes on, "if that other was the real Calam, she's sure ugly and fairly foul-mouthed, and I don't believe there is many men who find such a person attractive. As for fighting, I wouldn't think women was supposed to be good at it."

Caroline was kind of sneery at my innocence. "You'd be surprised," she says, "at how many fellows find a fighting gal mighty to their taste. I have had a good many admirers every place I have went, including, if you'd like to know, Mr. Wild Bill Hickok, of who I reckon you have heerd, only that whore you mention tried to steal him away from me. Now I'll tell you, what people recall about her is that name, it ain't her personal self, and 'Calamity' ain't her real name nohow, which is Jane Canary, but just let a bunch in some saloon hear 'Calam,' and they don't care who it is, they'll joke you and buy you drinks and you are real popular. I've had some hard luck in my time, Jack, and I don't mind being the center of a bunch of fun-loving fellows."

There was something real pathetic about Caroline. But I knowed what she meant about names: it was certainly true. Take me, and look at the colorful, dangerous life I have led in participating in some of the most remarkable events of the history of this country. I'll wager to say you never heard of me before now. Then think of Wild Bill Hickok, George Armstrong Custer, Wyatt Earp—names is what they had. Wild Jack Crabb, Crabb's Last Stand—it just don't sound the same.

But of course right at that moment I wasn't thinking of that, but rather about my erstwhile acquaintance Hickok, a remarkable coincidence.

"Wild Bill?" says I. "He is here in Cheyenne?" For I had not seen him since K.C. though having heard much of his renown in the years intervening.

But while she showed no particular sign on her own mention of the name, as soon as I said it Caroline commenced to sniffle and sob and abuse that man and I couldn't get no more out of her that was coherent on the subject, and did not understand the situation until the next day as I was walking down the main street of Cheyenne, who should step out of a drygoods store but Hickok himself.

He had put on a few pounds since I seen him last and was getting jowly; still wore his hair long, and was attired in his fancy town clothes of frock coat and all. He carried several boxes, of course under his left arm, and his eyes, which had seemed to get smaller owing to the fatness of his face, flickered up one side of the street and down the next.

I says, slow and easy: "Hiya, Bill. Remember me?"

He give me an equally slow once-over. I reckon he knowed me well enough right off, but had to check first as to whether I was about to pull a hideout weapon on him.

Then he says: "How are you, hoss? Still playing poker?"

I says not as much as in the old days, for I was fixing to go for gold.

So was he, he says, and instantly suggested that maybe we could go together. So we went to a saloon to drink on it, and that was when he says: "But first I am getting married."

Now, I realized that it was not to Caroline, and that was her trouble.

"To Calamity Jane?" I asks.

Hickok looked at me real funny. "Some people say," he allowed, "that Jane and I are already man and wife and had a baby daughter. But not," he added, "to my face."

I note this part of the conversation for what it is worth in historical interest.

"No," says he. "I am getting married to Mrs. Agnes Lake Thatcher, who is the widow of the celebrated showman William Lake Thatcher, now deceased. Agnes was formerly an equestrienne with the circus, riding standing up on the bare back of a white horse, prettiest thing you ever saw. A remarkable woman, hoss. I saw her perform some years ago in the state of New York, when I was traveling with my own show."

Now that was a phase of Hickok's career of which I had not heard.

"Oh yes," he says. "It was at Niagara Falls. I had a herd of buffalo, a cinnamon bear, and a band of Comanches. But the animals got loose and charged the audience, and the Indians had a real hunt on their hands before things settled down. It was a mess and I had to sell the buffalo to get fare back home."

"Speaking of Indians," I says, "I understand the Sioux don't like miners going into the Black Hills."

Bill disposed of that with a wave of his left hand. "Don't worry about it," he says. "The Army's going out to round them up."

"The miners?" I asks.

He looks impatient. "No, the Indians. You can't stop white men from going where they will. I happen to have heard," he said in a low voice, "that Grant sent out a secret order to the Army not to stop any more miners from entering the Hills. Instead, they are mounting a campaign against the hostiles in the Powder River country."

Mention of the Powder River give me an unpleasant feeling, which I don't believe I must explain if you have listened to my many references to that favorite area of Old Lodge Skins's.

"Led by George Armstrong Custer, no doubt," I says.

Hickok replies: "You are out of touch, hoss. Don't you know about the Congressional hearings?"

Well, I did not, being only a now-and-again reader of the newspapers, and considering politics to be a marvelous bore. It was only by accident that in later years I saw that notice about Amelia's husband.

For that matter, when I was acquainted with Wild Bill in Kansas City, neither did he take any interest in public affairs; so this new attitude of his must have been connected with getting married. You recall when me and Olga was hitched was the same period in which I participated in the public life of Denver.

Anyway, Bill told me there was a stink about the Army post traders in which Orvil Grant, the President's brother, was involved. Nobody else but authorized traders could sell anything on a military reservation, so naturally these fellows put no limit on their prices and was gouging the troops. They was also getting ahold of supplies that was supposed to go to the reservation Indians under treaty obligations and selling them to soldiers and civilians. Orvil Grant was believed to be illegally selling traderships to the highest bidder, using his brother's pull. Belknap, the Secretary of War, was in back of all this, etc., etc.

"Oh, is that all?" says I when Bill had apprised me, for to tell you the truth I thought all this was perfectly normal, having never known a case among white men where the fellows with authority and connections did not make the most of it. I think a good case could be made for the modesty of Orvil Grant's operations, considering whose kin he was.

"Well," Bill says, slightly irritated, "you asked about Custer. That's why he isn't going out after the Sioux: he went to Washington to testify in the hearings."

Now to show you how limited my idea of Custer was, I says: "Wants to get himself in good with the President."

Hickok shook his head. "You stick to poker, hoss," he says. "Politics is too much for you. Custer's going to testify *against* Belknap and Orvil. Grant will probably run him out of the Army for it."

"What's Custer want to do that for?"

And Wild Bill says: "Because he always does what he thinks is right. There are a lot of people who hate his guts, but there isn't anybody who can say that he doesn't back up what he believes in."

Then Hickok returned to the subject of getting married. "Agnes," he says, "is a fine lady, and not to be confused with the kind of women you and me knew in K.C. That's the reason why I have decided to go for gold and become rich. I hear you can pick it off the ground, practically." He ordered another round of drinks and we got to talking over what gear we'd need and whether we should take in other partners, for we was sure enough going as soon as he got hitched and come back from his honeymoon which he and the Mrs. was going to take back East in Cincinnati, Ohio.

Wild Bill had sure changed. In K.C. I could swear he never knowed the name of the President, let alone the ins and outs of politics he now spouted. Nor do I think he really cared about money in the old days. Obviously it was this woman of his that had made him more of a normal human being. I noticed he was learning to use his right hand occasionally to drink with, and he wasn't nearly so nervous about the other customers of the saloon; nor did he jump when I went into my vest pocket for a dollar.

I don't mean he was turning to butter. As a matter of fact, a day or so later he killed a man who drew on him in front of a livery stable. But there wasn't no question of his being under less pressure, or maybe in view of what he was going to do before the summer was out, just another kind.

I certainly didn't bother the man none about my sister Caroline, so I don't know to this day whether her romance with him was purely imaginary or had a basis, for I'll tell you something about that gal: she was losing her mind, poor thing. I should have seen it coming years back. Now that I thought of it, I remembered that everything I had ever heard about her unhappy love affairs come from her alone. It was right likely that Frank Delight, for example, never had asked her to marry him.

The point was that while Caroline survived them romantic disasters in her earlier years, she wasn't getting any younger. Indeed, she was forty-four if she was a day, and hadn't so far as I knowed ever got married yet, which she had been trying to do as far back as '52 when the drunken Cheyenne massacred our menfolk.

But you couldn't have told it from her appearance. She had looked much the same for twenty years except, as I mentioned, her front teeth was knocked out and her ear was some chawed up, etc. But I couldn't see a gray hair on her head; and her features, which had always been strenuous, didn't need to get more so as she went through life, as they usually do with the rest of us.

However, her mind had definitely sprung some bad leaks. For example, when I come back from that meeting with Hickok to the hotel where me and her had rooms, I decided to confront her with the truth, like slapping a hysterical person in the face to bring him out of it.

"Wild Bill is getting married," I says.

Caroline was setting on her bed, with her leg cocked up, a-scraping at the sole of her boot.

"And not to Calamity Jane," I goes on.

She lifted her head and folded up the jackknife and says, real smug: "I know. It is me that he is marrying."

Right then is when I realized she should be put in the booby hatch, though I didn't go right out and look for one then. But I should have, for once she fixed upon the theme of the wedding she kept it up day after day, and I guess was pathetic enough, for I had to lock her up in her room so as not to be embarrassed by a crazy sister in front of the other people I had got acquainted with in Cheyenne, and she would drape the window curtains about her like a bridal veil and parade around, etc., though never trying to bust out of the door or window, which in itself showed how far gone she was, for Caroline had never been able to stay in one place for long.

They didn't yet have a nuthouse in Cheyenne, and while there was surely one down in Denver, I hadn't been to that city since leaving it with Olga and Gus in '64 and would have felt funny returning there now with a loony sister in tow, so I took Caroline on the Union Pacific, which we had helped to build, east to Omaha.

She didn't give me no trouble, on account of I convinced her the wedding ceremony was going to be held there, for Wild Bill liked to do things up right and wanted to get married in a big town. Omaha was real big by then and had a gloomy home for the mentally defective, run by people who you would have took for the patients had they not been wearing uniforms. So it wasn't no pleasure to hand Caroline over to them, I'll tell you, but it had to be done, and I don't believe my sister was unhappy with the arrangement, for she immediately took that home for her own house and them attendants for her servants and become so involved with her wedding plans that she never even said goodbye to me.

That is how I happened to miss Wild Bill's real wedding, which took place in Cheyenne while I was gone, and I never did see his wife.

I never went prospecting with Wild Bill, either. In fact, I never laid eyes on him again. He come back from his honeymoon alone, leaving Agnes in Cincinnati, and went on up to Deadwood in the Black Hills where they was scratching for gold in that celebrated gulch, only he didn't do no mining. He played poker. On the afternoon of August 2, 1876, he took a seat with his back to the door, and in come a man named Jack McCall and shot him dead. Nobody knows why he left his spine unguarded that day, for the first and last time, unless it was that he had reached the point in life where he had to have confirmed what he always suspected.

Anyhow, what he was holding when he died has ever since been called the dead man's hand: two pair, aces and eights. R.I.P., J. B. Hickok.

It was April when I deposited poor Caroline in the nuthatch, and seeing as how Omaha lays on the Missouri River, I decided to go by boat up into Dakota Territory, maybe as far as Pierre, and then overland to the Hills. The river was just opening up from the winter, and I got me passage on a sternwheeler and rode it as far as Yankton, where I changed to another boat by the name of *Far West*. I did that so I could be at Custer's Last Stand.

I'm kidding. But you know how them things look later. The way it really happened was that the first boat had a little layover in Yankton, in the course of which I heard a lot of talk about the *Far West* and its captain, a man named Marsh who was famous along the Missouri. There used to be quite a body of legend about riverboating—captains who could navigate in a heavy dew, etc.—and Marsh was part of it, not having been hurt any by being a friend of an author named Mark Twain who wasn't noted for understatement.

Now I didn't have nothing for nor against Marsh, but what interested me was to learn that he was taking the *Far West* all the way up the Missouri and then down the Yellowstone, carrying supplies for the campaign against the hostiles who had, now it was spring, run off the reservations in considerable numbers and was thought to be in the Powder River region. Which of course was up in Montana and nowhere near the Black Hills. Actually, the Indians never did much at all to defend the Hills and I believe already counted them as lost by this time. They had in reality run away again, and the Army was going to hunt them down and whip them as at the Washita. You understand it was all wild country up on the Powder: there weren't no settlers there, nor even gold miners. It was the native place of many of them Indians, *but it was not the reservation they had been assigned.*

The latter was an important point to the Government, because it constituted a defiance of law. And then a lot of people had got sick by now of uppity redskins. It was after all the one-hundredth year since the Declaration of Independence, and they had opened a Centennial Exposition in the city of Philadelphia, featuring a deal of mechanical devices such as the typewriter, telephone, and mimeograph machine; and it did not seem logical for such a country to be defied by a bunch of primitives who had not invented the wheel. So President Grant okayed the campaign against them. He had earlier tried to treat the redskins nice by hiring a number of Quakers to run the Indian Bureau, but that had not worked out on account of most other people believed that brotherly love was cowardice and the Indians thought it was insanity.

Sitting Bull was up there in the Powder region and Crazy Horse and Gall, and a number of other famous Sioux, with a couple thousand of their followers, and as the spring progressed, more was leaving the agencies every day. If they was not quickly discouraged, it would become the fashion, for though the southern buffalo had been mostly killed off by people like myself, the northern herd was up in Montana and an Indian preferred that sort of eating over the beef he was issued at the reservation, which besides he was often cheated out of anyway by the agents and traders.

So the Army was sending General Crook from the south, Gibbon from the west, and Terry from the east, converging on the area where the Powder, Tongue, and Bighorn rivers flow into the Yellowstone. The idea was to gather the hostiles before the three prongs and if they showed fight, to hash them up. There was infantry, cavalry, and Gatling guns, and the *Far West* would penetrate as far up the rivers as it could, farther than any other boat ever had, for it was built for the purpose with a real shallow draft and two steam capstans for pulling off sandbars.

All this I found out in Yankton, but even bigger news to me was that Custer had come back from Washington and though Grant was sore at him for testifying against his brother, he had reluctantly agreed to let him go fight Indians. The other generals wanted Custer along, you see, owing to the reputation he had made in wiping out Black Kettle's village.

It has been ever so long since I have mentioned Old Lodge Skins and the Human Beings, whom I had not seen for eight years. The Southern Cheyenne had been quiet for a length of time now, down on their reservation in Indian Territory. The Washita and the other campaigns of '68 and '69 had settled the question for them: they since lived on Government handouts and scratched at a little farming and a few of them let their kids take schooling.

But if I knowed anything at all, it was that Old Lodge Skins and his band had not stayed down in the Nations. I could swear they had went back up to the Powder; either that, or the old man had gone under, for God knows he was old enough, but he wouldn't tolerate no farming nor do I believe he would stand for little Human Beings learning rot in a white man's school.

So Custer would be going once again to do to these people what he had done before. I commenced to look at it again as a personal matter. There I was in Yankton, southern Dakota Territory, in May of 1876, and the *Far West* was getting up steam to negotiate the upper Missouri and go help Custer to slaughter the Sioux and Northern Cheyenne.

I went onto the vessel and to the captain's cabin, and I says to Marsh that General Custer had telegraphed me to come as a scout for him, owing to my experience in that position at the celebrated Battle of the Washita where we wiped out Black Kettle and his cutthroats; and besides, I was ready to pay the fare.

Marsh says it was all right with him if I could find a place on deck to pitch my bedroll among the supply boxes and barrels lashed there, for the cabins was full up with all manner of persons, military and civilian, and there was even a sutler on board to sell whiskey when they reached the troops.

So the *Far West* dug its paddlewheel into the muddy water of the Missouri, and we headed north for the biggest Indian battle of them all. You know how a fellow says: but we never realized it at the time. Everybody knowed the tribes was gathering and that Custer would find them. Where we was wrong was in supposing they would run again; or if forced to fight, would lose.

CHAPTER 25 *Custer Again*

IT TOOK THE BETTER PART of two weeks to reach Fort Abraham Lincoln, up the spring-swollen, bank-crumbling Big Muddy; and when we got there, the troops had been gone for about the same length of time on their direct overland march to the Yellowstone, led by General Terry, with Custer as second in command.

Lincoln wasn't much of a place, occupying a sweep of treeless flat bottomland overlooked by bluffs from which the hostiles had been spying on the camp; you could see them little piles of stones behind which they'd conceal their heads.

No sooner had the boat tied up at the dock than two women come on board, and one of them was the prettiest female I ever seen in my life with one exception. And well-dressed and gracious, and oh my, what a remarkable sight up there in that barren land with the constant wind blowing across the flats.

It was Mrs. Custer. I recognized her though never having laid eyes on her before, with her winsome round face and beautiful sad eyes and wearing a dinky little velvet bonnet sort of like a derby, and she put her tiny feet on the rough gangplank the deckhands threw down, and walked over it like a bird. Them fellows just stood gawking; it was me who put a hand out at the other end, and she rested hers lightly upon the wrist of it as she stepped to the deck and looked squarely at me and never said thanks, but rather smiled it with small nose and a soft line of pearly teeth. I'll admit something: I would have killed every Indian on the plains if she had asked me to, or at least if she had been watching. Then she passed me by, for I wasn't nobody, and was short as her and, as a matter of fact, fair seedy after the time on that boat, where the washing facilities wasn't of the most improved.

Well sir, what did I do but follow along behind her like a personal servant or an idiot to which somebody done a kind thing, and there was that other woman, too, who was General Custer's sister and the wife of Lieutenant James Calhoun, though I couldn't have described her a second later.

Captain Marsh showed them into his cabin, and presumably getting after something on the heel of my boot, I lingered outside the door.

"Captain," says this whippoorwill voice, "I beg of you to let us come along."

"Forgive me, ma'am," Marsh says, "I cannot."

The same exchange, more or less, was repeated several times, but the captain stayed firm, and I moved away so as to hear no more of her distress. I was full of wonder at this wife of that glorious soldier, with his six hundred troops and his supply boat and Gatling guns. Bad worried she was, you could hear. Now women generally shiver at the thought of Indians, but not, you would think, one who was married to the victor of the Washita. Custer had whipped the Southern Cheyenne, and found gold in the Black Hills. He even survived the enmity of the President of the United States! He was hated by individuals, but was the public's great favorite, and Mr. James Gordon Bennett of the *New York Herald* had sent along a correspondent to be "in at the kill"—of the Indians, that is. Custer's wife was as pretty as a woman could get. So what ailed her?

I went onto shore. An old sergeant was there who had been left behind from the campaign on account of his retirement was coming up, watery-eyed old devil whose purple nose told me he had been doing much of his soldiering across the river in the saloons of Bismarck.

I says: "Why would the General's Mrs. want to come along, a fine lady like that?"

"Had a nightmare," says he, then honked into a bandanna and put it away. "Seen a big buck Sioux, bare to the G-string, holding up a bleeding scalp of long yellow locks. Might of been that was the reason why the General had a short haircut afore they left."

I says: "No, he never! . . ."

"All right then," says the sarge, "you just come upriver and you know better."

"Settle down," I says. "I ain't calling you a liar, I'm only confounded. I sure never thought Custer would slice off them golden locks. Now what will the Indians call him if not Long Hair?"

"Son of the Morning Star," says the old soldier. "That's what the Crow scouts named him."

"Was you at the Washita?"

"No," the sergeant says, "I had to stay behind in camp with a case of the screaming shits." He was clearly one of them fellows who find some way of missing all hazards.

At that moment Mrs. Custer and the other lady come off the boat, escorted by Captain Marsh, and got into a carriage on the dock and was drove off to the fort by an orderly. Marsh stood looking after it, and then he turns and says to me: "Poor thing, but I can't take along any women, especially now with this trouble between Custer and Grant. You know, Custer got court-martialed some years ago down in Kansas for running off a campaign to see his wife."

The old sergeant give a wheezing laugh and rubbed his stubbly chin: with the commander gone, I reckon he didn't bother to shave regular. He says: "He generally does what he wants. In the Grand Review at the end of the War, he galloped past Grant without salutin'. Claimed his horse bolted, but I seen him give it the spur."

Marsh, having himself some reputation for dash, didn't want to hear about this. He says: "Well now, take if Custer gets hurt, why, it would be all the worse to have her there."

"He has a charmed life," I says bitterly.

Well, Marsh went about the business of taking on more stores, and the old sarge invited me to cross over to Bismarck with him and we'd tie one on at a good hog ranch he knowed, which is what they sometimes called a whiskey joint, and he'd even let me buy if I insisted, for he had already went through his pay. On the last subject, he told me the men on the campaign wasn't to be paid until they got into the field, so that they couldn't spree in Bismarck. Custer didn't want to march out with a regiment who was all hung over. So the Seventh Cavalry was carrying two months' wages in its pockets through the wilds of Montana, around $25,000 in paper bills.

I had to turn down the invite, for the *Far West* was soon moving north again, up to the big bend of the Missouri and on into the Yellowstone River, with no significant layovers except the regular stops to cut wood to fire its boilers and a dropping off of supplies to an infantry column waiting at Glendive Creek. It was into the first week in June when we finally reached the mouth of the Powder, and that's where we found the Seventh Cavalry in bivouac.

All right, I had got there. Now what? There was quite an assemblage of Army thereabout. Besides the Seventh there was infantry and Gatling guns, and a supply train of 150 wagons; a herd of cattle, most of which however by now had been butchered and ate on the march in; a mule train; and a couple hundred civilian teamsters, mule skinners, and herders. Not to mention some forty specimens of an Indian for who the proper name is I think Arikara though they was mainly called Ree at that time. These Ree had come along as scouts, being hereditary enemies of the Sioux, though I believe that in time past they had been friendly with the Cheyenne when the Human Beings lived along the Missouri, for that's where the Ree still resided.

Right miserable-looking bunch, they was small and soot-colored, and I think a Ree would rather have cut his own throat than ever wash a particle of his person. Still, they was Indians, albeit enemies to them with which I was raised, and the mood I was in, I'd have took to anybody at the moment who was not white of countenance. I was thinking of Old Lodge Skins, see, and if he was still alive, and the Lakota tribes, the Minneconjou and the Hunkpapa and all, out there someplace to the west of us. Rumor now had it they was probably encamped along the Rosebud. I'll tell you about that creek: it got its name from the wild rosebushes along its bank. I reckoned its waters would run with blood any day now, like at the Washita.

The *Far West* had started to unload its stores, and I spotted a Ree what had come up to where that sutler was setting up his barrels of whiskey. This Indian was a dumpy fellow, dressed in filthy buckskins, and I would have took him for a degenerate imbecile the way he was a-studying them barrels.

But some trooper says to me: "Looky there at Bloody Knife, will you. He'd cut his Ma's throat for a shot of red-eye. You would never know he is Hard A—" He broke off, on account of he didn't know who I might be, being as I wore civilian clothes: among the herders and teamsters was Boston Custer, the General's youngest brother, and his nephew Armstrong Reed. The trooper had been going to say "Hard Ass," but changed it. "You wouldn't guess, from looking at him, that he was the General's favorite scout, would you?" He snorted. "Goddam old drunk."

But Bloody Knife wasn't drunk at that minute, nor for some time thereafter, for not even scout Indians was allowed openly to drink whiskey in front of white men. So he hung around hopelessly awhile and tried to talk to people in sign language, and at last, not able to stand and study them barrels without a chance to break into one, he trudged off as though from the burial of a loved one, so grief-stricken was his dark face.

I caught him up and, never speaking Ree, says in the signs: "You want a drink?"

He says: "All right." So I got a canteenful of that red-eye dispensed by the sutler, and me and Bloody Knife went on out one of the many ravines that cut up the country at the mouth of the Powder and set behind a sagebush, after the Indian had emptied his bladder so as to have a full capacity for drinking the whiskey. This pissing also served to run out a rattlesnake who had been sunning himself in the area: rattlers was abundant in that region.

I give Bloody Knife time for a good swallow and then took back the canteen. I says, watching a couple drops run down his chin and neck and flush out some bugs what lived in his collar, "What is Long Hair going to do?"

The Ree just kept his black eyes upon that canteen. "He has cut his hair," he says, making the slicing sign with his two dusky hands.

I signaled that I knowed that, but never saw what it had to do with the issue.

"It means," he says, "that he is going to die."

I give him the canteen again. I don't have to tell you at this point what importance an Indian sets upon human hair. Scalps are taken for a more important purpose than just trophies: a man without a skull-cover is considered powerless even when he reaches the Other Side. And whenever Indians saw a white man balded by nature, they believed him a coward who had deliberately shaved his head. I realized Custer had made a bad mistake for his own interests.

"That was not a good thing to do," says Bloody Knife, who was getting more depressed with every swallow. He looks up at the sun and signals to it: "I shall not see you rise many more times."

I knew that if I let him continue on that note he would commence to sing his death song at any minute and then I'd never get anything else out of him, so I says right quick: "But that will not happen until all those barrels of whiskey are gone, so drink up."

At which he was some cheered and filled his fly-trap again.

"Many Sioux and Cheyenne out there?"

He says: "Numerous as stars on a clear night."

I pointed back towards the camp. "But look at all those soldiers. And more will come from the west and south."

Bloody Knife shook his dirty head of tangled hair. It was graying some at the temples. "It does not matter," he says. "We will all be rubbed out. Long Hair will never be the Great Father in the chief village of the white men, as he wishes. I like him a lot, but his medicine has turned bad."

He goes on that Custer had come to him and the other Ree a night or so since, give them presents, and said he would whip the entire Sioux nation before the month was out, in return for which the American people would make him President.

Well, Grant was in trouble on account of them crooks in his Administration, and when you figured he had got to the White House by whipping the Rebs, a similar result might transpire for the man who sent the Indians under, for they was the only outstanding enemy of the U.S.A. at this particular time in the hundredth year of our Independence from the tyranny of the Old Country.

"I reckon he would like to get it all done by the Fourth of July," is what I wanted to say, but that is a hell of a difficult speech to make by signs. The Cheyenne know July as "the Moon When Buffalo Are Mating," but I didn't know what the Ree called it. However, I made the buffalo-horns, and the motion for screwing— which is the same as used by every white schoolboy—and for moon, and for the fourth day thereof. Still, what would a Ree know of the historical meaning. So I says the day when the soldiers made a lot of noise, shooting cannon and the like.

A look of dim recognition come over his dark face. "And get drunk?" he asks.

"Oh, hell," I says aloud in English. "What does it matter? Drink up, you poor son of a bitch."

He shortly passed out, and I took the precaution of unloading his rifle, in case he woke up before the effects had worn off.

I had learned what I wanted to know. I reckoned, in view of Custer's current needs, this upcoming battle would make the Washita look cheap. Bloody Knife's pessimism did not impress me. I didn't care how many hostiles had collected, I knowed they wasn't organized, never had much modern armament, and was living with their wives and kids.

Well, what was I going to do about it? That old childish idea of assassinating Custer was obviously out. Such a stunt, pulled off now, would just make the Seventh fight harder. They all hated his guts—no sooner had I got off the *Far West* than I heard the troopers grousing about him: they was particularly burned up that he hadn't let them be paid till they got into the field, which meant that even if they never found a hostile Indian, there'd be men in an outfit that size who would die of rattlesnake bite and the like, without having had a little celebration in town before they went on their last campaign. But once he had been shot by me, or stabbed in the back, he would turn into a hero. Anyway, General Terry was in actual command, so the campaign would not stop.

Now I had left Bloody Knife under the sagebush when, walking back to camp a-studying this matter, who should I spot but a figure out of the distant past, sitting on the bank just beyond where the Powder emptied into the Yellowstone.

His skin was darker yet than a Ree's and he wore a flop hat with an eagle feather in it. By God if he had changed much in twenty year.

I says to him: "Well, Lavender, this is some surprise."

For that is who it was, and he looked at me right polite and says I had the advantage on him.

"Jack Crabb," says I. "The Reverend Pendrake, in _____, Missouri."

He studies me careful and says: "Go on." Then he takes off his hat so he can see better, stands up, peers into my face, kind of groans, then laughs, and I grabs him and gives him a bear hug. I don't know why, it was more like finding a long-lost relative than when I had actually done so on several occasions.

After we got through with exchanging the pleasures of re-meeting, I says: "Tell me what you're doing here. Has the Reverend become a chaplain?"

"No, not him," says Lavender, who must now have been around forty-five years of age and had a few gray hairs when I looked him over close, but the mahogany skin of his face was still unlined. He was dressed in buckskin jacket and pants with fringe, and if I wasn't wrong, his belt showed beadwork in the Sioux fashion. "No," he says again, and then: "My oh my, I ain't thought on that Reverend for many a year. He died, Jack, not long after you run off. Et himself to death, is what happened. He packed away one of them gigantic dinners that Lucy made for him one noontime, then took a nap directly after, and some of that meal backed up and clogged his windpipe and he suffocated afore anyone knowed the difference, damn if he did not."

At that minute Lavender got a bite on his fishline, for he had set down again and lifted his pole, with me alongside, and he pulled it out and there was a real nice fish on the hook, which he unfastened and tossed flopping on the bank.

"Well," Lavender goes on, "the way I looked at it at the time, that man died happy, in the condition he liked best in all the world: stuffed with victual. I believe Lucy had cooked roast pork with applesauce that day."

I suffered something between indigestion and heart flutter as I asked: "And Mrs. Pendrake? I reckon she got married again?"

Lavender was threading another earthworm on his hook. "The Lady," he says, "no, the Lady closed up the shutters on that house and I recall never even attended the funeral. And the church got it a new preacher who was supposed to live in that house, but she never moved out and none of them white folks had nerve to ask her to do it, so the new one, he had to reside somewhere else, and as far as I know she is there yet."

I was thinking my own thoughts: even for a minute the impulse run through my head to pack up whatever I was doing here and head back down to Missouri instanter, but I was old enough by now to accept the better sense. I was thirty-six and had been through too much. Believe me, the real romantic person is him who ain't done anything but imagine. If you have actually participated in disasters, like me, you get conservative.

But while I was staring into the Yellowstone at the current making a sort of watery arrowhead around Lavender's fishline, he says: "I stayed on there for a year or so, but now it was a house of women, so I commenced to think again—" He slapped his hand upon the ground. "Sure," he says, "it was you yourself what had lived with the Indians. I recall it now, Jack. How you and me talked of it. Well sir, what I done—for I was freed and could come and go as I liked—I went on West one day, like I had thought of doing for quite a spell. Thisheer kin of mine had gone out with Captain Lewis and Captain Clark. . . ."

He went on about that slave York again, not having as good a memory as me. Suffice it to say he had had various employments and adventures before he found the type of Indian who met his needs, but he finally did, and who was they but the Sioux of Sitting Bull!

This news brung me out of my thoughts. "You didn't!" I says, and immediately regretted my choice of words, for you see Lavender wasn't a darky no more. I mean, he was of course still a Negro person by race, but he wasn't in any wise a servant nor had the mentality of such, and therefore was not any more used to having his veracity questioned.

He just looked at me with an evident pride which I immediately recognized as being Indian, and I said quick: "By God," I says, "by God, old Sitting Bull! It just surprises me, that's all. That's who they're going out after now, ain't it?"

Lavender looks sad. He says: "I married a Sioux woman of the Hunkpapa band and lived several year in a tepee made of skin." He shook his head and that feather quivered in the band. "They are real good people, and you take old Bull, I reckon for an Indian he is what you could call a genius. When he wants to see what is happening anywhere in the world, all he has to do is close his eyes and dream and he's got it clear."

"Yes," I says, "that's right."

The sun reflected off the lobes of Lavender's widespread dark nose. "You recall the Reverend Pendrake, Jack," he says. "How he was always spouting principles. They was good and even holy ones, I guess, and it was on account of them that he bought me from my old master and give me freedom. So I might be ungrateful when I say the longer I listened to him, the more I thought: he is a fool."

"So did I," I says, "even as a young boy."

"But why, Jack, why did we think that?" Lavender was real quizzical, and took off his hat and dropped it to the ground, showing his head of frizzy curls. "For I was black," he says, "but you knowed how to read and write."

I says: "Speaking for myself, I thought he was talking about how things *should be* rather than as they *was*."

"That's right! That's it!" shouts Lavender. "Whereas an Indian has it the other way around. . . . Well then," he goes on, "why did both you and me turn about in time and leave the Indians, too? Tell me that."

I says: "Because we wasn't born barbarians."

"You said it."

"And it don't work if you are aware of anything else," I goes on.

"It's perfect if you been born in a tent and carried on your Ma's back and lived with hocus-pocus since the day you was born and never invented the wheel."

"If you come from civilization," says Lavender, "to live among the savages, it is fine for a while and then you get so powerful curious as to what is going on back home, you can't stand it. You got to see, so you come back, and it might be good or it might be awful, but it is *happening*."

He pulled in his line and picked up his fish, and we went back towards where his tent stood at the edge of the bivouac.

"We got that straightened out," I says. "But what I wonder now is why you have come back to this country?"

Lavender looked sort of embarrassed at that. He says: "I ain't here to fight the Sioux. I signed on as interpreter. When they see this army, why, maybe they'll return to the agencies."

"You think they will?"

"No," he says. "And if they shoot at me, I reckon I'll shoot back."

The next day I finally seen Custer. I was still there unofficially and could have strung along that way for quite a time in a camp of that size, where as I have said there was lots of civilians as wagon drivers and such, and I considered so doing, for I was an enemy in this midst and it seemed less like treason if I didn't sign on for nothing. But then I thought that if I was around long enough, people would become aware I wasn't attached to any of the various services and begin to ask questions. I was afraid my sympathies might show up in any prolonged conversation with a white man, for you couldn't walk nowhere among that bunch without hearing how they was going to whip old Bull and his cutthroats, only good redskin was a dead one, etc. On that subject, the troopers would even forget their dislike of Custer and talk of what a fighter he was.

Then I still never knowed what I intended to do. The Indian camp had not yet been located, Major Reno and his command being out on a reconnaissance mission along the Tongue River at the moment to determine just that. I guess I had some vague plan when the village was found to slip off and get there before the troops and warn the hostiles, though it was too likely I would get killed long before contacting any Cheyenne who might recognize me.

The best move at present seemed to be getting hired as scout, and that required an interview with Custer. General Terry might be in official command, but I got the impression that he did the talking while Custer acted.

I went to the headquarters tent of Son of the Morning Star and bluffed my way past the orderly—a different man from the Washita striker—and walked inside to a little camp table, and there sat the General behind it, a-scribbling as usual. I don't know that anyone has ever pointed out what a writer Custer was: letters to his wife most every day, and he also done a whole series of articles for the *Galaxy* magazine while in the field. I believe he was writing such now.

He did look different with his long hair cropped off like a normal person's, a little weaker maybe, but then that might have been only the superstition of Bloody Knife. However, I saw something else before he lifted his eyes to me. It was day outside, but he was using a candle as additional illumination, and as he was bent over his papers, the top of his hatless skull lay directly in my sight and there, on either side of a sparse yellow forelock, long spearpoints of pink skin run back almost to meet at the crown. *Custer was getting bald.*

I felt a touch of human feeling for him on the sudden, which soon left while he made me stand there for quite a time without acknowledgment.

At last he scratches in a full stop on his writing, and he waits for it to dry, lays aside his pen, then stares coldly at me.

"State your business," he says in that raspy voice I had not forgotten.

"General," I says, a-trying to keep down the distaste that had again replaced that short-lived other feeling, "I was wondering whether you could use another guide or interpreter. There is Cheyenne out there with the Sioux, and I lived among—"

"No," he says, and picking up his pen again, called: "Orderly, show this man out."

That trooper entered the tent and stood aside for me to exit, but I got sore and wouldn't move and when he took ahold of my arm to assist my departure, I pushed him off and says: "Boy, you touch me again and I'll lay you open with my pigsticker."

Custer looked up at that and broke out in a dry laugh with more air in it than sound.

"You're peppery, aren't you?" he says. "I like that. All right, orderly, you can retire." Which the trooper does, glowering at me. Then Custer settles back in his camp chair with a superior smile and says: "Now then, what makes you think you might be useful to me?"

I was still riled, but I managed to mention some of my experiences with the Cheyenne while of course omitting everything about the Washita.

"Oh, Cheyenne," he broke in before I had got much out, "but not Sioux? Well, my good fellow, you are eight years late. As you may have heard, I trounced the Cheyenne in 1868 down in Indian Territory. You apparently do not keep up with things."

I tell you, it was his grin that burned me more than the substance of his comments, but I knowed that if I really let my temper go, I'd kill him.

So I says, level as I could: "There's still enough Cheyenne north of the Platte to give you a run for your money, especially if they have joined with the Lakota."

"Oh," says he, "a few stragglers, perhaps, have made their way north to join these malcontents, but I can whip the whole lot with one troop of the Seventh—unless the Indian agents have managed to equip them with the latest Winchester repeating arms, in which case I shall need two troops. In my opinion, a better campaign might be waged against the latter gentry, the scoundrels who, on the one hand, speculate in the Indian annuities and, on the other, excuse and prevaricate about the depredations of the savages under their protection."

On this subject he become genuinely exercised, frowning beneath them heavy pale brows and nose getting real pointy. "I find it quite sinister," he says, "that these men can connive—for that is what it amounts to—in the atrocities against their own countrymen. For example, the official at the Red Cloud Agency has been so lax with his barbarous charges that they lately, with murderous threats, frustrated his attempt to raise the American flag above his office!"

Then he caught himself, as if realizing it was not proper form for a brevet major-general of the U.S. Army to address a common frontiersman with high emotion.

"Well," he says, "I suppose this is all Greek to you. I'm sorry that I cannot give you employment as guide, but you can give extremely valuable service as herder or teamster or whatever you now do. Not everybody can ride at the head of the column: the feet are no less useful than the eyes."

Now you won't believe this, but it happened. I lost control at Custer's dismissing me so, and before I knowed what I was doing, I says very distinct:

"You bastard, I should have knifed you when I had the chance."

I was plumb full of horror once that expression was out—not because I feared for my well-being; no sir, I realized on the instant that now I would never get away to warn the Indians. I stood there for a time, the words still echoing in my head, and Custer says:

"But thank you for coming forward. I like your ginger. We need have no doubt of the outcome when even the civilians wish to serve in the van."

He returned to his writing, and I left the tent. Custer had not heard my comment, spoke directly to his face! As regards the outside world, he was like a stuffed bird under one of them glass bells. His own opinion sufficed to the degree that he had no equipment for detecting exterior reactions. That's the only way I can explain it.

Anyhow, that's why no roster of the men present at the Battle of the Little Bighorn ever contained my name. Custer thought I was a herder; and the herders and teamsters themselves figured I was an interpreter or guide, especially as I hung about a good deal with Lavender.

It was while we was at this camp upon the Powder that the Seventh Cavalry stripped off its excess baggage. All sabers, for example, was crated up and left there, so them pictures of the Last Stand in which Custer waves his sword while the Indians swirl around him is lies. And that famous regimental band which had so tormented me upon the Washita, they had come this far from Fort Lincoln, but for once they would not accompany the attack. Their gray horses was needed for a number of troopers who had made the march on foot.

A day or so later the rest of us moved forty mile up the Yellowstone to the mouth of the Tongue River. I got myself an Indian pony with a pad saddle and a rawhide halter from Bloody Knife, who had a few extra animals. As I recall the transaction, it cost me two or three canteenfuls of the sutler's whiskey, not the worst deal, but then that pony had seen better days and wasn't worth a whole lot more. He was a buckskin, right skinny and had a couple saddle sores, which I treated with an old Cheyenne remedy of boiled tobacco, bitter grass, animal fat, and salt.

My last memory of the Powder River encampment is of the band, on a nearby bluff, playing for our march out. Naturally, their selection was "Garry Owen," and it brung to my mind certain images of eight year before. I did not of course know that as the blare receded into the distance, it represented the fading out of Custer's famous luck as well.

I was riding at the rear, with the pack mules that had now replaced the wagons as supply train, and on ahead stretched the mighty blue column.

AT THE MOUTH OF THE TONGUE we found an abandoned Sioux village of the winter before, and the troopers poked about in it for trash, broken lodgepoles and the like, that they could use for campfires. Lavender found an old beat-up pair of discarded moccasins that he said he had known the owner thereof, recognizing the beading. I don't know if he did or not, for he was getting gloomier as we proceeded westward and it may have affected his judgment.

A little later he located a burial scaffold raised on poles painted black and red, the body still upon it in its funeral wrappings along with the other truck the Indians include with the deceased so he won't be naked and helpless on the Other Side: bow, moccasins, and suchlike; and as I come up, Lavender was a-standing there, one side of his hatbrim blown up against the crown by the persistent wind, for it was upon a barren bluff, and a-staring at the platform with his mouth gone slack.

Then up come some of the cavalrymen and tore down the scaffold for fuel and they took the moccasins and bow as souvenirs and left the body rest upon the bare ground. While this was going on, Lavender just stood to the side, and then he says to me: "I'm a-going fishing." That's what I mean by his getting queer.

But the next moment Custer himself appeared upon his prancing mare with three white feet, what was called "Vic," and he looks down upon the corpse and says to Lavender: "Uncover it." Which my friend then did, upwrapping the skins, and inside was a dead Sioux brave all right, who had been dead for a while, no doubt about that, but you could still see a big wound in his shoulder.

Custer says: "Dispose of it." Lavender lifted it into his arms and carried it like you would a small living person, a child or a girl, except it was stiff and being withered never weighed much. Down to the bank of the Yellowstone he went and pitched it into the water.

I figured the kind of person Custer was, he would not recognize me though we had the conversation recently, but I was wrong. He says: "Hello, teamster," and I touched my hat to him, instinctively respectful. I wouldn't have done it if I had thought about it, but the point is that when you were around Custer for a while, even if you hated his guts, you had to acknowledge that authority came natural to him.

Next a soldier reported to the General that they had found the remains of a white man in the ashes of an old fire down in the campsite, so he spurred off on Vic, and as I was afoot, by the time I got there they had uncovered a skull and most of a skeleton, though the bones was all jumbled together, belonging apparently to a late member of the U.S. Cavalry, which could be told from the device upon a couple uniform buttons also in the same fire, and thereabout was some big stones and charred wood clubs with which he had been obviously beat to death. I saw the Ree scouts telling this to Custer in the signs.

The General dismounted and walked to the pile of bones. A lot of troopers gathered around, and some said the poor devil must have been the man they lost in '73 in this area. It threw a hush over the soldiers, who had just lately been grousing about being sent on a wild-goose chase, for they didn't share the melancholy I had seen in Lavender and Bloody Knife. Not one Sioux nor Cheyenne had yet been seen in the flesh, and this campsite was half a year old.

But I'll swear this incident had its effect on Custer. I watched him as he looked at them bones. In the poor light of the tent I hadn't seen how old he had become since the Washita. He was only thirty-seven years of age, yet you could have took him for ten more. He had not shaved on this campaign, and his face was covered with a considerable stubble, his mustache and eyebrows ragged. He took off his gray hat, in respect for the dead, and that short haircut was amazingly rough-clipped for a man of his usual natty habits. The lines running from the nose to his mouth was deep as coulees, and he had not yet had time to wash up, so a lot of trail dust lay upon him.

As to me, it was now that for the first time I reflected that I might not want the Indians whipped, but neither was it my wish that these six hundred white men lost their lives, nor the Ree or Lavender, of course. It gets real complicated when you set out to monkey with mortality. If I tipped off the Indians, they might ambush Custer. If I did not, he would slaughter them.

I was watching the detail gather together the dead soldier's bones when Bloody Knife and another sloppy Ree called Stab come along and addressed me in the signs.

"Your friend, the Black White Man," says Bloody Knife, "threw the Lakota body into the river."

"Now," says Stab, "he is fishing in the same place."

"We think," Bloody Knife signals, "that he is using the corpse for bait."

The only thing you can do with an Indian in such a mood is what I says then: "I have heard you." They went off.

"You know what them Ree look like?" asks a voice at my shoulder. "Darky washerwomen."

I turned and seen a sergeant who looked familiar, I didn't at first know why.

He says: "Say, I could swear I seen you before. Did you ever serve with the cavalry?"

I assured him I never, and then I recalled the man. He was that corporal what found me just after I changed into Army clothes in a bush at the Washita, and took me in to the village where Custer bawled me out for having my coat unbuttoned. He had been promoted since, and had some gray in his hair and put on a pound or two around his gut, but was the same person. He had saved my life, and you don't generally forget that.

Memory of the incident naturally made me feel friendly to him, so I stuck out my hand and give my name, and he says his name was Botts.

"Well, Botts," I asks, "do you think we'll get a fight soon?"

He was smoking a short black pipe, which had quite a filthy odor even in that Montana wind. He puffs out some smoke, and says: "I reckon not. I think they'll run if they can, like the Cheyenne did at the Washita. Of course, nobody yet knows where they are at. Reno is out looking now, and Hard Ass is burning that Terry never sent *him*. He is afraid Reno will find and whip them afore he gets a chance, but I tell you he don't have to worry over that. Reno never has fought Indians, and he ain't got no stomach for doing it now. The only fighting he likes is between himself and a bottle. Hard Ass, on the other hand, will light into anything he finds with a red skin, be it a bunch of old squaws, so as to clear himself with Grant."

"I heard he might go for President himself," says I.

"Is that so?" Sergeant Botts give a horselaugh. "Well, he'd get two votes for sure: his own and Miz Custer's. Oh, and of course his brother Tom's—there's another bastard. You seen that specimen? Wild Bill Hickok put a head on him once down in Kansas and Tom pulled in his horns. And old Rain in the Face, when he was arrested a couple year ago for murdering three white men, he blamed Tom Custer for it and swore he would one day cut out Tom's heart and eat it. Tom's been pissing his pants ever since that Indian escaped."

You can see what a high opinion members of the Seventh Cavalry still had of one another. The only officers for which Botts had any use was Captain Benteen, who I remembered from the Washita, and Captain Keogh, a mustachioed Irishman; and even in the case of the latter, Botts never cared for the Catholic religion, he let on, and in addition Keogh was also something of a drunk, although he was naturally brave rather than drinking to get his courage up as with Major Reno.

I don't know where Botts got off condemning everyone else for boozing, for during my association with him he was himself invariably hitting a canteen which he had the sutler keep filled with rotgut. On the other hand, one of the main reasons he hated Custer was the General didn't drink nor smoke. He detested the whole Custer tribe and says the real menace on this campaign was getting surrounded by Custers rather than Indians, for in addition to the General and Tom, and that younger brother Boston and the nephew Armstrong Reed, Lieutenant Calhoun was married to the Custer sister.

Next I reckon Botts would have started talking abusively of Mrs. Custer herself, but I could not stand for that, whether or not he had once saved my life. That lady was pretty as an angel.

Most soldiers shared Botts's opinions, I found. Now they might have been right to feel such, but you take them Indians we was on our way to fight: if they had not venerated Sitting Bull and Crazy Horse and Gall, these individuals would not have been their chiefs. It never made no sense to redskins to be led by men they hated or contemned. That seems to be an exclusive white trick, and what it amounted to here was that the Seventh Cavalry had two formidable enemies at the Little Bighorn: the entire Sioux nation and—the Seventh Cavalry.

A couple days after our arrival at the Tongue, scouts come in from Reno's detachment which had reached the mouth of Rosebud Creek. He had found the Indians—or at least their tracks. A great trail half a mile wide, marked with the scratching of thousands of lodgepoles drug behind the ponies, led upstream in the Rosebud valley. So we all set out forthwith to join him where that creek emptied into the Yellowstone, the Seventh going by land and General Terry and his staff riding upon the *Far West*. Colonel Gibbon with his force was already in that area, on the Yellowstone's north bank.

It will help if you remember that the Yellowstone in this region flows southwest to northeast, and them tributary streams enter it from the south and are roughly parallel to one another. Proceeding westward, first comes the Powder, where I joined the campaign; then the Tongue, where we found the dead Sioux and the soldier's skeleton; next the Rosebud, where Reno was now waiting; and finally the Bighorn. Twenty-five or thirty mile above the mouth of the last-named is the forks, the eastward branch of which is the Little Bighorn.

Soon after everybody had collected at the mouth of the Rosebud, the leading officers, Terry, Custer, Gibbon, and their staffs, held a council on board the *Far West*, the results of which was circulated throughout the enlisted men on the bank before it was even over, for soldiers, like Indians, have their own mysterious means of getting news. I heard it from Botts.

"Here's the plan," he says. "The Seventh, under Custer, will go up the Rosebud to its headwaters and light into the Indians if they are there. If not, then we'll cross over to the Little Bighorn valley and come down it. Meanwhile, Terry and Gibbon will be coming upriver. If the Indians are there, they'll be caught between the two commands.

"But if I know Hard Ass, he won't wait for the others. With that infantry, it'll take them longer than us, and I'll owe you a drink if we don't have the Sioux whipped by time they show up."

That reminded him of his beloved canteen, and he took a shot from it, I refusing his proffer. "Maybe," he says, wiping his lips, "you was right, and Hard Ass *will* be President. On the other hand, I wouldn't be surprised if the Sioux had run off into the mountains. I never knew an Indin who had the stomach for a real fight. Down on the Washita . . ."

The point is that he wasn't alone in this idea. The Army still believed the Indians would run. What none of us knowed at this time was that while we was sitting there on the Tongue River, these very Sioux and Cheyenne had given General Crook's command a bad beating on the upper Rosebud. But armies then didn't have radios nor telegraphs, and we never knowed where Crook was located nor he us, though relatively close by, and he soon retired to the south.

Some say it was from the council on that boat that Custer returned in a depressed state of mind so different from his usual assurance. But I had seen the change in him when he viewed the skeleton of the soldier tortured by the Sioux. However, as the years have gone by, I have since come to believe the alteration commenced further back—when he cut his childish curls, maybe, before starting out from Fort Lincoln. He could hardly be the Boy General any more. We all know the type of man who hasn't no middle life; from a boyhood continued too long, he falls directly into old age, and it is pathetic.

There was a suggestion of that in Son of the Morning Star, so long as you understand he wasn't getting exactly humble yet. He refused an offer of Gibbon's cavalry battalion as reinforcement and also spurned them Gatling guns. And in this regard, as in few others, he got the support of Botts, for the sergeant like most soldiers tended to close ranks when the regimental pride was at stake.

"The Seventh don't need no help," Botts says. "I'll stand by Hard Ass on that matter."

So there at the Rosebud mouth we commenced to ready for the move upstream, and Gibbon's command marched off for the Bighorn, though the steamboat, which would haul the ranking officers, lingered awhile so the Seventh could be reviewed in parade. This was around noontime on that June day, a cold wind blowing from the north as we rode through the valley full of sagebrush, past black-bearded Terry and the others on the knoll, with all the buglers massed nearby a-playing the march while the mounts pranced and guidons fluttered.

Yet it was not a grand occasion when seen against the vasty

bleakness of the country, as the forward troops mounted the bench-land above the valley in a thin string of blue. I rode at the end of the column with the pack mules and after us come only a little rear guard. Custer had dropped off to say goodbye to Terry, leaning across his mare to shake hands with him and Gibbon, and just as I passed at the foot of where they was, I heard the latter say: "Now, don't be too greedy, Custer. Leave some Indians for us." This was spoken half in jest, I thought.

But Custer replied in sober face.

"Yes," he says, "yes," salutes, and gallops towards the head of his column, which already was dipping over the farthermost bluff. When I got to the high land, I looked back and seen them officers, small as flies, a-riding to where the *Far West* was tethered to the shore small as a floating leaf.

Well sir, the pack train started giving trouble when we was hardly out of camp. I was, by the way, still in my peculiar situation as to job, but now had more or less established myself, so far as the others went, as belonging to the little team of civilian packers. Looking at the way the supplies was lashed to the animals, you would have thought a woman had tied them on. Four or five packs fell off before we got twenty minutes out of camp. Now when you realize these mules was carrying ammunition that the Seventh was supposed to use against the Sioux, as well as the rations for a fifteen-day campaign, why, it was a serious deficiency, so Custer sent back a lieutenant to get things in order and in addition to the civilians there was a detachment of troopers to help out, but were the truth known, that pack train was never worth a damn from the minute it started.

The Rosebud ain't much of a waterway in quantity, being three or four foot wide and three inches deep throughout much of its length and even less in spots, but where we camped that evening was a deeper pool or two and some of the troopers went fishing in order to get a little change from the hardtack and bacon which was all that was provided in the way of food for the next two weeks. Hunting was not allowed from here on, for the discharge of a firearm can be heard great distances in wild country. But now that his favorite sport become so popular, Lavender of course abandoned its practice.

That's another example of the strange style of that man, as I have mentioned, and he was not getting any more normal as we proceeded further towards the Sioux. I'll tell you how he bedded down at night: we had left all tenting behind, traveling light as we was now, and the soldiers slept upon the ground, maybe scratching out little hollows for their hips. Luckily the weather stayed dry.

But Lavender, he made himself an Indian wickiup, which is a bush or a couple branches stuck into the ground and your blankets throwed over the top, creating a little hut therein. Now since it wasn't raining he obviously done that for privacy; nor did he invite me to share it with him though I was what at least passed for his only friend.

Wandering about that evening I spotted his establishment, off by itself. He had left the closure open at the top, and as I come up smoke was rising from inside. I thought he was cooking his bacon underneath, and thought: damn me, but he is *right* queer, for there was hardly room in that type of dwelling for a person to sit upright. But shortly I smelled tobacco rather than pork and figured: oh, he is just taking a smoke—still, I wouldn't burst in upon him, but rather I stamped my foot and called out, and the blanket slowly opens to reveal his dark face a-shining sweaty, for it was warm enough even outside a wickiup.

Lavender was holding an Indian pipe with two-three foot of wood stem and a red stone bowl, and he looks dully at me and never says a word.

Now I took this lack of hospitality amiss, for I knowed him from away back and had lived with the Indians myself and felt just as strange about returning with an army sent to punish them. But he was in a more compromising position than me; I had joined up under false pretenses, but he was getting paid. So for his conscience' sake he could play at Indian rituals, but in practical effect all that mattered was his membership in this command a-tracking down his former friends. . . . That's what it seemed like to me at the time, but I guess you are smart enough to understand, as I then did not, that when I looked at Lavender, I was seeing myself.

Yet right now I was annoyed, and says: "Well, if you are busy—" and starts to leave, but his eyes cleared and he says: "Come on and set." So I did and we exchanged that Sioux pipe now and again, and at length I says: "I guess it wouldn't do no good for us to run off."

"No," he says, "no, it would not."

I blew out some spicy smoke. He had got the real Indian mix somewhere, maybe from the Ree scouts.

"Look, Lavender," I says. "I asked you once and you never really answered: Why did you come on this campaign?"

He says: "I wanted to see this country again before I die."

I appreciated what he meant, though not everybody would have when they saw the cactus and sage and bullberry bushes, along with a few cottonwoods and box elders, which constituted the growth of that district, and the ravines and cutbanks of the terrain.

"Say," I asks, "did you ever find any descendants of that kin of yours who went with Lewis and Clark?"

"Not a one," Lavender says, "that I could verify, though some Sioux is right dark of skin. But I didn't look much, for the thing is, when you join the Indians, you got all the relatives you need. There might be people in the band what ain't overly fond of one another, but they save their real spite for the enemy."

Lavender had throwed back the blanket when I set with him, though that bush was still arched over us, and a tribe of mosquitoes was also sharing the wickiup. I had took several bites already.

"It is otherwise with this here bunch," I says.

"Oh my yes," says Lavender. "The way they hate General Custer, and they ain't nobody thinks well of Major Reno, who was slapped once in the face by Captain Benteen at the officer club at Lincoln. And Captain Benteen wrote the newspapers a bad letter on what happened at the Washita. And General Custer was a-fixing to horsewhip him for it, but the Captain put his hand onto his pistol and he say: 'Come ahead,' but the General decided not to."

Lavender shook his head. "I'll tell you this about Captain Benteen. Did you ever know he come from a Southern family what was Rebel in the War and called him a traitor when he joined the Union Army? His old Daddy put a curse upon his head, hoping he'd be killed. So the Captain worked it that his Daddy was arrested and throwed into a Federal prison till the War was over. Think of it!"

"The Cheyenne killed my Pa, but took me for a son." I don't know why I said that.

"I never knowed my Daddy," says Lavender. "My master sold him to another before I was born."

Then I got to telling him about Olga and Gus on the one hand, and Sunshine and Morning Star on the other, and as long as I had started, related the rest of it, Denver and Wild Bill and Amelia and, yes, the Washita.

"Well," says Lavender when I had finished, "I never knowed being white was so complicated."

"I don't reckon it is for everybody," I allowed. "Take General Custer. He not only knows who his family is, but he takes most of them along when he goes to war."

"That's right," Lavender says, and he looks uneasy.

I says: "You like him don't you."

His pipe had went out and he scraped the ash from it and took his time. Finally he says: "He has always treated me well, Jack. That's all I got to go on. You got to remember he is a soldier."

"Good at killing," I says.

"And dying, if it comes to that," says Lavender. He puts the pipe away into a buckskin bag, then says: "I wonder if you would write out a will for me."

So I went through the twilit bivouac and the soldiers lounging about digesting their suppers, and now the fires was all extinguished for a flame can be seen many miles after dark, and I had to ask quite a few before I found a man who could lend me a pencil and even then he never had no paper except a letter from his wife which he carried for good luck in a pocket over his heart, so I saw two officers a-coming through the gloom and purposed to beg a blank page from the order books they generally carried.

They was Lieutenants McIntosh, Wallace, and Godfrey. I found out later from Botts that Custer had held a staff meeting that night, in total distinction to his usual practice of keeping his own counsel. He explained why he never took the Gatling guns and cavalry reinforcements, on the ground that the Gatlings being hard to transport would detain the column, and as to the other horsemen, he figured they would cause more jealousy between outfits than give help against the foe. Then he talked some more about the campaign and asked for suggestions from the officers.

Now this was an unprecedented thing for Custer to do. He had always *told*, in that raspy voice of his, and never asked. Bottsy says he had heard the General sounded almost pleading. "That mean son of a bitch. I wonder why."

Anyway, this will make some sense of what I heard them officers say, as I remembered it later.

"Godfrey," says Wallace, "I believe Custer is going to be killed."

Lieutenant Godfrey asks: "What makes you think so?"

"Because I have never heard him talk in that way before."

McIntosh just looked from one to the other and didn't utter a sound. He was a breed, his Ma being an Iroquois Indian back East, and was noted for his slow-moving, cautious ways. He was the only member of this trio who was himself soon to die. He must sometimes have had interesting thoughts.

Well, hearing that, I did not ask them officers for paper, but waited awhile and along came Captain Keogh by himself, with his big black mustache and little pointy underlip beard, so I put my request to him.

Keogh was an Irishman what had served in the personal guard of the Pope in Rome before coming to the U.S.A.

"Ah, sure," he says, "go and tell Finnegan to give you a sheet from my writing case."

Finnegan was his striker, who according to Botts kept all of Keogh's money when they was at Fort Lincoln, lest the Captain drink himself to death on it. "Finnegan's more like his guardian than striker," Botts said.

I thanked him and started away, when Keogh put an odd question.

"Would you be writing your will?" he says.

"How'd you know that?"

He give a merry laugh, which was odd considering what he said then: "I made me own last night. But that was after Tom Custer and Calhoun took me at poker, so I don't have much to leave behind."

"Why then did you make it?" I asked humorlessly, for I was still under the influence of Lavender and them lieutenants.

"For the sheer hell of it," says Captain Keogh, and his eyes was bright even in the dusk.

So I searched out Finnegan and got the paper and come back to Lavender, and him and me made out our wills, leaving such as we had to each other, and then the problem arose as to who should keep it, since we'd both be going into whatever fight occurred.

"Give it to Bloody Knife," says Lavender. "Roll it up and stick it in a cartridge case and give it to him to keep."

"Why," I says, "he'll be in the fight too, won't he?"

"Not him," says Lavender. "He's a coward, like all Ree. At the first shot, he'll turn and won't stop till he sees the Missouri River."

That just goes to show you there ain't no race that has a monopoly on truth. In point of fact, Bloody Knife got shot in the head in the valley and his brains was blown all over Major Reno. However, that didn't matter so far as our wills went, for I burned that paper. To have such a document in existence seemed bad medicine to me. I wasn't the devil-may-care type of Captain Keogh, and maybe that's why I didn't get killed like he did.

Next day we marched thirty mile up the Rosebud, and within the first five we hit that Indian trail which Reno had found on his scout. Now I was still at the rear with them goddam mules, which was so slow that the main column would get miles on ahead, so when I seen the Indian trail, it had been overmarked in part by the iron shoes of the cavalry horses, but it was clear indeed that four-five thousand Lakota had made it, for it was no less than three hundred yards wide and the abandoned campsites along it showed the circles from a thousand tepees, not to mention countless wickiups.

Less than half the total population would be full-fledged warriors; but as you know, an Indian boy from the age of twelve onward can be quite effective with a deadly weapon.

In addition to the Ree, we had acquired from Gibbon's command a few Crow scouts—this area being home ground to that tribe. I figured Custer had plenty of advice on what could be read from the trail, so did not plan to offer my services again. Did not, that is, until I happened to speak to a lieutenant of the detachment that was guarding the pack train.

We had made one of our many stops so as to resecure the hard-tack and cartridge boxes that was always slipping off the mules, and I says to the lieutenant in command, pointing to the Indian trail that extended so far in width beyond our own: "Big village."

He smiles like I was a greenhorn and allows it showed a few hundred hostiles.

I asks if that was what the Crow and Ree scouts had reported.

"No, as a matter of fact it is not," says he. "But when you have been on frontier duty as long as I have, you always divide by three any estimate you hear from a friendly Indian. These Crows are good boys, but fighting is not their strong point."

Well, I have spoke about my worries for the Indians and then my disinclination to see these soldiers massacred, but I have so far not mentioned my growing concern for my own arse. I left that bastardly mule train pronto, and the lieutenant, figuring I was deserting, yells that I would never get my pay, but as usual he had the wrong slant, for I rode towards the head of the column.

Bloody Knife had sold me quite a broken-down pony. Indian-style, the animal was unshod and his hoofs had wore down real bad, so he was half-lame going over the rough terrain, the soil being flinty-hard and whatever grass had grown there was ate off by the immense pony herds of the Sioux. So it took me ever so long to pass the column and when I did, Custer wasn't at the head of it but rather a mile or two still beyond. He was famous for riding away out on point, in front of the advance guard and sometimes the scouts as well, and on other campaigns, so I heard, damn if he might not do a bit of buffalo or antelope hunting while he was at it. But he was looking for Indians now, and when I seen him upon a bluff at about three-quarters of a mile from where I was, it looked as if he had found them and got personally surrounded.

I whipped the Ree pony into a gallop and was halfway towards rescuing him when I recognized he was merely talking with the Crow scouts. By time I reached the bluff, Custer had gone off again, but the Crow was still there: White Man Runs Him, Half Yellow Face, Goes Ahead, and a young fellow named Curly. Also the guide and interpreter Mitch Bouyer, who was a breed of Crow and white.

I felt uneasy around the Crow, owing to my memories, and White Man Runs Him was old enough to have been a grown warrior in the days when I fought them. Indeed, he studied me from time to time, and while it was unlikely he really had my number, he must have Indianlike sensed something.

So I was glad to see the chief white scout come riding up from the other side of the bluff. This was a man named Charley Reynolds, a stocky, round-shouldered fellow, one of the few real good white scouts I ever knowed and no long-haired blowhard like Buffalo Bill Cody and some of them others.

The only trouble so far as talking to Reynolds went was that he was terrible quiet, keeping his own counsel to the degree that he got the nickname "Lonesome Charley."

"Charley," I says, and he immediately looks at the ground as was his custom when addressed, "have you told Custer how many Indians made this trail?"

He says: "Yep."

I says: "Because some of the officers think it is just a small band."

Charley shrugs and just keeps staring embarrassed-like into the ground while his horse stands dead still.

Mitch Bouyer comes alongside then and says, right rude if you considered him white, though understandably if you was conscious of his Indian blood: "What do you want?"

I answers: "To save my hair."

He says very factual: "That will be hard to do, for we are going to have a goddam big fight." He turned and rode back to the group of Crow a-sitting their horses all dejected.

Reynolds had looked up while Bouyer was talking, but when I turned back to him, he stared at the turf again.

"There's too many for him to take on alone," I says. "And I wager that's what he'll do. He won't wait for Gibbon and Terry."

"Nope," says Charley, in his soft voice.

"God damn it, man, you got to make him understand. I hear he'll listen to you."

"He won't," Charley says and knees his horse so as to move along, and I seen his right hand was wrapped in a bandanna, and asked if he was hurt.

"Whitlow," says he.

"Can you shoot?"

"Barely," Charley says and, by now exhausted with so much talking, he got away from me.

"Reynolds is just a yellowbelly," Sergeant Botts told me in camp that evening. "He begged Terry to let him off this campaign, claiming to have a pre-monition he would go under."

"Bottsy," I says, "you got a pretty poor opinion of most. I was wondering what you thought of me."

"Jack," says Botts, "there ain't a lot of you, but what there is, is all white."

Some men will get a great liking for you if you listen to them abuse others. At that moment, him and me was sitting within some bullberry bushes, getting drunk upon the contents of our canteens. I reckon it was the first real 100 per cent, lowdown, stinking, dirty case of inebriation I had been a party to since them days long ago as I wandered about the southern plains searching for Olga and Gus.

The result was that the next morning found me in very poor condition at the start of the longest day of my life.

CHAPTER 27 *Greasy Grass*

SATURDAY, JUNE 24, was a mean hot day, and the south wind served only to choke the men behind with the dust of them in front. It got so bad after a time that the troops was obliged each to march along a separate trail, so as not to stifle them following, and also to diminish the great cloud that marked our progress. For we was getting close to the hostiles, and it was just after the noon halt that we crossed the place where another great Indian trail, coming from the south, joined the one we had been on so far.

That was not long after we found the enormous abandoned campsite where the lodgepoles for a sun-dance lodge was still standing. On the floor of the latter was some pictures traced in the sand: lines representing pony hoofmarks on one side and them of iron-shoed cavalry horses on the other; between, figures of white men falling headfirst towards the Indian ranks.

My head was thumping, and the smell of bacon at breakfast had made me go off and heave. I felt so miserable of body that, in compensation, my mind rested somewhat easier than it had been. The Ree and Crow, however, waxed even unhappier than before, while looking at them sand drawings, and chattered to Fred Girard and Mitch Bouyer, their respective interpreters, for being Indians they was much affected by symbols.

Up come Custer shortly, and Bouyer tells him that the pictures meant "many soldiers falling upside down into the Sioux camp," which was to say, dead.

At that point I steps forward, saying: "General—"

But he interrrupts: "It's the teamster, isn't it? Well, teamster," Custer says, looking down his sharp nose, "I understood your place was with the mules." Yet he was not sore, but rather amused. "Or do I have it wrong?" he goes on. "I am only the regimental commander."

"Sir," I says, wincing from my hangover, "I don't know how good a job these scouts is doing. I believe the way they put their reports sounds to you like sheer superstition and you ignore it." Bouyer and Girard was giving me dirty looks.

"Whereas," I says, "the whole point of being an Indian lies in the practical combination of fact and fancy. These here drawings and bones was left purposely for you to find and be scared by. If you *are* frightened off, or go ahead and get whipped, then they will have constituted a prophecy. If you win, however, they will have been just another charm that never worked. But the important matter is that the hostiles know you are following them, and are herewith announcing they ain't going to run."

Custer had been showing a flickering smile. Now he throws back his head and makes a barking laugh. He once again seemed like his old self, rather than the sober figure he had become since leaving the Tongue.

"Teamster," he says, "I have the reputation of being a severe man. But I am also surely the only commanding officer who could stand and listen to the recommendations of a mule skinner. I have a partiality for colorful characters—California Joe, Wild Bill Hickok, and so on—in whose company I should say you belong. Charley Reynolds is a splendid scout, but he is too quiet."

He laughs again, taking off his gray hat and slapping his boots with it. "This campaign has been altogether too humorless! Very well," he says, "you wanted to be a scout. You are one as of this moment. Your orders are to stay with me, to say whatever comes into your head, and not to bother these other fellows."

So that's how I was appointed official jester to the commander of the Seventh Cavalry, as a result of merely telling the truth. Now you might think I took offense at it, but you would be wrong. It meant that I might be even more ineffectual than when traveling with the mules, for everything said by a man who is an authorized idiot, so to speak, is naturally taken as idiotic. But I would be at the head rather than the tail of the column. Maybe I could even jolly Custer out of the worst mistakes. So I accepted the position, and that threw the General into another laugh, and Girard and Bouyer got the idea, too, and laughed, and so did the Crow and Ree without understanding, but Indians is always polite if possible.

Now my orders might have been to stay with Custer, but that was unlikely for any human being, even one without a hangover and riding a better mount than my half-lame pony, for the General's reputation for energy had not been exaggerated. Back and forth he rode upon Vic and when he tired that animal out, the striker would bring up Dandy. Scouts was ever coming in with reports, but Custer would generally go out a mile or more to meet them. Then back he'd trot and maybe continue along the column to speak to one of the troop commanders. All the while, his adjutant, Lieutenant Cooke with the enormous mutton-chop whiskers, was writing out orders and sending them hither and yon by means of couriers, and replies come back and Custer'd read them in his quick, impatient way sort of like an eagle.

His brother Tom, a carbon-copy of the General with the characteristics less authentic—like he was more impudent than truly arrogant, with his hat on the side of his head, etc.—Tom was generally in evidence at the head of the column rather than back with his troop, and to get in on the importance he would also send messages to the pack train and so on; and the other brother Boston as well as the nephew Armstrong Reed, both young fellows, they was usually to be seen acting as if we was on a picnic outing.

So I was largely ignored and never had no more chance to amuse the General, had I wanted such, the rest of the day, nor indeed didn't talk to nobody except once or twice I tried to strike up a conversation with Custer's striker—not the man from the Washita, but a fellow named Burkman, but he was almost a moron, wearing his cap way down to his eyes, and a butt for everybody's wit.

We marched thirty mile and went into camp at eight o'clock of the evening, but in come the Crow scouts shortly with a report that the Sioux trail had swung west and crossed the Wolf Mountains in the direction of the Little Bighorn, or Greasy Grass as the Indians called it, so at about midnight we started to move again. I don't believe anyone had got a wink of sleep in the interim, for the news had soon went around that the hostile village was expected to lie in the river valley, in which case we'd attack it at dawn.

Of course during that halt, I encountered Botts, who had ate a quick meal and went wandering about sticking his nose in everywhere.

"What did I tell you," he says. "Hard Ass will pitch into the Indians tomorrow, a whole day before the junction with Terry and

Gibbon. And by the time they come up, he can deliver that village all skinned and gutted, compliments of the Seventh Cavalry. Curse his dirty heart," he says, "but you gotta hand it to him."

I warns Botts to keep his voice down, for we was right near the headquarters tent, but he says nobody would hear on account of Custer was holding a officer's conference there and was deaf to anything but his own voice.

Then Bottsy says he had to get back to his troop and take care of the men. I don't want you to have the idea he was not a good sergeant.

"Them recruits," he says, "is already dragging their tails from these long marches and some ain't fired a carbine more'n once or twice, nor seen a red excepting the coffee-coolers around the fort. If fired too fast, them Springfields heat up and the ejector sticks. I reckon the agents have fitted out the hostiles with repeaters, which can panic a man unless he realizes our pieces got twice the range of the Winchesters and Henrys."

Them recruits made up about a third of our force. Some was Irish, and some was Germans who come over here to dodge the draft in the Old Country, couldn't find no jobs, joined the U.S. Army, and was killed by savage Indians before they learned English: real peculiar experience.

As me and Bottsy was parting, we heard the officers in the tent sing some sad old songs: "Annie Laurie," and the like, and then "Praise God from whom all blessings flow," which took me back to my days at the Reverend Pendrake's church. As singing, it wasn't too good, I expect, but sounded very nice there in the wilderness and some of the enlisted men gathered around to listen.

Then, maybe to cheer people up after the plaintive and melancholic selections, they ended up with "He's a Jolly Good Fellow."

Bottsy says: "If they mean Hard Ass, then it's sarcastic."

So the column got into motion again and marched all night, going up a little creek off the Rosebud that led west towards the Wolf Mountains. It was right dark, without a moon, so them behind had to follow the leaders by the smell of dust and the sound of swinging equipment; whole troops kept getting lost, and there was shouts and curses and the banging of tin cups to locate them again, so when first light come about half-past two, we had done only some six miles and had not had no sleep since the night before.

However, we had reached the Wolf range by now, which really

ain't mountains but rather just bad country, steep hills and ravines and such between the Little Bighorn and Rosebud valleys, and went into camp in a coulee big enough to hide the whole regiment, where the idea was we could stay until the following morning, then cross the divide and at dawn strike the hostile camp which was expected to lie on the other side.

Now I had flopped upon the hard ground and tried to take a snooze, but never had no more success at it than most of the troopers. I wager to say that once again nobody slept during that halt: we was all too tired. The water thereby was so alkali the horses would not touch it; coffee made with such will take the skin off your tongue—which some of them recruits discovered there for the first time.

I don't think Custer sat down, except upon his horse, at any time during that morning, nor took a bite of food. He wore buckskin pants with a long fringe down the leg, blue-gray shirt, gray hat, and boots that come to just below the knee. Around his waist was a canvas Army belt holding two holstered English Bulldog double-action pistols and a hunting knife in a beaded scabbard. The stubble on his cheeks was substantial now, for he had not shaved in ever so long; and being fair, it looked white. I mean because his face otherwise seemed so aged, them hitherto clear blue eyes being bloodshot from loss of sleep, with pouches beneath.

But he wasn't slowing down none, and when word come in from the scouts that from a high point ahead they had spotted the Indian village fifteen mile upriver, he was washing the trail dust off his face from a bowl placed on a tripod. Quick he folded his collar back and leaped onto the bare back of Vic without even drying himself, for the air would do that as he rode: already in early morning you could feel it developing into a real scorcher. Off he went to alert the troop commanders, and within the hour we was on the trail again towards the pass across the divide.

The Crow and other scouts had stayed upon the butte from which they had made their observations, and when the column reached its vicinity, Lieutenant Varnum, the scout commander, come down and says: "General, our presence is known to the hostiles."

"No," says Custer. "No, it is not." He spurs Vic into a trot up the slope.

Varnum goes after him, shouting: "Sir, we encountered six

Sioux and gave chase, but they got away, riding towards the village."

Soon the ground got so steep and rough we had to dismount and walk the rest of the way to the top of the butte, and Custer still outdistanced everybody else. Varnum looked utterly perplexed.

"He won't believe there *is* a village," he says.

On the summit was the Crow and Ree, Mitch Bouyer, most of the white scouts, and Lavender. The view to the northwest, down the Little Bighorn valley, must have been good were the air clear, but at this hour it was obscured by the midmorning summer haze you get in that country.

Nor had Custer brung his field glasses. The Crow, however, possessed an old battered brass telescope, and White Man Runs Him handed it to the General.

"Look for the smoke of their fires," he says in Bouyer's translation. "And the big horse herds on the benchland to the left of the river."

Custer stares through the instrument for a minute. "I cannot see a thing," he says.

Goes Ahead says: "Look for little worms. That is how ponies look at this distance, like maggots upon a buffalo hide that has not been fleshed."

Custer gives the telescope back to White Man Runs Him. "No," he says, "there is no village."

Bouyer now speaks for himself, with an unhappy expression on his swart face: "General, there is more Sioux in that river bottom than I ever seen in thirty years out here. I swear it."

"No," says Custer, and walks briskly to where the orderly is holding his horse.

Back we went towards the column, and when still a half mile away, out rode Tom Custer and says to the General: "Armstrong, they have seen us!" A box of hardtack had fell off a mule, and when a detail of men went back the trail to fetch it, they found it being opened by a Sioux with his hatchet, had fired on him, but he escaped.

I don't know if Custer then changed his mind about the village, but so long as his kin had reported it, I guess he at least believed there was hostiles in the neighborhood, so had the trumpeters call in the officers and told them to prepare to attack immediately since surprise was so longer possible and the Indians would have time to scatter if there was further delay.

The weary troopers mounted their tired horses again, and the Ree called Stab spit on some magic clay he carried and anointed the chests of his fellow tribesmen as a charm against misfortune, and shortly we moved out and across the divide.

That was about noon on that fateful Sunday, June 25, 1876, in the hundredth year of this country's freedom, and though it be ever so long ago I recall it like it was happening this instant. I can get to sweating when I think of the heat of that day and how my flannel shirt clung to my back and how the dust got into my nose and coated my tongue, and I guess owing to my changed point of view that country did not look so attractive as my Indian memory of it, being chopped up and washed out with ravines and now and again tufts of reddish-brown grass or shabby gray sage.

Having crossed the divide, we reached the headwaters of a small creek that in spring must have been a tributary of the Greasy Grass, but now its bed was bone-dry pebbles. Right here it was that Custer made the division of his forces that a lot of people have criticized him for, but if you understand the situation as he saw it, what he done wasn't necessarily foolish.

He did not believe there was a village where the scouts said, though he did think it was likely the Indians was someplace along the river, between where we would reach it following the dry creek, and Terry and Gibbon's column coming up from the mouth.

It was however possible that the Sioux might be going upstream towards the Bighorn Mountains and would get around our left flank. Therefore Custer sent Captain Benteen and three troops to diverge from the main column on a left oblique and scout across the bluffs in that direction until he could see whether the upper river valley was clear.

My friend Botts was with Benteen's battalion, so off he went with the contingent. I never seen him again my life long, though I don't believe he perished.

Of the remaining eight troops, Custer kept five and gave three to Major Reno, and the two columns rode side by side descending through the timbered creek bottom which widened as it neared the river. I reckon we had come ten mile and two hours from the divide when we sighted that single tepee. There it stood, on the south bank of the creek, with some Indians clustered about it, and as often happened, we almost charged before recognizing they was our own scouts.

It was a Sioux lodge, and all about it was signs of a recently vacated camp with warm fire-ashes, and Lieutenant Hare tells Custer that when he and the Crow approached, they run off fifty-sixty hostiles.

Fred Girard rode up on a knoll from which he could look into the Little Bighorn valley, and he now waves his hat and shouts: "There go your Indians, running like devils."

"Bouyer," Custer orders, "tell your Crows to pursue them."

So Bouyer passes that on to Half Yellow Face and the rest, and they chatter among themselves for a time, and Custer gets furious at the delay and when Bouyer says the scouts refused, I thought from the General's expression he would have pistol-whipped them had there been time.

"They are afraid," says Bouyer. "There are more Sioux along the Greasy Grass than there are bullets in the belts of your soldiers."

"You are women!" shouted Custer, and them scouts knowed enough English for that and winced like they had been struck, yet still they sat upon their ponies while that blue dust cloud raised by the fleeing hostiles plumed above the valley.

I dismounted and went into the tepee. Inside was a body of a Sioux brave, dressed in fine clothing and resting upon a low scaffold, not dead long enough to smell, and there was Lavender, a-standing alongside.

I says: "Know him?"

He says he never, and turns away and ejects the shell from his Sharps, inspects and reinserts it, does the same for his revolver, and cleans his knife upon his shirt though it looked clean enough. Then some of the Ree set afire to the tepee, so we left it and mounted and Lavender bends over his saddle to give me his hand. His face was all powdered from the dust. He never said a word, nor did I, for there ain't no rules on going into a fight about how to leave your friends. Me and Lavender was just matter-of-fact, I expect, having gone over everything long since.

So he tied the feathered hat tight beneath his chin and trotted his bay pony after Reno's column, which had started to move briskly towards the river.

"Where they going?" I asked Custer's orderly for the day, a trumpeter named John Martin who was an Italian just come over from Italy, his real name being Giovanni Martini, and he didn't know English very good.

"Make-a de charge," he says.

"At what?" I asks.

It seemed that Lieutenant Varnum had gone ahead to a ridge and seen a village several mile downstream, so Custer at last believed there was such, when a white man told him, and we was going to attack it.

When Reno's rear troops had gone by, Custer's command fell in behind and followed till we neared the river. In later arguments about the battle, some said Reno expected, on fording the river and advancing up the bottom, that the General would come behind in support. I don't know about that; I never heard what orders Custer had give on that occasion, being inside the tepee with Lavender.

What I do think, though, is that he had an idea to use again the tactic with which he had had success at the Washita, where he also divided his force and struck the village from several points simultaneous, for we was still some distance from the ford which Reno was crossing when Custer turned right and led us off on a course roughly parallel to the river but behind some bluffs which cut off a view of it. It seemed to me that the plan was for us to get downstream a mile or two and ford over at that point and strike the lower end of the camp while Reno was attacking the upper.

I remember thinking then of how in a similar maneuver at the Washita, Major Elliot's command had got cut off, and right while Custer was elsewhere winning, the Cheyenne slaughtered Elliot. That incident was supposed to have touched off Benteen's hatred for Custer, and now Reno might be in similar jeopardy. Or maybe Benteen himself, for with only three troops he was away off to the left, and nobody really knowed how many hostiles there was nor exactly where they was situated.

For example, Custer didn't seem to be in no hurry. He had slowed his pace after that turn to the right—which was O.K. by me on that pony of mine, but looked odd when you consider Reno's fight was about to begin at any minute. Also I was uneasy at the sight of the terrain ahead. I did not claim any good memory of this stretch of the Little Bighorn from years ago, but what I did recall was that them northern rivers sometimes are bordered by real high bluffs that go on for miles without a break that will let you down to the water, and even when you arrive there you cannot rely on finding a ford.

Yet Custer was dawdling, and even stopped to water the horses at a little creek we come to. That was the place where I went up to him, and Tom was also there, and his brother-in-law Calhoun, and I thought again how he had sent off Benteen and Reno but was careful to keep his own family about him.

He looked quite drawn, I thought, and had his hat off to fan himself in the heat, and damn if I didn't wish at that moment that he never had cut his hair.

But soon as he looked at me, he started to smile. "Yes, teamster," he says, "do you wish to submit your plan of attack?"

"No sir," says I, "I don't mean to jest now. I know something of this country and it don't look to me like we are going to find a ford for several mile."

Tom pulls his blond mustache in annoyance and says: "Armstrong, why do you tolerate this idiot?"

"He amuses me," the General says. "Don't you, teamster? He is a frontier eccentric," he goes on as if I wasn't there. "You know I am partial to the type."

Then I noticed that newspaper correspondent Mark Kellogg, dismounted and holding his bridle over an arm while scribbling in a notebook. Now he says: "Would you repeat that last phrase, General?" "*Partial to the type*," Custer says very distinct and slow enough for it to be copied. I seen then that he was holding an interview right there.

"Thank you, General," Kellogg says. "Now would you care to characterize your mode of operation as we pause on the brink of battle?"

Custer brushed some trail dust off his shirt. "Very well," he says. "I have been called impetuous. I resent that. Everything that I have ever done has been the result of the study that I have made of imaginary military situations that might arise. When I become engaged in a campaign and a great emergency arises, everything that I have ever heard or studied focuses in my mind as if the situation were under a magnifying glass. My mind works instantaneously but always as the result of everything I have ever studied being brought to bear on the situation."

He was going to say more, I think, but at that moment his adjutant, Lieutenant Cooke, who had rode down to the river with Reno and stayed awhile on the near shore as observer, come dashing back, his whiskers flying like birds at his cheeks.

He reined in and shouted from his foaming mount: "Girard reports the Indians are coming out to meet Reno, and in force."

As if to exemplify his self-estimate, Custer leaped into the saddle of his mare and asked: "Where are the hostiles?"

"About three miles downstream when I received word," Cooke says. "By now Reno must have engaged them." And indeed a few seconds after that we commenced to hear the snapping gunfire.

"How big is the village?" Custer asked, but Cooke didn't know on account of the river bent like a corkscrew downstream and there was cottonwood timber in every bend which cut off the view.

The trumpeters sounded the order to mount, and there was some confusion getting the horses away from the water, but Custer didn't wait, he galloped furiously up the northward slope to a ridge beyond and everybody followed as best they could for two mile of rough travel which was brutal to the horses, and I believe several dropped from exhaustion and their riders stayed behind with them, thus being unwittingly saved from the slaughter soon to come.

Then we halted again, though the animals was so excited by now that a lot was out of control, especially in the hands of them recruits, and you had rearing, bucking, and a certain panic back along the column. But I must say for my own pony, who had looked to drop dead earlier at a smart walk, in an emergency he got himself together somehow and did right well: I guess his tough Indian breeding showed up, and then it was more his type of terrain than for them big cavalry beasts.

Now we had been traveling more or less parallel to the course of the Greasy Grass, but behind the bluffs, and Custer ordered the halt so he could go out to a high point and look down at the situation in the valley—his first such of the day, remember, excepting that morning long-range view from the Wolf Mountain Crow's Nest, from which he could not make out a thing. And up to this moment, he had still not seen one live, hostile Indian with his own eyes. It was real strange, as if some sort of charm was at work.

If so, the spell commenced to break now, for as we rode out onto the bluff above the river and looked into the western bottom, we saw enough Indians to satisfy any appetite. I'd say five-six hundred was massing against Reno's command, which had dismounted and gone into a skirmish line that appeared a thin blue necklace at our distance and elevation. He had only a few more than a hundred men. And we also seen where the enemy was coming from. There could be no further doubt as to the existence of a village: it started a mile or so downstream and God only knowed how far it went, for on account of them loops of the Greasy Grass, we saw only the lower end—though I still wasn't sure that Custer understood that. But figuring on the warriors charging Reno, and the visible tepees, the redskin population could not be far below two thousand souls.

Once that was realized, however, the situation was still not desperate in any wise. All together the Seventh Cavalry numbered some six hundred men, trained to fight in an organized way: for example, the efficient manner in which Reno went into the skirmish line. A very small party of dismounted men, controlling their fire, could handle many times their number in unorganized savage riders.

If we could get down to the next ford, Custer could strike across into the village and thus relieve the pressure on Reno, and Benteen would no doubt be along in time to reinforce either command. Also, back the trail the pack train was coming on with reserve ammunition and its cavalry guard.

Well, it didn't seem as bad to me as it might have been—though it wasn't no picnic, either—but I looked at Custer and seen he was hit real hard. He stared angrily into the valley, jerking his head a little and squinting in the sunlight. I figured he was mad at Reno, who had been ordered to charge the hostiles, and even though that was now manifestly impractical, it would have been like Custer to hold it against him.

But then the General suddenly takes off his gray hat, waves it into the air, and cheers. Since we others there with him—brother Tom, Lieutenant Cooke, the orderly Martin, and myself—never joined in, it sounded right odd. With that raspy voice of his, it might have reached the troops in the valley had all been silent there. As it was, it never had a chance, amid the firing of white and Indian guns, savage war cries, and the rest. Not to mention that you don't usually hooray at a defensive action.

Then he wheels Vic around and dashes back to the troops. Tom Custer's orderly was there, and the General barked at him: "Go tell the pack train to come directly across country to join us." In other words, not to follow the twisting trail we had made so far, nor to make no attempt to reach Reno, though he would soon need ammunition at the rate them carbines was firing.

Well, that was another man saved: I mean the orderly, Sergeant Kanipe. The rest of us started off again at a wild gallop across that upland country, following Custer's breakneck lead upon his mare, his personal guidon whipping along just after, the red-and-blue swallow-tailed pennant showing crossed white sabers, as borne by a trooper on a fine big sorrel. We detoured around the worst draws and steeper cutbanks, leaped some and negotiated others, but it was a horse-killing ride and again some animals dropped in their tracks, saving a few more lives as their riders stayed behind, though I heard some of them never did reach the rear but was ambushed on the way. For unbeknownst to us the Indians had started already to cross the Little Bighorn to our side and infiltrate the coulees.

I reckon we went more than a mile in that fashion and come just below a ridge that was the highest point in the region, when Custer called still another halt. Again he rode out and up for observation, and the same little party accompanied him as before, me included, and his nephew Armstrong Reed, too, who had come on the campaign for a summer outing. It was reflected on the latter's young face that, so to speak, I first seen the magnitude of that gigantic Indian camp which lay across the river.

I happened to glance at him as my pony reached the summit. Now Reed was a right handsome young fellow, like all the Custer clan, and his habitual expression was one which blended civilized breeding with eager interest. You saw that on a lot of Eastern lads who come West for adventure in them days, like the frontier was some type of exhibit put on for their education and entertainment, rather than the often mortal matter it was for us who lived there permanent.

Reed's officer-uncles had fitted him out in a buckskin suit like their own and hung some weapons on him, and a comely sight he was, a-sitting his fine animal on that elevation. But something awesome was murking his clear eyes and setting his beardless chin to tremble, and if you think I shall deride him for it, you are wrong, for then I looked myself into the valley, across that ribbon of river and beyond the fringe of timber dark in the sun, and saw the biggest encampment of savages ever assembled upon this continent.

Almighty God, it stretched farther than the eye could limit, five mile anyway of clustered tepees and on the benchland to the west grazed their herd of twenty thousand ponies. I give that figure, allowing it might have been bigger, for I couldn't see it all. But in my days along the Canadian River down south, I had observed them great masses of buffalo, and this was the closest thing to that vista.

How many Indians? I reckon the number was in the neighborhood of the pony population, for though certain braves might own several animals, there was always a multitude of women and children who walked. Say fifteen thousand individuals, four to five thousand of them warriors. And we was two hundred-odd with Custer, another hundred with Reno now fighting for their lives, about the same with Benteen, and another hundred or so back escorting the pack train.

But here's the queer feature: other than a few distant figures moving among the pony herd, and given the assumption that a great dustcloud downstream was raised by human beings, *we still did not see an Indian on our front*. There was not a soul in that part of the camp in our view. Was they all up engaging Reno? That field was now out of sight owing to the bluffs and the twists of the river. Or that cloud of dust downstream: was they, despite that strength, running away?

I'll tell you what Custer did. He waved his hat again, and damn if he didn't cheer once more!

"We have caught them napping," he says to nobody in particular, and it was appropriate that nobody seemed to hear him but all continued to stare down as if paralyzed, though Tom Custer was almost chewing off his mustache and Lieutenant Cooke jerked fitfully at his muttonchops.

Then for me the moment was broke when that Italian orderly Martin, or Martini, grins into my face and says: "They sleep, yayss? Is good." He never knowed the English expression, see, and anything his General said was literal to him.

Well, I didn't have no time to disabuse him, for as Custer descended to where the troops was waiting, I rode alongside. I had suddenly realized what the Indians was up to. They wasn't running or else the women would have been striking the lodges, for which there was ample time with us up in the high ground across river and Reno as distant as he was.

Nor was the force advancing on the latter nearly large enough to comprise all the warriors of a camp this size. Somewhere was a good four thousand more, and I thought I knowed their general situation: they had crossed our bank at one of the lower fords and awaited us in the ravines ahead.

No, Custer did not laugh when I yelled this at him. I don't think he heard me at all, just kept spurring that poor mare who had been hard-rode now for miles on a hot and dusty day and was lathered and just about blown, and when he reached the command, he cheers again and shouts: "Hurrah, boys, we've got them! We'll finish them up and go home to our station."

And them troops, who hadn't no sleep to speak of in more than twenty-four hours, a quarter of them green men who never faced a warring Indian, mounted on exhausted or panicky animals, they give a cheer back at him, a rousing sound that echoed off the ridge, and once more we went into the gallop, larruping down a wide ravine for say three hundred yards, then another halt. Which I reckon piled up the column again, but I didn't look back at them, it being no pleasure to study men who was about to be wiped out.

Oh, I knowed it for sure by then. That second cheer of his had done it for me: Custer had lost his mind.

Another type of person, seeing that huge village, might have admitted at least to himself that he made a mistake. Nothing shameful in it: in Indian-fighting a general seldom knowed the strength or disposition of the enemy. Some say Custer disobeyed his orders not to strike the hostiles until the time agreed on for his junction with Terry and Gibbon, the following day. But you can't count on that sort of thing in the wilderness, and besides, he believed from the incident of the Sioux discovering the lost hardtack box back in the Wolf Mountains, that they'd know our presence and escape unless he attacked forthwith.

But having once seen the village and not backing off and pulling Reno out and getting the whole command assembled— Well, I expect Custer was crazy enough to believe he would win, being the type of man who carries the whole world within his own head and thus when his passion is aroused and floods his mind, reality is utterly drowned.

I was near him on that halt, and his hat was askew from being put on and off in premature victory celebrations, sweat streaked the dust on his stubbled cheeks, and his eyes was glazed, their usual bright blue gone milky.

He called the orderly, and Martin came up and saluted in his Italian way. Custer then spoke rapid as the firing of a Gatling.

"Tell-Benteen-it's-a-big-village-and-I-want-him-to-be-quick-and-bring-the-packs."

I doubt Martin got it, but he gives another florid salute and is ready to start off, only Cooke cries: "Wait, I'll write it out," and scribbles in his order book.

This was the last message anybody received from Custer and the five troops that followed him north from the Lone Tepee. You can read in the histories that Martin made it, riding back along the trail we had come. Foreign as he was, he did not understand the situation and the Indians tried to bushwhack him along the way but it didn't bother him none even though his horse was hit. Shows what ignorance will do for you. Reaching Benteen, he told him we had the Sioux on the run, giving that officer another reason for not coming to our aid. I mean, besides his hatred of Custer.

From here on you have only my word for what happened to Custer and his five troops that Sunday afternoon, *for I am the only man what survived out of them 200-odd who rode down Medicine Tail Coulee towards the ford of the Little Bighorn River.*

If you don't believe it, go find another: one of them cranks who wrote letters to poor Mrs. Custer in later years, some of them still children in 1876; or the Crow scout Curly, who used to be exhibited around as the sole survivor of the battle. Except that Curly was not upon the field, but only watched a portion of the fight from a distant ridge, and the white claimants was either nuts or just plain liars. It has been amusing to me to hear of men who sought recognition for what they never done, while I have been at pains until now to conceal my true experience.

It wasn't long after Martin went that the ravine intersected with the big coulee called Medicine Tail, into which we turned left and descended a couple mile towards the river, with about one more remaining when it opened into a flat. We halted there briefly, for Mitch Bouyer and the Crow, on the high ground above, was waving their arms and Custer stopped to get their sign message. They could see the ford from that position and signaled that the enemy was crossing over.

Custer interrupted the report with impatient gestures, and with his hands said: "All right, you can go home now."

The Crow had not been hired to fight—and you remember that they had refused to earlier—but to lead the column through this country which they knowed. So you could see Bouyer dismiss them, and they sat their horses up there for a while as we started to move again, looking down at us in that redskin way that is always called stolid, and so it is, though that don't mean they haven't no feelings, but rather that there isn't much to be done about white men by even a friendly Indian. Them Crow always liked Custer, you see, and I heard that the whole tribe cried like babies when his death was known.

Bouyer could have left too, but being a breed his pride was involved, I guess, at the sight of men to whom he was connected by a portion of his blood, going to their death. He followed the others for a few yards, then with a sudden effort wheeled his horse and come down to join us, galloping to Custer.

Ahead the flat narrowed again to form a steep gorge the sides of which was almost perpendicular cutbanks, for this coulee drained the high ground in the spring thaws and rains. You couldn't have found a less congenial place for cavalry, which ain't worth a damn without room to maneuver.

Bouyer pointed at it, and says: "If we go in there, we will never come out." He was wearing buckskin and a broad-brimmed hat, but his black hair was long and he wore some Crow gewgaws, a bear-claw necklace and a medicine charm tied at his left ear.

Custer gives him a curious look. "I said you could go home," he says.

Bouyer lifts his glittering black eyes towards the sun, his face brown as a hide, and while he did not speak I reckon he was bidding goodbye to that great fire in the sky, Indian-fashion, though ready to die as a white.

We entered the gorge at a fast trot, the five troops in formation, column of fours, and along come brother Boston to join us; he had been in the rear with the pack train, where I suspect his kin had wanted him to stay for his health, but come action, no Custer could be denied it even by another of the same clan.

Within each company of the Seventh, the men rode matched mounts: Tom Custer's C Troop on sorrels; Troop E, gray horses; and the other three commands on fine bay animals. The guidons was swallow-tailed American flags with concentric circles of gilt stars within the blue field. They fluttered throughout the column, amid the rising dust as we descended that dry coulee, hearing nought but our own hoof-thunder.

I looked over my shoulder from time to time, for in a fight I like to know who's behind, and I can still see in memory that gray-horse troop, always easiest to distinguish, a-trotting in orderly fours. But Tom Custer's sorrels, in the leading company, was right handsome too, and almost red in the brilliant light.

God, it was hot along there. We had left the wind up on the

ridges, and I yearned to go into the gallop to get some breeze upon me. My hatband was sopping. I had the brim pulled down low to shade my nose, which was considerably burned from previous bright days. I had not shaved for a spell, and with dust and sweat intermingled, my sandpaper cheeks was right scratchy. I chewed a plug of tobacco to keep my throat wet, circulating the plug from side to side on my tongue, but suddenly it wasn't juicy no more but raspy as a cactus burr, and I could hardly hold the carbine, the metal parts of which was searing hot from the sun. Salt sweat stung my eyes, and Cooke's white horse ahead was too fiery-light to bear looking at.

We had reached some five hundred yards of the ford when we seen the first enemy on our front all day: several Sioux was riding in slow circles just this side of the river, either to tease us into chasing them or as a signal to others in hiding. The camp was now concealed owing to the stand of cottonwood along the far shore. Then the Sioux vanished, and from behind a little rise above the ford appeared four warriors. They brandished their weapons overhead and shouted at us: "*Hey-hey-hey-hey-hey*."

At which Custer forthwith halted the column.

I knowed that sound too well: it was the Cheyenne war cry. Then I done a funny thing. From unstudied instinct, I throwed my carbine to the shoulder and pulled off a shot. Missed them, and Custer started shouting at me, his eyes blooded and his face blackening with rage.

"You swine," he says, "who gave you that order to fire? *I* am in authority here. I'll have you shot for this. I don't care how highly placed your connections, you rotten spy, be they in the White House itself. This is what comes of your damned Indian policy, corrupt agents, venal politicians."

I think in his warped mind he had come to identify me with President Grant. Now he drew his pistol and I guessed was going to shoot me down, but like a madman will, he suddenly changed his whole mode of thought, and spurring his mare, cried: "Forward, the gallant Seventh! CHA-A-A-A-A-RGE!"

Now the trumpeter, spooked by this performance, sounded the Dismount call upon his instrument, but even that was too thin to be heard beyond the leading troop, and I reckon them behind couldn't see much for the dust, so what you had was Custer larruping down the coulee. then Cooke, Bouyer, and me strung out between, and then that first company climbing off their horses.

Meanwhile, down at the ford, five hundred more braves had swarmed across the Greasy Grass, and more was coming like bees out of a shaken hive.

CHAPTER 28 *The Last Stand*

IT WAS BOUYER who reacted first. Riding a fleet Crow pony, he overtook the General and detained him, seizing Vic's bridle. The Indians was firing at them, and Bouyer was wounded, I think: a dark stain showed on his buckskin shirt, but he never paid it no mind.

Cooke meantime got the troop remounted, after they delivered some answering fire as skirmishers, for it was obvious we would have to get out of that narrow place to where the cavalry could maneuver.

Now Custer suddenly recovered, the charge was sounded properly, and down Medicine Tail we dashed, almost to the water, and the Indians, most of them dismounted, fell back, though not so far we could have negotiated the ford against them, the Greasy Grass being clogged with warriors, hundreds on ponies and more wading chest-deep.

Another ravine opened at a forty-five-degree angle to the right, and we plunged into and up it, coming to a hogback ridge which we gained, galloping along the grass-covered bench under heavy Indian fire, though I don't believe we had yet lost many men, maybe a few near the ford, but the command was still in good organization, riding in column of fours. A mile or so north the ridge reached its summit, and I reckoned Custer was a-heading there as the best place to make his stand.

But when you run from an Indian, be it orderly withdrawal or not, he gets amazingly encouraged, figuring he has the momentum on you. We had started to attack the village and been stopped by four Cheyenne, then drove off: that's how them hostiles saw it, and events was proceeding to prove them right. I don't know why

Custer had halted at that first puny demonstration, four savages against our two hundred. Maybe in his crazy view he thought that was the entire enemy force and was caught by the idea that Indians was so brave. I don't think he could endure the thought of another person than he having the capability of courage in the grand degree.

Only they wasn't just four and had not showed foolhardy gallantry, but was rather demonstrating to gain time while others crossed the river behind them and still more lay concealed in the ground towards which we would be deflected. They was using strategy.

A peculiar reverse of roles took place that day upon the Little Bighorn. Reno had been sent to charge the village and instead was himself charged. Custer, going to envelop the enemy, had got it done to his own self. In their last great battle the Indians fought like white men was supposed to, and we, well, we was soon to arrive at the condition in which we had planned to get them, for this wasn't the terrain for cavalry and our order commenced to dissolve somewhere along that flight.

And now come a new host of Indians from the south. Led by the great war chief Gall, though we didn't know it then, who had just repulsed Reno and besieged him upon that bluff where Custer had took his first look at the village. They was at least a thousand strong, and riding in dread certainty.

Meanwhile, on the slope towards the river, the Gray Horse Troop was getting all cut up by Indians hidden in the draws along there, and finally they was run into a deep ravine and piled up on one another and slaughtered by Sioux shooting down from above, with only a couple of riderless horses left to plunge wildly up the vertical cutbanks.

Custer was still acting well. He throwed Calhoun's company against Gall as dismounted skirmishers, but them Sioux forthwith left their own ponies and advanced crawling through the sage, shooting arrows from concealment, hundreds at a time, which having reached the limit of their lofty arcs, descended in fearful volleys, piercing men who could not see an enemy to fire at.

Some Indians encircled the troopers detailed as horse-holders, every fourth man in the company, and leaping forth stampeded the mounts with screams and flapping blankets. So Calhoun was henceforth pinned in place. They then begun to diminish his line from both ends towards the center, knocking off the skirmishers one by one, and at last come out of the grass in a great naked brown wave, yelling *Hoka Hey!*, the Sioux war cry, from a multitude of guttural throats, and washed over him.

That's what struck me, the sight of savage flesh, for the Indians was stripped to the breechclout and most was not painted nor wearing their bonnets and other gewgaws usual to their battle costume, and taking no coups except upon the dead. Most fought afoot, with no frenzied displays of courage, and taking every advantage of cover. My God, there was a lot of the latter on that awful field: it was like a big sponge, with its gulches and draws, and now and again as if a mighty hand was a-squeezing it, it seemed to heave and savages would well out of every nook, drowning another portion of the command, then be absorbed once more into concealment.

But they took quite as much toll upon us when in hiding, with them arrow-volleys swishing through the sky, and had their rifle sharpshooters too, though there wasn't near as many guns on the Indian side as some people think; they simply used well the few they had, most of them not repeaters, either.

I had a seven-shot Winchester carbine, but would have give anything to trade it for the old Sharps single with which I had hunted buffalo, for we in Custer's party was now upon the summit of the ridge, farthest distant from the enemy as befits a general in defensive action. Below us and on a lower rise was Tom Custer's sorrel-mounted troop, and to the left, Keogh riding to fill the gap caused by Calhoun's collapse; then that deep draw into which the Gray Horse Troop had been run and slaughtered, and farther to the right, one platoon of Captain Yates's F Company, at this moment being rolled up by a great press of savages who shortly spilled through and engaged Tom and the remaining platoon of F.

So there was much to watch of the meanest kind of sight, and nought to do at that range. I mean for me: for Custer there was plenty, and he was so far doing it fine, though at the disadvantage of being by personality and training a cavalryman to the core, which is to say, having the offensive character. He had never been backed up this way before and denied the possibility of his beloved charge. Our horses was worthless here, and some of the men in headquarters detail had started to shoot theirs and make a breastwork of their carcasses, for any fool could see the ridge would soon be engaged. And to show you how normal the General was at this time, he had

Lieutenant Cooke take down the names of the troopers who did this and swore to court-martial them on the return to Fort Lincoln.

This was the next second after sending a courier to move Keogh against the Sioux what had run over Calhoun, who was after all Custer's brother-in-law and now evidently deceased, though as the time passed we could see less and less through the gigantic pall of gunsmoke and milling dust that was turning the middle afternoon into late twilight.

So when Keogh in turn got his, we knowed it mainly from the volume of hostile yells, and then come Tom Custer's men, dismounted and their horses lost, backing foot by foot up the rise towards our position.

Right about then, the first shot sounded from behind us, where there was a sharp slope to the northwest which fell into an encircling ravine. No one had paid that ground much mind, what with thousands of hostiles on the other three sides, so it had filled up unopposed with Indians who had traveled the long way around, another thousand if there was one, and now advancing up against us, they commenced to sound their cries: *Hoka Hey, Hoka Hey*, and some yelled the name of their great people, *Lakota! Lakota!* The Men! The Men!—but predominant even over these was the simple, throaty *Hey-Hey-Hey-Hey-Hey* that started like a funeral drum and then increased in tempo to where it was a madman's raving, though without disorder, a directed passion if you can imagine that, the wild and merciless fixed upon a single aim and undistracted. They was Cheyenne, and they was at the center of the world.

That first shot killed Custer's horse, hit white-stockinged Vic in her pretty sorrel head, under the left eye. She fell gradually, front legs as if in a dainty bow, giving the General time to step off before the hindquarters toppled over and crashed.

The most glorious cavalryman of all was now unhorsed. He looked a little bewildered, but was soon brung straight by the sight of the oncoming Cheyenne, so ordered the troops to do what he had but lately condemned: shoot the remaining mounts and arrange them into a breastwork. Before that was done, we had several casualties.

Utterly surrounded now, with C Troop backed up against a cutbank below our knoll and nothing in Keogh's direction but smoke and, when that parted occasionally in the slow wind, Indians, Indians, Indians, ever closer and in greater amount, the wonder being that there was ground enough to hold them, and I thought of Bouyer's prediction that they exceeded the number of our bullets. He had been a wise man and a brave one, and I seen him fall as we swung away from the ford, closest any member of the command ever got to the big village on the Greasy Grass, and him a breed.

The other Crow was long gone back to their people, though maybe that Curly watched part of our fight from a distant rise, for the next day he reached the *Far West* upriver and give a story of the massacre that no one believed. But he was not there upon our ridge. We had no friendly Indians left, the Ree having went with Reno. Nor did the Sioux and Cheyenne have any whites on their side, as has sometimes been said by them who wouldn't believe savages could fight so well: bitter ex-Confederate officers, squaw men, renegades, etc. Not so. Our adversary was 100 per cent red. It was simply that they no longer fought for fun, but was out to kill us in the most effective manner, with the least damage to themselves. Despite their swelling numbers, with your rifle at the shoulder you had hardly a target. They was creeping and crawling, and could vanish behind a tuft of grass no larger than your hat; a scrawny sagebush hid a score. But then go to reload and see them gain thirty yards.

Nevertheless, our boys was keeping the Springfields busy, until what Bottsy had mentioned as the weakness of that piece commenced to show: the action heated up under constant use, and the fiery sun, though blotted out by the blue murk, contributed no little, and them ejectors stuck, the spent shell locking in the breech. Some worked at it with their knives, breaking off the blades to no purpose. That type of thing might make for a panic while a hundred Indians slither towards you personally, but the fact is that I never saw no disorder among our troops once the situation turned desperate. The Sioux later claimed that a whole platoon down on Keogh and Calhoun's front committed suicide; I never saw such and won't believe it happened.

There wasn't no cowards up on the ridge. When the carbines jammed, the men used their revolvers, about as effective as spitballs like the schoolboys throwed back in Missouri. And the Indians being so numerous, it was hard to see a casualty among them when we dropped one, so had no encouragement from whatever toll we took.

Counting what was left of Troop C below the cutbank and those of us up top, I reckon we now numbered seventy-five to a hundred. No more firing could be heard from the direction of Keogh, and it had long since been silent towards the right, where Yates's command and the Gray Horse Troop had obviously gone under, though you couldn't see through the pall.

I was working my Winchester constantly towards the Cheyenne and might have hit a few from behind the carcass of that Ree pony, who I had shot in the forehead in necessity but regret, for he done a a fine job when the chips was down. I didn't know then that his old master Bloody Knife had been rubbed out down in the valley with Reno, but on looking back, I reckon *he* did: his big sad eyes showed a willingness to go when I pushed the Colt's barrel between them, and them saddle sores had rubbed open again in the course of that wild ride, so it was in several ways a favor to him. He continued right useful in death, being soon all porcupined with arrows, which in his absence would have perforated yours truly, now half under his belly, for them high-arching volleys was on the increase, hundreds of steel points descending through the murk, like it was raining razors. Fellow near me, sprawling flat, got stapled down in two, three places, but never killed until threshing about to free himself he fetched his head high enough for a bullet, collecting several, expiring still fastened.

That was the trouble: lay flat and you'd get pinned, stand up and you faced gunfire, roll under a horse's belly and you was temporarily safe but out of action, letting the Indians advance to where they eventually could walk in and kill you like a snake.

Now General Custer did not consider such a decision for himself. He was walking about through all this and had so far come untouched. And I don't mean crouching, but striding erect and pointing, sometimes with both arms out in different directions like a standing cross, in which case he must have been a target of maximum visibility against the sky for them Indians lower down. Occasionally he'd fire his Bulldog pistols, always with a classic stance he must have learned at West Point, elbow bending like a steel hinge, forearm rigid. Arrows flashing by him, lead singing, he was as if upon the firing range of some quiet fort.

He was a spectacle for fair, though strewn with dust from short-cropped head to leathern toe, sweat-streaked, blue shirt open at the neck, face like coarse stone from the stubble of beard. And smiling! By God if he was not, and you could hear his raspy voice going along the ridge, calling men to fill a gap here, commending some others for holding on there, ever confident and of good hope.

"Splendid, splendid," he says, standing there above me, and just as I took a breath, having missed a crawling Indian down the slope with the last three shots then in the magazine, and looked at him, a Cheyenne arrow come close enough by his neck to have feather-whipped it.

I says: "General, won't you get down?" But had no more luck with that than anything I had ever said to him in our whole history.

He stared back with eyes like blue gems through the dust on his countenance, fanatic as an idol, and says: "Splendid, boys! We have them on the run now!" And went along the skirmish line, kicking the troopers' boots in encouragement, only some of them covered the feet of dead men.

Well, his example might have been heartening to the ones who could see it. I recognized he had gone crazy again, like when charging the ford alone, which surely accounted for the failure of the arrows and lead to touch him, for missiles are reluctant to strike a man who has gone out of himself by reason of madness or medicine.

I turned back to shooting Indians, or trying to, as they squirmed through the tall grass below and their serpent heads popped up briefly, always slightly elsewhere than anticipated, for they was expert from birth at this type of fighting and though I had been trained to it myself, the advantage was nullified by our position on that gravel-topped ridge with no cover but the fallen animals.

Next we come under new fire from a neighboring rise sixty-seventy yards to the southwest, signifying that F Troop had definitely went under, for they had commanded that slope. The loud reports of Government carbines was heard everywhere, pointed towards us, quite a different sound from when they are with you, shooting away, and easy distinguished from the pop of weapons with a lighter load.

The hostiles grew better-armed by what they captured, turning our own weapons against us, not even troubled with them ejectors: having all the time in the world, they wouldn't fire so fast as to overheat the breech. They was getting plenty of ammunition from the saddlebags of the troops what had been rubbed out, whereas we was running low. The pack train was somewhere back the trail, and if you recall, Custer had sent it several messages to come on; but there was a nice problem in how it could get through the enemy host. Indeed, I supposed it had itself got wiped out by now, along with Reno and Benteen: not a stupid conclusion when you understand I reached it while riding a splinter, so to speak, on a roiling ocean of hostiles, amidst a smoke-fog which lifted now and again only to reveal a further loss.

Now it was C Troop, there below, all gone except a handful what scrambled up to us and fell behind the horse-corpse barricade, some hit in the back while so doing and belching blood onto the present occupants who pulled them in to add to the growing mortuary. Tom Custer was not of that number, so had got his, I expect. And young Reed was near me, one minute a-working his expensive sporting rifle and the next stone dead with his mouth open and tongue turning black, and I never saw Boston at all: he had probably dropped on our ride up from the river.

So as man, the General had lost two brothers, a nephew, and very likely his sister's husband; as commanding officer, the better part of five troops; as cavalryman, his mount. In smaller things, his hat was gone and one revolver; the other he was firing, down on one knee now. His pants was tore, and most of the buttons off his double-breasted shirt, where he had ripped it further open to relieve the heat.

Mark Kellogg, the journalist, lay on his face in the gravel, presumably gone under though there was not a tear on his back anywhere, and from his coat pocket protruded the rolled foolscap of his last dispatch, never sent. Sergeant Hughes, what carried Custer's personal guidon, was terribly hurt from a gut-wound that curled him up on the ground like a caterpillar around the point of a sharp stick, yet somehow he kept the banner from touching dirt. It hung limp except when feebly stirred by the passing of arrows.

I haven't mentioned my own wounds, though I had received a couple. I had been struck in the left shoulder by a ball from a muzzle-loader, I reckon, for it had enormous power behind it, lifting me right off the prone position, reversing my head with my boots, so my spine whomped onto the ground and I couldn't breathe for a minute. But I returned to place directly and got the Indian who done it, for he seen me go over and confidently exposed himself while reloading and nobody else was left to fire at him for thirty yards on either side of me. I give him one in the breastbone and let it go at that, having to conserve ammunition; down he went, and his pals pulled him back into the grass to die or recover, I would never know.

They done the same with all their casualties, whereas ours lay around us, and the dead horses, and owing to the heat the latter was ready to ripen soon, the laid-open flesh already growing dark, and there was even more flies on that hill than Indians, for commotion don't touch that miserable little beast. I had a few at my bleeding shoulder, feeling their tiny feet where I still could sense no pain. I had also been scored across the cheek by an arrow, at an angle so that the blood trickled into the corner of my mouth, from which salty taste I discovered it in the first place.

But that hangover, now, that was altogether gone, along with the depreciating effect of no sleep for two days: nothing like a massacre to clear your head. I don't believe my sight was ever keener, before nor since. Too bad there was nothing to use it on but savage enemies and sage, since I figured my seeing would soon end along with everything else. There couldn't have been over thirty-forty of us left. I don't know how long we had fought so far; sometimes it seemed like a whole lifetime and at others as brief as a sneeze since that gallop down Medicine Tail Coulee and then up onto the ridge.

I was conscious of somebody falling nearby and turned and seen it was Lieutenant Cooke, his magnificent whiskers a-swimming in gore; had been crawling along the line and got up too high for a second, his last. Then Custer come along, erect no more but his belly scraping the gravel. There was blood on him, too, splattered from someone else, I believe, for he was not yet wounded.

"Cooke," he says, and nudged the adjutant's lifeless form. "Cooke, take an order for Benteen." And then spitting the dust and stones out of his mouth, he says, "Cooke, write this down: 'Come quickly, and the day is ours.' . . . Have you got that, Cooke?"

"He's dead, General," I says.

"Get the name of the man who said that, Cooke," Custer snapped, his eyes red-veined and not looking either at me or the adjutant but towards the head of my fallen pony.

I don't know, I guess I felt sorry for him then, so I took up the role of Cooke and he never detected the difference.

I says: "Yes sir, I'll take care of it." And Custer mumbled some and rolled over on his back, his hands behind his neck, and looked into the sky and smiled as if at secret knowledge. Another of them great arrow-masses vaulted overhead, catching sunlight on the ground edges of their iron points, and coming down like sleet through his field of vision.

He never wavered—and as it happened, these was doing less damage now, for there wasn't many targets left to hit—but says in an easy tone of voice, like a genial scholar:

"Taking him as we find him, at peace or at war"—them arrows come swooshing down to stick upright all over dead men and horses—"at home or abroad," Custer goes amiably on, "waiving all prejudices, and laying aside all partiality, we will discover in the Indian a subject for thoughtful study and investigation."

I took time to discourage about fifty savages from advancing for a minute or two; I was fast running out of shells, for as our number dwindled I fired more frequently in compensation. And while I was so doing, Custer lay a-chattering away to himself.

As I reloaded, I heard him say: "It is to be regretted that the character of the Indian as described in Cooper's interesting novels is not the true one. Stripped of the beautiful romance with which we have been so long willing to envelop him, transferred from the inviting pages of the novelist to the localities where we are compelled to meet him, the Indian forfeits his claim to the appellation of the *noble* red man."

A rift opened up above him, and he smiled at the blue sky there revealed, lecturing at it with a dirty finger.

"We see him as he is, and, so far as all knowledge goes, as he ever has been, a *savage* in every sense of the word."

Well, he had an altogether appropriate subject, you could not deny him that, and his discourse was being embellished by the gunfire and howling of five thousand individuals of the very race; and I thought I could hear the devilish screeching of the women from the quarter nearest the river, and knowed what they was up to: clubbing the last sparks of life from our boys who lay wounded there, and mutilating all.

But that parting of the smoke took my attention then, for it lengthened gradually towards the southeast on some random current, and after a time you could see a good three mile across the stretch of ridges and bluffs by which we had come to this place, and the sun was on that far high point where Custer had took his second sight of the village, where I seen in Reed's young face the beginning of the death in which he now lay.

And a tiny flicker showed there! No Indian lance-pennon was large enough to be visible at the distance, no war bonnet would flutter so, a flapping blanket would be darker, bigger; besides, all the

Indians in creation was investing our hill. It had to be a cavalry guidon, I reckoned, had to be, though I surely could not verify the color at that range.

"General!" I says, yelling through Custer's monologue. "Look there, look there!"

Now you recall his crazy lone gallop towards the ford, from which Mitch Bouyer rescued him, and afterwards he turned normal again and done as good a job of leading as a man could under the circumstances. Well, he had seemed even farther gone at present, what with that raving, but I kept a-shouting at him anyway, and finally he moved his dull eyes towards the east, and then instantly they ignited.

"That's Benteen!" he snapped, and scrambled to his feet, erect again amid the hail of missiles and impervious to them. "Come on, boys," he shouted to the sprawling quick and dead along the ridge, "give a volley to direct him!"

Then caught up his own guidon from the lifeless clutch of Hughes, who had now expired, and waved it in great semicircles, and on the signal of one remaining lieutenant with an arm all bloodied, we sounded in unison whatever pieces still functioned, twenty carbines maybe and some pistols, enough to make a goodly report.

Then a bugler was called around for, but none was left. So Custer had us salvo again, and he was about to order a third when the officer informs him we wouldn't have enough shells left for another. Now I seen some of the Indians towards the outside of the throng against us, off a half mile or more, mount their ponies and head towards the peak where Benteen was supposed to be, and reckoned they had seen him too.

The distant flicker continued for a spell, getting no closer, and then the smoke from the volleys drifted across our view and cut it off forever. The last hope, and not a real one at that, maybe, for I expect he could never have got through with his hundred and Reno's similar number, and they too would have been slaughtered. Well, you can read how he made a try and was discouraged by that movement of Indians in his direction, and him and Reno retired to the hill where they was soon besieged by the host who had finished us off.

But I'll say this, and it might be biased on account of my own situation: Benteen never tried hard to relieve us. At this time only a few hundred Indians started against him, whereas we retained thousands. He had the pack train with its reserve ammunition; we possessed too few cartridges to sound a third volley. He hadn't done no fighting yet at all; our carbines was jammed.

Reno might have been a coward, but not Benteen, who wasn't afraid of nothing: not Indians, and not Custer, and besides, he was an honorable man, so well liked by the troops that I had got tired of hearing how wonderful he was. Which might have been my personal predilection against popularity, being generally alone in the white world as I had always been, but Custer was about to die now, while Benteen survived, and you have to admit that makes a difference.

So we fought on and no help came and one by one the remaining guns fell silent, but the Indians still didn't make no overrunning charge, just surged ever closer so that we was as if upon a diminishing island in a river at flood. Finally I fired my last carbine shell, broke the stock against the ground and poured gravel into the breech; it wasn't permanently ruined but at least no savage could turn it against me without some prior work. Then I drawed my Colt's and thought to get the knife out of my left boot-top, but discovered that arm was altogether lifeless owing to the wounded shoulder: no pain, just gone to board. Well, by time it come to blades I didn't reckon to be still among the quick, anyhow, so let the idea drop.

Around then, Custer come back. He had gone to the extremity of our position, still trying to signal Benteen with the guidon, I expect, and while there an Indian ball had splintered off the flagstaff halfway along, so he was now holding it by the stub. But as to his person, he was yet untouched by enemy fire, however ravaged by smoke and dust and heat and madness.

I looks up at him, and blue eyes glittering within that mask of dirt, still staring southeast into the white fog, he says aloud though to himself: "Benteen won't come. He hates me."

I had stopped worrying about him standing erect: it didn't matter much now whether he was hit, and then too it did provide some inspiration even for me, for I tell you it was absolute death from two foot off the ground on up, now. A fly couldn't have got through unsinged, so we didn't draw no more of that insect, though them that was there, feasting on our broken flesh, by the same token couldn't get away when engorged.

Custer wasn't singing, like Old Lodge Skins at the Washita, addressing his gods and walking in the magic way of the Cheyenne. No, the General stayed intact because he was Custer, better than anyone else, basically invulnerable even in defeat, and always right. You got to admire that type of conviction, even when you resent it. And I did both.

I says: "Hates you so much he would let two hundred others die to do you in?"

"Spite," says Custer slowly, "spite and envy. I've had to face them my life long."

He was speaking quiet, and there wasn't enough noise left of our firing now to obscure a word. "I would have liked to be his friend, but envy intervened. For each of my achievements I have paid bitterly in lost affection. People love only the weak, teamster. Now make a joke of that."

He was quite clear, you see, more so than at any time since we had come upon the ridge. He recognized me again, in my false role to be sure, but at least he wasn't talking to himself no more. He smiled through the dirt, and despite what he just said, not sardonic in any wise but as if in serene resignation. Then he fired several rounds from his pistol at what seemed, from his stance and firm aim, to be particular targets, still holding that battle guidon, now tattered, on its broken staff in his left hand.

He was hit then, just once, a tear in his shirt directly over the heart. He turned some to favor the force, dropped the banner, clutched at the wound as if rather in courtesy than anguish. Onto his back he fell, arms outflung as though crucified, but his closed mouth still showing the traces of a smile. He might have went to sleep at a picnic. I couldn't see he was bleeding at all, but he must have been, somewhere. I had finally accepted that fact that he was great—and he sure was, don't let anybody ever tell you different, and if you don't agree, then maybe something is queer about your definition of greatness—but it stands to reason he had blood.

There was about a dozen of us left when Custer went under, and we might have lasted a half hour longer. I can't say whether the rest of them troopers—the officers was now all gone—knowed that the General had died. They was right occupied with their own business, single particles of life scattered throughout the dead and dying, and over-all ideas of unit and leader and even race was hard to grasp by now, for fighting to the end is apt to make you awful single-minded. If Benteen had showed up at this time, we likely would have fired on him.

But he never, of course, and the bugle that commenced to sound on the slope towards the river was blown by a Sioux Indian who took it off a dead trumpeter, and he didn't know any of the calls, naturally, and just blowed sour blasts. They was many of them yelling, too, and singing in their falsetto, and now no longer conserving their ammunition, for there wasn't no need, so you had a lot of firing for the hell of it, with the smoke thick as pudding.

Still they did not charge. Finally I had only two or three cartridges left in my pistol, and I expect the rest had likewise or less, and we stopped firing altogether. I tried to look around once more to see who I was going to die with, but that stiffness from my shoulder had permeated my whole body now, and I was fair rigid, so lay my head upon my pony's belly, from which all warmth was long gone, my hand holding the Colt's alongside, and waited.

Waited, waited . . . Soon the whole field, a square mile of it, fell silent, so quiet I could hear the buzzing of a fly on my face-wound, and then I twitched my cheek, where the blood had dried like a strip of patent leather, and I could hear *that* crack. It would not have been hard to imagine everybody had gone home.

Ten minutes, fifteen—no chronometer could have measured that time, might have been thirty seconds or two hours, and then I heard a scraping on the far side of the pony and raised my eyes just as the head of an Indian, with one big eagle feather and a crimson parting of his black hair, reared slowly up across the animal's spine. He had a wide brown face and wore no paint.

The muzzle was damned near his nose when I fired, and his brains was blasted out before his eyes knowed it. Then shots sounded everywhere among us, scuffles and cries, and we was overrun.

Almost simultaneous, I got a thump on the skull and had the thousandth of a moment to sense that something landed on my back, light of weight yet all-enveloping. I figured it was Death, and thought: *you sneaky bastard, I might have knowed you would get me from behind.*

CHAPTER 29 *Victory*

I SMELLED SOMETHING SPICY, followed by a host of other scents, then commenced to hear drums, first only the big one in the back of my head, the beats of which at length smoothed out into one continuous dull roar, and then the regular smiting of them a distance off. And the voices, frenzied and ranging from a deep-throated howling to the highest quavering falsetto screech, almost at the pitch of a whistle.

I opened my eyes real careful, naturally expecting to find myself down in Hell, and first thing I seen was the flames, all right, and the next was the Devil himself, looking exactly like I had always figured he would or maybe worse: two horns sticking up from his forehead and his face was crimson-colored, and he had two big white fangs and the nastiest eyes you could imagine: they was outlined in white.

He was crouching alongside me and peering at me, and as I expected he might bite or something, and I too sore and weak to move, I was a-fixing at least to spit into his face, for I believe demons must operate on the same principles as people: show them you are helpless, and you'll get no mercy.

But before I had gathered enough spittle onto my tongue, the Devil says something to me in the Cheyenne language.

"Are you awake?" he says.

Well, that was fair: I had been killed by Indians, so had gone to the redskin Hell. I says: "Yes I am," and let it go at that, for I would have liked to sass him, but as you know there ain't no real curse words in the Cheyenne tongue, except to call a man a woman.

"All right," he says. "Then you know that you and I are even at last, and the next time we fight, I can kill you without becoming an evil person."

Then he leaps up with a whoop and runs out of the tepee—for

that is where we was—and other than that buffalo hat, G-string, and moccasins, he was naked though painted from head to toe. For he wasn't a devil but rather an Indian. Indeed, he was Younger Bear.

The flames was the little fire in the center of the lodge, of course, and the door flap was pulled back so I could see the glow of a bigger blaze outside, with the shadows of many moving bodies, the silhouettes of legs.

"He goes to dance," says a familiar voice nearby, "but you had better stay here awhile."

Old Lodge Skins sat there upon the buffalo robe, taking the fireshine onto his walnut visage.

"Do you want to eat?" he says.

I struggled up to the sitting position, feeling like a sack of loose meal, then tested with my fingers the stricken portions of my being. My left shoulder was all tied up with leather, moss, and stuff having a sweetish odor; and there was something that felt like raw mud upon my cheek-wound. My head was O.K.: that is, it ached awful, but the skull didn't have a break you could feel.

Finally, I says: "Grandfather, I did not expect to see you."

"Nor I you, my son," answers Old Lodge Skins. "Do you want to smoke?"

I says: "Then I guess I am not dead."

He reaches over and pokes me with a finger hard as horn. "No," he says, "if you were a spirit, my hand would go right through your arm as if it were smoke." The fact that I was talking to him, see, wouldn't make no difference neither way: he spoke a lot to the deceased, not only of humans but animals as well.

I asked him when it was as to time.

"The Human Beings and the Lakota rubbed out all those soldiers on the ridge," says Old Lodge Skins, "by the time the sun was here." He showed me on the horizon of his hand: looked like around five-thirty or six o'clock. "This," he says, "is the night following that, and everybody is dancing to celebrate the victory. Tomorrow we are going to kill the rest of the bluecoats on the hill downriver. It was a great day."

He sighs and goes on: "I am too old to fight any more, and as you know I cannot see through my eyes, but a boy led me up to Greasy Grass Ridge, which overlooks the place where the soldiers were. I could hear the battle and smell it and see a great deal in my mind, which is better than the eyes under those conditions, because I was told the smoke was very thick anyway.

"Almost the whole Lakota nation is here, and they are splendid warriors, the second best in the whole world. But naturally the Human Beings are foremost."

He was getting excited, commencing to sweat on his bare old belly, with that ancient scar, and his blind eyes was shining.

"The Hunkpapas have a wise man named Sitting Bull. Some days ago they held a sun dance on the Rosebud, and he cut his flesh a hundred times and saw a vision of many soldiers falling into camp upside down. Then we moved to the headwaters to hunt buffalo, and some soldiers shot at us, so we whipped them."

This apparently referred to the column led by General Crook, coming up from the south, and showed why Terry and Custer never made a junction with him.

"So then," Old Lodge Skins went on, and he now fetched out of the mess behind him a hatchet and was gesturing with it, "we moved here to the Greasy Grass, and some people believed those first soldiers were the ones that Sitting Bull dreamed of, but others said: 'No, because they did not fall into camp. More will come.' I did not join this argument, because while the Bull is wise, he is also easily spoiled by a lot of attention, and Gall was getting jealous of him. Which is not good."

I could agree with that, after my recent weeks with the Seventh Cavalry, and was kind of relieved to hear of it happening also among Indians. I did this in the forefront of my mind, though, for still deeper than all else, and it stayed so for many days, months, years, was them last moments with Custer on the ridge. You are not the same afterward when you should have died and didn't.

Well, Old Lodge Skins talked on and on, through the night while the drums kept on outside and the victory dance continued, the great fires illuminating the entire valley while Reno and Benteen's little command cowered up there on the bluffs. I fell off to sleep from time to time, having good reason for it if ever a man had, and I don't guess the chief thought it bad manners, for he was not necessarily addressing me anyhow.

After the Washita, his band and him come north, across Kansas, Nebraska, and into the Dakota Territory: some eight hundred mile, most of it on foot for you recall how Custer shot them ponies and the rest of that camp run off, so Old Lodge Skins and his surviving people could not obtain much help. If they got anywhere near ranchers and cowboys on that hike, not to mention soldiers, they was fired on automatically, so to speak; and whenever they sighted buffalo, why, there was white hunters with the long-shooting rifles that could kill either animals or Indians at a half mile. The Human Beings did not overeat on that long walk.

I asked about Sunshine and Morning Star, and the chief says they had not been with him and since he hadn't heard they was killed, he figured they must have joined the Cheyenne what stayed in the south with the Kiowa and Comanche. I never got a further report on them two, nor did I ever look for them in later days. If Morning Star is still living somewhere down in Oklahoma, he is half white and eighty-five years of age, and his Ma some twenty added onto that, and I have always hoped they owned a patch of land with some oil on it and never had to sell blankets to tourists to support themselves.

Then, without my asking, Old Lodge Skins said: "That yellow-haired woman of Younger Bear's died on the long walk north, and their boy, also with yellow hair, was captured from us by soldiers in a fight on Medicine Bird Creek. My son Little Horse was rubbed out at the same place, and many others too, and there was hardly anybody left when we reached this country.

"But once here, we met some more Northern Human Beings, and all the old troubles due to the mistakes of youth were now forgotten, so they welcomed us, and our friendship with the Lakota became very close because the great Oglala named Crazy Horse married a woman of the Human Beings. So we hunted and ate well, for there are still buffalo here, and more people joined us, warriors like Gall and Crow King, and the war chief of the Human Beings, Lame White Man, also Two Moon, and Sitting Bull made medicine, and last week we beat the soldiers on the Rosebud, and today we rubbed out even more on the Greasy Grass, and tomorrow we will kill the rest on the hill."

I expect you could say Olga had been another who died as a result of what Custer done at the Washita, but he was beyond my holding anything further against him, and anyway she had not been my woman for quite a time. Poor Swede girl: she had a strange life.

As to Gus, in afteryears I looked for him throughout the central plains, but there wasn't no white men nor Indians who ever heard of

Medicine Bird Creek, which must have been its Cheyenne name. So I could not get a line on him. But I should still today like to find my boy, and would pay a twenty-five-dollar gold piece to the person who can give me information on him.

And Little Horse gone too, never again to wear them beaded dresses and show his graceful ways.

"I guess it was Younger Bear who conked my head up on the ridge today," I says.

"Yes," says Old Lodge Skins. "Then threw a blanket over you and carried you across the river to my tepee. That was not easy to do, for our people went crazy with joy when the last soldier fell, and in the confusion, Indian was killing Indian, and many hands clutched at Younger Bear's burden so as to rip you apart, but he owed the debt, and also I have no other sons left now but you."

Finally I fell into a sleep of some hours, the first real rest in a couple of days of hardship and bloodshed. It might sound odd, but I felt safe and right in that tepee with the blind old man a-droning on, though outside, the savage exultation was ever mounting, and I reckon there was more than one Indian who had a sore throat next day and stiffer limbs from dancing than he had got in battle.

But they was most of them up again bright and early to invest that hill where Reno and Benteen was holding on. There wasn't nothing I could do about that at present though I didn't like to think of the fact that Lavender, Charley Reynolds, Bottsy, and my other friends was with Reno, unless they had been killed in the valley. But I was confined to Old Lodge Skins's tepee by my own desire, one white man somewhere in the middle of that enormous assemblage of lodges me and Custer seen from the bluffs the day before.

I woke up remarkably improved as to physique, though, my shoulder right tender but a lot of the stiffness had gone already and I could almost feel that moss or whatever it was drawing the rest of it out. I had thought the ball-joint had been busted, but if it was, it somehow healed too in the succeeding days and give me fewer twinges throughout the years since than that old wound in my other shoulder where I got shot in Dodge City.

My facial crease also was knitting up under the mud plastered there, and I didn't know I had it unless I laughed—which I wasn't doing much of at present.

Old Lodge Skins was still sitting there when I awakened and investigated my hurts. It was another warm, bright day outside, the sun half penetrating the tepee cover, the fire gone to white ash.

"Who was the doctor?" I asks him.

"Younger Bear," says he. "Do you want to eat now?"

One of them fat wives of his come in then from her cooking fire outside, bringing me a bowl of boiled buffalo. Everything was going on as normal, for Reno's hill was across from the upper end of the camp, whereas the Cheyenne circle was furthest downstream and out of earshot of the firing—the village was that big.

I took the bowl from her who handed it to me without expression, and ate some, and then I said: "Grandfather, do you want to hear what I was doing with the soldiers?" For he never would have asked.

"I am sure you had a very good reason," says he. "Let us smoke first."

So we exchanged the pipe, and then I says: "Do you know who led the bluecoats? General Custer."

He tried two or three times but was unable to pronounce the name, nor of course did it mean aught to him.

"Long Hair," I says. "Only now it is cut short."

"Now it is probably cut *off*," says he, laughing at his typical Indian humor.

"The Washita," I says. "He led the bluecoats there."

"Oh, yes." Old Lodge Skins nodded pleasantly. "I remember that fight. It was bad, but we rubbed out many soldiers in the tall grass."

Well, I was stubborn as him, and persisted: "Did no one ever talk about who led the soldiers there?"

"A white man," says the old chief. "They were all white, except for some Osage scouts, so it must have been a white man whom they followed, for nobody would follow an Osage." Then he got to telling experiences of his own in fighting the Osages as a young man, and it was ever so long before I could get back to the subject.

"This man used to wear his hair down to his shoulders," I says.

Old Lodge Skins asks: "Like a Human Being?"

"No, he didn't braid it."

"Then like a white woman," says the chief. "Was he a *heemaneh?*"

I was sure getting the worst of it. Now it may seem funny, but I felt I owed something to Custer. After all I survived him, and by God he was not 100 per cent to my taste, but he had impressed me, dying the way he did. He had worked out a style and he stuck to it.

He might have been a son of a bitch, but he was his own man, never whining nor sniveling nor sucking up to another, be it even the President of the United States.

But I guess I could never get that across to an Indian, for independence was the rule rather than the exception amongst them and thus not the occasion for any special merit. Nor could any one of them, no matter how exalted—not Crazy Horse not Sitting Bull nor Gall—order two hundred others to perish along with him. That was the difference. Whatever Custer believed, he did not die alone. So while as a Caucasian you could call him a man of principle, from the Indian point of view you might say he had no principles at all. Especially since soldiers, unlike savages, did not fight for fun.

I decided to drop the subject, but as I might have figured, Old Lodge Skins now got right interested in it. He says: "I want to go see this unusual man, or whatever is left of him, my son. Will you lead me to the ridge?"

I'd sooner have made my bed in a campfire. But Old Lodge Skins pointed out that the warriors was all miles upstream, and the women and children had got finished with most of their mutilating and stripping the bodies on the evening before, so it would be quiet there, and I could put on a buffalo hat like Younger Bear's and leather shirt and leggings, painting my face. Not to mention I would be with him.

Well, them wives of his helped me into the new getup, cutting down an extra pair of the chief's leggings, and a couple little kids was also there, his I reckon and only six-seven years old and him at least ninety by now, and I needed a breechclout, so one of them women handed me a company guidon of the Seventh Cavalry, which was a swallowtailed version of the Star and Stripes. I am happy to report for the sake of fellow patriots that I never employed it for this purpose. I don't curse in front of ladies and don't degrade the national colors, not even in an emergency: I used my old bandanna.

But those wives had got into the spirit of the thing now, giggling away as they disguised me as a proper savage, dropping necklaces and such over my head, and finally they come with a beaded belt to which they had just tied a number of fresh scalps.

I says, "No, no!" And they pushed it at me, with magpie noises, and my hand struck against one skull-cover, and it was real black and woolly of texture, and I caught it and held it up, asking: "Where did you get this?"

Traded it, they says, for a blond one which Younger Bear had give them, to a Hunkpapa Sioux who fought upstream in the valley against the first bluecoat attack.

I don't know if you can appreciate what it feels like to hold the scalp of a friend.

"It came," says the fattest wife, "from a Black White Man whom the Hunkpapa recognized as a person who once lived with his tribe and married a Lakota woman. 'What are you doing here?' asked the Hunkpapa in surprise. 'I don't know,' the Black White Man said. His horse had thrown him and he was lying on the ground with a broken leg, his rifle some distance away. 'Well, you were shooting at us, so I think I should kill you,' said the Hunkpapa. 'I think you should,' said the Black White Man, so the Hunkpapa did."

Even so, I reckon it was better than working your life long as a yardman back in Missouri.

Taking Old Lodge Skin's arm, I left the tepee and walked through the Cheyenne camp towards the ford, which was not far, for the Minneconjou village was just next door. As the chief said, all the warriors was up at the current battle and nobody was around but women, children, and aged men sitting in the sunlight and chewing their toothless gums. Some of the women was working as usual, but others was loudly mourning their dead husbands, sons, and brothers, for the Indians had lost some men themselves, only they didn't count them: maybe forty or fifty. They had erected a funeral tepee in the Cheyenne camp, with the bodies inside on scaffolds, and killed a number of horses, arranging the carcasses outside like spokes of a wheel.

The youngsters was playing in the sunshine. I seen a boy that had a little toy horse made from dried clay, and it wore a curious saddle blanket, a folded U.S. greenback. There was also other Seventh Cavalry souvenirs in evidence: one woman wore a blue jacket with a corporal's chevrons, some other kids was skimming a campaign hat through the air, and lying on the ground at one point was a pair of Army underdrawers, which had the name of the late owner stenciled across the waist. Further on, a shirt stiff as parchment from dried gore, torn canvas cartridge belts, discarded boots. Near to the ford the volume of this stuff increased, and small boys was watering pony herds there, among them a few big bays and sorrels with the conspicuous brand "7USC."

Nobody paid mind to us, not even among the Minneconjou

women who was washing clothes in the Little Bighorn, and me and Old Lodge Skins entered the river, fast-flowing and waist-deep, and waded across. I have mentioned my outfit, but not his: the chief had donned his full war bonnet of eagle feathers, which was a little moth-eaten if you examined it close but for all that a magnificent piece of headgear, each plume tipped with a puff of white down and little round mirrors at the temples, and trailing a long tail of more feathers which brushed the earth back of his heels. His face was painted crimson, and yellow lightning flashed across the cheeks. In one hand he carried a large bow, a special one, unstrung and with an iron lancehead affixed to one end. In his other hand he had that old medicine bundle I remembered from the Washita and further back: its skin wrappings was rotting away to dust in one corner and a bird-foot good-luck charm was protruding. I kept an eye on it but did not poke it back, for you wasn't supposed to touch another's medicine nor even know what it consisted of.

I saw where we had rode down Medicine Tail Coulee less than a day before. The ground was tore up with hoofs, and there was the marks of iron-shoed cavalry horses going right down into the water, but we hadn't got that far, so they must have been made by captured animals the Indians took across to their camp.

We walked a mile or more, up the diagonal ravine that Custer had took for his retreat, then onto the slope, proceeding ever higher towards that final ridge, and it was a good way before I seen the first body, though there might have been some that fell into the many gulches thereabout or been thrown there after being stripped and mutilated.

But soon they commenced to show up, at a distance pure white in the brilliant sun, like a field of boulders, one there, then two or three, others in groups of a dozen, lying where they fell and almost all by troops. Wasn't no sign of disorganized panic; they had been whipped but not routed. And when you thought of the proportion of recruits, the exhaustion of two days without rest, and the overwhelming strength against them, they had done real well.

Now Old Lodge Skins says suddenly as we toiled up the rise: "This fight has given me a better opinion of white men. I did not understand before that they knew how to die properly."

"Can you see them, Grandfather?"

"Almost," he says. "Their bodies shine so."

But as we come closer, the marble-white was not clear, but

streaked and sometimes drowned in red which the heat turned brown, and the smell was starting up too, attended by millions of flies, and the birds rose in great circles at our approach and coyotes scampered off to a safe range. There was also maybe a hundred dead horses spread across that square mile.

I gritted my teeth and held my breath and trudged on, with the ground as it were sucking like quicksand at my moccasins though it was dry as ash. Yet I continued, for Old Lodge Skins had some high purpose in coming here. He was hardly a ghoul. And I guess I realized that it was only through him that I could ever come to accept the fact of that awful ridge and make it a part of normality.

"Yes," he says, breathing deep through his ancient leathery nostrils, "they must be happy on the Other Side to have died as warriors rather than tenders-of-cattle or corn-growers or crazy diggers-of-yellow-dust or those-who-lay-down-iron-for-the-fire-wagon. I tell you, my son, I had thought for a long time that all white men were turning into women."

He stopped for a minute so's I could rest. True, that night's sleep had done wonders for me, and also the dressing on my shoulder; but it was remarkable I could walk at all, let alone climb uphill. Old Lodge Skins himself showed no physical strain, though out there in the sunlight you could appreciate his advanced age: them ravines in his face was so deep that a fly would think twice about treading the bluffs above them. Indeed, his visage was a sort of miniature of the ground on which we stood. And his withered skin, wherever it could be seen for the paint, made the hide wrappings of his medicine bundle look almost new.

He turned now and seemed to take a view across the entire panorama, holding the bundle to his chest and pointing with the lance-head-end of the bow, from which two eagle feathers dangled.

"There came Gall with his many Hunkpapa," he says, "and there Crow King. Down there, Lame White Man and the Human Beings, Minneconjou, and other Lakota peoples broke through the soldiers' lines, while the great Crazy Horse and Two Moon went downriver, traveled through the encircling coulee, and swept up from the blue-coats' rear.

"It was the greatest battle of all time, and there will never be another." His thick voice broke slightly and two tears rolled down the troughs alongside his heavy, crimson, yellow-traced nose and vanished into the vertical traces of his upper lip, his mouth being like a river system with tributaries above and below.

And despite all I had been through, I felt sorry for him and says, "Surely there will be more," though I did not consider what good they would do him since he was already too old to have been in this one.

"No," said he. "This is the end."

After a bit I gathered my strength and we climbed on, passing the remains of C Troop just below the knoll, and it ain't my purpose to dwell upon the particulars of the carnage, for I think I have said enough about how the Indian women would come out after a battle and deal with the wounded. Well, they was served up with such a banquet following the Battle of the Little Bighorn as to surfeit the worst glutton. There was so many corpses to deface that they actually got tired of mutilating after a time; and so, many bodies stayed untouched, some not even stripped for the clothing.

But Tom Custer had got it real bad, resembling something on a butcher's block. I would not have recognized him, except that his initials was tattooed upon one arm, along with an American flag and the goddess of liberty. His blond scalp had been ripped off down to the nape of the neck, his skull was crushed, his body opened from breastbone to groin, and his— I don't want to say any more; just let his example stand for all those ravaged, though he was about the worst I seen. Remember Bottsy's story that Rain in the Face swore to cut Tom's heart out and eat it? By the looks of things he could have done that, though in later years he denied it.

So it was in the greatest dread that I gained the summit of the knoll, Old Lodge Skins more leading me than I him, for if they had done that to Tom, what horrors must have been the General's lot?

We went up through the barricade of fallen horses, who was beginning to swell from the corruption, they having been dead for a day, the odor terrible, and there, strewn about like ears of corn, was the white bodies of the men who had died alongside me not twenty-four hours earlier. For a moment it was utter still, but I reckon that was an effect within my own head, for a light breeze blew up there and after a bit I heard a whispering flutter that traveled along the ground.

I seen what it was then: hundreds of dollars in greenback bills was scampering along the earth in the wind, now and again blowing over a naked corpse to give him some decency. It was that pay which Custer had held back from the men until they got a day out of Fort Lincoln. The Indians found it when stripping the bodies and flung it away as they did the other papers they come across, love-letters, orders, and the like, which added to the murmuring drift, giving the resemblance of an abandoned picnic ground to the area where none of the bodies had been violated and could have been sleeping but for the arrows erected from them.

One cheekful of Lieutenant Cooke's mutton-chop whiskers had been scalped, along with his head. Kellogg, the newspaper fellow, was lying where I seen him fall, full-dressed, unmarred.

Old Lodge Skins said: "Take me to the formerly Long Hair."

It ain't easy to identify men who are both dead and naked. They tend to merge and blur, like the people in a Turkish bath, only rigid as well.

But finally I saw General Custer, arms still in the crucified extension in which he fell, resting across the bodies of two troopers, where I guess he had been flung when stripped. There was a neat hole in his left chest, and another on the same side of his temple, very little blood from the first, none at all from the second, which I expect had been received as the Indians rode about the field when everybody was down, shooting each so as to make certain of him.

He was not scalped nor mutilated. What got me was his expression. I swear it was still a faint smile, slightly derisive, utterly confident.

"There he is," I told Old Lodge Skins, taking his hand in mine and pointing with both. And the chief went to Custer, stooped, and felt his head briefly. I would have opposed his doing anything nasty, but I knowed he wasn't going to: he was simply looking at the late General in a blindman's fashion.

Then he straightened up and says: "This was the man who brought the soldiers to the Washita?"

"Yes."

"And at Sand Creek before that?"

"No, that was another."

"Ah." He nodded his old head in the big war bonnet, and its feathers flexed in unison, like when a flight of birds unanimously changes direction in the sky. It was a beautiful thing, which I mention on account of the contrast with everything else in this place. There was no living thing throughout the field but him and me and the flies. The other Indians had finished up the day before, had fetched away their own dead, and would never return.

"All right," says Old Lodge Skins. He touched the lance-end of the bow lightly to Custer's bare white shoulder, taking symbolic coup upon it, and he says something to the corpse which I can't translate no better than:

"You are a bad man, and we have paid you back."

So that was that, and we started down to camp, only I was still imbued with the glory and tragedy of it all. Custer had had to die to win me over, but he succeeded at long last: I could not deny it was real noble for him to be his own monument.

So I expresses to Old Lodge Skins a thought that occurred to many other white men after the outside world learned of Custer's Last Stand—only I had it first because I was the first American to see him lying dead, as I was the last to see him live—a romantic thought it was, and appropriate in view of the General's heroic idea of himself that he imposed even upon a skeptic like me.

I says: "He was not scalped, Grandfather. The Indians respected him as a great chief."

Old Lodge Skins smiled at me as at a foolish child.

"No, my son," says he. "I felt his head. They did not scalp him because he was getting bald."

Back at the tepee I laid low, and you can read how the Indians continued to besiege the remainder of the Seventh on Reno Hill, that morning and afternoon of the 26th, but then some boys out herding horses come running through the tepees with news that more bluecoats had appeared, moving down the Greasy Grass from its mouth. So the warriors was called in and the women struck them countless tepees in no more than three-quarters of an hour, and we commenced to move south, everybody, thousands of Indians, tens of thousands of animals, in a column maybe four mile long, with the women and children on ponies which also pulled travois behind, and the warriors riding guard ahead and behind.

Still in my paint and buffalo hat, I stayed with the family contingent of course, riding one of Old Lodge Skins's ponies, him alongside on another, and also his wives. A few Indians had looked at me while we was moving out, but nobody said beans. I reckon they was tired of fighting by now and didn't want no more trouble unless forced into it. I learned a new thing: that Indians can't keep their attention very long even on winning. I mean, I knowed they was like that in warring tribe against tribe, but I hadn't ever seen them whip white men before.

It was early evening when the Cheyenne group passed through the valley across from Reno's position, for we was last in line, and I looked over at them bluffs but could not see a soul, for the distance was some miles. Also the Indians had earlier fired the grass to screen our movements, and smoke still drifted aloft.

The soldiers coming from the north was of course Generals Terry and Gibbon, on their way to that junction with Custer, a day late as he had been a day early, and now they would find him two days dead and the Indians vanished.

You can read about that, and also about Reno and Benteen's defense of their hill and the finding of the bodies of Lavender, Charley Reynolds, Lieutenant McIntosh the halfbreed Iroquois, and Bloody Knife the Ree, among others down in the valley. I come through that bottomland with the Indian assemblage, but fortunately didn't have to see any of my dead friends. I reckon they lay in the timber.

And of course you can read of the Little Bighorn battle itself in a couple hundred different versions, for it is being argued up to this time. First come the newspaper stories, and next there was a military investigation to determine whether Reno had been a coward, which heard a lot of witnesses and declared him not guilty—though some of the very officers who testified in his favor continued to blacken his name out of court. Even as a remnant, the Seventh Cavalry lived up to its glorious traditions, linking arms in public while privately slandering one another.

And then come the accounts of officers and men who served in the other part of the field, and that of the Crow scout Curly. Other fellows went about the reservations, interviewing Indians who had fought on the hostile side. This naturally resulted in a mess: no two savages could agree on what had happened in even their own particular area, seeing things different as they invariably did, not to mention the roles played by manners and fear. Some Indians thought they would be punished if they made it sound too bad; some, out of courtesy, told the investigator what they thought he wanted to hear. One would claim all Custer's men committed suicide; another, that the troops had crossed the ford, penetrated the village, and was driven out, with the General getting killed and falling in the middle of the river.

Last of all the scholars went to work, some setting up residence on the battlefield, which become a national monument, and going over the ground with tape measures and surveyors' instruments. Did Custer disobey his orders? Could Benteen have reached him in time to save the day? What was the exact route of travel taken by the five troops after leaving the Lone Tepee? For every question there are ten answers, pro and con on every detail.

But I alone was there and lived it and have told the God's honest truth so far as recollection serves. To this day I bear scars on cheek and shoulder from wounds I received on that ridge above the Little Bighorn River, Montana Territory, June 25, 1876, in the engagement with Sioux and Cheyenne Indians in which General George A. Custer and five troops of the Seventh U.S. Cavalry perished to the last man but one.

Why have I kept silent till now? Well, hostile Indians was never popular in this country, but for some years after the Little Bighorn their following dropped away to where it was outnumbered by admirers of the rattlesnake. "That's right," you can hear me say to a fun-loving bunch in some saloon, "I was saved by my friends among the Cheyenne."

Then I outlived that era, and along about 1920 I got to dropping a few hints to my then acquaintances but went no farther when I seen the look come into their eyes. What with being related to my Pa and Caroline, I am right sensitive to reflections on my sanity.

Oh, since I been in this old-folks' home and watched them Western shows on the television, I might have made a remark or two, for it gets on my nerves to see Indians being played by Italians, Russians, and the like, with five o'clock shadows and lumpy arms. Redskins don't hardly ever have to shave, and even the huskiest of them have smooth limbs rather than knotty muscles. As to feature, they don't look nothing like gangsters. If the show people are fresh out of real Indians, they should hire Orientals—Chinese, Japs, and such —to play them parts; for there is a mighty resemblance between them two, being ancient cousins. Look at them without bias and you'll see what I mean.

I guess my reasons for mainly keeping quiet boil down to this: Who would ever have believed me? But I am now too old to care. So if *you* don't, you can go to hell.

CHAPTER 30 *The End*

HARDLY HAD THAT vast Indian procession got through the valley where Lavender died when it commenced to break off in fragments which thereupon scattered in every direction, some east to the Tongue and Powder and some farther on to the Slim Buttes area where they was whipped in the following September by General Crook. Some even returned to the reservations.

Sitting Bull and his bunch of Hunkpapa eventually circled around and went on up into Canada, what the Indians called Grandmother's Land on account of Queen Victoria, and they stayed there awhile, where there was still buffalo, and the Mounted Police give them medals showing the Grandmother's likeness and says they was welcome as long as they didn't kill her subjects. Which they did not, for there was hardly any Canadians in that area, and Sitting Bull had such a grudge against Americans that by contrast he loved anyone else. But finally he come back to the U.S., and later toured with Cody's Wild West show for fifty dollars a week in wages, plus expense money, plus exclusive rights to sell photographs of himself.

Some said that while he had been spiritual leader of the Sioux on the Greasy Grass, he got yellow when Reno attacked the lower end of the camp, and hid out in the hills till the fight was over, not having faith in his own medicine. Gall spread that story, and I don't know if it was truth or just jealousy.

Getting back to those days immediately following that great fight: Old Lodge Skins decided to take his band south into the Bighorn Mountains. That is, he suddenly turned his pony in that direction, and those who wanted to come along, did. Which sure included me. I was relieved to see that Younger Bear, after thinking for a long time about it, sitting there upon his pinto animal, chose finally to go east with a number of other Cheyenne. He and I had really reached the end of our mutual relations, being square at last. He had never come around to see me again after that morning when he determined I was alive, and I certainly didn't seek him out.

He had had his great day, and these many years later it does my heart good to think about it, for the Human Beings he went with was badly whipped by General Mackenzie in the fall, and the remnants surrendered the following spring and was sent to that reservation down in Indian Territory where they got the ague and damn near starved. So they broke out, men, women, and children, and fought their way back north for hundreds of mile, under attack all the distance, threadbare and hungry, armed only with bows, for their rifles had been took from them. I reckon when the subject of manliness comes up, you can just say "Cheyenne" and be done with it.

Finally the Government understood that they would either have to be exterminated or let to stay in the country where they was born. So an agency was established on the Tongue River, and the Northern Cheyenne live there to this day.

But there was a lot of agony before that conclusion and I don't know if the Bear survived it. So I am happy he had at least one big win, and of course I wouldn't be here if he hadn't.

Some of the other Indians also went for the Bighorns, but we traveled separate from them and numbered only twenty-odd lodges. Apart from the chief, I didn't know none of these people. My old friends had all died and gone off. Though I was only thirty-four year of age, I felt in some ways older than I do now. Now it is only one man's life that is about to end; then it was a whole style of living. Old Lodge Skins had seen it all, up there on Custer Ridge, when he said there would never be another great battle. I didn't get his point immediately, and maybe you won't either, for there was many a fight afterward, and mighty fierce ones, before the hostile Plains tribes finally give up and come in permanent to the agencies.

One night in early July, it must have been, and we was camped in the foothills of the Bighorn Mountains and had got some buffalo and ate its juicy hump that evening, spicing it with the bitter gall of the beast, into which we'd first dip our knives. It had been a hot day, but cooled off rapidly at that height, and the fire was right cheery to feel against your greasy face, being made of pinewood, crackling and fragrant, for we was close to real timber. After a time it got so warm inside the tepee that them little kids throwed off their blankets and scampered around with their tiny brown arses bare.

The chief's fat wives was chewing on a big hide to soften it, one on each end, and chattering gossip between each bite, about the love life of Crazy Horse who had married a Cheyenne girl. I seen that great warrior once before we split off by ourselves: he had a face full of sharpened edges, wore no ornamentation whatever, no paint, no feathers; he was like a living weapon. He surrendered a year later to the military and was stabbed to death in a scuffle at the agency while his arms was being held by another Indian called Little Big Man. —Not me. He was a Sioux and therefore it was a different name though Englishing the same.

Old Lodge Skins wiped his knife blade on his legging and belched like a trumpet call.

I asked him then what he had meant by his remarks up on the ridge. For I saw it as queer that he had turned more pessimistic after the Indians had won than upon the many occasions when they lost.

"Yes, my son," he says, "it is finished now, because what more can you do to an enemy than beat him? Were we fighting red men against red men—the way we used to, because that is a man's profession, and besides it is enjoyable—it would now be the turn of the other side to try to whip *us*. We would fight as hard as ever, and perhaps win again, but they would definitely start with an advantage, because that is the *right* way. There is no permanent winning or losing when things move, as they should, in a circle. For is not life continuous? And though I shall die, shall I not also continue to live in everything that *is?*

"The buffalo eats grass, I eat him, and when I die, the earth eats me and sprouts more grass. Therefore nothing is ever lost, and each thing is everything forever, though all things move."

The old man put his knife into its beaded scabbard. He went on: "But white men, who live in straight lines and squares, do not believe as I do. With them it is rather everything or nothing: Washita or Greasy Grass. And because of their strange beliefs, they are very persistent. They will even fight at night or in bad weather. But they hate the fighting itself. Winning is all they care about, and if they can do that by scratching a pen across paper or saying something into the wind, they are much happier.

"They will not be content now to come and take revenge upon us for the death of the formerly Long Hair, which they could easily do. Indeed, if we all return to the agencies, they probably would not kill anyone. For killing is part of living, but they hate life. They hate war. In the old days they tried to make peace between us and the Crow and Pawnee, and we all shook hands and did not fight for a while, but it made everybody sick and our women began to be insolent and we could not wear our fine clothes if we were at peace. So finally we rode to a Crow camp and I made a speech there. 'We used to like you when we hated you,' I told those Crow. 'Now that we are friends of yours, we dislike you a great deal.'

" 'That does not make sense,' they said.

" 'Well, it wasn't our idea.'

"They said: 'Nor ours. We used to think you Cheyenne were pretty when we fought you. Now you look like ugly dogs.'

"So it was an emergency, and we had a big battle."

Old Lodge Skins shook his head. "Those Crow," he said. "They were good fighters in the olden time, but nowadays they are full of shame, riding with white soldiers. I heard they ran off at the Greasy Grass, and it did not surprise me."

Well, speak of shame, there was me. I still had not commenced to explain my presence with Custer. If indeed it could be explained. I had to try.

I says: "Grandfather, few people have your great wisdom. The rest of us are often caught in situations where all we can do is survive, let alone understand them. So with me, Little Big Man—" I realized my error soon as I said it.

"Ah," says Old Lodge Skins, "a person should never speak his own name. A devil might steal it, leaving the poor person nameless."

I apologized and started in again, but the chief yawns and says he was going to sleep, so he did.

Next morning when we had woke and took a wash in the cold, crystal stream that come down from the mountains, Old Lodge Skins stripping to the buff, immersing his ancient body, and splashing like a sparrow, and I was a-fixing to lay into a big breakfast, the chief dried himself on a blanket, wrapped another around him, and said: "My son, I have to go up to a high place and do something important today. Will you lead me there?"

He told me I could eat first if I needed to, but he could not. From which I knowed that the thing he had in mind was sacred; and though I might not be involved in it, I didn't want to mock his gods with a full belly. So I took no food either, and we started off.

Well, I regretted that decision after walking uphill for hours, for the place he had chose to go was a considerable peak. By noontime we had gained only about half of it, and had not brung along even a drink of water, and the higher we went, the less chance of finding one. I was still not thoroughly recovered from my wounds, and the air was thinner as we proceeded.

Old Lodge Skins climbed with a firm, powerful, even eager stride. He wore a single eagle feather and that red blanket, with nothing but a breechclout underneath. Far enough away so you couldn't see the seams of his face, I reckon you would have thought him a young brave.

Well, on we went, hour after hour, and I was so dizzy by time we reached the timber line that I thought I'd see double the rest of my life. Occasionally we'd stop so I could rest, but the chief never sat down then, just stood there impatiently, and soon he would say: "Come, my son, there are times to be lazy and times to be quick." So I'd drag myself off again.

It was late afternoon when we reached the summit. It was fair rocky up there, and only one peak among many in the range. I saw a bighorn sheep over yonder, leaping from crag to crag. To the west, the whole world was mountains, all the way to where the sun hung low over the final eminences. I don't think I ever seen a sky as big as that one, or as clear. Real pale blue it was, like a dome made of sapphire, except to say that makes you think it was enclosed, but it wasn't: it was open and unlimited. If you was a bird you could keep going straight up forever, fast as you could fly, yet you would always be in the same place.

Looking at the great universal circle, my dizziness grew still. I wasn't wobbling no more. I was there, in movement, yet at the center of the world, where all is self-explanatory merely because it *is*. Being at the Greasy Grass or not, and on whichever side, and having survived or perished, never made no difference.

We had all been men. Up there, on the mountain, there was no separations.

I turned to Old Lodge Skins to tell him I had got his point, but he had drawn off from me, dropped his blanket, and standing with his scarred old body naked to the falling sun, he yelled in a mighty voice that sounded like thunder echoing from peak to peak.

"HEY-HEY-HEY-HEY-HEY-HEY-HEY!"

It was the great battle cry of the Cheyenne, and he was shouting it at all eternity and for the last time. His blind eyes was crying with the ferocious fun of it, his old body shaking.

"Come out and fight!" he was shouting. "It is a good day to die!"

Then he started to laugh, for Death was scared of him at that moment and cowered in its tepee.

Then he commenced to pray to the Everywhere Spirit in the same stentorian voice, never sniveling but bold and free.

"Thank you for making me a Human Being! Thank you for helping me become a warrior! Thank you for all my victories and for all my defeats. Thank you for my vision, and for the blindness in which I saw further.

"I have killed many men and loved many women and eaten much meat. I have also been hungry, and I thank you for that and for the added sweetness that food has when you receive it after such a time.

"You make all things and direct them in their ways, O Grandfather, and now you have decided that the Human Beings will soon have to walk a new road. Thank you for letting us win once before that happened. Even if my people must eventually pass from the face of the earth, they will live on in whatever men are fierce and strong. So that when women see a man who is proud and brave and vengeful, even if he has a white face, they will cry: 'That is a Human Being!'

"I am going to die now, unless Death wants to fight first, and I ask you for the last time to grant me my old power to make things happen!"

That sheep I had seen earlier, or another, come into view on a neighboring crag with his magnificent scrolled horns and seemed to look questioningly over towards us. But this was not what Old Lodge Skins meant, and he couldn't see it anyway, so he give his war cry once more, and as it went reverberating across that range, an answering roll of thunder come out of the west, and that sky which had been crystal pure suddenly developed a dark mass of cloud above the sun and it begun to roll towards us across the vast distance.

I stood there in awe and Old Lodge Skins started to sing, and when the cloud arrived overhead, the rain started to patter across his uplifted face, mixing with the tears of joy there.

It might have been ten minutes or an hour, and when it stopped and the sun's setting rays cut through, he give his final thanks and last request.

"Take care of my son here," he says, "and see that he does not go crazy."

He laid down then on the damp rocks and died right away. I descended to the treeline, fetched back some poles, and built him a scaffold. Wrapped him in the red blanket and laid him thereon. Then after a while I started down the mountain in the fading light.

IT WAS SHORTLY after reaching this point in his narrative that Jack Crabb himself passed on, as I have described in the Preface. A pity that we will never get the account of his later years, which he led me to believe were no less remarkable than his first thirty-four. From various of his references, always spirited, I gather that he toured for a time with the Wild West spectacle directed by the late William F. Cody, "Buffalo Bill." He may have traveled to Europe with that company. His allusions were ambiguous, but it is possible that he went as far as Venice and was there photographed in a gondola with several Sioux Indians.

He seems in later years to have visited the Sandwich Islands—Hawaii, in our modern terminology—and there to have developed a taste for the female inhabitants, whose custom it was yet to swim in the nude. He led me to assume that he was no stranger to Latin America in the last years of the nineteenth, and the early twentieth, century. There were elusive references to Guatemala, Cuba, Mexico, generally in time of revolution—though as he has made so clear, Mr. Crabb was devoid of political convictions.

Which is perhaps as deplorable as his apparent approval of violence, from which I must dissociate myself. I am after all a white man, and believe that reason must eventually prevail, the lion *will* lie down with the lamb, if, though agnostic, I may use the idiom of the superstitious to express a serious moral proposition. I made such expression once to Mr. Crabb, and his answer made me shudder: "That's O.K., son, so long as you add fresh lambs now and again."

Jack Crabb was a cynical man, uncouth, unscrupulous, and when necessary, even ruthless. In sponsoring this his partial biography, I can in no way commend it to the overimpressionable. He must be seen as a product of his place, time, and circumstances. It was such men who carried our frontier ever westward to meet the shining ocean.

However, in concluding, I must make a frank admission. I have never been able to decide on how much of Mr. Crabb's story to believe. More than one night, I have awakened in the wee hours with a terrible suspicion that I have been hoaxed, have rushed to my desk, taken out the manuscript, and pored over it till morning.

It is of course unlikely that one man would have experienced even a third of Mr. Crabb's claim. Half? Incredible! All? A mythomaniac! But you will find, as I did, that if any one part is accepted as truth, then what precedes and follows has as great a lien on our credulity. If he knew Wild Bill Hickok, then why not General Custer as well? The case is similar when we suspect his veracity at a certain point: then why should he be reliable anywhere?

I can certify that whenever Mr. Crabb has given precise dates, places, and names, I have gone to the available references and found him frighteningly accurate—when he can be checked at all. There are exceptions: according to the best authorities, the only Negro at the Little Bighorn was a man named Isaiah Dorman, but he *had* earlier lived with the Sioux and he *was* killed in the valley while riding with Major Reno's command. There is no Sergeant "Botts" on the rolls of the Seventh Cavalry, though a Sgt. Edward Botzer appears upon the fatality list. As to Crazy Horse's not wearing feathers, we know that statement to be erroneous—his war bonnet, as mentioned in the Preface, presently reposes in my own collection; the dealer who sold it to me is a man of the highest integrity.

And so on. . . . But one name is missing from every index, every roster, every dossier. In my library of three thousand volumes on the Old West, in the hundreds of clippings, letters, magazines, you will search in vain, as I have, for the most fleeting reference to one man, and not a commonplace individual by any means, but by his own account a participant in the pre-eminent events of the most colorful quarter-century on the American frontier. I refer, of course, to *Jack Crabb*.

So as I take my departure, dear reader, I leave the choice in your capable hands. Jack Crabb was either the most neglected hero in the history of this country or a liar of insane proportions. In either case, may the Everywhere Spirit have mercy on his soul, and yours, and mine.

—R.F.S.